THE SCANDALOUS LETTERS OF V AND J

FELICIA DAVIN

Cover design by Felicia Davin. Detail of *Portrait de femme* (1787) by Adélaïde Labille-Guiard.

ISBN-13: 978-0-9989957-7-9
Copyright © 2023 Felicia Davin
All rights reserved.

PRAISE FOR FELICIA DAVIN

Davin's book feels genuinely, shockingly rebellious in its insistence on the beauty of transformation. If overhyped books are plastic necklaces, [*The Scandalous Letters of V and J*] is a string of natural pearls, each a luminous gem on its own but even more exquisite in sequence.

— THE NEW YORK TIMES

But bodies and identity are never a space for trauma in [*The Scandalous Letters of V and J*]—only for joy, attraction, experimentation, and play. Within their sexual and romantic relationship, Victor and Julien are perpetually trying on different roles, different acts, even different bodily configurations, unfettered by the constraints of what's allowable to a person of this or that gender.

— TOR.COM

CONTENTS

Content Guidance ... 7

Dedication ... 11

Preface ... 15

PART I
The Education of Young Denise ... 19

PART II
Landscape with Ruins ... 157

PART III
Young Man Writing a Letter ... 369

PART IV
The Emerald Necklace ... 445

Thank You for Reading ... 523
Sneak Peek ... 525
Felicia Davin to Readers Who Made It This Far, January 9, 2023 ... 539
About the Author ... 545
Also by Felicia Davin ... 547

CONTENT GUIDANCE

This series takes place in a violent, unjust world, and there are some abominable villains in it. I wanted to write fantasy that wasn't about armies or the fate of nations, but with more individual stakes. In practice, that means the villains deal in intimate violence. There is abuse in this book. There is also violent vengeance against the abusers. I can't promise that I've written things in a way that won't hurt you, but I hope this note helps you make the right choices for yourself.

Here is a more specific list of what you will find in this book. If you don't need to be forewarned and would rather avoid spoilers, skip it.

- A major character has been disowned by their family. It is primarily motivated by greed over inheritance, but not entirely unrelated to the character's gender and sexuality. This situation comes up repeatedly throughout the book.
- A major character changes their name as part of a gender transition, and their deadname occurs

CONTENT GUIDANCE

a few times in the text—when they strategically choose to say it, and not when it is weaponized against them by others.
- A major character has lost their mother to a long illness, years prior to the book. It is mentioned several times.
- A major character has been groomed and emotionally abused by an adult when they were a teenager.
- A major character is groped without their consent while they are magically stupefied, also without their consent.
- There is violence (stabbing and blood) and murder. There is also discussion of drinking blood and a brief discussion of antisemitic blood libel.
- A supporting character is in an abusive marriage. (She'll get a happy ending in book two.)
- There is sex in this book. Most of the scenes are explicit with regard to genitalia. Both main characters are nonbinary. One of them can shapeshift with magic; the other cannot. Nonbinary gender exists independent of what kind of body a person has. Though I have not always followed all of their advice, I am indebted to Xan West/Corey Alexander and their writings on trans and nonbinary erotica. May their memory be a blessing.
- Some of the sex scenes feature power exchange. There is some other light kink, namely roleplay (including some play with gender) and consensual bondage.

CONTENT GUIDANCE

A NOTE ON PRONOUNS

The main characters in this book use multiple pronouns (he/she/they for one of them, for instance). Singular they is perfectly correct in English. In contemporary French, there is now the corresponding nonbinary pronoun "iel," among several other options. Though nonbinary people existed in early 19th century France when this book is set, "iel" is a later innovation. French typically genders its nouns and adjectives as masculine or feminine, but the convention when referring to a nonbinary person is to write, for instance, "étudiant.e" (instead of "étudiant" or " étudiante") or "grand.e" so the word is both and neither. This convention didn't come up in the book I wrote in English, but it's cool, so I wanted to tell you about it.

The magic in this book breaks the laws of the universe as we know them in our own world. Since I had already flagrantly disregarded physics, history and prescriptivist grammar were trivial to me. Language is whatever we want it to be.

DEDICATION

On entre dans cette allée par une porte bâtarde surmontée d'un écriteau sur lequel on lit : MAISON VAUQUER et en dessous : Pension bourgeoise des deux sexes et autres.

One enters this path through a wicket gate, atop which a sign reads MAISON VAUQUER, and below that: *Boarding house for both sexes and others.*
—Honoré de Balzac, *Le Père Goriot*, 1835

Aux autres.
To the others.

PREFACE

NOTICE TO MY BELOVED READER

Here follows a collection of letters and diary entries arranged by date. They have been lightly edited for clarity and spelling, or decoded if necessary, but are unaltered, even when their contents are an outrage to decency.

Their story will be familiar to you. Where the events retold by these papers escape the boundaries of correspondence, an occasional scene has been inserted between letters. As you will no doubt recall, many other things were also inserted.

It is my hope that this collection will bring you pleasure, and that I didn't get you too wrong.

The Editor
Paris, 1828

I
THE EDUCATION OF YOUNG DENISE

1823

VICTORINE FAUCHEUX TO PIERRE FAUCHEUX, OCTOBER 2, 1823

POSTMARKED PARIS

Dear Father,

Aunt Sophie and I have taken rooms at the Maison Laval for now. I do not mean to imply that your allowance was ungenerous, only that perhaps you had not considered everything. I myself was quite surprised by how costly life is.

Now that you have our new address, it is my hope that you might find it in your heart to write to us. I would still like to know what I have done to anger you.

Your devoted daughter,
Victorine

PRIVATE DIARY OF V BEAUCHÊNE, OCTOBER 2, 1823

[*This diary entry and all others were written in a private cipher. They are printed here in plain language.*]

I will never sign another letter "Your devoted daughter Victorine" as long as I live. Every word of that is a lie. Abasing myself writing obsequiously polite bullshit to that bastard makes me want to punch a wall.

Aunt S is the only person in the world who loves me, which I know because she gave me a haircut. We did it by candlelight in the kitchen of my father's house and then swept a mountain of blond curls out the door. I imagine the sight shocked the servants who discovered it, but I'll never know because I don't live there anymore.

Aunt S also spent a fortune of her own money buying me suits so I could have something to wear other than the ill-fitting clothes I stole from Horace before we moved into the Maison Laval.

It's been several days since I've written and this is all out of order. I should start at the beginning: my father's announcement that, due to my mother's <u>alleged</u> adultery, he was disinheriting me and naming Horace as the sole heir to his fortune.

What makes me most furious—oh, the list is long—is that I did nothing wrong. Neither did my mother. She followed all the rules to her last breath and still ended up disgraced and with one child disinherited. Men can ruin your reputation even after you die. Intolerable. I wish she <u>had</u> committed this adultery that my father and brother have conjured from nothing. At least then I could rest assured she'd seized happiness where she found it.

And what a relief it would be if someone other than Pierre Faucheux were my father. The nose on my face dashes that dream.

I don't understand why he's doing this. I've begged and begged for an explanation.

After my father disinherited me, Aunt S and I retreated to my bedroom to cry and rage and pack my things in private. Fury splotched her cheeks red and she shook her head and gesticulated so much that some of the perfectly set silver-blonde curls in her coiffure came loose. I've never seen her so angry.

We had only a day to remove ourselves from the house where I have lived all twenty-one years of my life and Aunt S has spent the last few years, first caring for my mother and then protecting me from my brother and my father's increasing hostility. (Well, my father's increasing hostility. Horace has always been hostile.) She said she could make arrangements for us to take rooms in a boarding house, and that she would come with me to act as my chaperone since I was a young unmarried woman.

I was holding a dress in my hands—the white one with the multicolored floral embroidery and the short, puffed sleeves—and I thought, if I am not living in my father's house, if I am not my father's daughter, if I am not inheriting the wealth of Victorine Faucheux, then why should I bother to continue this charade?

To survive, I played the role in which I was cast. This performance did not protect me, and there is no satisfaction in knowing my own innocence; it cannot feed me or keep me warm.

Pierre Faucheux was, in a sense, paying me to be Victorine. Now that I have no promised dowry or inheritance, I refuse to do this work for free.

If I am to fend for myself, I want to be myself.

I had been silent for a long moment. The dress was crushed in my fists. Aunt S asked me what was wrong. We shared a bitter laugh when she added, "Other than the obvious."

I blurted out, "I'd rather be Victor than Victorine."

And she brushed her fingers over my cheek and said, "So be Victor, if that's what you want."

I don't know what jumble of words came out of my mouth, some combination of what, really, but I, you'd let me, and another really for good measure.

She laughed and said, "Let you? What does that mean? I'm your aunt, not a prison guard, darling. Close your mouth. I love you."

She embraced me. Aunt S gives the softest hugs. Stunned, it took me a moment to return the gesture. Could I have told her long ago? Perhaps she would always have understood. It made my throat close up.

"If I were a young man—not to say that I am, but if people thought of me that way, instead of as a young woman—I wouldn't require a chaperone. You wouldn't have to move to the boarding house with me. You'd be free to return to your life."

Aunt S so rarely displays anything other than sparkling cheer. She made a series of unaccustomed facial expressions, trying them on and discarding them like dresses that didn't suit her. At last she said, "Victor."

Hearing that was a pleasure.

"Are you asking me not to accompany you?"

"No!" How alone I'd feel without her. "It's only that I thought you might prefer…"

"If it's your desire to live more independently, I will absent myself whenever you wish," she said. "But while you might not be a young woman—and perhaps not exactly a young man—you are still a young <u>person</u>, one without means or connections. I think I can be of use to you. More than that, I like your company, and you're the only person in the world who misses Anaïs as much as I do. If you'll have me, I would like to remain with you."

"Oh," I said, because I wanted to say twenty things at once and I also wanted not to cry, and that syllable was the best I could manage. "I'd like that. I love you, too, Aunt S."

I'd never said that to her before. I haven't said it to anyone since Maman died. The words felt strange in my mouth. Light where I'd expected them to be heavy.

"Good. Now do you want to keep any of these dresses or are we pawning them all to buy you some suits?"

Aunt S was so at ease with the possibility that I might be a person named Victor who wore both dresses and suits. Whoever I was, whatever I wanted to wear, she was coming with me. The thought still suffuses me with warmth.

We'd amassed a colorful pile of fabrics, whites and pinks and lavender ruffles. I'd enjoyed wearing most of them—I do have a taste for luxury, and dresses never bothered me in the way that other social strictures did—but the thought of never seeing them again aroused no strong emotion. It was as though they already belonged to someone else.

"Let's pawn them. I want new clothes to go with my new name," I said. "I want a new family name, too. Can I have yours?"

"My sister did all the work of bringing you into the world," Aunt S said. "I think our name suits you perfectly, Monsieur Victor Beauchêne."

I bowed low. "My pleasure, Mademoiselle Sophie Beauchêne."

She curtsied in her dressing gown and then we slipped down to the kitchen so she could cut my hair. Aunt S doesn't know anything about cutting hair and it was dark, so it isn't a good haircut, but it's also the best haircut of my life.

We tiptoed back upstairs so I could admire myself in the mirror and Aunt S could tell me how exceedingly handsome I was.

"Let's get out of this house and go make a life somewhere else," I said.

"Let's," she said. She smiled at me, small at first and then wide and wicked. "Don't stay up too late reading. I promise to continue not noticing when you steal novels from my collection, you little thief."

While I was stuttering a denial, she disappeared through the doorway, calling "Goodnight, Victor."

So that was our last night in the Faucheux townhouse.

Now the two of us live in this hovel full of weird strangers and we barely have enough money to cover room and board. My brother's still at home living like the banker's son he is, waiting to inherit the whole fortune.

But I have Aunt S and I have myself.

JULIE MORÈRE TO ESTHER MORÈRE, OCTOBER 2, 1823
POSTMARKED PARIS

Maman,

You are so sweet to keep sending me money, but I have enough. I have paid Madame Laval for the room. I promise I'm eating. And sleeping. You don't need to worry about me. I have everything under control.

My studies are going well. I'm already quite well-versed in anatomy, and as you said, I don't <u>need</u> an official institution's stamp of approval, but it was worth it to come to Paris to study. It's educational to be in a room full of other artists—ones not related to me, I mean. And, if nothing else, my instructor has complimented my work. I don't require his praise to continue making art, but I'm still allowed to enjoy it, am I not?

I've enclosed a sketch of the Maison Laval and another of my room, so you can see where I'm living.

[*The first sketch depicts a stone building several stories high with moss creeping up the walls and a slightly uneven roofline. Puddles pool in the sloped cobblestone street outside the imposing wooden door. The second sketch depicts a small, spare room with a narrow bed and a desk. The desk is covered in piles of paper.*]

There aren't many other young people living at this boarding house, and my studies have kept me busy, so I've mostly kept to myself. But yesterday a young person named Victor Beauchêne moved in. I'd like to befriend him, but he will think—as everyone here does—that I'm Julien.

I find myself a bit shy in his presence. You would think, after months and months of self-portraits, that I would feel more confident.

Victor seems respectable. Nothing in my life has prepared me to speak to anyone respectable. He's probably a royalist. He probably goes to Mass. He's probably going to marry a marquise. Clearly it's for the best that I don't know how to approach him.

Thank you so much for sending me this copy of <u>Virginie</u>. Everyone is always talking about the author, Camille Dupin, and I can't wait to read it.

I miss you. I hope you and Papa and Georges and the farm are well. I wrote Adrienne her own letter. Give my love to everyone.

With affection,
Julie

JULIE MORÈRE TO ADRIENNE MORÈRE, OCTOBER 2, 1823
POSTMARKED PARIS

To my dearest <u>sister</u> ADRIENNE,

Adrienne, Adrienne, I'm so happy for you. And for me. I love having a sister. Adrienne is a beautiful name.

Do you think Georges feels excluded by the two of us, as unchanging as he is? I bet he has sculpted a few self-portraits of his own. Tell him I recall him being an exceptionally ungainly adolescent, and I don't believe there's any way he achieved handsomeness as an adult without some artistic intervention. (He'll probably just grunt and scowl at you.)

You've always been wiser than me. How did you know when you'd finished your work, Adrienne? I know you are going to write "it felt right." That's how it feels to finish a drawing or a painting, and I imagine it's like that. And I've finished a lot of drawings and paintings, but I don't think I've finished myself.

Maybe that's me, though. What I like best is the work in progress. I'm not interested in taking the canvas off the easel and framing it. (I hope you don't mind this metaphor, Adrienne. Your frame suits you perfectly.)

What chafes about being here in Paris, studying as Julien, isn't that I'm really Julie and I want to be her all the time. It's that I don't want to feel trapped into being one or the other when I've always been both. I want to make more self-portraits, but everybody at school knows this version of me, so any adjustments I make will have to be subtle.

I might stop growing facial hair. Shaving my face is bothersome. I might let my hair grow, too. That won't be too shocking. I like being taller than Georges, though, so please tell him I'm never giving that up. I spent all those years as the baby of the family and now I'm going to lord my height over the two of you forever.

The most beautiful person I have ever seen just moved into this boarding house. Victor Beauchêne, he's called. He has a set of rooms with his aunt Sophie, who gave me the direst glower just for existing. (I might have been staring.)

A sketch is enclosed. It's in ink so you can't tell he's blond, but he's blond. And small, but he takes up a lot of space somehow. He's just so—lively? I'm not good at describing people, this is why I draw instead. He smiled at me and I thought I might die.

Given that feeling, it's probably unwise for me to befriend him. I'd be willing to risk it if only I knew what to say. The two of them were dressed nicely, so I think maybe they used to have money? I don't know how you end up in the Maison Laval if you have money, but what do I know about rich people? Even less than I know about talking to men, that's what.

I don't know anything about talking to women, either.

How is it possible that I'm twenty years old and still don't know how to talk to men or women or anyone in between? Adrienne, how could you let me grow up without these skills? I'm depending on you now. Tell me what to do.

I'll be crushed if Victor is like my classmates. The only men I've ever spent any time with are Papa and Georges, and they didn't prepare me for this. I knew school would be difficult, but I thought it would be because of the rigor of the training, not the behavior of the other students. I don't find making charcoal drawings of casts especially challenging, even for hours a day in a crowd of fifty students and with hardly any instruction. (The master comes to the studio twice a week to offer a sentence or two of devastating criticism; so far he has mostly grunted in wordless approval when he passed my easel, though on two separate occasions, he said, "Good, Morère.") But the older students live to humiliate us. They take wicked delight in choosing one of us to go out for a celebratory dinner and then leaving that student with the bill, which was painful to me, but not as ruinous as it was for some of the others. They make us wash their brushes and clean the studio. On the first day, they made us strip naked, get on the model's platform, and fight a duel with loaded paintbrushes while they jeered. When I hesitated to attack my fellow first year, an older student shoved me so I stumbled and streaked his belly with blue. Auguste, my opponent, didn't like that, so then I had to defend myself. It took me days of scrubbing to find all the daubs of red paint afterward. Auguste was equally covered. We both lost.

Still, it was a sort of secret victory for me. They tried to use my nakedness against me, and I was not shamed. I've never been ashamed of any of the forms my body has taken. I don't think anyone else's is shameful, either, but to hear my classmates talk, I'm alone in that opinion. It's a horror, the way they talk about each other and especially about the women who model for the older students. I pity these young men, obsessed as they are with bodies, who can only think in parts and not in people. And the older students feel some superiority now that they've seen us naked, but we haven't seen them. As if they've learned some secret they can hold over my head.

The funny thing is that I would love to tell someone my secret. I know it's unwise, but I'm lonely. Don't tell Maman that. Sorry. I hate asking you to keep anything from her. But she worries too much already.

I feel foolish. I thought I was going to come to Paris and make brilliant friends who'd be just like me, except different, and we'd all only care about art and ideas and not these rules about whether anyone is exactly a woman or a man. Where are those people, Adrienne? This city is gigantic, so they must live here. How do I find them?

Anyway, I'm fine, really. I'm going to finish my studies and come home and make art with you and our family and we'll all get works accepted to the Salon and our collective genius will be celebrated (maybe my genius in particular, I'm not above wishing for that) and everything will be perfect.

Please tell me absolutely everything about your life, Adrienne. I miss you and love you.

Julie

PRIVATE DIARY OF V BEAUCHÊNE, OCTOBER 9, 1823

No word from Pierre Faucheux. I should stop bothering to record that, since it happens every day. On the day he writes to me, then I'll have something to record.

Only I don't think he's ever going to write to me.

I don't want to speak to him or see him. I just want him to tell me why.

I can't seem to think my way out of my own desperate circumstances, which is tiresome. To amuse and distract myself, I started writing an index of all the sex acts in Aunt S's obscene novel collection. Each book has a table that lists acts, number of people involved, and the pages where these things are described. An effective and oddly soothing project.

Happily, when I finish that, there will still be one other distraction available to me: a very handsome young man lives in this boarding house. We haven't spoken, but I've overheard the other boarders addressing him as Julien Morère. He's probably twenty years old, and very quiet and reserved at dinner. He's also tall, and dark-haired, and always a little rumpled. Maybe he's like me—maybe he used to have money, and servants, and that's why he isn't very good at shaving or tying his cravat. His clothes fit him quite well, though.

I think he's an art student, since I have seen him coming in and out with a large sketchbook. A few days ago, Aunt S and I took a stroll in the Jardin du Luxembourg, and I saw him drawing there. I wanted to stop and watch, but Aunt S hurried me along.

I don't know why. It's not as if I have a reputation to protect anymore—or as if Julien would want to seduce me.

It is a lovely thought, though. I would very much like to be seduced. Novels make it sound excellent, and what do I have to lose? Nobody is ever going to marry me, which would be fine—unlike seduction, marriage sounds terrible—except that we'll be out of money in a few months.

I have little education and very few talents. Here is a short list of things I am good at:

1. ~~Looking pretty.~~ (Never mind. I was good at looking pretty when I lived in my father's house and had access to money and servants. Now I have to start from the beginning and learn a new set of skills.)
2. Making dull, appropriate conversation.
3. Making lists.
4. Writing servile letters to my father. (I was going to say "begging," but to say I'm good at begging would suggest that he had given me any of what I asked for, which he has not.)
5. Knowing when someone is staring at me. (Julien definitely was, as was the other young man who lives here, his family name is Forestier I think,

but he's horrible so I ignore him. I don't know what to make of either of them.)

I don't see how I am meant to make a life—let alone earn a living—out of any of this.

Perhaps I can learn to make exciting, inappropriate conversation, and then someone (Julien) will want to talk to me. I still won't have any money, but at least I won't die alone.

LIST OF SEX ACTS IN THE EDUCATION OF YOUNG DENISE, ANONYMOUS, 1756

Act	Description	People involved	Pages	Comments
Self-pleasure	Denise spies on two nuns through a keyhole at her convent and touches herself	Denise	3-7	
Oral sex	Two nuns use their mouths on each other	Sister Agnès (giving and receiving), Sister Marguerite (giving and receiving)	3-5	
Fucking (with dildo)	One nun fucks another	Sister Agnès (giving), Sister Marguerite (receiving)	5-7	Where do you get a dildo?
Spanking, fucking (with fingers)	Denise is discovered and "punished"	Denise (receiving), Sister Agnès (giving), Sister Marguerite (giving)	7-35	This one isn't as good because there is a long philosophical speech in the middle about how virtue is meaningless.
Oral sex	Denise, having left the convent, pleasures a man with her mouth	Denise, a man	38-39	
Oral sex	One of Denise's clients pays to pleasure her	Denise, a man	40-41	The man likes Denise to fart in his face??

The remainder of this list and the others like it have been excluded for length.

PRIVATE DIARY OF V BEAUCHÊNE, OCT 10, 1823

This morning during my futile attempt to tame my hair into something respectably dapper, Aunt S swept into my room. She dropped the strangest little object on my desk. A glob of ochre yellow with a long tail of white string bounced silently to the wooden desk.

I gave up on my hair. Aunt S's gift was a sponge, fibrous against my fingertips when I squeezed it.

Aunt S said, "I'm too old to keep an eye on your young lusts. You can watch out for yourself."

I dangled the string. It was wrapped tightly around the middle of the soft, nubby form of the sponge. I had absolutely no idea what purpose such an object could serve, or what it might have to do with my "young lusts." There are no sponges in the obscene novels. It swung back and forth on the string, and I began to wonder if Aunt Sophie had given me some sort of bewitched charm.

"What is this?"

"Oh, you're in worse shape than I thought. It's a sponge, darling."

"I know it's a sponge, but what is it for?"

"To prevent pregnancy," she said, and then, as if that weren't shocking enough, she said, "I've never put one to the test, but I'm told they're relatively reliable. I'm also told sheaths are effective at preventing the pox, but I didn't have time to acquire one this morning."

"You think I'm going to get the pox?"

"Not if you're careful," she said. "Do you understand how to use the sponge?"

Until she asked the question, I confess I had <u>not</u> understood, but the placement—and the purpose of the string—dawned on me as she said it. I let the sponge fall to my desk. Clearly the forbidden novels have not taught me everything. I wish I had been brave enough to ask Aunt S if you can do things <u>without</u> a sponge. Only in the privacy of this journal do I speak freely.

I want to be like Aunt S, to talk about these things without clearing my throat and averting my gaze, but I didn't achieve that audacity this morning. Like everything else in my life, it will require practice. Maybe I should read some more books.

"Is this because Julien looked at me?" I asked, trying not to sound hopeful. He <u>did</u> stare.

"No," she said. "It's because you looked at Julien."

"That's the same thing, isn't it?"

"Not at all. I was prepared to drive away all your suitors, but I'm not prepared to deprive you of joy. Do as you please, but try to have some common sense about it."

Years of etiquette lessons didn't teach me what to say in such circumstances. What I wanted to ask was whether Aunt S thought Julien would be receptive to flirtation from a person of both masculine and feminine attributes such as myself, but I think I have to deduce that on my own. Anyway, I supposed that even in a wildly indecorous conversation, an expression of gratitude wouldn't go amiss. So I said, "Thank you."

"Be careful."

Then we made eye contact, and I wish we hadn't. Aunt S and I look alike, or rather, we both look like my mother. Aunt S is plump and fashionably well-endowed, and Maman spent the last few years of her life desperately thin, and I'm none of those things, but no matter. It's the blond curls, the blue eyes, the prominent cheeks, the bow in the upper lip, the brow that can rise like a Gothic arch. Most of the time, the resemblance makes me happy.

But not this morning. It should have been my mother revealing all this. Then again, if my mother had lived longer, perhaps I'd still be in my father's house. Nobody would be telling me to do as I pleased.

Averting my eyes caused me to catch sight of myself in the hand mirror, which I flipped over. "It's been three years," I whispered.

She touched my shoulder. "I miss her, too."

"Do you think she would have given me a sponge?" I asked.

Aunt S laughed a teary sort of laugh. "No. That would still have been me. But she would have wanted you to be happy."

Then she tousled my curls and somehow set them just right.

PRIVATE DIARY OF V BEAUCHÊNE, OCTOBER 11, 1823

Julien came to my room this evening.

That shouldn't have been a surprise. I planned it like we were in a book. At dinner I dropped my handkerchief so it fluttered to the floor at his feet. He didn't notice at the time. I thought he'd collect it at the end of dinner and perhaps offer it to me tomorrow as I passed him in the garden, in public and in daylight, at an hour we can pretend is civilized, a time when neither of us will have to acknowledge the vast effort I have expended imagining what it would feel like if he touched me.

Instead, he knocked quietly while I was writing this evening. Granted, I am always writing, so it was likely he'd find me in this position, but still I was unprepared for the sight of Julien in the doorway.

"Good evening, Beauchêne," he said.

"Good evening. Please call me Victor. Ah, that is, if you—"

"My pleasure, Victor. You may call me Julien."

Every aspect of his presence entranced me—his height, his dark brows, his quiet amusement, the way he'd folded my handkerchief into a neat square. How delicate the creased white fabric looked in his fingers. A feverish temperament (mine) might have briefly mistaken it for a love note.

Julien likes the look of me, I'm convinced. Knowing this makes me feel like I've had one glass of wine too many —happy, undone. Of course I myself think I am handsome, but someone else thinking I am handsome is a pleasure I have only just discovered. I want to spend as much of my life as possible with Julien looking at me.

"I think," he said, pressing the handkerchief into my palm and enclosing my hand in both of his, "you dropped this."

I should have been embarrassed, knowing that Julien had perceived my plan, but his bare hands were warm and just a little rough from work and my mind was blissfully empty, so all I said was, "Yes."

He withdrew. The touch had lasted a long time, but not long enough. I clamped my hand around his wrist before he could leave. I didn't know what I was doing. I tucked the handkerchief into my waistcoat pocket and said, "Uh. Do you want to come in?"

"I'd like that."

My room at the Maison Laval is stark. All the wooden furniture—a bed, a wash basin, a wardrobe, a desk, and a chair—is rickety and unornamented. The bedsheets and the drapes on the lone window are threadbare. The door to Aunt S's room hangs a little crooked in its frame. The whole place is colorless, dreary, and cramped. There is nothing of interest but my papers, which are private. (To my great relief, I'd hidden the sponge in a drawer.) If Julien entered and sat down, his choices were my bed or the chair at my desk. Both were bad, but the desk was undoubtedly worse.

I stepped back, jerked the chair away from the desk, knocking into one of its wobbly legs and sending an inkwell and a pile of papers flying. Frantic, I crouched to right the inkwell before the puddle could spread any further.

Julien, courteous and helpful, collected my journal and a few loose pages from the floor. I retrieved a rag from the wardrobe to mop up the ink and was on my knees cleaning before I remembered that I hadn't encoded those pages.

Julien replaced them as though they were a precious and ancient parchment that might crumble if handled indelicately. I wish they had. My meticulously ruled index of all the sex acts in The Education of Young Denise lay naked on my desk.

Why did I not write that idle curiosity in code? Why did I write it at all? Why is my life such a shambles that this is how I spend my time?

Above all, what does Julien know about these things?

To my horror, I discovered that I am a person who blushes. How the knowledge escaped me for the previous twenty-one years of my life remains a mystery; perhaps it is only Julien who holds this power over me. Regardless, a tendency to blush runs contrary to the brazen and seductive personality I wish to cultivate in Julien's presence.

Kneeling while he stood didn't help, either.

He did smile at me, though.

Well, almost. It was more like he pressed his lips together to hold in a smile, but not unkindly. With that abashed expression, he made it feel as though we were sharing something. "My room is a bit of a mess, too."

The only things out of place in my empty room were

the pages he'd just set on the desk, but I know when I am granted mercy. "I suppose your art requires that?"

He stuck out his hand. I could hardly believe he was allowing me to touch him again, but I didn't waste the opportunity. He pulled me to my feet easily, so fast I went dizzy with it. Before tonight, I'd never thought about how you can feel the heat from another person's body if you're close enough.

"I don't think it does," he said, dropping my hand. "Plenty of other students at the École des Beaux-Arts are neat."

Oh. Art. I'd said something about art. "Your art might have different requirements from theirs."

"That's... wise," he said. "I should have known you'd be smart. You're always reading and writing."

Desperate to avoid the topics of what exactly I'm always reading and writing, how profoundly pathetic and obscene those things might be, and how utterly uneducated I am, I searched for something intelligent and alluring to say. I settled on "I, um, not really."

Julien saved me a second time. "I'm sorry about your inkwell. You must go through a lot of paper and ink."

"I'm the one who spilled it."

"Still," he said. "At least your papers were spared."

God, I would willingly drown every volume of my journal in a vat of ink if it meant I could live a life without the knowledge of Julien's wide-eyed stare at my index of indecencies.

Or maybe I wouldn't. He looked, after all.

A little part of me likes knowing that.

I said, "They're not important, those papers. I was merely... distracting myself. As you've observed, I like to write. And to organize things."

"It was very organized," he said.

There was a note of admiration in his tone. It still makes me shiver, how calm and careful he was. Julien saw that page, realized its nature, and put it aside. He didn't mock, scold, pry, or immediately end our acquaintance. His behavior was as close to perfect as anyone could reasonably expect.

Not quite perfect, of course. He could have taken inspiration from pages 56-62, kissed me passionately up against the wall, and ravished me, but I suppose in order to know that, he would have had to spend more time studying my notes.

Instead, he said, "I was telling the truth about the mess in my room. Maybe I should let you organize my drawings."

This tantalizing possibility of a future connection between us made me part my lips in shock. His gaze flicked toward my mouth and I thought all is not lost. "What do you draw?"

"Everything. Landscapes. The streets of the city, sometimes." He paused to examine the floor. Julien has such long, dark lashes. "People."

"Models? People you know?"

"Both," he said. "And myself."

"I'd like to see your work," I said.

For the first time in our strange conversation, Julien appeared nervous. "Now?"

"No, no, just… some day. If you want to show it to me," I said.

"I would," he said. "I could draw you, if you want."

"I've never had my portrait done," I said. More or less true. There is a childhood portrait of Victorine Faucheux in my father's house, or there was before he evicted me.

Perhaps he threw that into the street, too. But nobody has ever drawn Victor Beauchêne. "I'd like it if you drew me. I also wanted to ask you, since you've been living here longer than me, if you'd show me the neighborhood."

"I'm not sure I'll be of much use. I spend all my time at school. That afternoon in the Luxembourg was a rare moment," he said, and then added quickly, "But I'd be happy to walk with you."

"I look forward to it, Julien," I said. Brazen and seductive might still be beyond my reach, but I certainly conveyed how eager I was. Grateful, as well, that Julien allowed our conversation to continue past its nadir. The obscene novels don't spend any time on these early stages. I've recorded in mortifying detail where I ought to put my tongue once we're in bed, but how do we arrive there?

Julien met my eyes and said "I look forward to it as well" in that low, smooth tone, which is not the sort of thing people say to each other in obscene novels, and yet it left me breathless.

JULIEN MORÈRE TO VICTOR BEAUCHÊNE, OCTOBER 12, 1823

LEFT OUTSIDE THE DOOR UNDERNEATH A BOTTLE OF INK AND A PACKET OF PAPER

Victor,

I wanted to give this to you, but you've gone out for the day. My apologies for being such a distraction last night. I hope this replaces your lost supplies.

Julien

VICTOR BEAUCHÊNE TO JULIEN MORÈRE, OCTOBER 12, 1823

SLIPPED UNDER THE DOOR

Julien,

I decline your apology; I am in dire need of distractions. But I thank you for the ink and the paper. I wish I could draw something for you in return, but that is not among my paltry talents. My handwriting is passable when I slow down, and I am quite good at spelling, but this note still seems a poor trade. I'll have to find something else to offer you.

—Victor

PRIVATE DIARY OF V BEAUCHÊNE, OCTOBER 12, 1823

It's late and I shouldn't be burning this candle because if Aunt S wakes up, she'll see the light under the door. But I'm too giddy to sleep.

I slipped a note under Julien's door and was halfway to the stairs when he came out and called my name. I was in my dressing gown and slippers. I hadn't intended to see him. Perhaps he drew shocking conclusions from my state of undress, though certainly not more shocking than what he read in my room last night.

(Those conclusions would not have been wrong.)

Regardless, he didn't question me. He let me right in. His room is just like mine, with a bed and a wash basin and a small desk, except full of piles and piles of drawings. I sat on his bed and he showed me a small, curated selection.

I know nothing about art, but I found them wonderful. Julien became adorably speechless when I said so.

It's possible that they're abysmal and my judgment is clouded by Julien's nearness, which is also wonderful, but I'm fairly certain they're good. They held my attention for a time despite my interest in their artist. Lively little sketches of market stalls and flower girls and café patrons and bridges over the Seine. His sketch from the Luxembourg was in the pile, and there were two quick, small silhouettes in it that I can imagine represent myself and Aunt S walking along the path. I wanted to see self-portraits, but he didn't show me any.

JULIE MORÈRE TO ESTHER MORÈRE, OCTOBER 12, 1823
POSTMARKED PARIS

Maman,

You're right that I should be more careful in what I record in writing. Thank you for the reminder. My first letter to Adrienne was very personal, so we must hope she burned it. (We both know she is too sentimental for that.)

And thank you for the novel. I enjoyed <u>Virginie</u> a lot. Did you know the author, Camille Dupin, isn't a man? Perhaps not a woman, either. Or both? Regardless, it's quite a scandal. Everyone agrees the novel is excellent, though. I suppose a genius may live however a genius wishes. I shall continue to work toward that goal.

I would love to meet Camille. The society of my fellow students leaves something to be desired. But my studies are going well.

I'm glad to hear you and Papa and Georges are in good health. I miss the smell of the air at the farm. I will spare you a description of what it smells like in the street outside the Maison Laval. Whenever I can, I go to the Jardin du Luxembourg. It's nothing like home, but there are plants, at least. I have enclosed one of my sketches of it.

With affection,
Julie

JULIE MORÈRE TO ADRIENNE MORÈRE, OCTOBER 12, 1823
POSTMARKED PARIS

My dearest sister Adrienne,

I <u>knew</u> you were going to tell me that you knew when you were finished because it just felt right. You are, of course, always correct. Perhaps change is what feels best to some people, and perhaps some people are astride categories, or outside categories. I am certainly glad to have you to discuss it with. Your letters fill me with such gratitude and reassurance.

I notice a number of references to a character named Léon in your letter, and I think it was cruel of you not to send me a sketch. He sounds very gallant. What does our brother think of him? Have Maman and Papa met this Léon of yours?

Maman has encouraged me to be more circumspect in my letters, so apologies in advance for the vagueness of this one.

I think I may have encountered someone who is like us —or me, and the particular use I have made of my Art. I want to tell this person the truth, or part of the truth, and hopefully be rewarded with truth in kind, but it's an intimate and delicate subject to broach with a new acquaintance. I like this person very much, so I would hate to cause offense. And I don't think this person knows how to paint, so I would hate to reveal anything that might put our family in danger.

It is very hard to talk about this without saying anything directly. I don't like being indirect. I'm going to tell you a story instead.

Do you want to know an embarrassing thing that happened to me? Of course you do, you're my sister. Last night, one of the other boarders came over and while he was in my room, I showed him my work. I was flattered by his interest, but it was an unusual encounter—especially because a fair amount of the work in my room is <u>me</u>.

Worse, a fair amount of the work in my room is <u>him</u>.

Just sketches of his face—I didn't imagine anything I couldn't see. (Normal sketches. Not like my self-portraits. Despite my struggles with writing evasively, you know I have learned to be careful with my Art.) But still, I didn't want him to know. We've only just met, and I didn't want to discuss my fascination with his face.

Only... now I'm wondering if maybe I should have let him see.

Nothing else seems as momentous as that, but I am happy to report that I have found two of my classmates to be tolerable. Their names are Laurent and Auguste. I had assumed that my classmates disliked me because I am uncomfortable around them and shy in all matters except telling them they should not speak so crudely about the women who model for us. But it turns out, as Laurent and Auguste have explained to me, that my classmates <u>also</u> dislike me because I am better than them.

This came as a shock. Not because I don't know my

work is superior. Anyone can see that. But because I didn't realize it would be such a source of resentment. It's not as though I've ever had the bad grace to say aloud that I'm the best artist of our class. I just complete my assignments and stay quiet.

Now that Laurent and Auguste have discovered I am willing to answer their questions, they seem to want to be friends, so I suppose we will be. If only things were so simple with my fellow boarder.

Send me more Léon stories, Mlle Adrienne Morère.

I love you and miss you a lot.

With affection,

Julie

PRIVATE DIARY OF V BEAUCHÊNE, OCTOBER 19, 1823

Still no word from Father.

I'm angry at him and at myself for writing him such a false and horrible little supplication and then waiting around for a response like a pathetic, spineless thing.

I want the truth. I want to write him a letter that will burn his hand when he opens it.

[*The remainder of the entry is illegible, even with the cipher, because the ink has blurred. There is a tear in the page where the pen nib has pierced it.*]

VICTOR BEAUCHÊNE TO PIERRE FAUCHEUX, OCTOBER 20, 1823

POSTMARKED PARIS

Pierre Faucheux,

I hope the lies you've told about your late wife haunt you every night, but I know you're not honorable enough to feel shame about slandering her or evicting and disinheriting your own child. You sleep peacefully, warm and safe, too rich to feel fear, untouchable.

Consider whether that will always be the case.

You wronged me because you thought me powerless. Perhaps you imagine I'll starve quietly to death and trouble you no longer. I won't.

By turning me out of your house, you have set me free. You have known my whole life. You fathered me, though I know both of us are unhappy to acknowledge it. Surely you remember that Horace stole my journals and read them until I invented a cipher—as a child. You know I stole his school books to give myself the education you denied me; he never caught me and all your efforts to stop me were in vain. Imagine what I might do with that sort of intellect and dedication, far from your surveillance and made desperate by your hand. Do you want to find out?

Here is what I want: a written response stating why you spread this vile slander against my mother in order to disinherit me—even if your only reason is "I am a cruel and selfish man who only loves one of his children," I want you to write those words—and ten thousand francs.

Give me that, addressed to the name at the bottom of this letter at the Maison Laval, and you won't hear from me again.

Victor Beauchêne

PIERRE FAUCHEUX TO VICTOR BEAUCHÊNE, OCTOBER 21, 1823
POSTMARKED PARIS

Victor,

Your threats are uncivilized and childish, and still I will give you half of what you ask. It will be the truth and not the money. Due to my recent infirmity, Horace has assumed control of the finances. Only he has the power to make withdrawals.

It's strange. He asked me not to speak of that, so I haven't, but I suppose I never promised not to write about it. I have no desire to tell you, either, as it shames me— you see that I do feel shame—but reading your letter inspired a bizarre compulsion to respond.

I know you wish to believe your mother was blameless. I do, too. I did love her, though I don't expect you to believe that. She poisoned you and Sophie against me. Perhaps you were easy to sway, not really being a child of my blood. That part is unquestionably true. I know because Horace told me.

It's why I had to turn you out. Your presence in the house was a stain upon our family honor. It was not right that you should inherit half of a fortune that was never yours to begin with.

    Pierre

PRIVATE DIARY OF V BEAUCHÊNE, OCTOBER 21, 1823

My father's letter was too strange to comprehend. I can't sort it out.

1. I only wrote my letter for my own satisfaction. Never in my life would I have expected a serious response. None of my other letters merited his notice. Why this one?
2. "Due to my recent infirmity" is nonsense. What infirmity? He's a perfectly healthy man in his fifties. There is no reason for my brother to assume control of the finances—and I cannot imagine my father letting him.
3. He says he promised Horace not to "speak" of the situation, but he can write to me because of a "bizarre compulsion." I certainly agree that it's bizarre. It's also not the way my very staid and practical father talks or thinks.
4. "That part is unquestionably true. I know because Horace told me." WHAT DOES THIS MEAN?

5. He seriously considered giving me ten thousand francs? A strong argument for writing more letters asking for money.
6. He made no comment about my name.

I would question whether he wrote it, but it's his handwriting. Is his "infirmity" that he now suffers delusions? It has only been a few weeks since I last saw him and he never showed signs of any such condition. He doesn't seem impaired in any other way. His writing is legible and coherent.

What does all this mean?

Perhaps I should perform the experiment of writing to Horace and asking for ten thousand francs. Though it's obvious at this point that Horace bears me nothing but ill will.

I can't even be angry about this. It's too strange.

(Well. I can, actually, and I think I will.)

PRIVATE DIARY OF V BEAUCHÊNE, OCTOBER 27, 1823

I haven't written to Horace. There has never been any affection between us, and if my father is telling the truth that it's Horace who is the architect of my eviction—and possibly that Horace has some means of controlling my father—then (1) caution is required and (2) I am too angry to possess any.

My father's comment about his "compulsion" to reply to my letter haunted me, so I explored it. Though I am alone in my room and I always write in a cipher, recording this makes me glance over my shoulder like someone might be waiting to laugh at me: I seem to have developed some limited ability to compel people's beliefs and behavior with my writing. It is possible that magic exists.

I feel absurd even writing it. Do we not live in an enlightened, scientific age? This isn't some backwards, once-upon-a-time village, where neighbors might have accused each other of witchcraft and been punished as criminals. We have street lights and factories. Stock markets. Steam locomotion. (Well, I've never seen that in real life, but I glimpsed some etchings over my father's shoulder once while he was contemplating an investment in it.)

Yet here I am tiptoeing cautiously around the notion that perhaps magic is... real?

And that I engaged in it?

Accidentally, no less.

I can confirm nothing beyond my own experience. I have mostly tested the claim by counterfeiting money in the simplest and most ludicrous of ways.

I felt so guilty about tricking my tailor, who has shown me nothing but kindness and didn't deserve to be drawn into my scheme, that I immediately returned to the shop to pay my debts with real money, though I could ill afford it. It was impossible to explain why I was trying to pay my bill <u>again</u>, since he believed I had already paid him, so I had to write a second letter that said "You will accept this money that I owe you for my purchases on October 26, 1823 and you will not ask any questions."

I didn't expect that to work, but it did. So now I have a new suit, no money, and a vague idea that I can do something terrifying.

Regarding the source of the power in this exchange of letters:

- It can't be the paper because I've had success with several different sheets now.
- It can't be the ink because I used the ink that Julien gave me in one successful note and borrowed Aunt S's inkwell for another.
- It can't be <u>me</u> because I've had failed attempts. (I wrote Aunt S a note that said "this is twenty francs." She laughed at me, said "If only we

could make money like this, my dear," and handed it back.)
- That leaves the pen. But I used the same pen to write all those letters to my father, and he never responded until I wrote him the furious one. So if it is the pen, perhaps I did something to it?

Further study is required. But for the record I am writing this entry, and all future entries, with an ordinary pen. Just in case.

PRIVATE DIARY OF V BEAUCHÊNE, OCTOBER 27, 1823

ADDENDUM: I am also writing all my correspondence with Julien—which I hope will be copious—with an ordinary pen. I am distressed by the notion of influencing him. If he feels any affection toward me, I want it to be his own.

V BEAUCHÊNE TO JULIEN MORÈRE, OCTOBER 28, 1823
SLIPPED UNDER THE DOOR

Julien,

Are you free this evening or are you feverishly working on a masterpiece? If it's the former, come down to my room and talk to me. I've read every book I own six times and I'm bored.

—V

J MORÈRE TO V BEAUCHÊNE, OCTOBER 28, 1823
SLIPPED UNDER THE DOOR

V—

I would come down, but I'm afraid of your aunt. Perhaps you could come upstairs?

—J

PRIVATE DIARY OF V BEAUCHÊNE, OCTOBER 29, 1823

Last night Julien invited me to his room. He claimed he was too afraid of Aunt S to come to our rooms, but I told him I had never heard anything so ridiculous in my life. He's twice her size and half her age. She does have an imposing presence, though.

Anyway, I went upstairs. I wanted to tell him about myself, but I was afraid. Aunt S behaved so perfectly, and I want to believe Julien would, too. But it would break my heart if he didn't.

I don't know how to tell him how I've been spending my time, either. It's difficult to say "by the way, I think I might accidentally have imbued a pen with some supernatural power."

It's funny, because I feel more at ease with Julien than I ever have with anyone else. I could almost imagine saying that to him. He would consider it carefully, just as he does everything else I say.

I can't tell if it's because I've spoken to so few men in my life (really just my father and Horace, what specimens), or if it's because everyone used to treat me as a frivolous heiress (I <u>am</u> frivolous, and I long to be an heir again), or if it's some quality that is particular to the two of us. I think Julien is <u>interested</u> in me, and I don't only mean the staring. He asks me questions and then listens when I answer. It's marvelous.

I asked to see more of his art and he showed me a few new sketches, all breathtaking. Julien liked it when I said so, I'm sure, even though tonight he was more difficult to fluster. Perhaps he is already inured to my compliments.

He did let me stay for a long time, though. The candle was burning very low when I left, and I had to be careful not to let the floorboards creak beneath my feet. (Though it's not as if there's anything untoward in one young man visiting another young man for reasons of friendship and art appreciation. At least, that's what I planned to say to anyone who asked me why I was awake, which no one did.)

I do appreciate Julien's art. His style is very decisive, and he never makes two marks where one will suffice. I told him I would like to watch him work, and he was quiet for a moment and then said, "Yes. Tomorrow afternoon in the gardens."

I don't think I will be able to sleep at all tonight.

JULIE MORÈRE TO ADRIENNE MORÈRE, OCTOBER 30, 1823
POSTMARKED PARIS

To my dearest, most marvelous, wretchedly foolish sister Adrienne,

Of course Léon likes you. How could anyone not like you? You are—in addition to being modest to the point of absurdity—kind and generous and thoughtful, and let us not forget, my hero. As if that were not enough, you are also beautiful, which I know you know, but which I will tell you again so you will not write me any more nonsense. Should Léon disagree with me on any of these points, or hurt you in any way at all, I will come home and hit him. I've never hit anyone before, but I have two perfectly functional fists.

I know you have fists of your own, but I owe you a rescue. I suppose Georges is already at home with you, and he does spend all day hauling stones for his sculptures, so he has the arms for throwing a punch. But Georges doesn't have the temperament. I do.

Now that I have forbidden you from writing more nonsense, I can fill this letter with my own. You are the only one I can write nonsense to. No, that makes it sound silly, when really it's serious: you're the only person with whom I can be my whole self. I would be very lonely without these letters, Adrienne.

Anyway, this afternoon I invited my fellow boarder, Victor, to watch me work. He asked to watch, I mean, and I accepted and suggested he might accompany me today. I'm not so egotistical as to assume people want to waste an afternoon staring at my hands. (I do like them, though. My hands. I had better, since it was a nightmare to draw and paint so many studies of my own hands <u>while they were changing</u>. On second thought, I retract my offer to punch Léon and substitute instead an offer to kick him, should he behave poorly. My hands are too precious to risk.)

Here is a quick sketch of Victor. His face is quite striking. Sharp and delicate. A nice contrast with the soft curl in his hair. He has a kind of unblemished symmetry that you rarely see outside of paintings. I think that's why I keep drawing him.

That, and he's so clever with a smile. It makes me feel like I'm part of a secret. I feel more alive in his presence. I know that doesn't make any sense. Either you're alive or not. But I feel quicker, more alert, and more interested and interesting when I'm with him. I swear today's light was crisper and brighter than it would have been otherwise.

He told me how he came to be in the Maison Laval. I was correct that he used to be rich—his father is a banker. But Victor has been disinherited in favor of his brother. Their father claims to doubt their late mother's fidelity. Victor, he says, is not his child. The only true heir is Victor's brother Horace. All of this is false, according to Victor, but it hasn't stopped his father from expelling Victor from the family home and fortune.

Victor's aunt—his mother's sister—came to live with him at the Maison Laval. She's the only real family he has left. Isn't that tragic? I told Victor the story broke my heart, but he seemed to take the whole thing in stride.

"I'm not happy about being disinherited, but there is a certain freedom in it," he said. "I will determine my own future."

This is a freedom that you and I have always had, to make our own choices, and we don't have to sacrifice the love of our family to do it. We may not be the children of bankers, but we're rich.

I didn't say that to Victor. I'm not quite sure how to talk about our family with other people, first because we're strange, but second because it's a bit like talking about how good my drawings are. "Oh, my parents love me unconditionally and so do my sister and brother, I can't imagine living any other way." Insufferable.

I did tell Victor that if he ever needed help, he could come to me, which he seemed to like. Other than the sad topic of his family, he was cheerful, and we had a pleasant conversation. He intuited that I don't like to talk much while I draw, for which I'm grateful, and seemed content to watch in silence and sit next to me.

Very close to me, I must say. I don't have any sense of these things, especially not between young men. Is it normal if his whole thigh was touching mine? And later, after my sketch of the landscape was complete and he'd just finished leaning over to look at it, he brushed his fingers over my cheek and said, "You didn't shave today. I like it. Have you ever thought about growing a beard?"

He smells good. Expensive. Like some kind of flower I can't identify. And his face was so close to mine, and his touch was warm, and [*The remainder of this sentence has been scratched out. The word "sketchbook" can be made out.*]

Sorry. Carried away. You take my meaning.

It is extraordinarily inconvenient to have these feelings. I don't know what to do with them. I just came here to study. I'm not prepared for anything else. And if I get distracted, I worry that I won't hold my tongue. It was a near thing, not telling Victor that I'm tired of my choice to give myself facial hair, except when he's touching it, and that I would grow a beard if he wanted me to. The degree to which I feel witless in his presence—especially when he is practically draped over my shoulder, or petting my face—cannot be overstated. Does Léon make you feel this discomposed, Adrienne? Am I singularly stupid?

Is this why it was so easy for Alphonse [*The previous, unfinished sentence has a single line through it.*]

No, let's not talk about that.

I couldn't be sure what was going to come out of my mouth if I said something, so I didn't answer Victor's question about beards. The terrible little choked sound I made didn't trouble him. He's good enough at conversation that he can carry one all by himself.

You're probably thoroughly horrified by this point, but there is worse to come.

Victor stroked his own face, which is youthful and smooth, and mused, "I can't grow a beard."

And I said—because I am a <u>fool</u>—"Would you like to?"

Happily, he interpreted this question as entirely hypothetical. "I don't know. Do you think I would look good with one? Or sideburns, perhaps?"

I choked again, and then told him that I thought he would look handsome no matter what he chose, just managing to stop short of saying something like "because your face is perfect." And then, thankfully, we went home and ate dinner in the company of the other boarders, where I wasn't required to say anything, and no one touched me at all.

How am I going to survive this, Adrienne? I have to stop seeing him. But I don't want to stop seeing him.

With affection,

Julie

PRIVATE DIARY OF V BEAUCHÊNE, OCTOBER 30, 1823

Julien is brilliant and talented and handsome, and I like him far more than he likes me. It's awful. I thought I was correct in thinking that I flustered him—I thought it meant he liked me—but in fact, it may indicate real discomfort. He was even quieter than usual this afternoon, even though I gave him lots of opportunities to say something or do something or react in any way.

Well, he did say I was handsome. But I prompted him.

Perhaps I was too much. But was it the flirting or the family story that ruined things? I think I can still salvage our friendship if I take a more sedate approach. Even if he doesn't want to kiss me, I still want to talk to him. I hate to think I've repulsed him.

I shouldn't be focusing on that. We are going to run out of money in a matter of months. I suggested to Aunt S that I might look for work and she was thoroughly amused. She actually said, "But you're useless, my dear." (I am reconsidering my love for her.)

Then I told her maybe I could marry a girl with a large

dowry, and she patted me on the shoulder and said, "If you find one, let me know."

Possible ways to get money:

- Work (I am indeed useless, but perhaps I could learn not to be? I do know how to read and write. Perhaps I could lie my way into the study of... law? Suffer nobly in poverty for a while and then earn a living—if we live)
- Marriage (innumerable problems with this, including both my first and last name and the unjust nature of the institution itself)
- Theft (like work, this requires skills I don't yet have; also, Forestier is a police officer and he lives in this house, so I would definitely get caught)
- Writing one of Aunt S's wicked novels (having utterly failed to get seduced in life, I am not sure I have the skills for this, either—and the legality of some of Aunt S's collection is questionable, so the problem of Forestier recurs)
- Magic (know nothing about it, am intrigued but slightly terrified by it, don't want to use it to steal from decent people like my tailor)

I wish this was a story so I could accidentally faint in front of the carriage of some aristocrat, flash a little ankle, and all my problems would be solved. To do: meet a rich person who finds me charming and will pay my rent. (And Aunt S's rent. She didn't abandon me and I'm not abandoning her.)

PRIVATE DIARY OF V BEAUCHÊNE, NOVEMBER 3, 1823

I've managed to have several very civilized and appropriate conversations with Julien, where I didn't touch him or say anything suggestive. It was difficult and I'm proud of my restraint, though I must say Julien seems a bit gloomy lately.

Still, I have maintained our friendship, I think.

In worse news, the pen is not as reliably persuasive as I had hoped. I tried to buy a book about magic from an extraordinarily surly bookstore clerk and he would not accept the note of credit I had written myself. (It was only a loan! I would have gone back later to pay in real money.)

I had to count out so many coins from my dwindling stash, all while the clerk glowered. I don't know if I can set foot in that bookstore again, which is a shame, as they have a lot of books on the occult.

Perhaps the clerk was alert to the possibility of magic, and thus defended himself against my deception?

Come to think of it, the laundry also only accepts coins, and so does the bakery. That makes me suspect that for smaller amounts, writing a note doesn't work, no matter how much conviction I feel when I do it.

My own conviction does play a role in the pen's effectiveness. I have to feel, very deeply, whatever I'm writing. You would think this would be sufficient to produce money—I want very badly to have some—but the laundress rolled her eyes at me.

Necessary conditions for success: (1) my own state of mind while writing, (2) the state of mind of my reader. People who expect coins and bills reject my handwritten notes. The most susceptible reader would be one who expected our transaction to result in being handed a piece of paper.

Say, if I were to go to my father's bank and make a large withdrawal from his account.

PRIVATE DIARY OF V BEAUCHÊNE, NOVEMBER 4, 1823

This book I bought fascinates me, and I hope it's not all lies. It has the unassuming title <u>A Catalogue of Artifacts</u>, but the catalogue itself is preceded by a treatise on magic. Here is what I have learned so far: magic is the purview of humans alone. No other living things possess it, although some animals may be able to sense its presence in people or objects.

The author (one J. L. A. Malbosc, he seems to have been a libertine thinker some two hundred years ago) expresses uncertainty as to why <u>some</u> humans possess magic and others don't. Malbosc theorizes that we are all born with the potential, but that some of us never unlock it.

Magic, he says, lives in the body and springs primarily from the will, but other deep emotions can release it. Intentions and emotions can permeate objects created by human hands, rendering them powerful enough to transform the world. In some objects, the power remains long after their creators die.

My pen may outlive me. I'm not sure I like the thought.

Malbosc gives all sorts of horrifying examples of cursed objects. It's a long list of knives that leave no trace of a wound but still kill, cups that turn any liquid poison, and shoes that prevent their wearer from running. Murderous impulses abound. There are non-violent things—baby blankets that protect from harm, jugs of oil that replenish themselves, good-luck dice that actually work, perfume bottles that make anything smell good, clothes that prevent their wearer from being seen, musical instruments that always play true, various magic paintings—but on the whole, Malbosc spends more time on the dangerous items. He writes with particular relish about an emerald necklace that collars the mind as well as the neck: whoever wears must obey the person who clasped it.

I wonder if Horace possesses something like that. Could that be how he assumed control of my father's finances? If he does have such an object, did he create it himself, as I did my pen?

My pen is not a knife or a poison cup. It has uses that don't result in death. And I have not yet done anything wrong—or rather, I have, but I paid everyone I was temporarily indebted to. Still, the pen could be put to terrible use. I know that.

I don't like the idea of my brother possessing such a power, even if it's hard to feel pity for the father who turned me out.

J MORÈRE TO V BEAUCHÊNE, NOVEMBER 5, 1823
SLIPPED UNDER THE DOOR

V—

Are you sick? You weren't at dinner tonight, and I haven't noticed you leaving your room much these past few days.

—J

V BEAUCHÊNE TO J MORÈRE, NOVEMBER 5, 1823
SLIPPED UNDER THE DOOR

J—

Are you tracking my movements? I'd accuse you of being like Forestier, except I think he really is tracking my movements. I know he lives two floors up, but he's always lurking in the oddest places.

I am not sick.

—V

J MORÈRE TO V BEAUCHÊNE, NOVEMBER 5, 1823
SLIPPED UNDER THE DOOR

V—

It's called worrying. What I'm doing, that is. I don't know what Forestier is doing. He makes me uneasy, too.

I asked after your health because I was afraid to ask if I'd offended you. It's been days since we talked. Sometimes people mistake my silence for condemnation, and I want you to know that's not the case between us. I think very highly of you. I'm just not as good at conversation as you are.

I can see the light from your candle in the gap under the door. I feel silly writing to you while you're standing right there, but sometimes it's easier to write than to speak.

If I haven't ruined everything, then I hope you'll come in. The door is unlocked.

—J

JULIE MORÈRE TO ADRIENNE MORÈRE, NOVEMBER 8, 1823
POSTMARKED PARIS

My dear Adrienne,

I'm so glad to hear your Léon is a sensible young man —for your happiness and also so I won't have to make good on my promise to avenge your honor with kicks. Good shoes are expensive.

There are no sensible young men in Paris, myself included. You were correct that I should stop seeing Victor if I can't trust myself to keep a secret around him, and I tried for a while. Or rather, we mutually avoided each other for a few days, me because I thought I had offended him somehow, and him because he was deeply immersed in reading and correspondence, which he says is a common occurrence.

But you were also correct that it's cruel to deny myself this friendship, and that I need a friend here in Paris. Laurent and Auguste are acquaintances now, but their company doesn't provide the same pleasure as Victor's. So I have resolved not to talk about our Art. I do it in the rest of my life and it causes me no consternation, but something about Victor makes me want to share everything.

I suspect he feels the same.

(Your mockery about how I made myself too handsome is the pot calling the kettle beautiful, Adrienne. You may be right that I underestimate my effect on other people, but go look in a mirror, you crimson-lipped, raven-haired fool. Besides, we are artists. We did not paint hundreds of self-portraits to produce unattractive work.)

Victor comes to my room every night now. Oh, I've just realized what that sounds like. We're only talking. I haven't let him get close enough to touch me since—well, it's too much for me, you understand, trying to work out who I am and what I want while also worrying about our friendship. It's like when you put a magnet next to a compass. Victor makes me dizzy.

He might be the smartest person I've ever met. He told me he keeps a diary in a cipher he invented <u>as a child</u> to stop his brother reading his private writing. (His brother sounds like an asshole.) No one taught Victor the idea of the cipher. He just didn't want to stop writing. He said "I was alone so much that my diary was almost like a friend"—everything I learn about his youth makes my heart hurt—so he found a way to keep writing in private. Then he spent twenty minutes trying to teach me to substitute one letter for another, but I found it laborious. I can't spell in normal French, Adrienne, can you imagine how incomprehensible my letters would be if I mixed up the alphabet to try to write in code? Victor told me that he's memorized his.

I think he finds me shocking. I let slip that we don't go to church and he called me a Jacobin. He was teasing, I think, but I explained that we don't go because our mother is Jewish, and then she married our father and they stopped practicing any religion but art, and that I do actually believe citizens have a right to govern themselves, and Victor stared at me like I'd grown another head. He didn't know much about the Jacobins, as it turns out. He had all sorts of questions, and I tried my best to answer them, and wondered how he could know so little about the history of our own country.

"Are you a royalist, then?" I asked.

He took a long time answering. "I don't think I believe in anything."

"Then you're even more radical than me."

"No, I mean you believe in things—the rights of man and citizen, good and evil, your art. What I want is to survive," he said. "It's not so much that I _believe_ in inherited wealth, it's that I can't survive without the money I expected from my father. Every aspect of my upbringing was designed to render me decorative and not too threatening. What few serious books I've read, I stole from my brother. I know nothing about the world, and they cast me into it. I don't ever want to return to my family, but I won't give them the satisfaction of quietly disappearing. I will live. Whatever allows me to live, that's what I believe in."

This was startling, and ferocious, and admirable, and I wanted to say how admirable, but instead I said, "That's rather Machiavellian."

Surely there exists a conversational middle ground between lovesickness and cold disdain, but Adrienne, I swear to you I couldn't find my way there even if I had a map. (Because of my faulty compass, you see? I can be clever in letters, but _only_ in letters.)

But I digress. The important result of my blundering

comment was that Victor hasn't read any Machiavelli—<u>The Prince</u> was not among the books he stole—and thus didn't know what I was talking about, which made everything worse. This discussion of his past supports a theory of mine. Wealthy young men are not customarily brought up to be decorative and harmless. They are not denied education. (Though many are uneducated in what matters.)

If I were to mention, very very carefully, that I am not an entirely masculine person, do you think that would be wise? I think I can do it without reference to Art. I would love so much to tell him even a small part of the truth.

I know you are going to give me a sensible answer, Adrienne, and we both know I'll ignore it, but I suppose by now it's tradition. Go ahead.

With affection,

Julie

PRIVATE DIARY OF V BEAUCHÊNE, NOVEMBER 12, 1823

I was raised by a banker and yet he taught me nothing of finance. Instead he tried to impart all that knowledge to my thickheaded and cruel brother, and even though that failed, he inexplicably <u>still</u> decided Horace should inherit the family fortune.

As with everything, I am going to have to teach myself.

But I will take my time—as much time as we have before things go from desperate to dire—because if I am going to do this theft, it must be done right. What concerns me is not so much the details of banking or finance or having money and turning it into more money (another kind of sorcery). Those things can be learned.

No, I have two worries.

The first is that I don't yet know the lasting effect of my work with the pen. I finished reading Malbosc's book and I have a better sense of what I can expect from magic now, and my theory is that if I dash off something that I don't believe—"this is twenty francs"—then the recipient may struggle to believe it, or may reject it outright. Perhaps a susceptible reader will be swayed by what I've written while the page is in their hand, and a very susceptible one might accept it for a few hours.

A matter of hours is enough time to exit the bank with money in hand, but not enough time not to get caught.

But if I write something deeply felt—that my father owes me the truth, for instance, or that my name is Victor Beauchêne—then my conviction is communicated to the reader. They feel it and act on it.

I need that money to live, and I'll make better use of it than my father or my brother. I've never felt more conviction about anything. The bank clerk will be expecting letters on the subject of withdrawals and transfers. These things work in my favor. But I need to produce a letter that will strike anyone who sees it, even years after the fact, as undeniably real. I need to write a letter that Horace himself could pick up and think "I suppose I did write this." A perfect forgery.

It's a shame that Horace finagled control of the bank. I have a letter of my father's handwriting to copy, but I'm going to have to write to my brother to obtain a sample of his. I can think of no one on Earth that I have less desire to speak to. Time to practice my obsequious and pathetic letter-writing again.

My second worry is that, per my father's bizarre letter, Horace may possess an object like my pen—something that allows him to exert influence on my father. This troubles me, but I don't know enough to act yet. I will see if I can get Horace to reveal anything to me in his letter—fingers crossed *he* doesn't have a way of influencing *me* through correspondence—and I will ask Aunt S to listen for gossip about him. And I will hope that things become clearer before our money runs out.

VICTOR BEAUCHÊNE TO HORACE FAUCHEUX, NOVEMBER 12, 1823

POSTMARKED PARIS

Dear Horace,

I deeply regret the events that have kept us apart these past few months and wish to make amends enough to communicate with you, if you deem it possible. In my humbled condition, even a fraction of your forgiveness would mean the world to me. You are, after all, my only brother. I am no threat to you. All I ask is an acknowledgement. Perhaps you might deign to write with some news of your life?

I heard recently that you took control of the bank; you must be very busy with important things. How does it feel to assume Father's place? He must be very proud. Did you celebrate? You probably did. Beautiful women probably fell at your feet. They must all be lining up to marry you, handsome and rich and powerful as you are. What are you doing to entertain yourself—still hunting? I imagine you must have quite the collection of trophies by now. Curiosity overwhelms me. You would be doing me a great kindness by answering any of these questions. Tell me everything.

I have nothing to offer but accounts of my humiliation, so I will not bore you with all the ways in which I find myself reduced. Correspondence with you would bring me just what I need to get through these difficult circumstances. One letter is all I need.

Your brother,
Victor

HORACE FAUCHEUX TO VICTOR BEAUCHÊNE, NOVEMBER 13, 1823
POSTMARKED PARIS

Victor,

I told Father that it would do you good to have to fend for yourself, and I see that I was right. You've always needed humbling. I'm glad to see you don't think yourself so smart anymore now that you're in the real world. I always said it's not your fault you were born such a weak and unmanly thing, but it is your fault you didn't learn to accept your lesser status, and instead you became conniving and insufferable. We just couldn't have you in the house anymore with your stolen books and your codes and your tricks. You were trying to overturn the natural order of things, and it was a disgrace.

All those years you thought you were smarter than me, and look at us now. Of course it's better this way. We're both in our right places. Now that you're showing the proper gratitude, we can talk honestly. Some people aren't suited to power and greatness and some are. You'll make a little life for yourself down there among the people you belong with. That's how it should be.

As for taking over the bank, that had to be done, too.

This is my rightful place. Father just doesn't know what's necessary anymore. You would have been able to deceive him if you'd still been in the house, so I had to make him listen. I had to make him respect me. He <u>would</u> be proud of me if he weren't a doddering old fool. At least we both know he isn't proud of <u>you</u>. That would be too much to bear. Maman liked you best because she was subject to useless feminine flights of emotion and she mistook you for a helpless weakling instead of the crafty fraud I knew you to be. But she's dead and you're in the gutter and I have all the money, so I was the smart one in the end and now everything's right in order.

You're right, lots of women do want to marry me. Even more of them want to fuck me. I'm rich and great-looking and nobody can say no to me—not even the frigid bitches who try to keep their legs closed—so I can have any woman I want.

I do still hunt, and you're correct that I'm excellent at it and could be bringing home trophies any time I wanted, but the passion that occupies me these days is collecting art objects. I've become a connoisseur. It's an expertise that not many people can acquire. I'm part of a very exclusive collectors' club. Even among them, I have the best taste. Soon, I'll have the best collection, too.

Horace

VICTOR BEAUCHÊNE TO HORACE FAUCHEUX, NOVEMBER 14, 1823

POSTMARKED PARIS

Dear Horace,

Thank you so much for your letter, a spark of light in my sad little life. It is worth a great deal to me. You will never know how much.

I know you are busy doing important things, and you are right that I need to make my own way in the world. Indeed, your idea about my independence is so brilliant that we should commit to it. I want to make my own way in the world and not rely on our relation for success. I have done my part to make this possible by changing my name.

For your part, if you never want to see me again, take the precaution of providing me with a list of the people and places you frequent, that I might avoid them and leave you free of my burdensome presence. I know our paths are highly unlikely to cross, as I don't move in such rarefied circles as you, but this list will assure it. If the list should fail and chance bring us together, let us agree to act as strangers.

Whether it be in the street or a parlor, allow us to be

introduced anew. Say nothing of our connection. You owe me nothing, so treat me as a person entirely unknown to you. Wipe the slate clean.

If anyone remarks on our physical similarity, laugh and say what a coincidence it is. I know that will be well within your ability. You did, after all, convince our father that he wasn't my father.

Victor

JULIE MORÈRE TO ESTHER MORÈRE, NOVEMBER 15, 1823
POSTMARKED PARIS

Maman,

Here are some small sketches—a bit macabre, the skulls, I know, but I like them. And I drew a scene in the covered market. My instructors dismissed it as insufficiently historical or mythological or grand, but I was very taken with the crowd of figures and the stuffed surroundings. All those barrels and overflowing baskets.

Of course I will come home in December.

As for your suggestion that I invite my new friend, I will consider it.

I miss you,

Julie

JULIE MORÈRE TO ADRIENNE MORÈRE, NOVEMBER 15, 1823
POSTMARKED PARIS

My dearest sister Adrienne,

Did you tell our mother about my new friend? It pierces my heart that you would betray me like this. I choose to believe Maman extracted the information in some devious way, and thus you are innocent—and also, I hope, <u>wracked with guilt</u> about what you've revealed.

Or perhaps you were so desperate to meet Victor yourself that you surrendered my secret willingly? I've never known you to be so cunning, Adrienne. This affair with Léon has changed you. I will invite Victor to come home with me if you promise to introduce me to Léon. It's the only way justice will be done.

I can't wait to see you in December.

With affection,

Julie

PRIVATE DIARY OF V BEAUCHÊNE, NOVEMBER 18, 1823

I haven't apprised Aunt S of my plans, with regards to the pen and the bank and Horace, though I did ask her about the list of people Horace so generously provided. She made a few inconclusive murmurs about one or two of the names being familiar, and something about how she was old and had been away from society for too long, and then said she would ask her friends.

It seems she's been making plans of her own. I've mostly known Aunt S as Maman's most devoted caretaker and the only living family member who gives a damn about me, but apparently she used to be rather sought-after company in certain circles—or rather, she still is sought-after, more so now that she's disappeared for a few years.

"A little absence does wonders," she told me, although it's not as if she left society by choice. She did it because Maman needed her. And now I need her. I know she's here with me by choice, but I still feel a bit selfish. Judging from her correspondence, a lot of people want to see her.

It's not what I expected from a *vieille fille*, but I suppose Aunt S is still quite beautiful—she's fifty-something, I think, though I will never ask—and why should old maids have to withdraw from society, never to be seen again? I don't know why Aunt S never married, but I tend to assume she's right about everything. Besides, when she was young, it was the Revolution and all that, and Julien has made me understand that those times were not at all like these times.

Anyway, she's been writing to all of her friends and connections on my behalf. When she first told me that, I guessed it was to gather invitations to places where I might be seen and subsequently proposed to—a marriage or a job, preferably the latter—but the idea caused her gales of laughter. I get the impression Aunt S's connections aren't respectable, and that makes me even more eager to meet them.

SOPHIE BEAUCHÊNE TO ISABELLE DE TOURZIN, NOVEMBER 18, 1823
SENT BY PRIVATE COURIER

My dear Isabelle,

I know it has been far too long since I've written. I have missed you dearly—yes, you recalcitrant old crone, my feelings of friendship endure, and you are powerless to stop me. Be as ill-tempered as you like. Tell me you have no interest in such sentimental weakness. I know you'll write back to this letter, and in all the decades of our acquaintance, you have only said no to me once. Never have I been so gently refused. You say you are without a heart, but we both know it isn't true. Don't worry, darling. I've never told anyone.

I write to you now because the misfortunes that have kept me away from society continue, and I find myself worried for my sister's child. Cruelly disinherited by Anaïs's toad of a husband, this young person is in need of help. A few introductions might help them find their way in the world.

Perhaps in January, if that could be arranged. I think we will be traveling in December.

Don't interpret this letter as me digging for information, you cranky old paranoiac. I know your heart, Isabelle, and that is a better secret than anything I could ever hope to learn about your work.

Your friend,
Sophie

ISABELLE DE TOURZIN TO SOPHIE BEAUCHÊNE, NOVEMBER 19, 1823

SENT BY PRIVATE COURIER

Sophie,
    No.
    Isabelle

JULIE MORÈRE TO ESTHER MORÈRE, NOVEMBER 21, 1823
POSTMARKED PARIS

Maman,

Victor and his aunt, Mlle Sophie Beauchêne, have accepted your invitation to come to the farm in December. I am very much looking forward to spending some time with all of you. I will be home soon.

With affection,
Julie

JULIE MORÈRE TO ADRIENNE MORÈRE, NOVEMBER 21, 1823
POSTMARKED PARIS

My dear sister Adrienne,

Victor and his aunt are going to visit the farm. I have acted perfectly calm in front of both of them, but <u>I do not feel perfectly calm, Adrienne</u>.

I can no longer distinguish excitement from panic. What have I done, Adrienne? What am I going to do? What do I even <u>want</u>? (Victor. I want Victor. I want to tell him everything and have him still trust, respect, and want me. It feels possible, but perhaps that's my feverish imagination.)

Promise you'll keep me from doing anything monumentally stupid in front of Victor. No, don't, I know you'll say it's too late.

With affection,

Julie

PRIVATE DIARY OF V BEAUCHÊNE, DECEMBER 2, 1823

Look at this drawing. Look at it. I can't reconcile my thoughts. I've never seen something so instantly recognizable as <u>me</u>, and yet I can't believe that it is me. That Julien has seen me so well.

At first glance, it is a study of a young man's head. A few short blond curls brush his forehead, and the rest of his hair brushes the tops of his ears. He has a straight, slender nose and a sharp jaw, but there is youthful softness in his smooth cheeks. And at second glance, one begins to wonder: is this a young man? Perhaps the jaw is not sharp, but delicate. Look at the indulgent curve of the bottom lip, at the luxuriant lashes. But the hair is short and the neck is clothed in a cravat. Some young men do have an androgynous quality. It is not unheard of for men to have thick lashes and soft mouths. The question lingers. It invites further study. After long looking, one discards the question in favor of others: what secret joy motivates that little smile? What knowledge lifts the arch of that brow? Is there an offer in this expression, or only mockery?

What a gift. I hope it is not mere flattery. Then again,

if the drawing is Julien's opinion of me, there is pleasure in that, too. I would very much like for Julien to flatter me.

I did have to bully him into drawing me, though. He suggested it weeks ago and I only cajoled him into it today. I brought it up every time he mentioned models—I know full well that they usually take their clothes off. He didn't accept <u>that</u> offer. He hasn't been refusing, exactly, just quietly demurring and changing the subject. Julien is so reserved. Perhaps the idea of my nudity makes him uncomfortable. For now, I have retreated from that battle, and my strategy has been rewarded, since he did such a handsome little portrait.

A few days ago, I met his classmates Laurent and Auguste and they teased him about being cold and arrogant. I insulted them for being so wrong, and I think Julien was ill at ease because he turned his face away. But I couldn't stop myself from correcting them. Julien knows he's good. He never says so, but he doesn't have to. That's confidence, not arrogance. I can't believe the École des Beaux-Arts lets in such dullards.

And having spent all afternoon with Julien watching me, I know he isn't cold. It's rare to get a glimpse of what's under that calm, quiet exterior, but it's more fire than ice. It was delicious to have him stare at me for so long, and to see the drawing he produced is even more so. Julien knows me, as I know him.

I wish I could draw him. It feels so inadequate to describe a person in words. Julien's <u>exemplary</u>, like a marble statue made flesh. He's not enormously broadshouldered, but he's bigger than me, and that suits me. (I confess not knowing <u>why</u>, exactly, it matters to me. I suspect we could enjoy ourselves perfectly well together if we were the same size. So why do I care that he's big? Do I want him to pick me up? Or pin me down?

[*an unintelligible blot of ink*]

Well. Writing does bring clarity to the disorder of the mind.

Anyway, I look at Julien and I think yes.)

He has such long legs. His clothes aren't usually very tight, but I have dedicated myself to the study of his thighs and his arms, the muscles of which can sometimes be seen when he moves.

I'm so crude. Julien drew me a beautiful, personal study of my face, and here I am waxing poetic about his ass. It deserves poetry, though.

His face is equally wonderful, broad and angular with thick, dark brows, but with such a soft gaze. His resting expression is serious and contemplative, his chestnut-colored eyes a little mournful. When he smiles—I wish it happened more often—it's usually crooked.

He's still and deliberate, except when lost in thought, and then he runs a hand through his hair. Some of it always flops back onto his forehead. It's the color of dark wood, or coffee, and it's just long enough to show the beginning of a wave. Every time he touches it, my hands itch to do the same. His hair looks so soft.

Julien also has the most beautiful hands I've ever seen, but I think I must stop describing him, because my own hand is beginning to cramp and I haven't even written the most important thing that happened, which is that he invited me (and Aunt S) to spend two weeks at his family farm at the end of the month. Not counting those few months at that school, I've never left the city, but when I say my imagination fails me, it is not the countryside I'm trying desperately to envision. Is this a gesture of friendship? What will we do for two weeks at a farm?

In other news, I have forged many letters, but none perfect enough. Aunt S has called on some "old friends," but I haven't been invited to join them. So there is nothing to occupy my thoughts except this visit to the farm, and Julien, and this portrait, and the hours of attention he lavished on my face this afternoon.

SOPHIE BEAUCHÊNE TO ISABELLE DE TOURZIN, DECEMBER 3, 1823

SENT BY PRIVATE COURIER

My dear Isabelle,

I wasn't afraid of you in 1794 and I don't intend to start now. You are twenty-nine years too late to scare me off, and it's a waste of time for you to keep trying.

I should have been clear. Anaïs's child has already entered your world, and being a creature of powerful curiosity and little sense, will blunder toward danger unless some guidance is provided. You will invite us to your home and introduce us to some people who might furnish Victor with a measure of caution. (I would make my own list of names, but I haven't kept up to date with which of our mutual acquaintances are still working. You know who I liked and trusted.)

Name a date in January.

I remain

Your friend,

Sophie

ISABELLE DE TOURZIN TO SOPHIE BEAUCHÊNE, DECEMBER 4, 1823
SENT BY PRIVATE COURIER

Sophie,

Age has not dimmed your impertinence. Were I your friend, I might find it reassuring that your spirit has emerged mostly unscathed from the trials of the last few years, but as you have noted, I am a recalcitrant old crone. I don't trouble myself with friends.

I also don't trouble myself with senseless young people who stumble into forces beyond their comprehension, and I have no interest in educating your sister's child. I will remove myself from this situation <u>immediately</u> following the evening of January 5, 1824, when the two of you may come to Nouvelle-Athènes for dinner with Béatrix and Dominique. I cannot claim to like or trust either of them, but neither of them has betrayed me yet. That will have to suffice.

You will find me at number 9, Rue Branoux.

Isabelle

SOPHIE BEAUCHÊNE TO ISABELLE DE TOURZIN, DECEMBER 5, 1823

SENT BY PRIVATE COURIER

My dear Isabelle,

I'm touched. Thank you for your generosity. You've chosen the guests well. I'm delighted to know that Béatrix and Dominique are willing to meet with us, especially Béatrix. She never cared much for your particular domain and I assumed she had devoted herself solely to performing.

You'll love Victor—just as you love me. You love Béatrix and Dominique, too. Don't waste the ink on a denial, darling. It won't change a thing. It will be wonderful to see you in January, since, as you know, I will always be

Your friend,
Sophie

PRIVATE DIARY OF V BEAUCHÊNE, DECEMBER 15, 1823

My letter worked.
   [*This page is marred by a splatter of ink.*]

PRIVATE DIARY OF V BEAUCHÊNE, DECEMBER 15, 1823

I ruined my first page in my excitement, and then I had to get up and pace my room until I was calm enough to sit again. I'm overcome. I did it. Aunt S and I are saved.

The affair was simple. After much meticulous practice forging my brother's style and signature, I used the pen to compose a letter requesting a transfer of ten thousand francs to an account in my name—at a bank Horace doesn't control, of course.

It was brazen to put my own name in these proceedings, but I can't wait for him to know. I want him to find the paperwork and read exactly what it says. My only fear is that the amount of money I took—reclaimed—is too small for him to notice. First of all, I can't imagine my brother going through the books voluntarily. Second, my father's annual income is fifty thousand, and his income is inconsequential compared to his accumulated wealth, and presumably all that is under Horace's control now.

I was tempted to take more, but my early experiments with the pen suggest that asking for an extraordinary amount of money would invite too much skepticism and scrutiny. It is hard to believe, after these months of counting every centime, that ten thousand francs is an ordinary amount of money to my former family, and that they might well be indifferent to its disappearance, but it's true.

Besides, if this first withdrawal doesn't cause me any trouble, I can always repeat it. Though I'm more interested in stealing whatever objects might be in my brother's possession. I haven't forgotten the disturbing line in his letter about nobody being able to say no to him. It's only that I need to know more. Going near Horace if he truly has that kind of power terrifies me.

But I can't let him use his power to harm people—and I cannot imagine Horace having power and _not_ using it to harm people—so I _will_ stop him.

I think it might be rather enjoyable.

This first success elates me—almost as much as the prospect of traveling with Julien in a few days. Both leave me a little bit breathless.

I feel powerful and alive and almost fearless, but not quite enough to run upstairs and kiss Julien.

DECEMBER 20, 1823

The farm wasn't far outside of Paris, according to Julien, who was a damned liar. To Victor, the gently sloped pastures, the bare-branched orchards, and the slow-flowing river might as well have been the wilderness of Canada. They might as well have been Jupiter. Everything outside of Paris was the same distance away from the city: too far.

"What's that smell?" he asked Julien as they walked toward the farmhouse.

"What smell?" Julien asked. "Fresh air? The absence of stale piss?"

Victor's aunt Sophie—his very rude aunt Sophie—let loose a rich, full-throated laugh. He glared at her, and she only doubled over and wrapped her arms around her middle.

Sophie ought to have been as out of place against that wide, cloudy grey sky as Victor was, but instead her round cheeks were pinked with joy. A spiral lock of silvered blond hair brushed her neck under her bonnet. Considering the jolting, tiresome, two-day journey they'd had, she still looked neatly put together, though her outfits were all a little shabby.

Come to think of it, Sophie hadn't worn anything new or fashionable in years. She'd always been stylish, before. He hadn't heard her laugh so loudly in a long time. Nursing her sister through those last few years of life had taken a toll on Sophie, and living under her brother-in-law's roof had made it worse. (Victor couldn't imagine any scenario that would be improved by living with his father and brother.)

And Sophie was still, after all of that, trying to protect him. Just like she'd protected his mother. She deserved better than the Maison Laval.

Never mind the ten thousand francs he had waiting in his new account. Victor could rob his family until there wasn't a single, dusty centime left lying in the vault, and it wouldn't be enough to repay Sophie. Still, he had to start somewhere. He wanted happiness for her, and independence, and an obscenely lavish new wardrobe. Money could buy two of those things.

Victor hadn't told her—or Julien—about their new circumstances. The right words hadn't come yet.

Julien's family had money, he thought. It had been difficult to determine. Victor had bounced between having almost everything—a fortune multiplied by investment, but controlled by his father—and having almost nothing. What lay between those points remained a mystery.

And Julien's family was so eccentric that comparisons were impossible. All four older Morères were moderately successful artists, and Julien intended to follow in their footsteps—or outpace them. Their farmhouse wasn't the dilapidated, one-room affair Victor had expected, but a

THE SCANDALOUS LETTERS OF V AND J

simple, well-kept building of limestone, its windows framed by neat wooden shutters. The planters outside the door were empty, since it was winter, but even so they lent a welcoming air. It was nothing like the imposing Parisian townhouse where Victor had grown up.

Instead of a servant, a grey-haired woman who could only have been Julien's mother opened the door. The two of them had the same broad smile, although Julien kept his in reserve.

Madame Esther Morère greeted Victor and Sophie like she'd known them both for ages. It was warm beyond the threshold, the hearth in the parlor crackling, the afternoon light giving the floorboards one last caress. Potatoes and leeks simmered in a nearby kitchen.

Julien introduced them to the three other people in the parlor—Henri, Georges, and Adrienne—unmistakably Julien's father and siblings by their eyebrows and their intensity. Henri and Georges made Julien seem like an unstoppable chatterer in comparison, but Adrienne was cheerful. She inspected Victor with particular interest, which he returned. She was Julien's most frequent correspondent, he knew. Her hair was black, as opposed to the chestnut shade of Julien's, and her skin was a touch paler, but the resemblance was strong. The two of them leaned forward in the same way when they listened. Adrienne served enough questions about the journey that Victor and Sophie were able to volley, so the conversation flowed smoothly.

Had such pleasantries not been among his very few skills, Victor might have fallen as silent as Julien. It was not one of Julien's companionable silences, but a stiff, wary one. Perhaps he regretted inviting Victor here.

When Julien expressed a desire to go for a walk before

the last of the light faded, Victor jumped to his feet. A tramp through the muddy fields and the biting wind sounded terrible, but he would endure it to be alone with Julien.

No one else offered to join them, predictably, but Adrienne watched the two of them leave with an interest so avid it bordered on rude.

It took them a miserable eternity to cross a pasture and end up on a hilltop. Victor's cheeks were stinging with cold by the end. In better light, there might have been a view of the surrounding river valley, but twilight had already washed over the horizon.

"I've made a grave error," Julien said.

"By inviting me here?" Victor asked. It wasn't the cold making his throat seize up.

Julien hardly seemed to hear him. "There is something I must confess to you. I should have told you before you came here, and I regret that I did not. I assure you that if what I say means the end of our friendship, you will still find shelter in my family's home tonight. It is my hope that our separation will be peaceable. I hold you in high esteem, and will do so even if you no longer wish to speak to me. I hope you will remember that, and respect that what I am about to tell you must be kept in confidence."

"Julien," Victor interrupted. The formality of that little speech distressed him. "There is *nothing* you could tell me that would make me not want to be your friend."

Evening painted the uncertainty of Julien's expression in shadow.

"Nothing," Victor repeated. "Nothing, do you understand me? You can tell me you murdered someone—"

"I'm not a man."

"That's the best possible thing you could have said."

Victor grinned. He would have thrown his arms around Julien, but they'd never done that before, and Julien still looked stiff with terror. So Victor said, "Neither am I."

"Oh," Julien said, shoulders easing down. "I'm not a woman, either. Or I'm both, I suppose."

"If you want to discuss the finer points of this distinction, perhaps we could go somewhere warmer? Suffice to say we have something in common."

Julien graced Victor with a wry smile. "And you haven't committed any murders?"

"Not yet," Victor said.

"My name is Julie. Well, here it is. In Paris, I'd like you to call me Julien and 'he,' at least for now. He or she, I don't mind either, but I wanted you to know."

"It's a pleasure to meet you, Julie," Victor said, and on impulse, grabbed her gloved hand and kissed it, an impudence that Julie allowed. His face ached from smiling. "My name is still Victor, and I'd rather be 'he' than 'she.' I don't think of myself as a man, but it suits me for the world to treat me as one. Oh, Julie, this is marvelous, no wonder we're such good friends, there's so much I want to discuss—"

Julie cleared her throat.

"Yes?"

"I wasn't finished," she said.

Victor made a sweeping gesture. "By all means, continue."

She didn't.

The wind rose again, and Victor shoved his hands into the pockets of his greatcoat. He had to lift his head away from his upturned collar so his voice wouldn't be muffled when he said, "Need I remind you, again, that there is nothing you could say that would make me not want to be your friend?"

"That's just it," she said. "It's not friendship that's the problem."

The gap between his heartbeats grew dangerously long.

"Perhaps I'm guessing wrong, but I think you want me to kiss you," she said. "If you do, I need you to know that I have not always looked like this, and I will not always look like this, and if that troubles you, or if it's only my body that makes you want me, then I don't think we should kiss at all."

"I haven't always looked like this," Victor said cautiously. "And we all change as we get older. But that's not what you mean, is it?"

"No, it isn't."

Victor's heartbeat had come pounding back. He was dying to ask questions. Even though it was wretchedly cold outside, there was heat quickening inside him. His too-tight clothes, perfectly comfortable a moment ago, rustled against his skin.

Julie's gaze was on him, hot and dark and waiting, and it was that, more than anything, that made Victor blurt, "I don't think there's a way you could look that would make me not want you. That is to say, I do like your body—really a lot, and also your face, and everything about you—but I think I would always like you, no matter what—you listen to me, and you have this passion, this genius and—and because it's *you* and I like you, and also because I've read a lot of dirty books and I'm equally interested in *all* the illustrations, but maybe that's more than I should have said, but you brought it up and I'm being honest—"

"Victor," Julie said. "I'm going to kiss you now."

"Oh, thank God."

Julie never drew two marks where one would do, and she didn't dither about kissing, either. There was no slow approach, no wavering, no leaning close enough to taste, hoping something would happen. Victor had tried that last tactic without success.

Julie just kissed him.

There was an economy of motion to it—that single, firm, warm press of her lips against his—or maybe *grace* was the word. Exactly as much as necessary, and no more. Her extraordinary confidence drew him in. She'd decided. She'd acted. And she'd done it right on her first try.

All those weeks of staring at his face that Victor had mistaken for idle dreaminess, Julie had been like a general with a map, plotting her campaign.

Her lips parted. The tip of her tongue teased at the seam of his mouth, and he let her in. She tasted clean and sweet like water, but her tongue was hot against his. That, too, was Julie: powerful and direct, but still gentle. If this was the kind of decision she made, Victor would submit to all of them.

Julie hauled him by the hips until they were pressed together. Cold stung him everywhere but where they touched. Victor leaned into her, crushing their woolen coats between them, imagining the burning heat of her skin. Everything inside him was taut, but his knees had gone weak. He'd melted against her.

"We should go inside," she said, ending the kiss as decisively as she'd begun it. "It's getting dark."

Victor didn't let so much as a wisp of air pass between them. "Can we do more of *that* inside?"

"When we're alone, yes."

"And when will we be alone?" Victor asked. It was a shame to develop such a fierce resentment of Julie's family within hours of meeting them, since they seemed lovely, but if they were going to prevent him from further kissing, then it couldn't be helped.

"All night, if you like," Julie said. "We're sleeping in the same room."

DECEMBER 20, 1823

Julie loved her family, but dinner was interminable. Victor must have felt the same, since as soon as the meal came to a close, he yawned and stretched.

Julie didn't believe for a second that he was tired, but it was nicely done. They excused themselves from the table and Julie led him to the guest room. Adrienne had arranged for the two of them to have this room, while she shared her own room with Victor's aunt. That, too, was nicely done.

Georges had moved into the cottage last year when he married Jeanne. Julie didn't think he'd done that for her benefit, but she was still grateful to have the room to herself.

And Victor.

The privacy was a luxury, but it struck her that the rest of the room wouldn't impress Victor, the child of a banker. The bed was an unadorned wooden frame, its mattress not especially downy or large. Paintings covered the walls, but the lone candle in Victor's hand didn't show them to their best advantage.

Victor stopped in front of one and stared anyway. The painting depicted a young, dark-haired woman from the shoulders up, her face in three-quarters view, her gaze distant. Her simple clothes didn't mark the era, so he could mistake the woman for a young Esther Morère. Or it could have been Adrienne with browner hair and slightly harder, more angular features—the nose too prominent, the mouth not soft enough, an imperfect likeness.

"It's you," Victor said.

Julie smiled. She didn't paint imperfect likenesses.

"Is it a self-portrait? It must be—I recognize your style."

"Yes," Julie said, flattered that he knew her work so well. "One of many."

"That's how you change? Self-portraits?"

"Yes," she said, braced for shock or horror. She'd never told anyone. Her whole family knew, and it was too dangerous to raise the topic with outsiders, so she never had.

"You maintained the family resemblance," Victor said.

"It's important to me."

Contemplating the portrait with candlelight burnishing his hair and the planes of his face, Victor might have been a painting himself. Darkness brushed away everything beyond him.

He set the candle on the bedside table and turned toward her. "Julie," he said, wrapping his arms around her neck. "I love your work."

She wanted to pour herself against him. Still, she hesitated. "You don't have questions? Objections?"

"What could I possibly object to? I have the opposite of objections. Approval. Enthusiasm. Esteem. I *do* have questions, like 'will you show me everything you've ever painted?'" he said. "But it's dark right now, and you promised to kiss me again."

She'd been waiting hours—no, she'd been waiting since October. It was delicious to have him so close at last, nothing left to worry about. His mouth was hot. The lingering sweetness of wine met her lips, its flavor a sheen over the deeper, earthier taste of Victor. He made a beautiful little sound in his throat when her fingers found purchase in his hair.

A slow exploration unfolded between them, their tongues sliding over each other and their hands skidding over their clothes. They pushed against each other, and it was startlingly wonderful just to press their bodies together, to feel the friction of every twitch and rub. When they dropped to the bed, it was unspoken, almost accidental. Julie laughed softly and her attention caught on how low the candle burned. They were well into the middle of the night.

Victor had ended up straddling her lap. His attention was not on the candle.

"Is that for me?"

"No," she said, "it's for the *other* person who's been kissing me for hours."

He rolled his hips, trapping her arousal between their bodies, and she sucked in a breath. He fitted himself against her, then licked his lips, and said, "It's for me."

"Well, yes. But I can ignore it. We can go back to kissing. Or go to sleep. This is just a thing my body does—it doesn't have to mean anything."

"My body also does things, you know," Victor said. "I don't want to ignore it. I want us to take our clothes off and *attend* to it."

"If we do that, there could be consequences."

Victor was flushed from all the kissing, his eyes bright. "Like you'll fall irrevocably in love with me because I'm so irresistible and then no one else will ever truly satisfy you as long as you live?"

"I was thinking of pregnancy, but I suppose that's also a risk," Julie said.

"Oh." Victor grimaced. "Aunt S gave me a sponge for that, but right now I just want to look at you. And maybe use my hands. Or my mouth."

Julie was well-acquainted with her own hand, but the latter suggestion was something she had only seen in books—or rather, in Victor's meticulous notes on an obscene work she hadn't read. "I didn't know people did that in real life."

Victor busied himself shucking his waistcoat and shirt, leaving himself bare-chested. Julie wanted to kiss that slender expanse of smooth skin, and to touch the stiff pink peaks of his nipples, but Victor was talking as he unbuttoned the fall of his trousers, so she waited.

"They do. We could. Will you undo your trousers? I'm dying to see your..." He made a vague downward gesture.

"I've never known you to be shy," Julie observed.

"I'm not *shy*," Victor said. He huffed. "I was worried *you* were shy. You're the one with all your clothes still on."

Julie laughed, removed her shirt, and dropped it on top of Victor's discarded clothes. "I'm not shy, Victor. I like my body. I worked very hard on it. But it's going to change, and I needed you to understand that before we started. You can touch me anywhere you want."

He ran his hands over her chest, admiration in his gaze. Julie had wondered before if she'd been too generous with her own body hair—it had intrigued her at the time, and then the novelty had worn off—but seeing Victor's wide, dark pupils and his fingers spread through it affirmed her choice. Her sex swelled against her trousers, which were now far too tight.

Victor's hands meandered over her shoulders, around her biceps, down the sensitive skin of her stomach. "It's marvelous to touch you, and it would be no matter what, but knowing that you fashioned yourself... has anyone else ever seen you, Julie, or is it only me?"

"Only you."

"That seems a shame, but it's also thrilling," Victor said. He stood to take his trousers off, and she did the same. He continued, "No one's ever seen me, either, but I'm not so spectacular as you."

"I'll be the judge of that," she said, curving her hand around one hip and aligning her thumb with the angle of his waist. The wiry hair around his sex was as golden as the hair on his head, almost king's yellow, a beautiful complement to the rosy color—aurora red, or peach blossom red, maybe—that spread down his chest as she studied him. Even in the low light, the effect was radiant. His body was so sleek and lithe, like she could bend him any which way. "You could be Girodet's *Endymion*, if only we had moonlight instead of candles."

"I assume that's a painting," he said. "I hope it's a good-looking one."

"Not as good-looking as you."

"I don't know much about art, Julie, but you're better than anything I've ever seen. Besides, it's bad manners to go to museums and do this." He reached between her legs and cupped her.

The heat of his hand made her suck in a breath instead of laughing at the joke. After a moment, she managed to say, "Yes, it's frowned upon to fondle the sculpture."

Victor's fingers were playful, just the barest of touches, making her ache for more. Keeping his tone equally light, he said, "I might not know art, but I'm well-read. I know a lot of words for these things. What would you like me to call it?"

"I don't care what you call anything as long as you keep touching me," Julie said. The question gave her pause. "Are there things you don't want *me* to say?"

"You, Julie Morère, can say absolutely anything you want to me." Victor touched himself between the legs. "You can call this a cock or a cunt. Talk about my tits if you want."

The vulgarity shocked Julie—it was like how her awful classmates talked about their models, except it wasn't. People could say what they wanted about their own bodies. Victor had chosen his own name, and now he was naming himself again. Maybe tomorrow he'd name his body differently, just like maybe some day she'd have changed, too. She smiled.

Victor lifted his hands to his chest and casually groped himself. "Not that my tits really deserve the name. They're barely there—not at all in pleasing balance with my backside, I'm told."

"I like your backside. I like these, too," she said, dragging a finger down his sternum, well clear of his small breasts.

"Oh, I do too," he said. "Their size is convenient, and it feels nice to touch them."

"Is that a hint?" she said, laughing. "I rate them a bit higher than 'convenient.' They're perfect, Victor."

She caressed his chest with both hands, kissing him, kneading and squeezing the softness there, relishing the slight weight in her hands. Then she rolled one nipple between her thumb and forefinger, and he gasped.

She slid her other hand down to that golden thatch beneath his navel and, despite Victor's permission, found herself hesitant to name anything. She asked, "What about here? Can I touch you here?"

"God yes," he said.

"Get on the bed," she said.

He dropped gracefully to his back and let his legs fall open. *Not shy* didn't begin to cover it. She knelt on the mattress between his spread knees. Her hand didn't tremble as she reached for him, but a shiver ran through the rest of her as soon as her fingers made contact. She wanted this so much, it didn't seem real that she'd been allowed to have it.

She dragged her fingertip down, parting the short curls that were already dark with wetness, revealing a pink so vivid and saturated she'd never be able to recreate it in oil paint. Everywhere was supple and slick. She dipped her finger inside and the heat invited her deeper, so she moved with slow caution until Victor lifted his hips and ground down on her hand, engulfing her finger to the root.

Her breath caught. It was impossible not to imagine that sensation sheathing her cock. And if Victor made that same, satisfied sound, she might die of happiness. Fuck, she was dripping already.

"You like that?" she asked. He'd made himself clear already, but she wanted to hear him say it.

"I love it."

He squeezed her finger and her mind went perfectly blank. Fuck. Julie met Victor's gaze and said, "Do you want another?"

"*Please*."

It came so easily to him, that unabashed desperation. She liked that he was shameless, that he writhed and sighed as she slipped another finger in and began to thrust. He was noisy. If they weren't in her family home, she'd aim to make him scream. The temptation to make him scream even though they *were* in her family home was devilishly strong.

Instead she shifted so they were lying alongside each other and she could swallow his moans with kisses. She kept her fingers moving steadily until he wrapped his fingers around the shaft of her cock.

She closed her eyes to stem the rush of sensation. It didn't work.

"*You* like that," he teased.

"I do."

Her sincerity, or maybe the rough depth of her voice, stunned him into momentary silence. His hand kept moving, finding the wet slit at the tip and smearing the liquid until she was almost as wet as he was. Victor didn't seem to need instructions—maybe it was all that reading —and his hand was gliding up and down in no time. He was clever with it, adding a slippery twist, and she made a wordless noise in her throat. She wouldn't last if he kept that up, but she didn't ask him to slow down. She matched her own hand to his pace, using her thumb to circle his clit, and when he cried out, she kissed him.

She stroked her free hand down his back, palming the curve of his ass to draw him closer. Her hand, she noted with satisfaction, was the perfect size.

Victor was panting into her kisses. "Julie, I need—"

"I know," she said, and worked her fingers until he came. It was spectacular. He arched into her touch and clenched down furiously on her hand and groaned. Then he went boneless—except for the grip he still had on her cock.

She'd been forcefully ignoring her own arousal, trying to outlast Victor, but it had been so overwhelming to feel him finish on her hand. She'd done that. He'd come for her.

"Do it on me," Victor said. "I want to see it."

She got to her knees and he guided her toward his chest. Julie had never imagined this, but Victor wanted it, and that made her want it, too. A few quick strokes tipped her over the edge, and she came hard, streaking his skin with her release. Everything went from heavy and aching to light and tender. She sat back on her heels, dazed.

Victor swiped his fingers through the mess and then brought them to his mouth and sucked them.

She stared.

"I was curious," he said. "People do that in books sometimes."

Julie couldn't help laughing. Her own fingers were still sticky from touching him, but she refreshed them by sliding them down his sex and then brought them to her mouth. The taste was slightly salty. It was strange, too, but she didn't mind it.

Victor had talked about people putting their mouths on each other. He was watching her now, and she knew he was thinking about it, too. She held his gaze as she slid her fingers out of her mouth, and his lashes swept down as he looked away.

She didn't know why she liked that—staring at him, making him avert his eyes, knowing that even as shameless as he was, she *could* fluster him—but she supposed it didn't matter. She liked it, and Victor, with that tiny smile on his face, clearly liked it too.

"We could do that again later," she said. "We could do other things."

"I'd like that," he said, and then, "The only question is how I'm going to survive tomorrow with your family, knowing what we could be doing if we were alone."

"I'll be on my best behavior," she said.

"I hope not."

Julie felt a smile curve her lips, unbidden. She could make tomorrow very long indeed.

DECEMBER 21, 1823

"I dreamed that you touched me," Victor murmured, half-asleep. Julie was pressed against his back, radiating heat. Morning light slitted through the curtains. He hadn't even fully opened his eyes.

"That wasn't a dream. I did touch you. We touched each other."

"No," Victor said, burrowing deeper into the pillow. He shouldn't have brought this up. He wouldn't have spoken of it if he'd been fully awake. Julie would laugh at him.

Julie draped an arm over his waist, trapping him, and then propped herself on her elbow and peered at him. "What did you dream about?"

"I was asleep." Julie wasn't the only one radiating heat. His cheeks burned.

"That is usually when dreams occur. Now tell me what happened."

The pillow wasn't nearly fluffy enough to disappear into. "No, *in* the dream, I was asleep."

"And I touched you?"

"Mmf."

"Like Endymion and the moonlight," Julie murmured. She'd moved her hand from his waist to his hip, which she was now stroking. Her fingertips dragged up and down, methodically, inexorably, making him sigh. "Did you finish?"

"No."

"Would you like to?"

"Yes," he said, maybe too eagerly. Was it possible to be too eager if they were both in bed and already naked and her fingers were traveling ever closer to the apex of his thighs? His brain was too fogged to work that out.

"Go back to sleep, then," she said.

His eyes flew open. "What?"

"How else am I supposed to make your dream come true?"

God help him, but Julie teasing him squeezed something inside him, made his whole body tighten with desire. The way she'd patiently elicited the details from him, the way she was offering to do it—he might well still be dreaming.

Except he was wound too tightly now. "I don't think I can fall back asleep."

"Pretend, then," she said. "Close your eyes and take a deep breath."

Quiet settled over him as he followed her instructions. She combed her fingers through his hair and ran her hand down his back for such a long time that the ache between his legs receded a little, and his thoughts drifted. Here in the soft, warm darkness, he could relax.

There was a touch against his chest, so light it might not have been real. A slow, careful circling of one nipple and then the other, until both were stiff and pointed, and then again, intensifying until he was breathless with it, and then again, but this time something warm and wet sucked at the side of his neck. He whimpered. The hand slid down his stomach, branding the center line of his body, aimed unerringly at the place where he ached. He pulsed with a second heartbeat there, all the heat of his body gathered into a red-hot line, and the touch made him gasp and open his eyes.

Julie's hand on him was almost too much. His eyelids fluttered shut and she dragged him against her body, which ran even hotter than his own. He squirmed and she grunted. Her other arm banded his chest, keeping him close.

She ran her fingers along the slick, swollen flesh between his legs and he felt her lips curve against his neck. She liked it. That only made him press himself more urgently into her hand. She answered with a rough caress, and then set up a thrusting rhythm that made him spend into her hand in no time. He shuddered through it. She tightened her arm around him and kissed his jaw when he was done.

It was only then that he became aware of the hot liquid dripping down the small of his back. Julie had come, too.

He grinned, delighted. "Did you enjoy that, Julie?"

"You wriggle a lot for someone who was supposedly sleeping," she said. "But yes, I did enjoy it. You too, I hope?"

"We should do that every morning," he told her, and she laughed and kissed him.

"If we did that every morning, I would never get out of bed."

"I fail to see the problem," he told her. "Let's stay in bed forever."

"As lovely as that sounds, I want breakfast," she said.

She extricated herself from him and got out of bed. She bent over, magnificently naked, the light from the window caressing all the contours of her body, and picked through their discarded clothes. "And you told me I could torment you all day, which I'm looking forward to."

"*Torment*," Victor repeated, sitting up and clutching the sheets to his chest. "Who knew you were so wicked?"

"You did."

"Oh, I didn't. I hoped. But you should have seen my diary, Julie. In October, I was worrying that I'd offended you and despairing that you didn't like me."

Julie paused in her dressing and studied him. He'd pulled the sheets to his chest in a melodramatic gesture. Her attention made his fingers clench in the fabric. The sheet revealed more than it covered, and his nipples had already tightened to hard little points. Being looked at like that, it made all the ink run together in his thoughts. It was like dipping a freshly written letter in a basin of water —everything diluted and blurred into blankness. It rendered him useless.

She finished tucking her shirt into her trousers, moving as though the moment hadn't affected her, but Victor could see that it had.

Julie sat on the bed, the collar of her shirt still open, and reached for him. She took him gently by the chin and brushed her thumb over his bottom lip.

"You don't need to worry," she said, "about that."

Victor had entirely forgotten what they were talking about.

DECEMBER 21, 1823

After dinner, when it was full dark, Julie took Victor to her studio, one of the farm's many outbuildings. It was distinct from Adrienne's studio, or Georges's, or her father's, or her mother's, Victor learned. Even having met the Morère family, he couldn't believe they were real. It wasn't so much that all of them were artists, or even that some—possibly all—of them possessed magic. It was that they loved each other.

Julie's parents would never have disinherited her.

Victor didn't miss Pierre Faucheux, who had never offered much in the way of affection, but he did miss his mother. He wouldn't ever stop missing her as long as he lived.

"You look sad," Julie said. She'd been lighting oil lamps all over the room. When she'd methodically transferred the flame from her lantern to the kindling for the stove, the smell of the smoke had sparked in the air. The wooden floor creaked under her boots as she came to stand by him.

"I don't want to talk about it," Victor said.

She'd almost offered him an embrace. He could read it

in her posture. It wasn't tenderness he wanted, but distraction. He was grateful that she'd kept her word and tormented him all day, since her ceaseless flirtation had prevented this episode of spleen. She'd found ways, when they were in company, to say things in a particular tone of voice or linger over a word or to press her leg against his under the table. Sometimes all she did was watch him, and that was enough.

He'd been a desperate wreck all afternoon. It should be easy enough to fall back into that state.

"Show me your work," he said.

She encompassed the room with a gesture. "What do you want to see?"

The oil lamps she'd lit reflected in a psyché, a large free-standing mirror, and glinted off the textured surfaces of oil paintings, daubed or polished. There was work all over the studio, including a half-finished charcoal figure study on the easel, which must have been waiting there the whole time Julie had been living in Paris. Painted canvasses and wood panels leaned against the walls and drawings hung above them or lay on the table and the top of the flat file like a fall of leaves. If a surface wasn't covered in sketchbooks and loose pages, it was covered in brushes, sticks of vine charcoal, chamois cloths, pieces of wood, and tools Victor didn't recognize. A pile of pillows and crumpled drapery sat atop a mattress. A smock hung over the back of a threadbare armchair. Dried flowers, books, vases, wine bottles, birds' nests, bones—the calm, decisive aspect of Julie's work and personality was a façade for chaos. The studio was even worse than her room in the Maison Laval. Victor itched to sort through it all. He liked neatness, but it was more than that. Julie's work shouldn't been treated carelessly. It should be in the Louvre.

"I want to see all of it. Everything."

"We'll be here all night, or possibly until next week."

"Good," he said.

Julie could remain unruffled during a full day of surreptitious advances, but here, Victor had the upper hand. All it took was a few compliments on a still life or a landscape to make her swallow her tongue. Victor wasn't even trying. He was being sincere.

He let Julie arrive at the self-portraits in her own time, but arrive she did. He'd recognized her in the one hanging in the bedroom, and he saw her again in the works she presented now, even the ones that didn't show her face. Some works were life-size, half-length portraits or studies of her limbs, her torso, her shoulders and the back of her neck. Those canvasses she left propped against the wall, but there were smaller works, too, and not all paintings.

There was a particularly breathtaking series of her hands, over and over again, an alphabet of gestures in charcoal. She'd cleared a space on top of the flat file to spread those pages out, so her hands were right next to their likenesses.

Victor had heard Julie's classmates complain about the difficulties of drawing hands. He smiled slyly at her, and she returned it.

"You know how good you are," he said.

"I do."

"You don't need me to tell you."

"You don't *need* me to kiss you," she countered.

"On the contrary, I need it intensely."

She grabbed him and kissed him then. Fast and rough, her hands jumped from his shoulders to his hips. When she pulled him closer, they bumped the cabinet, jostling the pages.

Victor broke away. "Julie—your drawings."

"They'll be fine."

"Julie," he repeated, bending to pick up a page that had fluttered to the floor. Her hands, palms down, fingers spread. The drawing trembled because he couldn't keep his own hands still while he laid it atop the cabinet. Charcoal dust and paper, these things were delicate. Fragile. "These drawings are—they're *you*. Er. Aren't they?"

"They depict me. But no, they're not me. I'm me." She lifted her hands and wiggled her fingers. "You could smudge it or rip it in half—"

"Don't!"

"—and I would still be here," she finished. "Really, Victor, they're just drawings. Nothing will happen to me if they get erased and reused, or lost, or burnt, or any number of other fates. And I can make more any time I want."

He'd put an arm out protectively to bar her from ripping a page in demonstration. He withdrew with reluctance. "How does it work, then? You did say you used the self-portraits to change."

"I did. They help me focus. But the magic lives in me, where it belongs. It's extraordinarily dangerous to transfer magic into objects."

Like his pen. Like Horace's collection. Like the catalog in Malbosc's book. Victor didn't move. This was the first time he'd heard Julie say the word *magic*. A terrifying confirmation. As nonchalantly as possible, he said, "How so?"

"The same reason I don't go around telling people what I can do," Julie said sternly. "You can't trust people to do the right thing with it."

"So it's not... it's not as though transferring power into

an object would kill the person who tried," he said. "Hypothetically."

Julie drew her brows together. "I don't think so."

"So they might not all be dangerous," Victor said.

"Anything can be dangerous in the wrong hands. Anyway, imbuing objects with power is unnecessary. It's not that difficult to use an object to focus and simply channel the energy back into yourself."

For the first time, Victor began to understand why Julie's classmates resented her natural abilities.

"And it's a bad idea to create them, so I don't," Julie said with finality.

"Who told you that?"

"Maybe we should sit," she said.

The only place for two people to sit was the mattress on the floor, once Julie had pushed aside the tangle of drapery. An hour ago, Victor couldn't have imagined sitting on a mattress with Julie and remaining fully clothed, but the only thing more powerful than his lust was his curiosity. He'd put it aside last night. He didn't want to wait any longer.

Julie took a deep breath. "I don't want to keep things from you, but I also feel as though I shouldn't be telling you this. It's not my place. I trust you, though, so here we are. My whole family can do this."

"Change their appearance through self-portraits?"

"Yes. We can change other things with our Art, too."

"You drew me."

She perceived the unasked question. "It requires choice —intention, will—to affect the nature of what I draw. It's a difficult and prolonged process. I have only ever done it to myself. It's nearly impossible to effect lasting change on another person's appearance. It can be done, but it requires agreement, not merely between artist and subject but between subject and work. For the change to endure, you have to represent people the way they see themselves. A person's own understanding of themselves is a powerful thing. More importantly, it would have been wrong for me to do something to you without asking."

"And—" he smiled "—we both know I cannot be improved."

She laughed, but it faded quickly into seriousness. "If you ever want a change, I'll help. Anything, Victor."

"A generous offer," he said, touched. "But I wasn't joking. I'm happy at the moment. What I *really* want is to know how it works."

She shrugged. "Magic."

"What an unsatisfying answer," he said. "Surely there's a whole field of study on this. How did you learn? How did the rest of your family learn? Who else can do this? Are there other kinds of magic? There must be."

"My family taught me," Julie said. She narrowed her eyes. "You adapted to the notion of magic easily. Almost as if it wasn't new to you."

"It isn't," he said, the confession a thrill coursing through his blood. "It's not fine art for me, though, it's writing. I write and people believe me. I haven't used it on you, I promise. Just like you can draw without affecting me, I can write to you without affecting you."

Julie evaluated that statement for an excruciating moment. Victor couldn't prove it to her. He felt a pang of guilt for eliding the existence of the pen, but he was embarrassed by her declaration that his way of doing magic was dangerous and unsophisticated.

"I liked you long before you wrote to me," she said at last. "If I ever doubt it, there's a pile of sketches in my room at the Maison Laval that can serve as evidence. Not to mention all the letters and drawings I sent to Adrienne."

"You drew me before we'd even spoken. My God, you were *pining*." So much for research; the glee he felt was impossible to contain.

"Hush."

Julie punctuated this objection with a warning shove at his shoulder. Victor was twenty-one years old and all of his friendship and curiosity and longing and lust were concentrated in the staggeringly beautiful person sitting next to him on the mattress. That touch was a spark. All he wanted to do was fan it.

"You were wasting away, sick with yearning in your little bedroom in the Maison Laval, making drawing after drawing, torturing yourself over me," he continued. "I *am* irresistible to you, Julie-Julien Morère."

She flattened him with a single motion, and then he was trapped between Julie and the lumpy straw mattress. She moved his arms so they were over his head and then pinned both wrists with one hand. His breath quickened.

Her face was very near to his. The light glinted off her white teeth when she smiled and said, "Speaking of irresistible, I don't feel you resisting."

"You won't," he said. He hadn't been this excited since —well, since this morning. But still. It was delicious to play at being immobilized. He wriggled beneath her, wanting to rub against something.

"I need more than that," she said. "If you want this, you have to tell me you like it."

"Like I told you I liked your paintings?"

"With more moaning," she suggested.

He gasped out a laugh. "I'm enjoying myself, but if it's

moaning you want, you have to give me something to moan about."

Julie dragged her hand down his chest, over the layers of his waistcoat and shirt. She didn't pause over his stiff nipples or bother undoing any of his buttons. She slid her hand between his clothed thighs and cupped the heat she found there. The motion was leisurely and exploratory. Even through his clothes, there was no doubt how aroused he was. Everything about it felt filthy and illicit. She stroked him a few times and he whimpered.

"Oh, that's good," she said, stamping her approval on the pathetic sound he'd made. "Remind me, which of us can't resist the other?"

He meant to laugh, but it came out airless. It shouldn't feel this good, what she was doing to him. She hadn't removed a stitch of his clothing. But her hand kept moving. His response was undeniable, desire screwing tighter with every rough stroke.

"You know what I think?" she asked in a low, conspiratorial whisper. "I think you wrote in your diary about me. I think you sat alone in your room with a single candle burning, writing furiously about how much you wanted me. About how you couldn't stop thinking about me. And then I think you went to bed and stuck your hand between your legs."

"I didn't always make it to the bed."

As a joke, it fell flat, but as a confession, it worked wonders.

"Right there in your desk chair, with your pen still wet?" Julie asked. "That *does* sound desperate. You poor thing."

Victor made a wordless noise of agreement, and then another, sharper noise when she finally undid his trousers.

All she needed to do was touch her hand to his bare flesh and he'd be done for, but instead she peeled his trousers down to his ankles, forced his knees apart, and laid an open-mouthed kiss on him.

His hips jerked. His feet splayed uselessly, his ankles caught in his clothes. He'd told her about this, people using their mouths on each other, but it had been somewhere between a boast and a dare. He hadn't actually thought—sweet fuck, her tongue was hot and wet and rough and *relentless*. He couldn't have imagined this. But of course she'd committed. That was what Julie did.

He was going to die if she stopped, or if she didn't stop, or—God. By now there was no turning back. He was going to die. Right here on this mattress on Julie's studio floor, half-undressed, clenching his fingers in the sheets and groaning. However it looked, it would feel glorious. He'd never wanted anything more.

She closed her lips around him and sucked, and he fell all the way apart. Sensation blotted out everything else. It rolled over him in waves, cresting and ebbing, making him shake.

Julie wiped her hand over her mouth and she looked almost as pleased as he felt.

"Write about *that* in your diary," she said.

"Oh, I will."

She dropped down next to him. On further study, he suspected she was in need, but she hadn't mentioned it.

"Now it's my turn," he announced, and lust darkened her eyes. Good. That fine fracture in her composure called to him.

It took him a moment to remember how his limbs worked, but he collected himself and got to his knees. Julie lay on her back. He reached for the fall of her trousers.

Victor didn't bother to tease her, since it was evident she'd riled herself up. He drew her clothes down and sank his teeth into his lower lip appreciatively. He didn't know what he was doing, but that had never stopped him before.

Besides, judging from how wet she was, it wouldn't take much.

She'd loved tasting him. Selfishly, he hadn't even considered that while it was happening. *Considering* hadn't really been within his power. And he was still a little dazed, because he'd mistaken her quiet for calm. She'd done a good job because she did a good job at everything, he'd thought, but that didn't account for the slick heat under his hands.

Victor bent down to take her into his mouth. He licked her up and down and she curved her hand around his head and guided him where she wanted him. It was gentle. It didn't need to be.

He paused for a moment so he could swallow and say, "More. Harder."

She raised her eyebrows. "Isn't that what I'm supposed to say?"

"You won't need to," he promised and went back to work.

Her skin was impossibly soft against his tongue, and the feel and taste of her drove him wild. Julie made strained little sounds above him. Her grip on the roots of his hair betrayed her silence—she was as wild for this as he was, she was just a lot less noisy about it.

She came in a rush. One long sigh and all the tension poured out of her. He stayed where he was, absorbing every last shiver, until she said, "Come up here and kiss me."

He wouldn't disobey that order.

Afterward, she laughed and said, "I can't believe we didn't even get all our clothes off."

"You can't?" he asked. "I can't believe I didn't ask all my questions."

"You can ask me anything you want." She yawned. "Tomorrow."

DECEMBER 29, 1823

The days passed easily. Julie and Victor weren't subtle about spending a lot of time alone together, but Maman and Papa let it happen with only a brief, private, thoroughly unnecessary warning to be careful. When Julie reported that to Victor, his jaw dropped and she had to scold him to adopt his pose again. He was seated in the armchair in her studio, ostensibly gazing into the distance while she drew him.

Except right now, he was staring at her. "Your family is *so strange*."

"Why do you say that?" Julie asked, storing her charcoal in the easel tray. She rubbed her thumb over her fingertips, smoothing the fine grit of charcoal dust into velvet smudges. "Sophie knows about us. She gave you the sponge."

"Yes, but she's *Sophie*."

"My parents are eccentric artists with radical beliefs. It's not any different."

"Can I ask—the warning they gave you," Victor began. "Was it about sex or magic?"

"Both. They know I've brought you here." She pivoted and waved a hand at the studio walls and all the self-portraits. "It's not hard to guess that I told you everything. I'm not much good at keeping secrets."

She hadn't told him everything. But she hadn't lied. A few careful omissions, that was just being judicious. If she could prevent Victor from getting too tangled up in this business of artifacts, he wouldn't need to hear any cautionary tales.

The afternoon light illuminated the pale golden column of Victor's throat so it was impossible to miss his swallow.

"What is it?" Julie asked. "Don't look down. You can talk and hold the pose. Angle yourself toward me again. Now stare out the window. Yes. That's it."

Victor didn't answer her question, so she filled the silence with the rasp of charcoal on paper. The round form of Victor's head took shape on her page. She worked in large arcs, and then in blocks of shadow and light, saving all the details for last.

She didn't forget their conversation, so it didn't startle her when he spoke again.

"I've been considering leaving the Maison Laval."

"Because you can't pay room and board?" Julie asked. "I'll help you, Victor. How much are your rooms?"

Victor's eyes were such a deep blue that in shadow, his irises were indistinguishable from his pupils. They looked huge and dark—and under the delicate wrinkle of his brow, puzzled. The effect left Julie as tender as a bruise.

Victor asked, "You'd pay our rent?"

"Of course," she said, stung by his surprise. "I don't know if I have enough, but I'll help however I can. I won't see you thrown out of the boarding house, Victor. I'm sure the rest of my family will offer as well, now that you've charmed them."

"That's very generous of you, but it's not necessary. I wasn't talking about a lack of funds. Rather the opposite. I'm going to seek out better lodgings."

"Has your father finally changed his mind? That's a relief."

"No," Victor said. "But we've come into some money."

Julie paused in her drawing. Enough money to move into better lodgings was a large amount of money to acquire at once, and that boded ill. "I don't understand. You would have mentioned finding work, surely. Did someone else in your family help you?"

"No."

His satisfied smile didn't ease the thread of worry that had pulled tight in her gut. "What did you do?"

"Magic."

The thin twist of vine charcoal snapped between her fingers. She laid the two pieces in the easel tray and gave up the pretense of drawing. "Victor. What *exactly* did you do?"

"I saved myself and Aunt Sophie from destitution," he retorted. "It wasn't dangerous, Julie. There was hardly anything to it. I opened a bank account and wrote a few letters, that's all. The worst that could possibly happen is that my brother will notice and try to take the money, which will return me to the same predicament I was in before—if he succeeds, which I doubt he will."

"The letters," Julie said. "Are you transferring magic into them?"

"That's an interesting question," he said, as though this were a university class and they were engaging in a hypothetical discussion. "I think the answer is no. There were a few times early on where people would only believe what I wrote while they were holding or reading the page. But I've refined my technique so the effects last. I worked on this plan for months, you know. I didn't just dash off a letter. Give me some credit."

Julie could only respond with a grimace, but Victor didn't take any notice. He'd risen from the armchair and was pacing around the room, animated by curiosity.

"The pen seems to have retained some magic. Certainly, the process only works with one particular pen. I haven't been able to replicate it with any others. But you know, I don't think these transfers are as risky as you say, Julie. I read a book about it and there are thousands of magical artifacts in the world. Not all of them are bad."

Julie rooted herself to the ground to keep from going after him and shaking his shoulders. "The point isn't that all of them are bad, Victor. The point is that you made a pen that makes people believe whatever it writes. What if someone takes the pen?"

"I'll be careful, then."

"Yes, you've been very careful so far."

He stopped right in front of her. "Oh, don't scowl at me. So you're telling me the only acceptable way to do magic is the way *you* do it? That's convenient."

"It's too dangerous. You have to destroy it," Julie said.

"That pen is my only protection against my family—in particular my brother, who, by the way, has a collection of his own. And the pen is my best source of knowledge about magic. I'm not destroying it."

Julie ran her fingers through her hair, pressing against her scalp. "Victor."

"How will we ever learn more about it if I destroy it, Julie?" Victor asked. He ceased gesturing and took one of her hands into both of his. "I've scraped together a future for myself out of *nothing*. I thought you'd be relieved and happy for me. Proud, even."

"I want to be," she said, squeezing his hands in return. "I think you're brilliant and I *am* happy you've found magic, Victor. I'm not asking you to stop. For fuck's sake, right now I'm not even asking you to stop using your magic to rob banks—though I do think we should revisit that later. What I'm asking you, very specifically, is to destroy the cursed artifact you've made."

He scoffed. "Calling it a 'cursed artifact' makes it sound so much worse than what it is. There's no harm in what I've done."

"No harm to you," she corrected. "Yet."

"Don't tell me you're feeling pity for my brother," he said. "Why don't you trust me to do the right thing?"

"Of course I'm not worried about your brother. And it's not that I don't trust you. I'm imagining the deception you perpetrated against your brother being wielded against someone else—you, perhaps. Do you know what happens when you make a powerful artifact and flaunt it, Victor? Bad people notice. They come looking."

"I didn't flaunt anything. I carried out a simple, effective, carefully planned, *successful* transfer of funds."

"For how much money?"

"Ten thousand francs," he said.

"Ten *thousand?*" Julie opened her mouth, closed it again, and finally brought herself to speak when she was sure she could do it with relative calm. "You and I have different definitions of 'flaunt.'"

"It's far less than I would have inherited," Victor said. "It's easy to follow the rules when you have everything you need, Julie. Who would you be if you didn't have your family? Their love and support? *Financial* support? Try to understand my circumstances."

"I do understand your circumstances, and I'm telling you I would give you *anything*, Victor. I might not have ten thousand francs, but we could get by with less. More importantly, we'd be safe. You don't need that pen for protection because you have me. You have all of us."

"So I should sit idly by while you pay my rent?" Victor dropped her hands and walked toward the window. The air was cool where his touch had been. "You think you understand, but you don't."

This conversation was an overturned carriage, wheels spinning the air, the rest of it sinking into the mud. Julie took a deep breath. "Maybe we should go back to the house to see if Adrienne wants to visit Léon or play cards."

"I can't afford to play cards with your sister again."

"I heard you can," Julie said.

Victor looked over his shoulder and returned her tentative smile with a lift of his eyebrows. "Oh, are we making jokes already?"

"It seemed preferable to continuing our argument," Julie said. "I'm not angry with you, Victor. I'm afraid."

"And I'm telling you that you don't need to be," Victor said. "I have everything under control."

II
LANDSCAPE WITH RUINS
1824

PRIVATE DIARY OF J MORÈRE, JANUARY 5, 1824

I've never kept a diary before, only a sketchbook, but I'm too upset to draw.

Bothering Adrienne with this is out of the question. I've put her through enough.

I did my best to appear content for the last of the visit home and the two days on the road with Victor and Sophie, but I wasn't. Victor knew—I avoided his touch. My tossing and turning probably kept him awake. He didn't ask why.

As soon as we had a private moment at the Maison Laval, I told him we couldn't sleep together as long as he refused to destroy the cursed artifact he made. His pursuit of magical knowledge might kill him. I can't sit idly by while he endangers himself and others, even if it breaks my heart. He made all the same points as before—that I have a loving family, and money, and don't know what it's like to live without either. That I'm being rigid and close-minded, thinking my way to do magic is the only right way.

I've done it the wrong way, too, but I don't know how to tell him. I've made a mess of things, because if I had only explained myself earlier, he would have understood. Now it's too late. The truth will make him even angrier with me.

We're still speaking, but barely. Nothing is as easy or as comfortable as it was. The loss hurts.

I haven't seen him much since that conversation. Every time the house creaks, I wonder if it's Victor moving around in the room below. I don't know what he's doing. Keeping more secrets, probably. Taking stupid risks. He wasn't at dinner tonight.

My room never used to depress me. It's a relief to go out, and I need to find a place to rent as a studio in any case. I haven't told anyone, not V or my family, but I'm thinking of leaving school. It's tedious.

The other tenants never irritated me so much, either. Yesterday at the dinner table, Forestier asked if we'd had a pleasant time in the country and I snapped "Why do you want to know?" in front of everyone. The ensuing silence was sharp. I had to apologize. I may not like Forestier, but he was only making polite conversation. It's just that his manner puts me off. Maybe it's only because I know he works for the police, but he treats everyone as a suspect. Even the most innocuous conversation has the feel of an interrogation. And I haven't forgotten those times he was lingering outside Victor's room.

No, my bad mood is making me imagine things. Enough of that.

I regret that Victor and I argued, but I don't regret what I said. Why doesn't he understand that I want to protect him?

PRIVATE DIARY OF V BEAUCHÊNE, JANUARY 5, 1824

Here's something I never expected to write: today my father came to visit me at the Maison Laval. Aunt S and I had gone for a walk in the Jardin du Luxembourg and when we returned, he was waiting for me in the little parlor.

I thought he'd discovered my theft. What a chill.

"I need to speak with you, Victor," he said in a trembling voice. He appeared like some specter from the past, and I do mean like a specter. He looks like someone drained the life out of him. Stooped from his former height, with his blond hair washed to white and his eyes pale and watery. His skin hangs off him in folds. He stood unsteadily from the worn armchair. "Only you, not Sophie."

"Whatever you have to say to me, Aunt Sophie can hear it, too," I said and was glad to have her standing behind me. I didn't need to see her face to know she was glaring.

"Can we at least adjourn to a more private space?" he asked. "Your rooms, perhaps?"

"If you wanted to speak to me in a private space, you could have allowed me to continue living in your home," I said. "Why are you here?"

"Your brother is killing me," he said. "You have to stop him."

Aunt S put a hand on my shoulder.

"You're not dead yet," I said, though he looked a lot closer than he ever had. He used to be in robust health. There was no sign of his muscular form under his suit. "What are you accusing him of, poison?"

"No, it's far worse. There is a certain artifact in our family. A ring. Horace took it from me."

"The cameo ring," Aunt S said with certainty. "With the woman's profile in white relief against the orange shell. You used to wear that all the time."

"It grants the wearer influence over people," he said. "It's a subtle effect most of the time. I didn't give a lot of direct commands. Just suggestions. It's like a luck charm. Smooths the way."

A leaden weight collected in my stomach. The artifact my father described, its effect isn't so different from the pen I created. I hate resembling him in any way. Knowing about this ring casts my whole life into doubt. It's not a question of whether he used it on me, but how much.

It makes me almost grateful to have been disinherited and evicted.

"Horace took this ring from you, you said. But how is he using to kill you?"

"As I said, I didn't give a lot of direct commands. I wielded my power carefully. Your brother does not. And when he gives commands that go against my wishes, I resist. That is what's killing me."

"You didn't want to give him control of the bank," I

guessed. "And that's why your health is deteriorating? Because you resisted Horace?"

He gave a sharp, decisive nod. "I wanted to tell you about it, but when I'm near him, I can't defy his will. I hardly even know what's true, living in that house with him."

Aunt S had removed her hand from my shoulder, but I could feel her vibrating with fury behind me. "You're saying that resisting the magical influence of this object gave you a mysterious illness that might kill you."

As ever, my father is the only thing that goads Aunt S to fury. Writing this, I realize that she didn't stumble over the concept of a magical object. At the time, I was only concerned with the horrible revelation about my mother's illness.

"Sophie," he said placatingly. "Anaïs was sick, Sophie. Sometimes people get sick."

"You killed her," she said. "My sister. My only sister. I hope Horace is killing you. I won't lift a finger to stop him."

Aunt S stalked out of the room. I don't blame her for leaving me alone with him. She wouldn't have, except that any mention of Maman's death ruins her composure. I heard her slam the door to her room down the hall.

"It isn't true, Victor. I loved your mother. I didn't kill her." His body abandoned him then and he collapsed back into the armchair. He clung to its arms to keep himself from sliding to the floor. His voice, already rough, thinned until it was almost inaudible. "She just got sick. I didn't mean for her to die."

If I'd had a gun in my hand, I would have shot him.

He looked up at me with red-rimmed eyes. "Help me, Victor."

"You killed my mother and slandered her memory in order to kick me out of your home," I said, rage searing down my skin. I've never been so angry. He crushed her will with his magic for years, over and over, until she sickened and died resisting him. He evicted and disowned me. And then he asked for my help.

"I didn't, I tell you I didn't! I loved her. It was an accident. The rest, that was Horace, he told me those things, he wanted you gone. You have to help me, Victor. I know you can. I know about your little theft."

That was what I'd feared when I'd first seen him sitting in Madame Laval's armchair, but in the wake of his other news, it meant nothing.

"I won't tell Horace and he'll never notice, he has no interest in the accounts," my father continued. "You keep the money and we'll consider it payment for you helping me retrieve the ring."

Sheer force of will kept me from grabbing Madame Laval's ceramic vase of half-wilted flowers and chucking it at his head. "I was rightfully owed that money—and more. And no, I won't help you retrieve the ring you used to imprison and poison my mother. How could you come here expecting that after you ejected me so many months ago?"

"I couldn't get away. He doesn't like to let me out of his sight."

How hard it is to reconcile this cringing coward with the authority who deemed me no longer part of his family. I took no pains to hide my disgust. "You weren't sick when you evicted me. Does that mean you weren't resisting him? You fought harder for your bank than you did for your second child?"

"The trouble accumulates over time. Your mother, she

was fine for years. It was only once you got older and started misbehaving that she—"

"Shut your fucking mouth."

It's possible I shouted that. Madame Laval probably heard it.

I'd like to think I stalked out of the room as coldly as Aunt S, but I think I might have run. It was pitiful and undignified rather than furious and impressive. I spent the rest of the day in Aunt S's room, both of us distraught. Even writing this, my grip on the pen is painfully tight.

I hate my father. I hope he dies.

But he's right about one thing: Horace shouldn't have that ring.

I have to rob my brother—again. It will be harder to divest him of a ring he wears night and day than of mere money. Fuck, I wish I had someone to talk to, but Aunt S is taking a nap before we go out tonight and J is already angry with me. Hearing about this disaster won't improve that. Also, I've been crying and I don't want anyone to see.

V BEAUCHÊNE TO J MORÈRE, JANUARY 6, 1824
SLIPPED UNDER THE DOOR

J—

I know you're angry with me, and we're at an impasse, but now that I've met you, I simply can't conceive of my life without you in it. I miss you.

So I thought I'd write to you. Yes, even though we're only one floor apart. I could come upstairs and talk to you, but there's a chance you won't open the door. You think I'm reckless, but there are risks I cannot bring myself to take.

I do love writing to you, though. And talking to you. For so many reasons, but a notable one is that when we talk to each other, it's just <u>I</u> and <u>you</u> and we don't have to bother with <u>he</u> or <u>she</u>. You know, when I think of you, sometimes I think <u>iel</u>, "they." How do you feel about that? I wouldn't mind if you referred to me that way, at least in private, or if you're writing to Adrienne.

There's still the problem of adjectives, and whether I should tell you that you're <u>beau</u> or <u>belle</u>, but perhaps your beauty is too great to be contained with a single word, and you require both. That, or you're <u>splendide</u>. If we write enough letters, we'll come up with our own language.

I shouldn't assume you'll write back. But if you don't want my letters, you should return this one to me so I'll know to stop writing. That would be the decent thing to do, so I know you'll do it.

And speaking of decency, I'll make myself clear. This letter is written with an ordinary pen, and every future letter will be, too.

—V

J MORÈRE TO V BEAUCHÊNE, JANUARY 6, 1824
SLIPPED UNDER THE DOOR

[*This note is scrawled at the bottom of the previous letter.*]
I know. If you'd used the pen, I wouldn't still itch to tie you up to keep you from doing anything else foolish.

You can write to me.

VICTOR BEAUCHÊNE TO HORACE FAUCHEUX, JANUARY 6, 1824

POSTMARKED PARIS

Dear Horace,

I am sorry to trouble you with further correspondence, but I think I perceived in your last letter that the "art objects" you collect often have <u>unusual properties</u>, and I have recently come into some information about such artifacts. As you are my brother, I feel a duty to share it with you, though your knowledge is undoubtedly already far superior to mine. Consider this paltry offering a repayment for the education you so kindly provided me when you removed me from your house.

It will likely surprise you that I have one of these unusual artifacts in my own possession. An accident, but as I have recently learned, not a happy one. My particular object is a pen that grants me persuasive powers. Like a fool, I thought it would save me from life in the gutter. I wrote so many letters with it. People gave me whatever I wanted. The pen never left my hand.

But I have had to stop using it.

You'll note the sad quality of my handwriting in this letter. The strength has gone out of my hand. These objects, when worn or used too often, drain one's vital forces. Mere exposure can damage one's health, but use—sustained use especially—is the worst. Now I can hardly breathe except to cough blood. My hair and teeth have all fallen out. My bones have weakened and bent. People often mistake me for a very old person, and I cannot blame them. You would not recognize me, shriveled and pale as I have become. Merely sitting up in bed exhausts me. I fear I will die soon.

In the twilight of my life, I regret our separation more deeply than ever. I should have been a better friend to you. I could have learned from you.

Now, perhaps, you can learn from me. This letter is all I will accomplish today, but the fatigue will be worth it if I can spare you this fate. Should you have an especially beloved artifact, you must take care not to use it all the time. Remove it from your person or even from your room at night. In this way, you might slow its ruinous effects.

Victor

V BEAUCHÊNE TO J MORÈRE, JANUARY 7, 1824
SLIPPED UNDER THE DOOR

J—

You gave me a scare by returning that same page, but I forgive you. Please elaborate on this fantasy of tying me up.

I am relieved that you will permit these letters. I'd miss you terribly if you didn't, and of course I wouldn't have anyone else to tell this story to, and that would be a shame.

You recall I missed dinner two days ago? (I do hope you were rude to Forestier again in my absence. That was magnificent.)

Aunt S took me to the strangest place. It was across the river in a neighborhood they're calling Nouvelle-Athènes. It's perhaps fifteen minutes by foot from the townhouse where I grew up, but instead of bankers and industrialists, there are artists and musicians and other eccentrics. The city peters out there, narrow streets giving way to open spaces and scattered freestanding houses, rather than the cheek-by-jowl construction you find around here. There are no street lamps; there are hardly streets. Some of the houses are worn-down old stone things, all their corners rounded, but the one we went to was new and square, set a long way back from the unpaved street.

I'm getting ahead of myself. Aunt S fussed over my cuffs and my cravat and my hair before we left the Maison Laval, which she never does. She also never takes me anywhere, so it wasn't hard to see she was nervous. Her nerves contaminated me, although my own nervousness wasn't the clammy, stuttering kind, but instead a buzz under my skin. I wanted very badly to know what had interrupted Aunt S's usual unconcerned cheer.

Asking where we were going had only elicited the brief, useless answer that we would be dining with an old friend she hadn't seen in a few years.

We had to hire a cab, and on the way over Aunt S said, "The people we're about to meet may tell you shocking things about me."

"Shocking things like how you've aided your niece-nephew in perverting the social order and defying nature itself?" I asked.

"Oh, is that what you're doing?" Aunt S said. "The social order seems intact to me. And if it's your goal to defy nature, you might have to put in a bit more work."

"I don't think your friends can shock me, Aunt S."

"Well, even if they do, try not to give them the satisfaction of showing it."

We exited the cab and walked up a long gravel path lined with hedges. It was dark by then, but Aunt S forged ahead, and soon I could see the illuminated windows of the house in front of us. As I said, it was new construction, clean and angular.

"I don't quite know how things will be in there," Aunt

S said, and I wondered exactly what she had meant by <u>old friends</u>. "These would be good people to have on your side, Victor."

"On my side of what?" I asked.

But the door opened then so she didn't answer. We were ushered into a high-ceilinged foyer with a grand staircase. The dark wooden floor disappeared under a thick, muted red carpet woven with a white floral pattern. Brocade wallpaper and gilt-framed portraits glinted in the lamplight—I know you wish I was describing the paintings, J, but I only saw the foyer in passing, and then we were in a parlor, which of course had more paintings, but I couldn't look at them when there was such an extraordinary woman in front of me.

Our host and the owner of the house is named Madame Isabelle de Tourzin. (Monsieur de Tourzin, if he exists, was nowhere in evidence.) She is of medium height and build, with an olive complexion, and I judge her to be about forty years old. Her hair was mounded into a twist on top of her head, except for a few curled locks framing her face, glossy black stranded with silver. She has a large nose and powerful eyebrows and she does not smile. Perhaps this does not sound captivating, but she is. I wish I could draw her for you.

I have no idea how Madame de Tourzin and Aunt S know each other. Mme de T is younger, in my estimation, and she didn't look pleased to be reunited. That ought to be damning in and of itself—who wouldn't be delighted to be in Aunt S's presence? All she does is say witty, occasionally inappropriate things and try to make other people happy.

But anyway I'm a terrible judge of character because I saw Mme de T standing there in her wine-red dress and was struck speechless. Saying my own name in our introductions was almost beyond me—Aunt S had to nudge me. Even if I could draw, it wouldn't explain anything. She's a little too rough-hewn to be a classic beauty, Madame de Tourzin, but she has this air of knowing everything.

There were two other guests, both interesting in their own right. One was a laughing, statuesque Black woman named Béatrix Chevreuil with her hair wrapped in a gold silk scarf that matched her dress. The color made her deep brown skin glow. She said "<u>Sophie</u>" in this warm voice like my aunt was her long-lost sister and then took both of her hands.

When the two of us were introduced, I tried to call her Madame Chevreuil. With amusement lighting her eyes, she told me that it was still Mademoiselle after all these years—she must be the same age as Aunt S, though she doesn't look it—and then said she would be pleased if I called her Béatrix. So I shall. Béatrix turned out to be an opera singer, which explains her voice, but not how she knows my aunt.

The other guest was a thin white man in a fitted black wool frock coat and trousers. In this century, frock coats aren't weighed down with silver and gilt embroidery, but I still know a rich man when I see one. Remarkable finery aside—the ornate knot of his white cravat, God, I've never managed one that good—he might have escaped my notice, especially in the company of such striking women. I judged him to be a little older than Aunt S, with silver hair and elegant lines at the corner of his eye. Yes, one eye —the other is hidden beneath a black eye patch. The tail end of a scar scored his cheek. No matter how dignified and sober his clothes, that scar tells a story of a more dangerous life.

Madame de Tourzin introduced him as the Vicomte de Savigny. "This is the <u>Vicomte</u>," she said, like she was fatigued beyond measure. Can you imagine?

I know you don't care about anyone's nobility, J, but not all of us can be so passionately ideological all the time. I grew up rich but not titled, having it impressed upon me that this noble status was the one thing out of my family's reach—unless I was beautiful enough to marry a man such as Savigny, which I maintain that I still am. Marriage no longer interests me, that's all.

I suppose the five of us ate dinner, and it was probably finer than anything I've had at the Maison Laval, but I paid it no attention. Aunt S was right that these people wanted to shock me, and Savigny wasted no time.

The first thing he said was, "Beauchêne, my young friend, in 1795—we called it Year Three back then—I saw your aunt arrive at a ball naked and barefoot."

"I wore a dress," Aunt S protested mildly.

"A completely transparent dress."

"It was always too warm at those balls," Aunt S said.

"Ever so practical, our Sophie," said Béatrix. "I recall you used to bathe in strawberry juice."

"It was only the once," Aunt S said. "You'd know that if you'd accepted my invitation."

"Was I invited, then?" asked Béatrix, leaning forward.

"You'd be invited now if only you'd say yes," Aunt S said. "Hard to find strawberries at this time of year, but I hear the Vicomte de Savigny and Madame de Tourzin can get their hands on anything."

It was at this moment that I began to suspect my aunt was flirting. Having just written all that down, you will think me as dull as a stone for not noticing earlier, but in my defense, there was a lot to take in. I can't help but wonder if, thirty years ago, my mother partook in this association of... revolutionaries? witches? I'm not quite sure what I witnessed. It was probably only Aunt S, though. My mother was younger than her and led a far more sedate life.

"Enough of this," Mme de T said, spreading her hands.

Even the Vicomte sat up straighter at the sound of her voice.

She continued, "We are not here for idle nostalgia. I agreed to meet young Beauchêne here because Sophie told me it was urgent. Tell us, monsieur, what have you done?"

I had no idea what Aunt S had written about me. All I had to work with was her warning not to give them the satisfaction of shocking me—and, I suppose, your caution influenced me. So I said, "I've done nothing. I came here to meet an old friend of my aunt's."

"'I've done nothing' isn't the sort of thing people who've done nothing have to say," Savigny observed.

"You might as well tell her," Béatrix said, tilting her head at Mme de T. "She'll figure it out regardless."

Aunt S, who had sat in unhelpful silence the whole time, nodded vigorously.

Still wary, I said, "There's nothing to tell."

You must understand, J, that I hadn't told Aunt S <u>anything</u>. You're the only one who knows the truth. So this conversation bewildered me.

Béatrix said, "I don't care for any of this secrecy and mystery. I stay away from magic and anyone who's interested in it as much as I can. But I have a particular talent —my voice is quite literally enchanting—and I'm here in case you need to be trained not to hurt people by accident. If that's not the case, then I'm here for Sophie."

Béatrix struck me as sincere, but I think the others

wanted to determine if I posed a threat to them. Instead of saying so, I pinned Savigny with my gaze and asked, "And what can you do?"

"Oh, nothing," he said, giving me a quick, sharp smile. "Like all inveterate old gossips, I'm terribly dull in my own right."

"Do not play cards with him," Béatrix said.

Savigny gave a shrug so boneless that the motion ought to have sent him pooling to the floor. I began to understand his careless posture as a desire to be underestimated. He possesses some magical ability, I have no doubt.

I turned my attention to our host, mustered all of my courage, and said, "And you?"

Mme de T's only answer was a long, dark-eyed stare, followed by the tiniest lift in her brows. "No one has asked me that in a long, long time. But I won't be helping you. My home is a meeting place for tonight, nothing more. Address yourself to Mademoiselle Chevreuil and Monsieur le Vicomte."

Neither of the other two guests was forthcoming on the subject of Madame de Tourzin, and Aunt S was too busy mooning over Béatrix to be of any use. But I had other questions I wanted answered, and nothing to lose by asking them.

"How many people can do things like this? Magic?"

"The number is unknown," Savigny said. "We suspect everyone has the potential, but only a small fraction unlock it. Those who do tend to be secretive about it, either because secrecy benefits them, or for fear of reprisal."

"That, or they accidentally get themselves killed one way or another," Béatrix said. "As a favor to Sophie, we'd like to stop that from happening to you."

"Is there no community, then? No King? No Emperor? No Directory?"

"You imagine a republic," Savigny said, amused.

"No," Béatrix said. "We find each other, that's all."

"It's better to be found by some than others," said Mme de T, locking eyes with Aunt S. I know I'm missing something important. But I sensed they wouldn't tell me if I asked.

I'm glad it was you who found me, J. Even if we never repair things, I'll always be glad of that.

"What about objects?" I continued. "How many magical objects are there in the world?"

"Why do you want to know about cursed artifacts?" Mme de T said.

As steadily as I could, I said, "My initial research suggests that there are thousands." I've only read one book about magic, but "research" sounded more impressive. Watching the other guests, I continued, "They're dangerous and likely all over the city. Someone ought to keep track of them. I think they're worthy of study."

Savigny laughed. "You and half the rich men in Paris. Though it's not study that interests them—there's a thriving artifact market. Everyone wants a trinket to show off."

Béatrix said, "'Show off' is putting it too lightly. Most of them want to do harm."

"Either way it's obscene," Mme de T said severely.

"Well," Aunt S said brightly. I nearly jumped. She'd been quiet for so long. "This has been a fascinating evening. I think we should be going now. We'd be delighted to keep in touch—perhaps you'd permit us to call on you?"

"Of course," Béatrix said.

"Yes, I think so," said Savigny, and then we left.

There you have it. I have been wondering what it all means ever since. Does this story make you want to tie me up? At least then something worthwhile would have come of such a strange encounter.

—V

PRIVATE DIARY OF V BEAUCHÊNE, JANUARY 7, 1824

That was perhaps more than I should have told J, and I still didn't tell them everything. I also asked Aunt S's strange friends about this ring my brother supposedly has, and his list of friends and associates, though I also didn't tell them everything.

Savigny confirmed for me that all of the names on my brother's list are known collectors of objects and counseled me to stay away from them. There is also a curio shop on the list, a place on the Quai de Voltaire where objects are bought and sold, and Savigny told me not to go there, either. He was blunt. "You don't want to get involved in this affair. You're likely to end up dead."

I don't think I have much of a choice.

I didn't name my brother or my father in the story I told, which caused Aunt S to narrow her eyes at me from across the table. She didn't gainsay me, though. The ring was unknown to Mme de T, Savigny, and Béatrix, but they agreed that the story sounded likely; the details of my father's account overlap with what they know of other persuasive artifacts. When I asked where they'd learned that, they said it was experience. There aren't very many books about these topics. The people who know the most tend to be avid collectors, so they don't care to share their knowledge. I said I'd like to write a book, and they seemed to find this amusing, which I didn't like.

If they hadn't been so condescending about that, I might have explained that I wrote to my brother to convince him to stop wearing the ring at night so my chance of stealing it will be better. (I would have asked him to send it to me, but I think such a request is beyond the powers of my pen. I can't force people to do things they have no inclination to do. I can only nudge them.) But I thought they would pat me on the head and tell me not to get involved, even though I <u>am</u> involved whether I like it or not, so I didn't divulge my plan to rob my brother or the existence of my pen.

I did ask, "This hypothetical ring—is there a way to destroy it?"

"There may be," Madame de Tourzin said. "Cursed artifacts are all different, but they tend to be volatile. Trying to destroy them physically often fails. Even when it succeeds, destruction unleashes a burst of energy. An explosion, I mean. It can be done safely, but it shouldn't be tried carelessly."

"What do you do with a cursed artifact that can't be destroyed?" I asked.

"Keep it upstairs," Savigny said and laughed.

I don't think he was joking.

V BEAUCHÊNE TO J MORÈRE, JANUARY 8, 1824
SLIPPED UNDER THE DOOR

J—

I waited all day and you didn't write back to me. Have I upset you?

—V

JULIE MORÈRE TO ADRIENNE MORÈRE, JANUARY 10, 1824
POSTMARKED PARIS

My dear Adrienne,

There is only one thing worth reporting in my life, and it's that CAMILLE DUPIN BOUGHT A DRAWING FROM ME. Yes, the author of <u>Virginie</u>. The genius. That Camille Dupin.

When I'm not at school and the weather's not too miserable—so, almost never—I sketch scenes of the city. I showed some to my instructor once and he deemed them a waste of my time and talent, too "small" and "unworthy" to be real art. But Camille Dupin passed by me and bought one right out of my sketchbook. Specifically, a little study of a butcher's stall in the covered market. Camille Dupin saw it and touched it and paid me genuine currency for it. Camille said it was "arresting" and "real."

Yes, <u>Camille</u>. We're on familiar terms now. I even asked how she liked to be referred to, after she introduced herself, since some of the papers have printed "he" in their novel reviews. She laughed and said "I suppose 'she' will do, but your uncertainty is appreciated."

And then she looked me up and down—in this form

that I crafted to avoid ambiguity—and said, "How do you like to be referred to?"

"Oh, anything suits me," I said, smiling as if it were a joke.

She said, "I like you, Morère."

Camille is about five years older than me, lean and daring, with hair the color of rosewood. As you've no doubt read in the papers, Camille prefers trousers and frock coats, usually in black, but she wears her hair long. On the day we met, it was in a simple bun. She is not a beauty by conventional feminine or masculine standards—a long nose, a narrow face, close-set eyes and a mouth that only draws attention when pulled into an irreverent smile—but I found her wonderful to look at, and I have included a sketch. She speaks deliberately, often quite slowly, even when making a quip. Her voice is low and resonant.

I sound smitten. I don't mean to imply that anything passed between us other than conversation and the sale of a sketch, but it's hard not to be smitten when you meet someone you admire and she buys your work and tells you that you have a great deal in common, as artists, and that she hopes to befriend you.

We're going to a salon together next week. I still can't believe it.

So, as you can see, things are going well here and there's no need to worry about me. I hope you and everyone (and Léon) are well.

With affection,

Julie

ADRIENNE MORÈRE TO JULIE MORÈRE, JANUARY 15, 1824
POSTMARKED VÉZY-SUR-OISE

My dear Julie,

I am thrilled for you that you met Camille Dupin. She sounds wonderful and I hope you become the best of friends. For your happiness, of course. And if it so happened that through your close friendship, I was privy to Camille's next novel before it was published, that would be the happiest of coincidences.

Everyone here is fine, but I refuse to write more until you answer the question you have been avoiding. A certain name—a name that has been repeated in <u>every single letter</u> for the past few months—is missing from your latest missive. Did something happen?

Are you well, Julie?

Love,

Adrienne

V BEAUCHÊNE TO J MORÈRE, JANUARY 16, 1824
SLIPPED UNDER THE DOOR

J—

Until you employ our agreed-upon signal of returning one of my letters unopened, I will continue to write to you. Your absence renders me pitiable. (Your presence renders me pitiable, too, but I like that.)

That is to say, I miss you, and these letters make me feel better.

Upon reflection, I see that my last letter must have upset you because it made clear that I am pursuing my inquiries into magic, and that through Aunt S's connections, I have stumbled upon people who may be collectors of the objects you fear. You wish me not to associate with them, and I will inevitably disappoint you.

I won't claim that greed and ambition play no part in my choices. I don't need you to think me more virtuous than I am. But you of all people ought to respect ambition, since you have it in abundance. Can you not sympathize with mine? My life has had no purpose until now, J, and this phenomenon calls to me. I want to understand magic. Never have I felt such a fire to educate myself.

If you cannot accept that, perhaps you will accept this: these objects exist. If you picked Paris up and shook it, a rain of artifacts would tumble out. We cannot stop people from creating them, whether by design or by accident. We can only determine what happens after their creation. As my last letter demonstrates, other people are already hard at work collecting and cataloguing these objects. My cruel brother is among them. Wouldn't you rather it were me?

—V

J MORÈRE TO V BEAUCHÊNE, JANUARY 16, 1824
SLIPPED UNDER THE DOOR

[*This note is scrawled at the bottom of the previous letter.*]
I would not.

V BEAUCHÊNE TO J MORÈRE, JANUARY 16, 1824
SLIPPED UNDER THE DOOR

My dear J—

Your tenderness overwhelms me.

Your miserliness with your pages overwhelms me slightly less, but we all have our faults. I will not be swayed from my course; you will not spend a fresh page or more than one sentence writing back to me.

Do you miss me as I miss you, J? Do you miss touching me? Do you think about how I'm one floor below you, alone by candlelight, and no one would know if you crept down the stairs to come see me? You've already come once to deliver your last letter. You should come again—or you should unlock your door when I deliver this one.

I know you think the two of us are a bad idea, but what if it's only tonight? Let go of your principles and hold me instead. I won't tell.

—V

J MORÈRE TO V BEAUCHÊNE, JANUARY 17, 1824
SLIPPED UNDER THE DOOR

[*This letter includes a drawing that would get this book banned from publication, were it destined for such a fate.*]

I was asleep when your last letter arrived, V, but if you insist on tormenting me, then I will torment you in return.

V BEAUCHÊNE TO J MORÈRE, JANUARY 17, 1824
SLIPPED UNDER THE DOOR

My dear J—

"Asleep" is a likely story, but since you've outdone yourself by offering me one whole page, I will accept your version of events along with this breathtaking gift. I assume the two people depicted are you and me, though you've made a few changes. I like them very much, your changes.

Rest assured, J, that I am quite talented at tormenting myself.

Should your hand start to ache—from all the drawing—you know where to find me.

—V

PRIVATE DIARY OF V BEAUCHÊNE, JANUARY 20, 1824

Having carefully repaired my correspondence with J after nearly scaring them off, I have decided that from now on, I won't discuss my work with them. I want to preserve our friendship and this is the only way to do it. So I resort to this diary again, lacking for confidants in real life.

I don't know how I will determine if my letter to Horace had the desired effect. I told Horace I was dying, so I can't let him see me. The safest choice is to write to my father and ask him to check. The thought turns my stomach.

Aunt S and I have been out almost every night, dining and chatting and being introduced to four hundred new people. (That is to say, I'm being introduced. Everyone already knows Aunt S, as she regularly demonstrates.)

This socializing is nothing like that time at Mme de T's house. Nobody talks about magic, and if someone insinuates they know something I don't, it's usually just gossip. Not that I mind gossip—I just prefer it to be magical. Who possesses supernatural abilities, who collects artifacts, who's supplying my horrible brother with the tools to subjugate other people, that sort of thing. I haven't met anyone in Horace's circle, but I do have quite a list of the extramarital affairs of the Parisian elite in my head now, though, in case I ever need that.

Last night, after we descended from the cab that brought us back to the Maison Laval, I finally told Aunt S everything. Between the social engagements she's arranging for me and all the time she's spending with Béatrix, it's been remarkably difficult to find time alone with her.

"Aunt S, can you come into my room? I need to talk to you," I said.

"Who are we killing?" she asked, laughing. The bed dipped as she sat down next to me and took my hands into her lap. "I like Julien, but if he broke your heart, I'll do it."

"No, it's not that. It's the other thing. We need to talk about magic."

"Ah," she said. "I'm afraid I won't have the answers you need. It's Béatrix or Isabelle or Savigny you'll need for that."

It took me a moment to connect "Isabelle" with the intimidating Madame de Tourzin, who I have not seen since I met her. "I don't trust them—except maybe Béatrix, and that's only because you love her. I want to talk to you."

Aunt S gets pink in the face so easily. It's a little discomfiting to think about my own face doing the same thing.

"Of course, darling. What is it?"

"You know I did something."

"Yes," she said. "As soon as you handed me that letter that said 'this is twenty francs,' I knew. I've been around magic before. So I knew you'd need help."

"But you don't possess it yourself?"

"No. And fifty-two years is long enough to discover whether I could enchant people with my voice, or always win at the gaming tables, or that sort of thing. I've known a lot of people with rare talents."

It strikes me, writing this, that Aunt S underestimates herself. To live through such upheaval and come out the other side alive is one thing, but to come out the other side still everyone's favorite person, all your warmth and friendships intact, that's a minor miracle. The way Aunt S cares about people, and the way they respond to her, that is nothing if not a rare talent.

"It's writing for me," I explained. "I, um... I took back some of my inheritance."

I was braced for disapproval, having only told J, but Aunt S beamed and said, "Good for you. Your shit of a father has too much money, and God knows your brother doesn't deserve it."

"I have enough for us to pay rent," I said. "Somewhere much nicer than here."

"Oh, darling, I'm sorry I teased you about being useless. You're clearly very clever. But for God's sake, be careful. This is a dangerous thing."

"I know. My father knows about the money. He said he won't tell Horace, but he wants me to help him retrieve the ring. I stormed out of the room without telling him yes. I haven't heard from either of them."

"In a just world, they'd kill each other and leave the two of us alone," Aunt S said. "I hope they choke on that awful ring. I've never had my own magic, but I've come across a trinket or two. I never wanted anything to do with all that. Béatrix has such a horror of cursed artifacts."

"How long have you known Béatrix? Were you two always—"

Aunt S laughed at me. "Did the most beautiful woman in Paris always want me? No. They were lining up for Béatrix back when we were young. They still are, I suppose, but my point is that I don't think she noticed me until later. We were both preoccupied with other things—she's dedicated to abolition, you know, and her art of course takes a great deal of her time, and she had other lovers. She never pined for me, not like I pined for her. But she missed me when I went home to care for Anaïs and was happy to see me again at Isabelle's. It was actually Isabelle I met first. That was in 1794. I was twenty-two."

"Madame de Tourzin must have been a child then." A serious, silent one, most likely.

Aunt S held my gaze. "She looked exactly as she does now. Forty years old, perhaps."

"But that's impossible. That was thirty years ago. What—how did she do it? How old is she?"

"I don't know," Aunt S said, answering all of my questions. "Béatrix doesn't know either, before you ask, and Savigny might know something, but I doubt he knows all of it. I don't think anyone knows. Isabelle doesn't talk about it."

"Béatrix could use her voice to find out."

"Victor," Aunt S scolded. "Isabelle is our friend."

"Your terrifying friend who doesn't age," I said. "Myself, I'd like to know what that's about."

"You will **not** ask her," Aunt S said. She can be very severe when she wants to. "And you will not ask anyone else, either. We owe her, Victor."

"For what, introducing me to Béatrix and Savigny? I only like one of them."

"No," Aunt S said. "We owe her because Isabelle kept Anaïs alive for five years."

"What," I whispered. I'd intended to shout. The revelation froze me, made me sluggish to speak even as my mind raced. Isabelle de Tourzin had kept my mother alive? How? And more importantly, "Why did she—"

"As for why she did it in the first place, I suppose she owed me. As for why she stopped—" Aunt S paused to swallow. Her voice was soft when she said, "Anaïs decided it was time."

"It wasn't time. I wasn't ready."

"I know," Aunt S said. She squeezed my knee, and then abandoned the pretense that neither of us was going to cry and wrapped her arms around me. "I wasn't ready, either. But Anaïs was. She'd been sick a long time, Victor. In pain a long time. Isabelle was helping, but she didn't have a cure. We didn't know it was the ring. We only knew she wasn't getting better. I think your mother only held on as long as she did—"

Aunt S didn't finish her sentence, but I didn't need her to. My mother held on for me.

It was a long time before either of us spoke. At last, I pushed myself away and said, "So Madame de Tourzin doesn't age and she can keep sick people from dying? She has some kind of ability."

"That's the extent of my knowledge. Anaïs knew more, but it was a condition of Isabelle helping her that she didn't tell me or anyone else. And Isabelle made it clear to me that I shouldn't talk about her with anyone. She sees very few people, you know. It's extraordinary that she agreed to meet you."

"Why did she? And why did she owe you?"

"As I said, we met in 1794," Aunt S said. "It was a turbulent year."

"The Terror."

"I was peripherally involved with some people who were... well, it's hard to say what anyone was trying to do then, except survive. But there was a sort of network, and sometimes someone would ask for a favor. Occasionally a stranger would stay with me for a few days, and then be shuffled off somewhere else, presumably to avoid execution, though I never asked."

"You were a counterrevolutionary spy," I said. I wasn't scandalized for myself, but because I knew J wouldn't like that. J is the only reason I even know the word "counterrevolutionary."

"Me? A spy?" She shook, fluttered her hands in the air until they landed on her décolletage, and beamed at me, immensely cheered. "You have the most entertaining notions. Espionage is dreary, all silently following people day after day and waiting in the rain for hours. I don't have the patience and it would have ruined all my favorite dresses. I just went to a lot of parties and knew a lot of people. I had some interesting friends. Savigny was one of them."

"So the Vicomte de Savigny was a counterrevolutionary spy," I said.

Aunt S exhaled something like a laugh. "No, actually, he believed very strongly in the Republic. At least, at first he did. He went by 'Citizen' then. We all did—we had to — but he really meant it. He did have some quibbles about method, as he told me."

"So he used to believe in something but he retired to enjoy his obscene wealth alone?"

"I'm not sure any of us believed in anything by 1795,"

Aunt S said. "What he was doing was neither here nor there with any of the political factions of the time. It was a chaotic, violent moment, when the contents of many wealthy people's homes were suddenly dispersed. Savigny worked hard to keep track of the worst of the cursed artifacts. To find them and lock them away, if he could. And sometimes there were people who needed to go somewhere, which was how I helped."

"People with magical abilities?"

"That would be a very rude thing to ask a guest," Aunt S said. "I'm getting it all out of order now. One morning in 1794, Savigny showed up at my house and asked if I'd be willing to host someone for a little longer than the usual few days. He'd been out of town for some time on one of his errands, so I knew whoever he'd found must be important or dangerous or both. By that point I'd become quite good at batting my lashes and playing empty-headed whenever an unwelcome knock came at the door. So I said yes. Savigny and three other men carried a cask made of oak into my home. There was a woman inside."

"Isabelle de Tourzin."

"They'd found her in the wrecked remains of a château," Aunt S said, nodding. "She only survived the attack because she was mistaken for dead. Savigny told me he'd been 'out for a stroll' and come across her."

"He strolled right into someone's ransacked mansion? Or... he was there the night before, participating in the destruction?"

"There's a reason I'm so well-liked, you know," Aunt S said. "<u>I didn't ask</u>. I did what needed to be done. Savigny and his comrades had done their best to clean her up and treat what ailed her, but she'd been listless and silent for their whole journey. They swore she'd been covered in blood and nearly dead when they'd found her, but she had no obvious wounds and didn't seem to be sick. It was inexplicable. Savigny felt sure magic was involved, and he had a sense that she was important, and he never ignores his suspicions. Beyond that, I don't know what lies between Savigny and Isabelle. A fraught sort of partnership. He seemed genuinely distraught on the morning he brought her to me—a rarity for him. As for Isabelle, I'm not sure she's ever forgiven Savigny for seeing her at her lowest moment, but he also saved her life. I suspect she regards me in much the same way.

"Anyway, Isabelle stayed with me. She didn't get out of bed for months. She barely spoke to me. We lived together, if you can call it that, for two years. I'd like to tell you that I helped her heal, but I'm still not sure that I did."

"She seems in good health," I said. "And wealth."

"Yes, but I don't think she wants to be alive," Aunt S said, troubled.

"Obviously she suffered something terrible, but it's been thirty years, surely she's recovered. Why would she have lived for thirty years—" I stopped myself before something unforgivably callous exited my mouth. In the silence, it dawned on me, what Aunt S really meant.

She believes that Isabelle de Tourzin <u>can't die.</u>

This is not a problem I've ever had to think about before. I didn't know what to say then and I don't know what to say now.

VICTOR BEAUCHÊNE TO PIERRE FAUCHEUX, JANUARY 20, 1824

POSTMARKED PARIS

Pierre,

Please call on me when you have the opportunity.

Victor

V BEAUCHÊNE TO J MORÈRE, JANUARY 20, 1824
SLIPPED UNDER THE DOOR

J—

I know we saw each other at dinner, but when we're both under the watchful eyes of priggish Madame Laval, the nosy old gossips who live here, and skulking, hawk-eyed Forestier, it hardly qualifies as being together. I miss you. Asleep or awake, no matter what you've been drawing, you didn't come to me or let me enter your room the other night. Will tonight be different, if I knock? I fear the answer. I think you fear it, too.

So we'll write instead. Tell me about your life. What are you drawing, other than dirty pictures of us? How are things with your dullard classmates? How is your sister and the rest of your family?

—V

J MORÈRE TO V BEAUCHÊNE, JANUARY 21, 1824
SLIPPED UNDER THE DOOR

V—

It's not that I don't want to see you. On the contrary, it's all I want. I miss you all the time.

Our problem has a simple solution. Give up this quest of yours that's only going to get you entangled with thieves and killers, and I'll happily fuck you until the whole Left Bank has heard you come. I'm including an illustration.

I can't write a paragraph about my family with that drawing enclosed. It feels too strange. Life is good with one exception, which is that my preferred person in all the world is as stubborn as a mule and foolishly following a path that will end in violence. But we've discussed that.

There is one thing I wanted to tell you. It won't be half as good as your letters about people you met, since I don't have your talent for storytelling. But it's still good.

I met Camille Dupin. You remember the novel I told you about, <u>Virginie</u>? The one I loved? Camille Dupin wrote it, and happened to pass by me one day while I was sketching in the covered market, and bought one of my drawings. Even better, we spoke at length and have since become friends. Camille is the friend I've longed for, the person with an infinite appetite for discussing art and ideas. We went to a salon together and I met so many people. Writers and actors and musicians and thinkers. I think you'd like them—you're better with people than I am—and I think many of the attendees were, for lack of a better word, like us.

Camille is, too. I asked how to refer to her, and she said "she," but she appreciated the uncertainty. And she asked about me! I told her some of the truth—that I'm at ease being called he, she, or they, though we didn't discuss the last one—which I've never done with anyone but you. I didn't explain any of it because I was nervous, but I think she understood. The press called her "he" for a while, since her name is ambiguous, and I don't think it bothered her. On the contrary, I suspect the grammatical chaos she's sown pleases her.

I hope some day that I will have to consider what the press will call me—I have been signing all my work J Morère. I suppose there is time to reflect on this before widespread acclaim changes my life. Perhaps it never will—at the risk of failure, I've decided to stop attending school and simply make my own work. I remain in touch with a few of my kinder and more interesting classmates, but I've rented a studio. Meeting Camille felt like a sign.

Camille is fascinating. Not merely for her ideas, but also for her presence. She's very stylish. She's shorter than me, but manages to give them impression of being not merely tall but long-legged. Maybe it's the trousers. But she keeps up with me when we go places together, and I don't know how, except that she seems to be strikingly competent at everything, whether it's writing a novel or taking a walk. I feel reassured to know she's in the world. At least someone here knows what to do.

It's absurd to be shy about anything, given the drawing I'm including, but I feel silly committing this thought to paper, let alone sharing it with you: I hope some day that I emanate that same sense of calm, unshakeable confidence. That's how I want people to think of me. I don't much care what name they use, as long as they're expressing that I'm a person with a vision and the skills to accomplish it.

And as long as I'm making confessions, I'd like to introduce you to Camille, but I worry you'll like her better than me. This fear is in direct opposition to my desire to be perceived as imperturbable, but being the source of all my troubles, you already know how very perturbable I am.

—J

V BEAUCHÊNE TO J MORÈRE, JANUARY 22, 1824
SLIPPED UNDER THE DOOR

J, darling—

I wish you were perturbed enough to come downstairs. If you did, I would demonstrate to you how very attractive I find your implacable (stubborn!) demeanor, such that you could not possibly believe I would ever prefer another person to you.

Even a person you lavished with praise for so many paragraphs. If you meant to inspire jealousy with that description of Camille, you failed. You can fuck all of France and I will still want you. That said, I do hope you're writing forlorn letters to Camille about the infuriating little blond who lives below you, source of <u>all</u> your troubles, the one you can't stop drawing or writing to. Who's <u>fascinating</u> now?

Perhaps I am a bit jealous.

But I am also happy for you to have a friend. What excess, to have more than one emotion at a time. My nervous fibers will vibrate too much and I'll expire slowly and incurably like a respectable virgin in a novel.

Still, I would like to meet Camille, if you can tolerate

my presence in person. I will refrain from ripping your clothes off in public, though you make it more difficult with each new drawing.

That said, I admire your commitment to making me desperate enough to come crawling to you, and I encourage you to continue. The drawings are treasures. Your plan may yet work.

Up there all alone in your little room, can you hear how much I like them? I like them at least once a day, and I assume you know that sound well enough to recognize it, even through the floorboards.

—V

J MORÈRE TO V BEAUCHÊNE, JANUARY 22, 1824
SLIPPED UNDER THE DOOR

[*This letter is yet another erotic illustration.*]

I don't think you need to worry too much about the fates that await respectable virgins, V.

PRIVATE DIARY OF V BEAUCHÊNE, JANUARY 27, 1824

I've had no response from my father. Were I capable of worrying about him, I'd be losing sleep. Now I am simply not sure what to do. Infiltrating the house is too much of a risk without more information.

I have seen both Béatrix and Savigny again since our first meeting. Béatrix confirmed my hypothesis that my emotional state while writing with the pen affects the outcome, and she taught me her strategies for better control. Her power is astonishing; she has to be careful even when speaking lest her voice influence someone by accident. She swore, long ago, only to use her ability intentionally—to protect herself and others. Perfecting her control has been the work of a lifetime.

"I understand that you've sometimes not known your own strength, but does the opposite ever happen? Has your ability ever failed you when you need protection? What if you tried to influence someone who also had magic? Could it fail you?" I asked.

"I suppose it could, if I came across someone whose

will was stronger than mine." She smiled. "That hasn't happened yet."

"If I knew of someone who possessed a cursed artifact that they shouldn't—"

"I'm sorry, Victor, but these matters are too dangerous for me. My other work requires a great deal of time and focus, and I can only do it if I'm alive. If you need help with an object, you have to ask Savigny or Isabelle. That's their line of business."

I didn't take it too hard, though I almost feel guilty for asking. Evidently she has had to refuse requests like mine before. She was very gracious about it.

Béatrix and Aunt S are corresponding and spending time together without me. I'm happy for them, though when the three of us are in a room together, the two of them are so in love they forget I exist.

Anyway, I took her suggestion about asking Savigny. Béatrix is so warm toward me that I naïvely assumed Savigny would be as well. He lives in the Faubourg Saint-Germain. Everything outside and inside the house is just as it should be. It's clear he has a lot of money.

There was a dazzlingly handsome Asian man on the parlor sofa when I arrived, and Savigny introduced him as Quang Nguyen and said he was a friend. I was presented to Quang as "an acquaintance of Béatrix and Isabelle's." (The former may be true, but the latter isn't. I've only seen Madame de Tourzin once.)

Quang said "Oh, this is about <u>that</u> business, I'll leave you two to talk." He must be like Béatrix, adjacent to the world of magic but with no wish to know more. I struggle to imagine that life.

Quang left by going <u>upstairs</u>, so I think it's likely that he lives in the house. He may be Savigny's lover, but

Savigny didn't offer any further information, so when I got home, I asked Aunt S. She said Savigny never takes anyone to bed, it's simply not his nature, but she learned from Béatrix that he and Quang are in love. She also told me that Quang runs a shipping business with his sister, and Savigny is an investor in it, and a number of other details that she seemed delighted to know.

Savigny did chastise me for staring at his beloved. I tried to explain that I was staring because Quang's jaw was like something from a sculpture and his arms were as thick as my thighs, but I stopped halfway through; staring because someone is beautiful is still rude.

"I'll apologize to him when he returns," I said.

"When I said I would see you again, I did not mean you could knock on my door whenever the impulse took you," Savigny said. "Why did you come here today? I hope you intend to surrender whatever cursed artifact you blundered into making."

So we didn't begin well. I asked for his advice on retrieving a magical object from a dangerous person, and he said, "I told you: don't get involved. You're young. You could have a long, happy life."

That frustrated me and I cut our conversation short. Not counting Savigny's love affair, I learned nothing from that visit and am reluctant to contact him again.

It does make me laugh to have crossed Savigny's threshold now, without my father's help, knowing how Pierre Faucheux would have salivated over the connection (money _and_ a title) if it had arrived when I was still his child.

Most aristocrats are no good with money. They have it because they were born with it. Given what Aunt S said about his investments, I suspect Savigny's fortune owes something to his cleverness—or his unknown ability. I've considered asking for his help with my ten thousand francs, but then I'd have to reveal to him that I possess ten thousand francs, and I don't want to answer his questions about that.

Savigny owns a lot of paintings. So do Aunt S's other friends. Perhaps I can get them and their connections to buy J's work. Will J find that upsetting? I have no way of knowing.

V BEAUCHÊNE TO J MORÈRE, JANUARY 28, 1824
SLIPPED UNDER THE DOOR

J—

Is that last drawing a sketch of me as Endymion? I've been educating myself, so I recognize these things now. If you're yearning to play the role of the moonlight and enter my room while I sleep, I've enclosed a copy of the key. Consider this a standing invitation to slide it right in. Nothing is stopping you but you.

Here is a story to make you jealous. I've met dozens of rich, titled, important people in the past few weeks—Aunt S knows <u>everyone</u>—and almost all of them want to fuck me. I think I could make a career of it, if I wanted. Perhaps I'll sleep my way to security and wealth. Would you prefer that?

Apologies, that was too cruel. I regret that our difference of opinion on my career has driven us apart, and I will try not to mention it again.

I was serious about the rich people, though. Their interest stems from the fact that I am a stranger—they've all already fucked each other—and has nothing to do with any quality of mine. You would not believe the seduction attempts I have endured. Dull, aggressive, dully aggressive, aggressively dull.

There's the occasional good one, of course, and I won't say I don't enjoy it. There was an older widow last week who had quite a smile. (The flirtations come from men and women equally. I have yet to meet a rich person who openly defies categories, though surely they exist, and when I meet them, I hope they will flirt with me, too. I wouldn't mind any of this if only people were subtler or more charming about it.) I told the widow I was flattered, but pining for someone who won't have me. She gave me her card.

And here is something to make you smirk: all your radical beliefs about how rich people don't deserve their money are true. You would not believe the hideous decor and awful paintings I have been subjected to, J. Bad suits, bad gowns, bad taste everywhere. And bad behavior, of course, but that goes without saying.

I am only interested in bad behavior if it involves you. I hope your nights have been more interesting than mine.

—V

J MORÈRE TO V BEAUCHÊNE, JANUARY 29, 1824
SLIPPED UNDER THE DOOR

V—

I locked your key in my desk to prevent anyone else from using it. <u>Please</u> destroy any other copies you possess. It's not safe to have so many keys loose in the world, given the value of what is in your room. I'm serious, V. Be careful.

On a less dire note, say yes to your widow if you need to, but don't forget that I'd be happy—ecstatic—to satisfy you, if only you'd accept my very reasonable terms.

I'm not as good with words, so another drawing is attached, in case I haven't made myself clear.

Your letter does explain the sudden parade of people through my new studio, all struck with a whim to drop in and ogle my work. I've sold four paintings. I assume that's your doing. If your rich friends are flirting with you and buying my art, their taste is impeccable.

What do you say to a drink with Camille some time soon? I'll be fully clothed and as staid as possible to make it easy on you.

—J

V BEAUCHÊNE TO J MORÈRE, JANUARY 30, 1824
SLIPPED UNDER THE DOOR

J—

Thank you for the drawing. Is that what you intend to do with the rope? I'm intrigued.

I'm enjoying this fiction of yours, the idea that you being "fully clothed and as staid as possible" won't be vividly erotic to me. (And to you, you big liar.) I have an entire drawer full of beautiful obscenities from your hand. Even if we both behave perfectly, I'll know what you're thinking and vice versa.

Naturally, I won't miss it.

Poor Camille. Perhaps you should warn her.

—V

PRIVATE DIARY OF V BEAUCHÊNE, FEBRUARY 1, 1824

The private parts of people's houses are so much more interesting than the public parts.

Perhaps that is true of people themselves, though personally I like people's outsides—their clothes, their hair, their faces—just as much as their insides, whether that means secret wishes and fears or something more tangible. But perhaps I only like people's outsides because I'm studying them to find an unobserved hallway that will let me slip into the bedroom, so to speak.

I've managed it a few times recently, the hallway trick. I'm practicing. Each house has its own plan and each soirée its own schedule, but with patience, an opportunity always arises. Everyone thinks me delicate, since I so frequently excuse myself for a breath of fresh air or a moment to myself, but I don't mind. Stealth is its own reward.

I've overheard quite a few conversations that weren't meant for me and glimpsed even more bedrooms to which I wasn't invited. Until last night, I hadn't met any members of Horace's artifact-collecting club.

Aunt S and I were invited to dinner at the Taillefers'. They're industrialists, the sort of people my father met with all the time, but our paths had never crossed before. I suppose they find Aunt S's whispered reputation titillating, and my presence adds even more mystery. Maximilien Taillefer's name was on Horace's list; thankfully my brother was not present last night, but the contents of Taillefer's house confirmed my suspicions.

On first glance, Taillefer isn't much like my brother, except that they're both rich men. He's older, though neither wrinkled nor grey-haired, and certainly smarter, although that's hardly a measure of anything when it comes to Horace. There are paving stones with more curiosity. In any case, Taillefer has aspirations of being seen as an intellectual. He goes to salons. Sophisticated in dress and manners, with dark brown hair and a small, neat beard, he might seem likable if only I hadn't actually met him.

He invited the men to drink brandy in the parlor after dinner, myself included. (There's a lot of—theater, or pageantry, I suppose are the words, in these affairs of "men" and "women." Nobody else seems to find it humorous.)

Naturally I took my time in the corridor between the dining room and the parlor, letting everyone else stride ahead.

The glow of oil lamps lit the corridor, and a painting caught my eye. A landscape, one of those ones that are supposed to be Italy, with a few verdant hills in the background, a little stream, and some scattered marble columns in the foreground. A minuscule shepherd and shepherdess, no sheep in sight.

For as long as I stared at that painting, I ought to have

more to say about it. J would comment on the brushwork or the quality of the light or something. I don't remember any of that.

What I remember is the sound of the stream.

Faint giggling, too, and a breeze to relieve the oppressive heat. Paintings, no matter how good, can't do that. I wish I had realized it sooner, or witnessed one of the other guests being lured in, but instead I stood there, rooted to the ground but lost in the distance, until I felt a hand slide down my backside.

I jerked. The corridor closed in, the air too cool and quiet. Where there had been sky and horizon, there was only a painting. Behind it, a flat expanse of silvery grey brocade wallpaper glinted dully in the lamplight. The plush carpet under my feet had absorbed the footsteps of the man who loomed behind me.

When Taillefer spoke, his breath curled in my ear. "Does it please you?"

"Where did you get it?" I said, stepping away from him.

"It's been in the family a long time."

I bit my tongue to keep from asking if previous generations of his family had also used the painting's hypnotic effect to grope their guests. I wish I'd asked for the artist's name, or the date, or any other details, but Taillefer startling me hadn't fully swept the fog from my head. If I could reproduce the image for J, I'm sure they could tell me about it, but I've never been any good at drawing.

Taillefer leered at me the rest of the evening, and I let him. If he'd only asked for what he wanted, I might have given it to him. I have no interest in him, but I'm not above trading sex for a chance at some answers, as long as we were clear about our terms. However, I don't like being manipulated, and I'd wager that his collection contains worse artifacts. He seemed practiced with the painting, and I don't care for the idea of Taillefer repeatedly tricking his guests. What if I hadn't noticed his touch? Is that possible? How long can the effect last?

If I saw that painting again, could I protect myself from it?

VICTOR BEAUCHÊNE TO MAXIMILIEN TAILLEFER, FEBRUARY 2, 1824
POSTMARKED PARIS

Monsieur Taillefer,

Thank you so much for your gracious invitation. Your hospitality was unforgettable.

I was captivated by a painting in your home last night, and I write to ask you about it. I'm sure you'll recall me studying the small landscape in the hallway. Who is the artist? How did the painting come into your family's possession? Satisfy my curiosity with the truth and tell me everything you know about it, including its uses.

I would like to study the painting further. If you'd do me the kindness of lending it to me for a series of experiments, there is much knowledge to be gained. Imagine what you could do if you knew its secrets. You could cover your walls with enchanting works. Perhaps other objects could be made to exert similar effects. I have some expertise in these matters and if you deliver the painting to me at the Maison Laval, I will discover everything I can.

Please accept, monsieur, my most distinguished salutations,

Victor Beauchêne

J MORÈRE TO V BEAUCHÊNE, FEBRUARY 3, 1824
SLIPPED UNDER THE DOOR

V—

Alas, Camille has withdrawn to her country estate to finish her novel. I don't know when she'll return to Paris, but I'll arrange for the three of us to meet.

I wouldn't mind spending time with you and you alone, you know. Not passing you in the hallway or staring at you from the opposite side of the dining table or channeling all our pent-up lust into these absurd little notes, but taking a walk or having a conversation. Sex isn't the only thing I want from you. It's just that I can't imagine a private encounter between the two of us that doesn't involve it, and I don't want to test my self-restraint against my principles.

Perhaps if we met somewhere public?

No. Look at this, you've made me desperate enough to contemplate loopholes in my own rules. I'm having a moment of weakness because it's sleeting outside and I didn't want to get out of bed this morning. I would still be lying there—missing time at my studio, can you imagine? —if only you were there, too. I could wrap my arms around you and bury my nose in your hair and kiss the back of your neck. You'd smell like that orange blossom soap, the one you insisted on using even when you couldn't afford it, before you decided to enrich yourself at the risk of your own life. I guess you have as much of that as you could ever want now. If you fuck that rich widow, I hope she appreciates the scent.

Anyway, we could be warm in bed together, but instead I'm awake and shivering in my shirtsleeves, writing you this damn note so I can slip it under your door. What a waste, V. Sometimes I wish we weren't so entangled, because maybe we'd both be happier, but I've never met anybody else who makes me feel like you do, and I won't give up on you just yet.

Speaking of costly little luxuries—and being all tied up with each other—somebody left a paper packet of satin and velvet ribbons outside my door. They're pretty, but at the moment, I don't have any use for them. It's a shame.

—J

MAXIMILIEN TAILLEFER TO VICTOR BEAUCHÊNE, FEBRUARY 3, 1824
POSTMARKED PARIS

Monsieur Beauchêne,

Please find enclosed the painting you mentioned, a capriccio by Nicolas Tilleul entitled <u>Landscape with Ruins</u>. I believe it was painted in 1740, or thereabouts. I told you last night that it had been in my family for a long time, but in fact I acquired it two years ago from an antiques shop on the Quai de Voltaire. They specialize in unusual objects and have become quite fashionable among a certain set.

I will entrust the painting to you for a time because I am eager to learn its secrets. The artist, Tilleul, isn't well-known. Mine is something of a rarity. Its allure is lost on anyone who would pass by a painting without a second look, but obviously you are not in that number. It took me perhaps three months to accustom myself, and now I can choose whether to enter the scene. Its potency varies from viewer to viewer, but always wanes with exposure. Some guests have remained transfixed for hours, impervious to a picked pocket or a hand inside their clothes. Trifling entertainments, nothing to fret over. I never got caught—except by you.

A hard shove can end the trance, but most people remain disoriented for an hour or two. Sometimes people become bizarrely emotional. I always tell them they overindulged in brandy. You were remarkably alert. Perhaps that's why I feel you are the right person to study it.

Please accept, monsieur, my most distinguished salutations,

Maximilien Taillefer

PRIVATE DIARY OF V BEAUCHÊNE, FEBRUARY 3, 1824

Taillefer's painting is sitting in my room, wrapped in sackcloth, and my hands are trembling so much that it's hard to write.

It's not only the painting. It's not the ease of acquiring the painting or forcing Taillefer to tell me the truth. It's not even the knowledge that Taillefer is a disgusting rapist who deserves far worse than what I've done.

It's the letter J sent this morning, the one where they wavered a little bit. It made me waver, too.

I could try to forget everything I've learned, set aside all the fears I have about my brother, ignore all my questions, stop seeing Aunt S's more eccentric friends, and constrict my life until it suits J's notion of what's moral and acceptable. Then we'd have each other, which I long for more than almost anything—the sex, yes, but also the conversation, the companionship, God, that description of the two of us lying entwined in bed almost made me run upstairs barefoot—but no matter how much I want J, I'm not willing to become someone else for them. I've already lived for years under someone else's idea of who I should be. I won't do that again. I don't think either of us would be happy in such an arrangement, just as we're not happy now.

Is J right that we might be happier without each other? It's true that neither of us is likely to change our mind, but the prospect of living without them feels like a knife to the gut.

I don't know the answer and I hate it.

Besides, now I have this painting and I have to do <u>something</u> with it. I can't send it back to Taillefer. That would be unconscionable, given what he might have done to me and what he has done to others. I suppose in J's view of things, the painting has to be destroyed, but I don't know what that entails, and I don't want to try anything until I'm sure it's (1) necessary (2) possible (3) safe. I need to discover how these things work.

V BEAUCHÊNE TO J MORÈRE, FEBRUARY 3, 1824
SLIPPED UNDER THE DOOR

J—

You can't think of a use for the ribbons? Are you not an artist? A genius, no less? You may not have faith, but I do.

—V

PRIVATE DIARY OF V BEAUCHÊNE, FEBRUARY 4, 1824

Aunt S has gone out for the day—with Béatrix, no doubt—so it's just me and <u>Landscape with Ruins</u> by Nicolas Tilleul, circa 1740. I intend to discover everything I can.

Questions:

(1) How long can the trance last?

(2) What events can end the trance?

(3) How much exposure (in minutes, or in times viewing the painting) is required for the trance to become voluntary rather than involuntary?

These questions will require more than one day, and more than one experiment, to answer. The simplest trial would be to sit in front of the painting, become entranced, and wait. Aunt S will return just before seven in the evening, at which point she will enter my room so we can walk down to dinner together. Regarding (2), given that being touched has ended my trance once before, I assume Aunt S will be up to the task.

It is currently ten in the morning. If the trance lasts nine hours uninterrupted, then it might last indefinitely.

Remaining entranced longer than this might endanger my health, so I will consider the question answered.

Regarding (1), Taillefer reported that the painting has no effect on anyone uninterested in art. My interest in art is present and unquestionable, as the painting has already worked once, but it could best be termed "naïve." It is not clear whether expertise or naïveté matters, or if interest alone suffices. I doubt I can persuade a person with more art expertise to undertake this experiment with me, so the matter will remain unresolved.

Regarding (3), Taillefer (male, thirty-odd years of age, serious interest in art) reported that the trance became voluntary after "perhaps three months." I (person of both masculine and feminine attributes, twenty-one years of age, slack-jawed rube) have already had a promising response to being startled out of the trance, remaining, in Taillefer's words, "remarkably alert" after my first exposure. It is my hope that today's long trance will render the painting less powerful for me, making future study easier.

~

Holy shit. Aunt S had to shout at me and shake me, and I still don't feel fully awake. She's covering the painting and frowning at me as I write this. Dinner now. (It's seven in the evening, as predicted.) Notes later.

~

It's been two hours and everything still feels slightly unreal. I don't feel as dazed as I did when Aunt S shook me, and I was hungry at dinner, which reassured me. Nothing more real and grounding than the urge to shove a hunk of baguette into your mouth. I had to piss like a horse after Aunt S woke me, that was also very grounding.

I'm exhausted, but not sleepy. Writing this is a trial. My hand is heavy and my head is empty and the rest of me feels... hollow, I suppose? Sad, even. This is germane because I have no other reason to feel sad, so it is undoubtedly a consequence of the trance. Now that it is recorded, I don't intend to pay this feeling any further attention.

It didn't feel like any time passed while I was looking at the painting. I am persuaded that the trance is indefinite. The painting undoubtedly has the potential to be very dangerous, but I find myself reluctant to destroy it. The object itself is not malevolent. It's a work of art, and its creator imbued it with power. I don't want to rid the world of powerful art. If <u>Landscape with Ruins</u> could be kept somewhere where its owner wasn't putting it to ill use, and people would always be warned before looking at it, and if I could learn to control my response and then teach others to control theirs, then I can't see that there would be a need to destroy it. These conditions would be difficult to meet, but not impossible.

I want very much to tear the sackcloth off and look at it again. Again, I'm noting my own feelings for the sake of the record. Indulging the urge would clearly be a terrible idea.

I just want to know if spending nine hours entranced has given me any control over my response. It's not a desire to return to the landscape, or the trance.

I'm rational. I think.

V BEAUCHÊNE TO J MORÈRE, FEBRUARY 4, 1824
SLIPPED UNDER THE DOOR

J—

I know this breaks the rules we've made for ourselves, but would you mind terribly if I spent an hour in your room? I swear this isn't a proposition. I need to be somewhere else, that's all.

—V

FEBRUARY 4, 1824

Julie opened the door an instant after reading the letter. Surprised, Victor swayed on their feet, dressed but disheveled, eyes glassy. At dinner, Julie had wondered if Victor was drunk. After reading that note, she knew better.

"You did something."

"I know how you object to me doing things."

"You're not distressed enough to be sincere, I see," she said, and pulled Victor into the room. The door latched, she took them by the shoulders and held them at arm's length. "Tell me."

"Julien," Victor said.

"Julie," she said softly. "She." The door was closed. This was private. And Victor was about to tell her something she wouldn't like.

"Julie," Victor began again, and then halted. "I shouldn't tell you. You won't like it."

"Oh, I'm guaranteed to hate it. But I didn't leave you in the hallway, you'll note."

"I looked at a painting."

In the coolest, most controlled tone possible, Julie said, "Not, in itself, an error."

"For nine hours. Without moving. And now I want to look at it again."

Shit, she thought, her heart seizing in her chest, *it's my fault*. And then, before she could betray this absurd fear, Julie gave herself a firm instruction not to react.

Her instruction didn't quite work. She made a dissatisfied noise. A grunt. If she said any words, she might regret them. She needed to put Victor somewhere, but the desk chair had a stack of sketchpads in it. The other option was the bed. No, she'd move the sketchpads, as long as Victor didn't collapse when she let go—

Victor sucked in a breath and released a long, ragged exhale.

Oh no. No, no, no. Julie was wrestling with anger and panic and guilt. Victor crying would be, perhaps all too literally, the drop of water that made the vase overflow.

The horror on Victor's face mirrored her own, but a sudden flood of tears washed away their expression. Their shoulders shook under her hands. It was silent, and it shouldn't have been.

"Just cry," Julie ordered. No use sighing over it. The two of them were in this now, Victor in tears and her in sentiments. She pulled Victor into an embrace, closing her arms around them, and just barely managed to stop herself from burying her nose in their curls. It had been so long. They smelled like orange blossom soap, the little shit.

"Don't do this in-between thing where you pretend you're not crying," Julie said, because if she didn't talk, she'd kiss the top of Victor's head, and that was a bad idea. "You're no good at it, anyway. If you're going to cry, do it right."

"I don't want to—" Victor's breath caught on a sob. "I never cry. I hate crying."

"Should've thought of that before you spent nine hours staring at that painting," Julie said. It sounded convincingly stern and unsympathetic, but one of her hands had started rubbing circles into Victor's back. Her thoughts skipped across the surface of what she was doing, of what Victor had said, of what she had just repeated. *Painting. Nine hours.* No. This was not her affair.

Julie continued, even more severely, "They're called cursed artifacts for a reason. Maybe next time you'll think twice."

That wasn't believable for either of them. Victor convulsed with sobs.

"There you go. Good, let it out."

It was easy to rock back and forth a little while she held Victor, squeezing tight and murmuring nonsense, and when her thoughts troubled her, Julie took refuge in sensations. Victor had soaked the open collar of her shirt with hot tears, and now the damp fabric was sticking to her skin. Her chest ached. Victor had caught her in her shirtsleeves and waistcoat, and meanwhile her fingers were wearing tracks into the smooth weave of their frock coat.

The crying slowed, but Julie didn't let go.

"I didn't—" they paused for a ragged inhalation "—come here to cry, I—"

"You came here because that *thing* is still in your room," Julie said. "At least you had the sense to get away from it."

Face still buried in her chest, Victor sniffled. "I don't know why I'm crying. Or why I can't stop. This despair just swallowed me—like I spent all my happiness while I was entranced, and now there's none left. I have to make a note of this."

"Mm," Julie said. "A note. In your notebook. In your room. Where the painting is."

"I didn't mean right now."

"Oh, I see, you meant in the future, when you continue this reckless experiment of yours," she said. "Nine hours, Victor. What if a candle had tipped over and caught the building on fire?"

"I'm sure a fire would have been enough to wake me, and besides, I knew Sophie—"

"Stop," she said. Mentioning fire had been a bad idea. "I preferred it when you were sobbing too hard for words."

After a subdued pause, they said, "I ruined your shirt."

"It doesn't matter."

She sat them both down on the bed, one arm around Victor's shoulders. They blotted their face with a sleeve—should've used hers, it was wrecked already—and breathed.

Julie didn't know how long the two of them sat there. She was in a sort of trance herself, listening to Victor breathe, forcibly keeping her mind blank of all the things that could have happened, or all the things that could still happen, or whether and how she could tell Victor the truth. The texture of Victor's coat under her fingers no longer registered, that was how long she'd been rubbing her hand in circles.

Eventually, Victor slumped against her, asleep. They woke when she worked the tight sleeves of their coat down their arms, but only briefly. She soothed one hand over their forehead and they folded toward the mattress. Removing their shoes and lifting their legs onto the bed didn't trouble their unconsciousness.

Julie stood, rolling her shoulders and pressing her

fingers into the back of her stiff neck. She intended to extinguish the candle and go to bed, only... Victor.

For such a small person, they took up a remarkable amount of space.

She had a key to Victor's room. She could sleep in their bed downstairs. The painting was there, though. The painting and God knew what else. Victor had said the painting was covered, but they'd been dazed. It was the middle of the night and she didn't want to take the risk.

This wouldn't be the first time she'd shared a bed with Victor. It would be the first time either of them was clothed.

She wouldn't feel so tangled up if this were the first time. If they'd never slept together. If she didn't know how much she liked it. If she didn't miss it every day.

She was too tired to feel so conflicted. She'd sort herself out tomorrow. Julie put out the candle and went to bed.

It was still dark when she woke, Victor wrapped around her like a monkey climbing a tree. Maybe three hours had passed, but it was that strange suspended moment in the middle of the night. Even the city was quiet. No cart wheels on the cobblestones. No sign of dawn. The best thing would be to fall back asleep and not do anything she'd regret, but Victor was nuzzling her neck.

The warm drag of lips on skin softened her resolve. The tip of their nose, a touch cooler than their mouth, nudged her ear and tangled in her hair, unbound for sleep and grown long in the past few months. Teeth scraped her earlobe.

Julie's hand, unruly thing, brushed through Victor's short, soft hair and cradled the back of their head. *This might be a dream*, she told herself. *You might still be asleep. Enjoy it and don't think about it too hard.*

After that, it was easy to twist and kiss them, a swipe of lips and tongue over their salt-streaked lips and into their mouth. Easy to push aside the blankets and strip off her clothes and theirs, in the dark where nothing was quite real. Easy to lay her body down on theirs, one long warm line of contact, nose to chest to belly to thighs.

"Don't think," she whispered, her words as much as instruction for herself as for Victor.

"I never do."

A sliver of moonlight let her catch that bright flash of smile, sharp as a shard of glass. Piercing, pretty, impudent, too much to be resisted. That was Victor.

Fool that she was, she was glad to see them smiling. It won them another kiss, this one softer and deeper. With long strokes of her tongue, she kissed them until they squirmed beneath her, hips lifting and curling like she'd drawn them taut with a string. In time, she'd get there. Patiently and methodically, she covered their throat and collarbone with kisses, keeping them still with one hand on their shoulder and the other on their hip. It was the gentlest of holds, one they made no attempt to escape, though their breath quickened and their hips twitched as she closed her mouth over one tightly furled nipple and sucked.

Victor responded to her attentions with a quiet intensity. Their ribs swelled and emptied and their belly quivered as she trailed kisses down toward their navel, each one a taste of the velvet warmth of their skin. How many kisses would it take to make them understand how precious they were?

Julie slid her hands so they framed Victor's hips, then

pushed their thighs wide. The darkness was good cover for bad decisions, but she regretted the loss of this view and the palette of pinks—carmine red mixed with snow white, sometimes a little cochineal red, a little hyacinth red—that it would have offered.

But she hadn't come here to stare.

She lavished a few more kisses on the sensitive skin of Victor's inner thighs, then wrapped her arms around their legs and lifted, tipping their hips so she could dive in. Their sex was slick before she ran her tongue over the folds, and dripping by the time she plunged inside. The taste of it was like the tide rushing in, washing over her lips and her tongue. Stroke by stroke, she lapped it up, the languid heat of Victor's body, listening as their gasps and moans grew louder and more insistent.

Their fingers tangled in her hair as she closed her lips around the swollen peak of their sex. It was ripe and heavy against her tongue, and she savored the shape of it, the feeling, licking and sucking until Victor screamed and clenched around her. The orgasm came in fierce waves, one after another, and Julie didn't let go until the last of it had subsided and Victor had sunk into stillness in her arms.

She rubbed her face on the inside of their thigh, leaving a smear, then dropped a kiss there and laid them down while they sighed in satisfaction.

She joined them on the mattress, expecting nothing more than for Victor to drift into sleep next to her, and was surprised when Victor sprang up.

"What are you doing? You can't go to sleep in this condition," they said, clambering up and straddling the condition in question, sliding back and forth along its length to make their meaning excessively clear. "It's an injustice. We believe in equality, don't we?"

"Do we?" she asked, more breathless than deadpan. Victor had fit their bodies together tantalizingly close, the soaking apex of their thighs perfectly aligned with her cock.

"Oh, we do," Victor said. "Unless you don't want me to, in which case I'll demonstrate my fervent belief in hierarchy, whether it puts me over you or under you."

"Over *or* under, that sounds like equality to me."

Victor hummed, then reached a hand forward to stroke her hair, the tips of which were now down to her chin, and then to draw a finger along the smooth skin of her jaw, her throat, and her chest. "You changed your hair."

"I know you liked it the way it was," Julie said, stopping just short of an apology.

"I like this, too. I like that you can be however you want, and you do it for yourself, not anyone else."

Victor traced the valley of her sternum, and then under one pectoral toward her nipple. Her chest was sensitive, its contours a little softer and fuller than last time Victor had touched it, but she enjoyed the tiny spark of pain because it meant Victor hadn't withdrawn. There was tenderness—reverence, almost—in the light brush of their fingers.

It was dangerous, this moment of quiet exploration. They were no longer two people having wordless sex in the dark—they never had been, but she could almost have made herself believe her own excuses about the late hour, and the haze of sleep, and the difficult circumstances. Now there was too much thinking. Too much feeling. There was Victor leaning forward to kiss her nipple, and then her mouth, like she was something rare and precious.

The gesture brushed something tender and aching that

had nothing to do with her flesh. It was the same jolt of pain-edged pleasure, only in her heart instead of her chest. She'd missed Victor. She wanted more than this one night, but the two of them would never agree, so she'd have to take what she could get.

The new position laid Victor against her. She curved her hands around their bottom, sank her fingers into the softness and filled her palms, and said, "God, you have the finest backside in all creation."

Victor laughed, and there was a bitter edge to it. "I wish you were the only one who thought so. You're the only one invited to touch it."

Julie stilled her hands. "Did something happen?"

"No, no, nothing," Victor said. "You know, I didn't know how it was going to feel, wearing trousers. But I wouldn't give it up for anything."

Deliberate misdirection, but Julie couldn't help her response. "The sight of you in trousers is as stunning as any masterpiece in France. Please convey my appreciation to your tailor." Julie gave Victor a squeeze, making them groan and kiss her neck.

She pulled and Victor followed, letting their bodies slide against each other, catch, and slide again. Luxuriating in the heat and weight of Victor's thighs on her, the wet kiss of their bodies, she let the teasing drag on while they kissed. The contact tied something up inside her, twisting and tightening, and finally she rolled the two of them so Victor was beneath her, then tugged at Victor's hips until they flipped onto their stomach.

They went so willingly that her heart did its own little flip. Victor delighted in this, wanted to please her in even the smallest of motions.

An intuition lived between the two of them—there

was no sponge tonight, no sheath, but if they spoke of it, the absence would only remind them that tonight was unplanned. Julie didn't want to think of her noble plans not to fuck Victor. She wanted to straddle Victor's thighs, slide her cock into the tight, warm cleft of their ass, and rut until she came.

Victor canted their hips toward her eagerly and she rocked forward, thrusting against them, slipping through the hot, sticky evidence of her own want. This was no slow teasing. She wanted it fast now.

Victor writhed beneath her, pushing back. "Feel how wet you are. You *love* this. I bet you want to spread me open and bury your cock in my ass."

Her own desire, sudden and sure, surged forward and nearly choked her. "Do... *you* want that?"

"I do if it's you."

Julie sucked in a breath, exhaled a quiet "fuck," and came so hard her vision went dark.

The next thing she heard was Victor's soft laughter. "I think you got the back of my neck."

"Sor—"

"Don't apologize," they interrupted. "*That* was a revelation."

"Well," Julie said, not quite embarrassed, but not comfortable, either. The two of them had stumbled upon yet one more thing they wanted to do with each other—yet one more thing she'd yearn for, like the ribbons and every damn fool illustration she'd made, if they couldn't work out their differences. Even her darkness-swaddled, sex-soaked bed wasn't safe from incursions of the outside world.

She got up, dug through her belongings for a handkerchief, and did the best she could to wipe Victor and herself clean. Then she tumbled into bed, wrapped her arms around them, and inhaled the scent of their hair like it could clear the worry from her mind.

No fragrance, no matter how delicate and alluring, was that powerful, just as no sex was good enough to solve the problem. Julie didn't want to be the comforting distraction every time Victor got themself into trouble. She wanted a partner, someone who respected her opinions. Victor was unwilling to do that.

They might remain so even after she confessed the shameful truth.

The sun gradually weakened the darkness from ink black to watery ash grey. Daylight spilled through the crack in her curtains, and Victor roused from her arms, pressed a sleepy kiss to her cheek, and said, "Thank you, Julie."

"Thank me by removing that cursed artifact from your room," she grumbled.

Victor dressed efficiently in their wrinkled clothes from last night. "And putting it where?"

"Somewhere it won't hurt anyone."

"An excellent idea. We're in complete agreement," Victor said, beaming at her and slipping out of the room before she could say a word.

PRIVATE DIARY OF V BEAUCHÊNE, FEBRUARY 5, 1824

Taillefer did tell me that the painting made viewers "bizarrely emotional." I supposed I've confirmed that now, though I wish I hadn't done it in front of J.

The aftermath wasn't so bad, though. If J always went to bed with me after I cried, I wouldn't hate crying so much. I might even learn to like it.

A night in J's arms works wonders. Still can't comprehend why we've been denying ourselves the pleasure, but surely J will come around now.

Anyway, while I felt much better prepared to resist the allure of the painting by morning light, I still chose not to look at it. The painting can only teach me about itself, and I have other unanswered questions. So I went to the antiques shop on the Quai de Voltaire specializing in magical artifacts, one my brother and Taillefer both mentioned.

It was a dreary day for a walk, the sky as grey as the stone. The wind, once I reached the Seine, was piercing. Still, better to be out in the world and feeling real—if unpleasant—sensations than slowly starving to death in the pleasant haze of <u>Landscape with Ruins</u>. That thought kept my pace brisk.

I had to wander a bit before I found the shop. Horace and Taillefer technically told me the truth of its address, as the building is on the quai, but there's no sign and no number. I lingered outside the long row of nearly identical buildings, pretending to be taken in by the river and the île du palais, as though the early morning chill is perfectly suited to appreciating such views.

In fact it is. I don't usually venture out at such uncivilized hours, but things are quieter then. The only people in the street, other than myself, were paid to be there: scrubbing steps and washing windows.

I had simply wanted to <u>find</u> the shop, confirm its existence, perhaps peek in the window if there was one. I didn't expect a curio shop with wealthy clientele to be open so early in the morning, or to keep regular hours at all.

But then a small, well-dressed man briskly bypassed one of the people scrubbing the steps—an old woman whose ribs could almost be counted even through all the layers she wore. He nearly stepped on her in his haste. It was an action so breathtakingly inconsiderate that I began to suspect he might be just the sort of man I was looking for.

He'd pushed open the heavy wooden door without knocking and then disappeared up a set of stairs. It was unlocked, then.

I nodded at the old woman as I passed her. She didn't stop me from entering.

I guided the door silently back into place and paused in the entryway to listen, but everything was inaudible from the bottom of the stairs.

If it was the curio shop, I reasoned, then I could pretend to be a client like anyone else. And if it wasn't, then it didn't matter and I would be on my way.

I drew in a breath and went up.

The door nearly swung into the back of the man I'd followed. I slipped in while he was berating me, though towering piles of objects obstructed my efforts to get farther away from him. We were trapped in a narrow lane between the entrance and a long wooden counter, behind which stood another man, this one tense with distaste. The wall behind him was a grid of small wooden drawers, and above them, open cubbies, each one stuffed. I saw candles, books, mirrors, inkwells, magnifying glasses, a sextant, a lute, glass vials, various vessels and dishes in clay and porcelain, and many, many knives.

A fortune of jewelry sparkled on the counter.

The shopkeeper swept all of it into a velvet-lined tray and shelved the tray behind the counter. The motion defended against my intrusion, in case my intent was to steal gems—I <u>hope</u> I would be more subtle about it, if it were—but more than that, it knotted the tangle of my suspicions into certainty. He hadn't used his hands to clear the counter, but a wooden dowel.

A rough way to treat precious jewelry. But perhaps a wise way to treat magical artifacts.

"Who're you?" the shopkeeper grunted.

"A client."

"No, you're not. It's by appointment only."

"This is <u>my</u> appointment now," I said, flicking a dismissive glance at the small, well-dressed man.

The shopkeeper's glare and the confinement of heaps of potentially deadly objects, all of which he likely knew how to use, made me sweat. Still, though, it was a thrill: I'd found exactly what I was looking for.

"The brooch," the small, well-dressed man said. "Have it sent to me. Good day, Aveux."

He nodded and shut the door abruptly on his way down the stairs.

Aveux didn't watch his client leave. He didn't remove his hands from under the counter, either. "What do you want?"

"That brooch you plan to sell him," I said impulsively. "Give it to me instead."

He laughed.

It works better with the pen, my little trick. Perhaps some day I'll be like Béatrix, able to carry the power in me, but for now I'm just a person.

An insufficiently convincing person.

I had taken advantage of Aveux's momentary laugh to glance around the shop. A great deal of furniture was stacked there, as well as a saddle and four wagon wheels and what I think was the disassembled wagon but might, for all I know, have been assorted lumber. A coffin stood upright in the corner. There were two fully clothed mannequins in the extravagant dresses of the Ancien Régime, surrounded by twenty fairytales' worth of discarded slippers.

It was an inopportune time to notice the taxidermied crocodile on the floor. I turned away as if I saw one every day.

"Let me give you my card," I said, thankful I'd taken to carrying around a case of them. They say "Victor Beauchêne, contact me at the Maison Laval." It's not a suggestion.

Aveux grunted again. He touched my card with the

same dowel he'd used to move the jewelry around, but he read it. His watery green eyes narrowed and then he trained his snakelike gaze on me.

"You think I spend all day in here, surrounded, without protecting myself? Magic won't work on me, not unless it's strong."

My writing always sits better with those who are inclined to believe what I've written. I was no match for Aveux's skepticism—or whatever object he was using to defend himself. But his confirmation that it is possible to protect oneself was precious to me. Certainly worth sweating through one of my better shirts.

Aveux is a strange, coiled-up man, always ready to spring. Curiously, my attempt to manipulate him with magic seemed to have made him like me better.

"Most who come in here, they don't have their own," Aveux said. He flicked my card with the dowel. "What'd you need me for, if you can do this? I'd be drowning in pussy, myself."

"That's one thing I prefer to come by honestly," I said. "Why use the dowel if you're already protected against magic?"

"I'm not stupid, am I," he said. "And I said it won't work unless it's strong. Plenty of that in here."

"Do you have anything that could protect me?" I asked.

"From what?"

"Say someone else tried to compel me. Could I render myself immune?"

"Of course. It'll cost you, though." Aveux raked his gaze over my clothes. "Don't think I have anything you can afford. And don't try anything with that funny writing of yours."

We argued about that for a while, and he did name some objects and some prices, but eventually I was forced to admit he was right. Unless I rob my brother again, I can't afford the kind of protection Aveux is selling.

"Do you have any paintings by an artist named Nicolas Tilleul?" I asked. "Eighteenth-century landscapes. Capricci."

"Tilleul," he said, scratching the grey-brown scruff on his chin. "If I do, you gonna pay me with coin or paper?"

"My banknotes are real." Most of them, anyway. I slid a stack of gold louis across the counter, assuming he'd be suspicious of any paper I offered him.

He grunted and it was almost a laugh. "That wouldn't be near enough."

"Would it buy me what you know?" I asked. At his hesitation, I pulled a second fistful of coins out of my coat pocket.

He leaned both elbows on the counter and said, "As it happens, I don't have what you're seeking. I've only ever sold one signed Tilleul. An obvious forgery, but the magic was real."

"What do you mean, a forgery?"

"Papers that came with that painting said it was from the 1740s, but the green's not right. The artist used a modern pigment. Don't look at me like that, boy, I don't sell wares I haven't examined."

"I'm not a boy," I said, although I wouldn't have minded being called one in the right circumstance, which this shady little curio shop was not. My heart beat fast and shallow for all the wrong reasons. What I most wanted to know was what object permitted Aveux to inspect the paintings and set aside my card without being affected, but

I doubted he'd tell me. I swallowed. "So what does that mean, then? Why forge a painting by an unknown artist? Who would do that? Where did that painting come from?"

"Haven't found any evidence that a painter called Nicolas Tilleul existed at the time," he said. Then he shrugged. "Hard to know for sure. As I said, the magic works. Got another little painting in the same lot as that Tilleul, and it's a nullity. Well, almost. Doesn't do anything except give people a feeling of unease. Doesn't look like the others, either. Unfinished, unsigned. Portrait, not landscape. Nobody wants it. Should probably have tossed it already."

"Show me."

For all his hunching, Aveux revealed himself to be a large man. He exited the space behind the counter and navigated the labyrinth of his shop nimbly despite his size. On his return, he laid a small canvas on the counter.

As he'd said, the painting was unfinished. Brown underpainting and white canvas showed at the naked edges. It was a head study of a man I judged to be in his thirties, skin the color of pale wood and hair like honey. He was handsome, but the intensity of his gaze filled me with dread.

"Don't know anything about the man, so don't bother asking."

My mouth was open, but I had formed no sounds. Something about the style—those deep shadows, those careful, almost indistinguishable brushstrokes, the depth and dimension and sheer feeling in the man's face—something was familiar to me.

I was, for a brief instant, enraged that Aveux would call this brilliant little portrait a "nullity." Its impact on me was nearly as strong as <u>Landscape with Ruins</u>, but for different reasons.

This painting had been in a lot with a landscape by Nicolas Tilleul, a painter who didn't exist, whose alleged work was more recent than it claimed to be. This portrait, then, wasn't that old. Perhaps painted by a living artist.

Perhaps painted by the living artist who rented the room above mine.

"Where did you get this? Who sold it to you?"

"They came together as a lot. The seller had no particular connection to them, and the person who'd sold them to him didn't know anything, either. Papers were fake, as I said, but that happens in this line of work. When you specialize in objects with unnatural origins, people don't like to say where they came from. Might be stolen, might just be cursed. A fair number of things that end up in my shop are here because people begged me to take them. I free them from their burden."

"Generous of you," I said.

A flash of teeth. "Not really."

"The client who bought the Tilleul painting," I said. "Have you sold him other items?"

"What would become of my reputation if I betrayed my loyal clientele like that?" Aveux said, clucking in disapproval. "But since you seem like the curious type who'll eventually be begging me to take some object off your hands, and I can tell you want this null painting, I'll—"

I interrupted before he could finish. "No bargains, no favors. I paid for the information, and I'll pay for the painting, and then I owe you nothing."

"If that's how you want to do it," he said.

Having revealed my interest in the painting, I had to empty out my pockets to bring it home, but it doesn't matter. I couldn't simply leave it there. I tucked the small canvas under my greatcoat to protect it from the elements and descended the stairs.

Cold air rushed into the landing as I pushed the heavy outer door open. It was still early enough that the street was mostly empty.

There was a figure loitering at the opposite edge of the street, pretending to stare down into the water, just as I had. Their clothes had faded from black to grey, and their hat was so battered as to be nearly shapeless, but a tuft of red sideburn stuck out between the hat and the high collar of their coat.

As I shut the door, they turned to look at me, and I locked eyes with Forestier.

I clutched the painting tight, my arms hidden under the folds of my greatcoat. I don't know why I felt such concern that he not see it. I broke away and marched back toward the Maison Laval. There was no reason for my chest to seize at the sight of Forestier. I'd just survived a much more dangerous encounter. And he couldn't possibly know where I'd been or what I'd been doing.

But if that's true, then why was he waiting on the quai? It's too much of a coincidence to be believed that we might encounter each other in the deserted early morning, far from the Maison Laval. Forestier wasn't wearing his police uniform, and I've rarely seen him in other clothes, let alone such disreputable ones. Either he was following me or he was watching the shop.

I don't care for either possibility, but I also don't want to inquire into Forestier's business. First of all, it would involve talking to him. Second, I have two paintings to study now and many more intriguing mysteries to solve.

PRIVATE DIARY OF V BEAUCHÊNE, FEBRUARY 6, 1824

Second experiment with <u>Landscape with Ruins</u>, allegedly by Nicolas Tilleul, allegedly 1740.

I can no longer rely on Aunt S to shake me from a trance, as she was angry at having been unknowingly involved in my last experiment and will be even more infuriated if she learns of this one. There is no one else both willing and trustworthy, so I will have to continue alone, but I have taken precautions, described below:

The painting sits on my desk, leaning against a wall, and I will sit in my desk chair to observe it. There is sackcloth covering the painting, which I won't remove until I'm ready. In order to end the trance, I have wrapped a book (<u>Thérèse philosophe</u>, but this is not relevant) in twine and strung that twine over a ceiling beam so that the book is suspended over my head. I have also made a stack of other novels (they were the resource at hand) to raise a candle to just underneath the string. When the candle is lit, the flame will burn through the twine and the book will drop onto my head. This should be sufficient to end the trance.

FIRST TRIAL

Partial success. My book-twine apparatus successfully woke me, but the twine burns so quickly that I hardly had time to become entranced—though even that brief minute was enough to know the trance is still powerful.

The pain is startling (necessary) but not lasting.

SECOND TRIAL

I lowered the candle flame, but it didn't provide me with much more time. No change in the trance.

Concerns: If I repeat the experiment many more times, dropping a book on my head will either become too painful or, alternately, I will become accustomed to it, which is more dangerous.

Also, I will run out of twine.

THIRD TRIAL

Ow.

I have altered the setup. Instead of the books, twine, and candle, I have procured a small wooden cask from the kitchen. It is filled with water and the tap is barely open, so a thin trickle drips into the washbasin I have perched on the edge of my desk. (The basin is tilted thanks to Thérèse philosophe, a more useful book than I knew.) The washbasin will fill slowly and eventually spill into my lap. The shock of cold water should be enough to end the trance.

I will have to be judicious about how many trials I perform with this method, as too much water on the floor will cause a puddle that will be difficult to hide or explain.

FOURTH TRIAL

Spent half an hour with the painting. The trance wouldn't have ended without the water, so it is still quite powerful, but I feel less distressed than I did after my nine-hour session.

Though it requires partial nudity, this method is promising.

FIFTH TRIAL

No change. I have started to shiver from the water. I don't notice the cold when I'm entranced. Break for dinner.

SIXTH TRIAL

No change. The most unpleasant part of these trials is the water. I keep having to go fetch more.

I understand how the painting is dangerous, but I don't think it was made with malicious intent. It's beautiful work. I'd like to find some way to preserve it.

SEVENTH TRIAL

I left the trance before the basin spilled because I heard the sound of a piece of paper whispering along the floorboards.

The note is from J. I ran to the door and opened it, but they were already gone.

J MORÈRE TO V BEAUCHÊNE, FEBRUARY 6, 1824
SLIPPED UNDER THE DOOR

V—

I wish I knew how to use one of those ciphers you mentioned. I can't believe you memorized them. I wouldn't be smart enough on my best day, and today is not my best day.

I'm ashamed that I didn't tell you this earlier. I'm ashamed of everything in this letter. But I wanted you to like me. I was hoping you'd listen to my warnings about the cursed artifacts and not repeat my mistakes, and then I'd never have to tell you. I suppose you can't learn from my mistakes if I haven't told you what they are.

You'd have written this letter in code and you'd still have managed to compose something compelling, whereas I have only simple French—please don't tease me about my spelling, V, I know it's bad—and no excuse for the chaos I am about to scribble.

I was a quiet, gawky adolescent. The other children in Vézy-sur-Oise never knew what to make of anyone in our family, so for most of my life I had only Adrienne and

Georges as friends. You might think our family was isolated, and in a way we were. But I met a lot of people.

My talents as a painter have been apparent from a young age. My parents were proud, and they told all their artist friends, who made me into a sort of legend. Sometimes friends of friends would visit the farm and want to meet the remarkable child. Word spread.

It sounds strange now that I write it down, but it didn't feel that way at the time. It was just my life. I had my brother and my sister and a stream of admirers I'd never met before and would probably never see again. Some of them only wanted a glimpse of my work, and others wanted to teach me. I had many teachers, and I still appreciate all of them.

One of them wanted <u>me</u>.

Or so I thought. I was fourteen and hardly knew any better, but his interest in my work seemed to extend to an interest in my person, an intoxicating novelty. No one else had ever felt that way. I wasn't sure anyone ever would. (Maybe that surprises you, V. I wasn't born with this confidence; I had to create it.)

Anyway, I craved it. Alphonse's attention, his praise, the way he looked at me.

Maybe I misinterpreted everything. Alphonse—that's the name he told me to call him—never touched me. I might have invented all of it. Extended my own desperate adolescent feelings to him. His praise was always for what I could do. We never spoke of anything but cultivating my talents.

And what would a man like him have wanted with me? I never knew Alphonse's age, but I suppose he was in his thirties, and he was handsome, his features an appealing mixture of the bold and the delicate. I don't think he had much money, but he dressed well, choosing colors that flattered his pale complexion and cuts that displayed his long legs and slender hips. Beyond his looks, his passion and knowledge called to me, as did his desire to see my work fulfill its promise.

Alphonse was only unusual in his appeal. I had met many other artists who wanted to teach me. My parents weren't concerned by the time we spent together; their network of friends had never failed them. That, and he was charming. A gifted conversationalist. A pleasure to have at the dinner table. We were all taken in—everyone except Adrienne.

Maybe it's because Adrienne is charming herself, and her own charm springs from her warm heart, so she recognizes falseness in others. I don't know. But she never liked him. He tried to persuade her and even at sixteen, she never fell for it. His honeyed brown hair and blue eyes didn't work on her, and neither did his silver tongue.

I wish I'd listened to my sister.

I didn't, though. I spent time with Alphonse, and he taught me the true power of my work. My parents had educated all three of their children in magic, but in the ethical kind I now practice, the kind that only touches me. Alphonse taught me to use my paintings and drawings to affect other people, whether they wanted it or not. It was intoxicating, learning to exercise that power, having his full attention, being told the whole time that I was a genius such as he had never seen before. He played my ambition like an instrument.

I told myself we were not hurting anyone. The paintings captured people's attention, which is what all good paintings do. My paintings were a bit harder to look away from, but what of it? They brought contentment.

It took time, this education. Alphonse had come to Vézy-sur-Oise for the summer, renting a house in the village, but he stayed into autumn and then into winter. At first, he came to our house all the time, and was often at our dinner table, but as the months wore on, the two of us spent all our time in an outbuilding on the farm where we'd set up a studio.

Alphonse dabbled, but he wasn't much of a painter. This isn't a judgment made in scorn, after the fact. We both knew it at the time. I had the talent and he had the vision. He knew more about magic than anyone I'd ever met, even though awareness of magic was common among my parents' eccentric and radical friends. That knowledge was one of many things I found captivating about him. He promised me acclaim and recognition, but first, he said, we needed money.

An amusement, that was what he called his scheme. We'd make paintings that resembled those of the Ancien Régime—picturesque imagined landscapes, dotted with attractive ruins, perhaps a tiny figure or two—and sell them under a false name, claiming they were valuable antiques. The paintings themselves would lull people into believing our claims. They'd be irresistible. We'd earn money and the satisfaction of feeling cleverer than anyone around us. And Alphonse would tell me how brilliant my work was, which was what I really wanted.

There was a linden tree outside the studio window, so we named our fake Ancien Régime artist after it. Tilleul, we called him. A private joke that now makes me sick.

By the time we embarked on this scheme, I was already adept at creating paintings that entranced their viewers, thanks to long practice. Alphonse was a demanding teacher. It wasn't hard to imitate the style of landscape he wanted, but I quickly grew bored. His scheme offered me none of the satisfaction he'd promised. I chafed at the restrictions—I wanted to do my own work, at my own pace, not churn out Tilleuls hour after hour. Sometimes Alphonse didn't let me sleep. He claimed I was better at channeling magic into the work that way.

What he really wanted was not paintings but brushes. He wanted me to create tools for him, to pour magic into my brushes until they'd paint the thoughts of whoever held them, or make a work that appeared ideal to whoever beheld it, or create a painting that could generate whatever it depicted—there would have been endless still lifes of gold bars in my future if I'd managed that, I think. But I couldn't do it. The magic paintings were easy enough, but magic brushes were beyond me.

Or perhaps deep down I knew that I shouldn't hand him that power.

We fought, but he always cajoled me back into doing what he wanted. I don't know if it was his innate powers of persuasion, or if he had some object that made it easy to trick me, or if it was the fact that I was barely fifteen and he was at least twice that. Maybe all three.

He kept me away from my family as much as he could, so there was little opportunity to share my concerns. I was afraid to speak to them anyway, since as he often reminded me, all the magical paintings in the studio—the evidence of wrongdoing—had been made by my hands. If he was at fault, then so was I.

Unable to voice my worries, I made another small painting during those last few months, a portrait of Alphonse. I never finished it, but even unfinished, its unsettling effect conveyed a warning to any receptive beholder. Alphonse, of course, wasn't receptive to a warning about himself. He didn't perceive the portrait as anything other than flattery, since it accurately depicted his handsome face.

But Adrienne knew.

My sister never stopped coming to the studio to check on me, even though she and Alphonse hated each other, and he made every effort to discourage her. She'd become alarmed by how much time I spent in his company, but she had no proof that I wasn't there of my own choice. I rarely showed Adrienne what I was painting—either because I knew what Alphonse and I were doing was wrong or because I wanted to protect her from the effects of my work—but on one of her visits, I showed her the portrait. She understood.

The next time she came back, she marched up the hill to the studio armed with a kitchen knife.

Her furious knock on the studio door wasn't enough to wake me, passed out on the cot as I was. It was mid-afternoon, but what little light that March day had offered was already waning. Alphonse let her in.

Adrienne told him that he was no longer welcome, and probably a lot of other things, too. I can almost hear her saying "slimy" and "manipulative." I wish I'd witnessed it.

It's easy to imagine Alphonse's little nods and remorseful, acquiescent expressions, lulling her into thinking he'd go peacefully.

Instead, he showed her the painting.

The paintings only work on people who are already receptive—interested in art, first and foremost, but also in the right frame of mind to accept the effects. This was how Alphonse explained his control over his own reactions. Adrienne, being an artist herself, has a great interest in art. That Alphonse was able to soothe her from knife-wielding anger into a state where she'd look at a painting is proof of his skill.

Then again, Adrienne had come to the studio out of concern for me, and she'd learned something valuable from the one and only painting I'd revealed to her. In the end, the whole thing is my fault. She wouldn't have looked if not for me. She wouldn't have been there if not for me. But she was there, and she cared, and she looked, and my unconscionable painting captured her full attention.

I don't know how long Adrienne remained entranced. Not long, I think.

Fire moves quickly.

I can still taste the sour sting in the back of my throat and the sharp burn in my nostrils. Smoke shrouded the room. Even with the fire lighting up one corner of the room, it was impossible to see, but I knew my way through the mess. I dropped from the cot to my knees, crawled across the floor, knocked the painting off my easel, and shook Adrienne until she came to.

She didn't understand where she was, I think, but we couldn't talk about it. There was no air, and besides, fire is much louder than you might think. Things were crackling and bursting all around. Showers of sparks split the smoke.

Alphonse had shut the studio door behind him, and the metal handle was too hot to touch. We only got out because I shattered a window with a chair. Fortunately the building had only one floor. It was still hell getting out—Adrienne confused and emotional, glass shards everywhere, fire in my throat and tears streaming down my face—but we did it.

The whole building burned, along with everything in it. I haven't seen Alphonse since.

But I'm not fool enough to think him dead. Even if he was, the world is full of people like him.

There you have it, V. The story of how my selfish ambition nearly killed my sister and myself. Why I no longer dabble in artifacts. I could write more to try to convince you to give up your course, but remembering all this has upset me. I have to stop here.

—J

PRIVATE DIARY OF V BEAUCHÊNE, FEBRUARY 7, 1824

I couldn't leave J alone after the confession in their letter, so I dressed, marched upstairs, and knocked briskly.

The door cracked open. "Victor, I'm not in the mood—"

"Not why I'm here. Can we please have this conversation in private?"

The door latched quietly behind me. "Julie?"

"Julie," they confirmed, their gaze directed at the floor. "And 'she' or 'they.' Though I don't want you to call me anything or think about me, because I want you to go away."

"I will, if that's what you want. I just wanted to see you for a minute," I said. "I need you to know that it wasn't your fault. You were fourteen years old—"

"Fifteen, by the end."

"That makes no difference. You were manipulated by someone much older and more knowledgeable than you, someone who used you for your abilities, and God, Julie, I like your parents, but <u>how</u>—"

"They didn't know. I didn't tell them."

"Adrienne knew. And she was, what, sixteen?"

"Seventeen when I nearly got her killed." Julie dared me to deny this with a stare.

"Seventeen when you rescued each other from awful circumstances."

Julie let out a long breath, then sat on the bed and put their face in their hands like their resolve had collapsed.

I waited a moment to see if they were going to ask me to leave, and when they didn't, I said, "Can I sit with you?"

A single nod. The mattress dipped, bringing our hips together, and I pressed my knee into theirs. They didn't move away.

"Would you hate it if I put my arm around your shoulders?"

"No."

It would have been difficult if Julie had been sitting up straight, as tall as they are, but they were leaning so heavily on their elbows that I managed without too much trouble. My blue dressing gown sleeve drooped over their linen-clad shoulders. (I should have dressed more properly to go to J's room, but it was late and nobody saw me. Besides, this silk brocade is the perfect shade of my eyes, so anyone who sees me should feel lucky.)

"We don't have to talk about it," I assured them. "I just didn't want you to be alone."

"We can't talk about it," they said. "We'll have another fight."

"How do you know your heartfelt confession didn't affect me?"

They raised their head so I could see the curl of their lip. "Oh, are you planning to destroy all the cursed artifacts in your possession?"

"Would you help me if I said yes?" I asked. "After all, you made two of them."

"I—no, that's not possible. I told you. There was a fire. Everything burned."

"You were unconscious when the fire started, and since you didn't see Alphonse's body, we should assume he escaped," I said. "And given what's in my room, we should assume he took two paintings with him. At least."

Wide-eyed and stricken, Julie paled.

I pulled their hands into my lap and squeezed. "The portrait of Alphonse isn't dangerous—on the contrary, it will help anyone who sees it to be wary of him when he comes back. That's what you think will happen, isn't it? You didn't want me to flaunt my magic because you fear Alphonse. So that just leaves <u>Landscape with Ruins</u> to handle, and since you made it, I'm sure you can unmake it. There's no need to look so horrified. This is a little bit of a mess, I know, but we're in it now and there's nothing to be done about that. Besides, we're both fine, I removed the more dangerous painting from its owner, and now we can work together to make things right."

Julie withdrew from my grip and dropped their head into their hands again. "This is all my fault."

"Oh, it's at least half my fault," I said cheerfully.

"You were in distress and cried all over me because of <u>my</u> painting," they said, ignoring me.

"In terms of fates I could have suffered, a few tears is nothing. And I recall you kissing it better. That was so good I'd learn to cry on command—"

"Stop," Julie said. "I hate this."

They seemed to need a moment, so I stopped talking and instead rubbed slow circles into curved expanse of their back. I missed touching Julie. When they didn't move for a long time, I slid my fingers into the thick, brown waves of their hair and began to comb in long, luxuriant pulls. My hair always tangled too much for that motion to be pleasurable when it was long, but Julie's is loose and sleek. They relaxed under my touch and then risked a glance at me, their dark eyes filled with worry.

"Are you angry?"

"That some villain abused you? Yes, I am."

"That wasn't my question and you know it."

It was easier to speak steadily when we weren't looking at each other. Julie's suffering was like smoke in the air, making my eyes water. I controlled myself and said, "You asked if I was angry and I told you what I was angry about. It was a perfectly comprehensible exchange. Now, do you still want me to leave?"

"Life would be simpler if I did," Julie muttered. "But no, I don't."

"Um," I said, momentarily floundering. The combination of complex grammar and sudden, unexpected acquiescence made me lose my hard-fought composure. "Could you maybe say what it is you do want, then?"

"Stay, Victor."

So I stayed in Julie's room last night, and we were quiet and held each other and I didn't suggest a peek at the painting or an adventure with all those very expensive ribbons I know are sitting tragically unused in one of Julie's bedroom piles. I didn't even take my clothes off.

I have no idea what to do about any of this.

PRIVATE DIARY OF V BEAUCHÊNE, FEBRUARY 8, 1824

Yesterday I was too consumed with thinking about J to record my progress.

My experiments worked.

Granted, I discovered this in the most dangerous possible way—J would be upset if they knew—because I left the painting uncovered when I received J's letter. I ran out of the room after reading it. We spent the night together, and I came back and voilà, there it was, staring at me.

But now I can stare back.

It's a little bit of a shame. I rather liked the feeling of peace and contentment the landscape provided. I suppose I'll just have to find those things elsewhere.

J MORÈRE TO V BEAUCHÊNE, FEBRUARY 8, 1824
SLIPPED UNDER THE DOOR

V—

If you give me the landscape, I'll try to undo it. The painting's not a danger to me. I might be the only one for whom that's true. I feel sick, thinking it's been out in the world all this time. I am responsible for the damage done.

Do <u>not</u> misunderstand me. I don't sanction any part of what you're doing, and I don't want to be involved in anything else. This is the first and last time I help you with this nonsense.

—J

V BEAUCHÊNE TO J MORÈRE, FEBRUARY 8, 1824
SLIPPED UNDER THE DOOR

J—

Understood. Collect the work from my room at your leisure. I would be very interested to know what approaches you'll use to change the painting, if discussing such a topic doesn't break your self-imposed rules.

And, as it so happens, you're not the only one safe from the effects. Its previous owner told me that anyone uninterested in art can pass by unaffected, and I have learned to control my own response to it.

You will need another pair of eyes to know whether you succeed in changing the painting's allure, and since you cannot safely show it to anyone else, I offer myself for your use.

—V

J MORÈRE TO V BEAUCHÊNE, FEBRUARY 8, 1824
SLIPPED UNDER THE DOOR

V—

I suppose I don't mind if you watch.

—J

PRIVATE DIARY OF J MORÈRE, FEBRUARY 9, 1824

I don't use this journal very often. V told me to write down what I did today in case I have to do it again with other paintings. I hope I won't, and this might not be helpful even if I do come across another Nicolas Tilleul, but I've decided to be thorough.

This morning we wrapped the canvas to protect it from the rain and carried it through the streets and up many flights of stairs to my studio, which has tall enough glass windows that even on a day like today, clarity pours in. The windows chill the room, and V made a show of complaining about air currents and tutting about how I work all hours in unbearable conditions, and naturally when they sat down on a rarely used armchair, a cloud of dust poofed into the air. They sputtered.

V has such strong reactions to everything, and because I'm terrible, <u>indignant</u> is one of my favorites. Their brows draw together and their mouth makes this open, round shape, and their lips get this rose-madder flush. It's lovely.

And this morning it made for a nice contrast, since they were looking so feline and dapper—it's easy to be dapper when you have ten thousand francs—and put together, with the blue in their waistcoat matched to the blue in their eyes. (Ultramarine. Of course V would have irises of the most impossible color, and the most expensive pigment. If I ever painted the color accurately, people would say I'd made it up. Too beautiful to be real. If I tell V this, they will tease me for the rest of my life—but I know how to get the upper hand with them whenever I want it.)

I said to V that they probably shouldn't wear their nicest waistcoat to a room full of oil paints and charcoal if they were worried about a little dust, and they stuck their nose in the air and told me it wasn't their nicest. I just barely kept myself from saying that was good because it would look better on the floor.

We'd never have started the session if I'd said that.

As it was, I was worried I'd never get any work done with all our chatter, but I didn't say so. I knew in my heart that I was provoking V for the same reason I was mixing my paint very, very slowly: I was scared to try fixing my mistakes. I hadn't seen any of those damn Tilleul paintings since Alphonse bamboozled me into making them, and I never liked them anyway. They're good for what they are, but we deliberately settled on a dated style that wouldn't resemble the work I made under my own name. That should have been a clue that Alphonse wanted the paintings for bad reasons, but I didn't understand back then.

I put <u>Landscape with Ruins</u> on an easel and stared at it for a while. I'd painted it in an all-consuming trance of creativity, a stretch of hours where the paintbrush became part of my body and the image poured out of it. I was a channel, a conduit. Some trace of the power of my trance had remained in the painting to trap viewers. I hadn't wanted to harm anyone. It was meant to be pleasant. Tranquil.

What would make it less dangerous?

I picked up a scraper and thought about wrecking the whole thing, but V jumped out of the chair and stopped me, their hand landing gently on my arm. If they were willing to touch my dirty painting smock, it must be urgent.

"Objects imbued with magic are volatile. Physical destruction can unleash a burst of energy. If you want to destroy it, we can, but we should render it inert first."

The fire Alphonse set in the studio had burned faster and more violently than it should have. There was hardly anything left of the building afterward. I suppose that was my fault, too.

"How did you learn so much about this?" I asked. Just a few months ago, V had been begging me for explanations.

"I'm tenacious."

"That, I knew," I said. "Go. I can't work with you hovering over my shoulder."

They bit down on a smile. "You're snapping at me because you don't know what to do."

That didn't seem like anything worth smiling about, but V got excited. We have a lot of differences, the two of us, but maybe the most important one is that I like knowing things and V likes <u>not</u> knowing things. The unknown makes most people nervous, but V charges right toward it. I am never going to understand.

"I've spent the last few years training myself not to paint like this." I waved a hand at the canvas. "And I don't mean frivolous little landscapes. I mean the technique of deliberately producing a dangerous object."

"It's not frivolous," V said.

"That's the least pertinent part of what I just said."

"No, it's not. I know this isn't your preferred style, but it's pretty and it makes people happy. Don't dismiss that. Not all art has to address grand subject matter, or represent real life, or be morally instructive and tragic."

My face is less expressive than V's, but still they could tell I was surprised by their vehemence.

"Those times when you and your boring friends talked about art, I listened," V said. "Your friends have terrible opinions. I'm right."

"Fine," I said. "Tell me how to fix this not-at-all-frivolous, entirely worthwhile artistic endeavor so it doesn't get anyone killed, please."

V interrogated me about the conditions of the painting's creation, and I explained the feeling of being a conduit as best I could, and then they said, "So you painted this in a sort of trance and it induces a trance in susceptible viewers."

"Sometimes that feeling of pure concentration happens when I paint or draw other things," I said. "I... like it, I suppose. My best work happens in those moments. The intensity doesn't always transfer to the viewer."

"Because ever since you made these, you take care not to create dangerous objects," V said. "But when you made this, you <u>wanted</u> to communicate a certain experience—a feeling of peace, happiness, ease, that sort of thing. A beautiful day. A pretty girl flirting with you."

Even though I am the one who made the painting and I ought to know exactly what it does, it still startled me to hear V express such an understanding of the work. I suppose they did spend nine hours with it. I always hope that my work will inspire understanding, but in this case, it made me uneasy.

And it's embarrassing to think about myself at fifteen, painting this and yearning for a pretty girl—or anyone—to flirt with me. I would prefer that V know nothing of that, but it's too late now.

"You made something that makes people want to keep looking indefinitely," V said. "All you have to do is change it so people don't want that."

I've never responded well to being told what to do, and this sort of command without instruction, from someone without technical knowledge, is what irritates me most. I am a little bit ashamed to record that I grumbled, "Yes, thank you so much for your expertise. Perhaps you'd like to paint it yourself?"

V regarded the brush I'd thrust toward them. "That's not why I'm here."

I shivered to think of why they'd come. I had only ever seen one person affected by my work, and it was Adrienne after Alphonse tricked her. My hand tightened on the brush; I thought of picking up the scraper again and carving right down to the weave of the canvas.

"You're here to paint," V continued. "I'm here to watch. I think we both know what to do."

I wanted to contest that, but instead I picked up my brush and palette. It always takes some time to enter the flow of work. At first I dabbed here and there, glancing at V every so often, waiting for a vision of what I ought to do with this damned canvas.

V tracked my brush. They made no comment, but their interest was evident in the lively movement of their eyes. I saw the moment they submerged themself. Everything softened. Their gaze, their stance, their breath, the set of their mouth.

It was exactly what they'd come here to do, and yet I couldn't keep myself from shouting, "Victor!"

I shook them and they blinked at me. "Yes?"

"Oh," I said. "You... you're there."

"I told you I have control," V said. "If I'm entranced, assume it's on purpose."

"Are you sure you want to do this?" I asked. "You don't have to."

"You know it's pleasant, right? The effect of the painting."

"I've never experienced it," I said, though in theory I did know. "It distresses me when you disappear. I worry that something will happen to you."

"Nothing will happen to me. I can exit at will. And you're here." Their voice dropped. "I'm enjoying myself."

That should have soothed me. We were alone in the studio. I hadn't seen Alphonse in years. V was doing this knowingly and voluntarily. Still, I frowned.

"I grant you permission to drag me away and wake me by whatever means necessary should anything go wrong." They accompanied these words with a half-smile, as though we were sharing a joke. I tried to return it. "I'm going in again. Is that all right with you?"

"I suppose so."

The change was quick. I pulled the armchair in front of the easel so V could sit, but by the time I had it in position, their eyelids had already dipped to match their drooping shoulders. I maneuvered them into the chair with a few gentle tugs and pushes. They went along with it without noticing.

Their strange, absent presence unnerved me at first. I would have preferred distracting chatter. But after a dozen glances revealed V still breathing, I accepted the situation. As I became absorbed in my work, V's presence felt more and more companionable to me, and soon enough I knew what to do. I mixed a series of greys on my palette and darkened a few of the clouds, cloaking them with the threat of rain.

Changing the sky had a cascading effect on the colors of the landscape, so then I had to correct those as well. As it was happening, I had no sense that it was taking a long time, but since I am recording this after the fact, I know I spent three hours making small adjustments. When I finished, the painting remained the same in composition, but radically different in tone. The sunny idyll was fleeting, soon to be stormy. The shepherd and shepherdess would need to seek shelter. They could not stay there.

"Nicely done," V said, scaring the life out of me.

"You shit," I said and painted a streak of greenish grey across their cheek.

They were too slow to dodge, having been motionless in the chair for hours. I studied V for signs of deterioration and found none. Their lips curved. I passed them a rag to wipe their face and they accepted it.

"It's less powerful, but I don't think it's powerless yet," they said. "Let's see how long the trance lasts now that you've made these changes."

I nodded. They drifted away.

After that I stood around tapping my feet, wishing I'd brought a watch. A break in the patter of rain outside the windows made the silence in the studio grow heavy—but there was a ticking. V had a watch. The delicate gold chain stood in contrast to the blue of their waistcoat. I tiptoed closer, pulled it out, and flicked open the case as carefully as if I were a pickpocket. Silly and unnecessary, since V probably wouldn't have noticed if I'd ripped it off the chain.

V probably wouldn't have noticed if I'd undressed them, but even writing the thought makes me feel filthy. I don't want V to be absent or unconscious when we go to bed together, though there was something thrilling about the trust they placed in me today. They were willing to hand me so much power. I want to be worthy of that.

I studied the watch face and half a minute later, V emerged.

"How long was I gone?"

"I'm not sure. Ten minutes, maybe."

"That's good," V said. "I could have woken when you consulted my watch, but I chose not to. I wanted it to happen on its own."

Draining the painting of the last of its allure was a slow process, less meditative than my earlier session, but Victor asked me a lot of questions about changing the painting and whether their presence or my emotional state had affected my work. I answered yes to both, though probably not articulately enough for V. They didn't make me feel inadequate, though. Thinking back on it, despite the circumstances, I enjoyed both the work and the discussion we had. Sometimes I underestimate V, maybe because I find them so attractive or so frustrating, which is unfair. It's exhilarating to watch them apply their mind to complex questions.

In the end, it was simple: I darkened the sky, faded the grass, withered the trees, sullied the ruins, and the little landscape lost its power. It was quite a funny thing when I finished, an unappealing parody of the genre. V could find no way to become entranced.

"That isn't to say I don't like it."

"But why would you? It's hideous."

"I think it's witty," V insisted. "If you still want to rip it apart or burn it, then that's what we'll do, but I think I've developed a sentimental attachment now. Now that it's a nullity, we could keep it."

"It's just one mediocre painting. I've made dozens of better ones."

V stood from the armchair and took both my hands. It was hard to take them seriously with that faint smear of paint on their face, but they gave me such a grave look. "Say the word and we'll set it on fire."

I suppose they were concerned the painting might be tainted by my memories of Alphonse, and it was, though looking at it right at that moment, all I could think about was the work we did today to transform it. Still, I shrugged and we decided to burn it.

"You know I will make you a better one—one without any potential danger—any time you want."

"I'm touched," V said. "It was good, you know. In both its incarnations. You're always brilliant."

That was unexpected. I had not been painting with an aesthetic goal in mind.

"Did you know the only time you ever look bashful is when I compliment your work?" V asked. "Thank you for letting me be here. It's fascinating to learn more about your process."

That was it. V didn't start talking about how we could scour Paris to make sure none of the other Tilleul paintings are out there, or how if I could alter this magical object, maybe I could do that to others, or how well we work together. They didn't ask me if I thought I could perform this same process on someone else's painting. (I could, I think.)

If they'd said any of that, I would have had to say no. I made that very clear in the note I wrote when I agreed to this. But they respected my wishes. No rhapsodizing about possibilities. No imagining our future success. They didn't push me. They didn't ask me for anything.

I wish they had.

I almost said that if they ever come across another Tilleul, or any painting with magical effects, that they should tell me and that I would help. (I won't deceive myself: V will continue seeking out these things.) But I was afraid. I don't think it's the actions we might take together that I fear. Changing my mind scares me. How will I know who I am if I do this? How will I know what I'm doing is right?

Anyway, we walked home. I don't think the rest of what we did after that is relevant, but it was <u>very</u> good.

PRIVATE DIARY OF V BEAUCHÊNE, FEBRUARY 9, 1824

J let me watch her work this afternoon, which would have been enough of a gift, but then we came home and she said, "Let me make you a better drawing."

And then she took my clothes off and tied me to her bed.

I suppose the obscene novels led me to believe it would be rough, hard, merciless, and I thought that was what I wanted. Instead it was almost unbearably tender, the way she posed my arms above my head and looped a velvet ribbon around the headboard and my wrists. She loomed over me, her shaggy brown hair curtaining her face, bottom lip bitten in concentration. I couldn't see the ribbon, but I could feel the long tails of it brushing the insides of my elbows. I know from her drawing that she tied a decorative bow instead of a practical knot. Nobody in the novels I've read ever does that. They don't tie people up for the way it looks.

Then again, the characters getting tied up always struggle against it. They protest. Even if we'd been play-acting that, I'm not sure I could have found the words. I wanted to be there. My breath quickened every time she tugged the ribbon a little tighter. I hope it was as obvious to her as it felt to me.

She moved to the foot of the bed. I lifted my ankle and it was less of an offering and more of a plea. She selected another ribbon, knotted one end around a bedpost and then cradled my ankle in one capable hand. The ribbon looped several times, crisscrossing the slender length of my ankle, and then J pulled it snug against my skin. I sucked in a breath; her small smile spoke volumes. She moved to the other bedpost and I spread my legs to offer her my other ankle.

It sounds backwards to say this might have been the single most erotic moment of my life, given that a while later J fucked me until I whimpered, but the anticipation of those few, deft touches of her fingers interspersed with the whisper of the velvet nearly killed me. To be handled like that, with competence and an almost impossible patience, I didn't even know how much I wanted it.

And then she sat down in her chair and began to draw. The actual drawing is quick and spare, revealing that J's patience and concentration are not so glacial and infinite as she implies. But it felt like I lay there for hours, trying desperately not to squirm. I thought she was capturing every wrinkle in the sheets and every last quivering tendon in my arms. It was marvelous. I will shiver at the sound of charcoal on paper for the rest of my life. I can't write any more about it; I am too discomposed.

She did say something I think I ought to write down, though. It was before we started. She sat in that little wooden desk chair—every chair looks little when J spreads her thighs so deliciously improperly—and stared at me so hard I couldn't move.

"This can only happen if it's a game," she said.

She unfolded the paper packet of ribbons, set it on her thigh, and removed one of blue-grey velvet. Most of it lay coiled among the others, but she pulled its long tail free and ran her fingers over it. "I don't want to be a person who ties you up to stop you from going somewhere or doing something in real life, do you understand? I hate the idea."

"But you do want to be a person who ties me up?" I asked, full of hope.

"If you want that, then yes, I want it, too. But only if we're playing."

"You don't want to do this if you're angry with me," I said. "In that case, I will do my utmost not to upset you."

J's mouth drew to one side. I don't think either of us believes that this state of affairs—me not upsetting her—can last, but she took full advantage of it this afternoon and I'm grateful for it. More than that, as I think over this brief moment of conversation, I believe J inadvertently revealed to me that she enjoyed our time in the studio. In her note, she told me she didn't sanction my studies, but she wasn't angry with me at the end of this afternoon. She said herself that she wouldn't have used the ribbons if that were the case.

J likes working with me. That thought discomposes me almost as much as the sex.

JULIEN MORÈRE TO CAMILLE DUPIN, FEBRUARY 10, 1824
POSTMARKED PARIS

My dear Camille,

Your return to Paris is a welcome change. I enjoy your letters, but am eager for your company. I'd love to introduce you to my friend Victor if you're available. You choose the café.

Your friend,
Julien

PRIVATE DIARY OF V BEAUCHÊNE, FEBRUARY 11, 1824

Had J not recently tied me up, produced an erotic sketch of me naked, and then fucked me vigorously, I do believe I would be jealous of Camille Dupin. The three of us went to a café together today. J is obviously on intimate terms with France's beloved androgynous literary genius. Apparently the two of them keep up a robust correspondence about art or something. I felt out of my depth in our conversation even though I have listened to J and J's boring art school friends <u>several</u> times.

Camille wears trousers, even in public, but keeps her hair in one of those architectural styles with buns and cascading curls and which I am so, so relieved to be free of. Hair like that requires a servant, but Camille is rich. She earns money from her writing and is also the great-granddaughter of some foreign noble whose name I didn't retain.

It's good to be highborn and rich and famous. You can walk into a café dressed however you like. I don't think J and I would be afforded this same courtesy if we didn't adhere strictly to masculine standards of dress. (And J's hair is already longer than is fashionable even among eccentric artists.)

Reading over this, it sounds as if I resent Camille. I don't wish to. She's lovely. In fact, any time the conversation strayed too far into aesthetic philosophy, she changed the subject to include me. I feel obliged to note her warmth and attention in the interest of equilibrium. She's much more interesting than J's other friends, I should note that too.

And I am always glad to meet someone else with whom I feel at ease. I didn't explain myself to Camille, but she knows the truth about J (except for the magic, I suppose) and has been accepting and discreet.

She flirted with me a little. Obviously I flirted in return. Another mark in her favor.

Rumor has it that Camille has many lovers. I can't work out if J is among them. Would it be my affair if J were Camille's lover? It's titillating to contemplate, even if I do feel foolish and naïve being ranked against a famous novelist. J finds Camille's intellectual pursuits admirable and unobjectionable, no doubt.

I'll have to work out how I feel about her, since we are likely to meet again. And I'll have to work to convince J that I am, and always will be, worth the trouble.

FEBRUARY 11, 1824

Julie didn't know what to expect from Victor. They'd made a sort of peace. Since the hazy late afternoon with the ribbons, she'd hummed with desire to draw that scene again. Preferably from life, if Victor would let her. Foolish, to feel shy about proposing it when she wouldn't feel shy at all once they'd begun the game. Her hard-won confidence in her art didn't transfer to every arena—yet.

There was no need to propose anything. After dinner, Victor slipped into her room and said, all in one breath without greeting or preamble, "You always make drawings for me and I feel terrible that I can't return the favor, except perhaps I can. I think I've come up with something I could do for you."

Julie raised her brows.

"Remember what you said about the ribbons—that we could only do it if we were playing? I want to do more of that. And you know those... novels."

"Your collection of obscenities, yes, you've mentioned." Julie had catalogued every single time the topic had come up in conversation as though someone were going to test her on it one day.

"Uh, well, technically it's Aunt S's collection of obscenities, but let's not talk about that. I was thinking I could tell you a story. I do that for myself sometimes. If I'm not looking at a picture or reading, that is. I imagine things. I know it's not as good as drawing it or writing—"

"I would like that very much," Julie said. She stepped closer and took hold of their cravat. "Can I undress you while you tell me the story?"

"Yes." Victor's breath caught. "I wasn't sure you were going to say yes."

"Why wouldn't I want to hear what you think about when you touch yourself?" Julie asked. She unwound the cravat and draped it over the back of her chair. Then she set to work pushing the sleeves of their frock coat down their arms. "Please begin."

"I will, I just don't know which one to choose. I tell myself a lot of stories."

"We can do this as many times as necessary, Scheherazade." Julie divested Victor of their frock coat, hung it on the chair, unbuttoned the fall of Victor's trousers and went to her knees to deal with their shoes.

Victor preferred a tighter, more fashionable trouser that had straps under the arches of the feet to preserve the fit and display the line of their leg, so their trousers and shoes had to be removed in succession. Soon they stood in their shirt and stocking feet, very fetching. Half-dressed was almost better than naked. A person might be unclothed in a painting—acceptably, classically nude, maybe with a carefully placed bit of drapery—but never half-dressed. Victor lifted their arms, allowing her to pull the shirt over their head.

Inspired, Julie discarded her own shirt and the linen she'd been wearing beneath. She heard a tiny intake of breath from Victor and smiled.

"Do you like them?" she asked, cupping her breasts. Tender with new growth, they overflowed her hands. She could have kept them smaller and more discreet, but she hadn't. The current fashion in suits prized a narrow waist and a puffed, rounded chest, so hiding them wasn't so difficult, but that convenience hadn't mattered. She'd wanted this and she'd given herself the gift. It was that simple.

Since Victor had seen her every day recently, the difference shouldn't have been noticeable, but they stared like it was a gift for them, too. Victor reached forward.

Julie caught their hand in her own. "I was promised a story."

"You were. Right. Here's a story. I'm Victorine in this one and it's during the brief period my parents sent me to convent school."

"Convent school," Julie repeated.

"Don't worry, in reality I came home at Christmas after my first few months there and cried in front of my mother, then marched into my father's study completely dry-eyed and told him that all the girls at school were insufferably middle class and provincial. Both my parents agreed I simply couldn't go back. I did the rest of my education, paltry as it was, with a private tutor. Anyway, this is a work of fiction. You know I'm not Victorine."

"I don't want you to tell me a sad story," Julie said. She pushed Victor to sit on the bed and then joined them and took their foot into her lap so she could gently unclasp their garter and roll their silk stocking over their calf.

"You're still worried about young Victorine, I see. Well,

she's in a worrisome state. There's this other girl at the school, and her name is Julie."

"*I'm* at the convent school? I'm willing to be a girl for your story, but my radical parents—one of whom is Jewish —*sent me to convent school?*"

"Shh. I'm not a girl, either. This Julie isn't you. She's just a girl with your name and your face and your personality and your beautiful, perfect breasts," Victor said, tracing a line between them.

Julie hummed in permission and encouragement. Victor's fingers curved under one breast and then the other. She picked up their other foot and worked their stocking over their calf, down to their ankle, and off their foot. When they were naked at last, she pushed them flat to their back and loomed over them, her arms straight and the fullness of her breasts directly over Victor's face. It ached, this position, but she could hold it. Victor continued to touch her lightly, as though they knew more would hurt.

"Even under our ugly, boring school dresses, I— Victorine—have noticed Julie's breasts. Every time we're in the same room, I look. I can't stop looking. At first I tell myself I'm only curious because they're so much bigger than mine, and I'm wondering what it would be like if mine were that big. And then I tell myself I'm interested because the other glimpses I've had of Julie—we live in the same dormitory, there's no privacy—reveal that her limbs are sculpted and muscular. I've never seen the like. Julie is strong. The convent school won't be able to mold her."

Victor ran their hands down her arms, displayed perfectly by the pose she'd adopted. She couldn't hold it much longer, so once Victor had finished admiring her, she dropped to the mattress beside them. They rolled to their side to face her.

"She looks wild, free, like a girl who's spent a lot of time running around forests or tramping through pastures or maybe even riding horses astride." Victor stroked her shoulder. Their voice dropped into a conspiratorial whisper. "Thinking about her straddling a horse makes me feel funny in a way I don't understand."

"Oh, you don't, is that so," Julie said.

Their eyes sparkled with amusement but they shook their head very solemnly. "My thoughts have never run away like this. I've always been the girl they wanted me to be, you understand—pretty, dutiful, untroubled by opinions and strong feelings, utterly without curiosity. A little posable doll that needed feeding. I have no idea why I'm always staring at Julie. I know it's rude. I've never had any trouble with manners before. It's furiously embarrassing, but it's beyond my control. Her body is so different. Mine has the softness that comes from a life confined to drawing-room indolence—"

Julie had always liked Victor's arms, both the undefined upper portion, which gave under her touch, and the slender forearm, its radius and ulna as obvious as an anatomy lesson. She hadn't expected her fingers stroking from Victor's shoulder to their elbow to interrupt the story. It wasn't as though she'd pinched their nipple. She dragged her fingers over the shallow curvature of their chest.

Victor continued, "But I have a modest, unremarkable bosom—"

"I disagree. I'm remarking on it right now."

"Hush. I only meant it's easy for mine to disappear under layers of clothing, which is true. Whereas her body is so firm, carved with muscle everywhere—except for her lovely, fat breasts. They seem like an indulgence, though I'm not sure for whom. I have the strange, silly thought that hers ought to belong to me, and mine to her. Why else would I find them so distracting? Sometimes at night, I lie in bed and think about it. And since it's strictly for purposes of comparison, I measure my own with my hands."

Victor demonstrated, covering their breasts with both hands. Julie moved her own hand to rest on their belly, which had the same, sweet, undefined give as their upper arm.

"Oh, I—" Victor swallowed.

It amazed Julie that Victor could tell this wicked story so well and yet be driven astray by a single affectionate touch. Fictional, virginal Victorine could never tell her own story, but Victor could, perhaps, embody something of her.

Victor resumed touching Julie, hands encircling her breasts. "I wonder if I could cup them in my hands and still not cover everything. How heavy would they be? They're probably soft... warm... I bet her skin feels like satin. I bet it would feel good to press my whole face in between them."

Julie laughed and combed her fingers through Victor's hair as they bent their head to pepper her breasts with kisses. The two of them shifted so Julie lay on her back and Victor pillowed their head on her chest.

"Around then, or maybe at the moment when I wonder what color her nipples are, and if they make little hard points like mine, I start to realize that my feelings about Julie's tits have nothing to do with envy."

"How observant."

"Hardly. I can't even begin to say what I'm feeling. I think maybe all this time spent making a careful, scientific study of my own breasts in the dark has given me a fever, because I feel hot all over, and I ache, and I can't seem to make it stop. And even in the daylight, when we're supposed to be paying attention in class, I stare at Julie and just the line of her back, her proper posture, makes me feel like I might pass out. My heart races and I feel so restless, I can't sit still in my chair. I get scolded by the teacher."

"You poor thing."

"That's exactly what Julie says to Victorine," Victor said. "But not yet. It goes on for days, this suffering, and I try very hard not to think about Julie's breasts, but it's too late, because now I think about the rest of her and get the same feeling. Every time I think about the intense way she stares at her book and bites her lip when she reads, or the fearless, long stride of her walk, or her strong, graceful fingers holding a piece of charcoal, I get a funny sort of squeezing feeling in my middle, like I want to clench my thighs together, which I have to because there's this—this wetness."

"I gather Victorine hasn't read any forbidden novels. Or tried sticking her fingers between her legs."

"Not a one," Victor said. "And of course not. I'm a good girl—or I used to be. Either way, I'm naïve and I'm going to suffer until someone takes pity on me and helps."

"I see. And has Julie noticed the state you're in?"

"She has. Julie, you see, *is* very observant. And very clever. And she's a very talented artist, so nobody minds if she spends all her free time in the studio where drawing lessons are taught. She's a good girl, too, so nobody checks on her while she's there. One day she tells me she's going to draw my portrait. I was going to say 'invites' but it's not an invitation. It's very firm. I couldn't say no even if I wanted to, which I don't really, except I'm a little bit terrified at the prospect of spending time alone with Julie, because I know how feverish it's going to make me feel. She makes me sit in an armchair to pose, and I keep imagining that I'm going to soak right through all my skirts and leave a wet, sticky spot on the seat, and I'm swimming in all this hot, squirmy shame, but the last thing I want is to leave. She's so beautiful. Even in the old, paint-flecked smock she has on over her dress, she's so beautiful. There's all this afternoon sunlight streaming through the window, making her dark hair glossy. I can't imagine anything better than Julie and I looking at each other for an hour—"

"You're not very imaginative."

"Oh, I'm quite empty-headed. Haven't got a clue. And I'm no good at posing for a portrait. I keep losing the pose and then Julie has to come over and help me find it again. She touches me so carefully and respectfully, adjusting my shoulders and my arms and my hands in my lap, turning my face until the angle is right, and I feel like I'm going to die, so of course I can't hold still. And then we have to do it again. She arranges me just so, and then she walks back to her easel and my gaze just follows her. I don't even realize I'm doing it. I'm hopeless.

"She comes back for a third time and I think she's going to be rough now, angry, but she's got this endless well of patience and she's so slow and gentle about everything and somehow that's worse. I can't string two thoughts together. Everything is suspended, like the flow of time has turned from water to honey. Either Julie is lingering or I've lost my mind.

"It doesn't matter how many layers of modest clothing I have on, because everywhere she touches me, I can feel my skin burn. My face is hot, flushed, and my breasts feel all swollen and my nipples are scraping against the fabric of my clothes, and I can smell her and it's making me dizzy and I can't quite breathe, so I think: it's really going to happen this time, I'm really going to faint."

"And that's when she says 'you poor thing.'"

"Exactly. And I don't understand because I'm worried she's frustrated with me for being such a bad portrait subject, but the next time she grips my chin, instead of turning my head for the pose, she angles it up so she can kiss me. And it's heaven. I've never felt anything so good in my life. I want to drink in the taste of her like she's the cure for everything I've been suffering—except, of course, the kiss fans all the fires."

"Like this?" Julie took Victor by the chin and kissed them deeply. Heaven, exactly as described.

"Just like that. And I moan into her mouth, and I can't even be embarrassed about the sound, because it feels so good. She breaks the kiss, and for a moment I worry I've done something wrong, but then she scoops up my legs, sits down in the armchair, and pulls me into her lap. Before I know it, she's pushing my skirts and petticoats up. She trails her hand up my stockings. Touches my bare thigh. Her hand is hot, but I freeze because I realize she's about to discover the wetness. Then she kisses my mouth again and her fingers just slide right in—"

Julie sat so her back was against the wall, dragged Victor into her lap, and imitated her fictional namesake. In Victor's pause, she said, "Like she's been waiting *forever* to do that."

"Yes," Victor said, breathless. "And when she feels how

wet I am, she groans like it's the most perfect thing she's ever felt, and I understand because her fingers belong there. I've been missing them, aching for them, this whole time. And suddenly instead of being ashamed of how soaking wet I am, I feel good about myself. Proud. Like I did it on purpose. For her."

"Good girl," Julie said, curling her fingers in a way that made Victor gasp. In the beat of silence that followed, she stilled her hand and said, "And then what happens?"

Victor sucked in a breath. "She kisses me and pushes her fingers into me, in and out, and I pant and whimper and make all these helpless, blissful noises, and I keep trying to move against her hand like there's something more I want, even though I don't know what it is. But Julie knows. She just keeps thrusting her fingers into me, and it makes me so wild that in between kisses, I pull apart the tie at her waist that holds the smock closed. I pull at the neckline of her chemise and undo buttons in her dress until I can push everything down her shoulders and kiss the tops of her breasts, which are as satiny and as soft and as warm as I dreamed they would be. Nothing could be better than this, I think, and then she presses her thumb down right on this spot and starts rubbing it in a little circle—"

"Like this?"

"Yes, that's—that's right."

"Keep talking."

"And then, with my face in her breasts and her fingers in my pussy, I tip over an edge I didn't even know existed, and I almost scream with it. I let out this high-pitched sound and she grips the back of my head and pushes me down into her tits to muffle the rest of it, and I come and I come and I come and—"

Julie grabbed Victor's head then and reenacted the end of the story until they were shuddering and clenching down on her fingers. When they'd finished, they lifted their head and said, "And then she told me to get on my knees in front of the chair, and she pulled up her skirts and spread her thighs, and I'll show you what happened after that."

"Victorine couldn't figure out masturbation but she instantly understands cunnilingus?" Julie asked. She was still wearing her trousers, so she set Victor aside to strip them off. Then she lay on her back and opened her legs so Victor could sit between them.

"Oh no," Victor said. "She just stares at first. But Julie pulls her by her hair until she's nose deep in it, and then tells her when she's doing a good job, which Victorine likes *very* much, and that's how they get through it."

Julie took a fistful of hair at the back of Victor's head, pushed them to the apex of her thighs, and said, "Stick your tongue in there. Lap it up like you're thirsty for it. Yes, like that. Good. Oh—yes, good, don't stop."

Victor didn't stop. Julie's orgasm crested, broke, and washed over her.

"Fuck, you're good at that," she said.

"And that," Victor said, "is how Victorine got an education at the convent school."

J MORÈRE TO V BEAUCHÊNE, FEBRUARY 12, 1824
SLIPPED UNDER THE DOOR

[*This letter consists of an erotic illustration.*]

V BEAUCHÊNE TO J MORÈRE, FEBRUARY 12, 1824
SLIPPED UNDER THE DOOR

J—

You are quite competitive. The whole point of me telling that story was that I was offering you something <u>in return</u> for all your previous drawings so that we might reach an equilibrium, but I see now that you must always have the last stroke of the pen. It's an uncivilized quality and I wish I didn't find it so overpoweringly seductive.

The illustration is exquisite.

—V

J MORÈRE TO V BEAUCHÊNE, FEBRUARY 12, 1824
SLIPPED UNDER THE DOOR

V—

If you insist on telling me another story to even the score, I'll suffer through it somehow.

But the drawing was meant in the spirit of cooperation. I think we work best together, don't you?

—J

PRIVATE DIARY OF V BEAUCHÊNE, FEBRUARY 15, 1824

Remarkable how much life improves with J in it. We're spending time together again, in bed and out of it, and I can't recall ever being happier in my life. There is such freedom when we're together. Nobody else has ever known me like J does.

I can't stop thinking about how J was able to change the nature of the painting. I wonder if we could do that to other objects. If J can change their body through the medium of painting, is it possible to transform other things? Could J render dangerous objects inert? It would be of value to acquire some and study them.

Speaking of the acquisition of objects, I never heard back from my father. I don't want to address the problem of my terrible family members; I am as happy not thinking of them as they are not thinking of me. Happier, now that J accepts me again.

But my father killed my mother, accidentally or not, with a cursed artifact. Now my brother has possession of that same object, and there's no telling what he'll do with it—but it won't be good. It's time to take it from him.

JULIEN MORÈRE TO CAMILLE DUPIN, FEBRUARY 21, 1824
POSTMARKED PARIS

My dear Camille,

It's such a pleasure to see you in person. I'm not a conversationalist or a writer like you, so I'm glad you're still willing to see me and read these scribblings. I'm glad of so many things lately. I think I didn't know it was possible to be this happy. Have you ever felt that way?

Sorry. I'm rambling. I know we're meeting at that salon two days hence, but I'm writing to ask if you'd like to visit my studio and see my latest work tomorrow? I'd be honored to show it to you.

Your friend,

Julien

PRIVATE DIARY OF V BEAUCHÊNE, FEBRUARY 21, 1824

Shit, shit, shit, shit, SHIT.

Aunt S heard from Béatrix who heard from a friend that Pierre Faucheux is three days dead.

Horace's manipulations finally killed him.

Is this my fault? I don't care about that. I'm angry, though. Angry I never had the chance to have the kind of father I could mourn, instead of a cowardly, controlling piece of shit whose death is both a relief and a complication to my plans. Angry that Horace couldn't be bothered to send us a note.

Angry enough to do what I should have done already.

PRIVATE DIARY OF V BEAUCHÊNE, FEBRUARY 22, 1824

I forged myself a letter in my father's handwriting, thinking I might need it if I was caught entering my former family home, but in fact I slipped in through the kitchen and no one stopped me. The household staff must not care if Horace gets murdered in his bed—or robbed.

I used to creep through that house in the dead of night all the time. It was the best time to steal Horace's books for school. A victimless crime, since he wasn't reading them. But those nighttime excursions from my bedroom never made the back of my neck prickle the way tonight did.

I didn't want to get caught, and I was halting and holding my breath at every unaccustomed sound, but that wasn't what sent fear sliding over my skin.

Objects like my pen and the Tilleul paintings have a certain presence. It hums in the air around them, inaudible and intangible but undeniably there, and I have learned to sense it now. The whole house was seething with magic.

Horace—or possibly my lying father, may the worms

eat him and shit him out—collected far more than just the ring.

All the wrong people have power in this world. Or maybe it's the power that makes them the wrong people. Either way, I shudder to think what use my brother is making of his wealth, status, and hoard of magical artifacts.

My steps whispered up the stairs and down the hall to Horace's bedroom. I pressed the door handle down silently and then stood on the threshold of a musty, unused room. With the hearth unlit, it was like a tomb in there—but empty.

Horace had moved into our father's bedroom. It's possible he did it while our father was still alive, simply for the spite of it. Regardless, the house belonged to him now.

This time when I stood in the doorway, I took a moment to plug my ears with beeswax. I don't know if Horace's ring works only on the ears or if its influence can penetrate the mind in other ways, but the wax seemed harmless enough. I'd needed my hearing to make it to his bedroom unnoticed, but I hoped not to need it for the theft itself.

Darkness dimmed the imposing size and opulence of the bedroom, flattening its wood paneling, brocade wallpaper, and oil paintings into nothing. The windows were blocked by heavy curtains and the banked fire in the hearth provided hardly any illumination, but I knew by heart that the massive wooden bed was in the center of the room, flanked on either side by a small table. A decoration for symmetry's sake only, as my mother had never slept in this room—she had been so sickly for most of my life that she always needed rest and solitude, which she'd taken in a smaller, separate bedroom adjacent to this one.

Which side of the bed would Horace use? Right, mostly likely. I crept closer, my heart booming in my muted ears, each beat shaking my ribs like the toll of some huge bell. I groped for the edge of the bed, followed it with my hand, feeling the covers wrinkle and rise over Horace's sleeping form. I'd chosen correctly. I was standing next to him.

It was horrible to be without sight or hearing in that moment. As much as I'd like to imagine that my feelings about Horace are only hatred and anger and scorn, he will always be the person who hit me and ripped up my journals when I was a child, and I will always be a little afraid of him. Even when he is asleep and I am awake, even when I know where he is and he does not know where I am, that sharp little shard of powerlessness and fear remains embedded in my heart. I wished for a candle, even though one would have given me away.

I would have liked to feel like a hero in a myth, creeping next to a sleeping beast. I didn't. Perhaps they didn't, either. Perhaps all they knew was terror and urgency. I brought my fingertips to the edge of the bedside table and traced its shape, drawing my hands over every square centimeter with silent lightness. I found a shallow ceramic dish and within it, a ring.

There was no time to be thankful that my letter had worked and Horace wasn't wearing the ring to sleep. The metal band must have clinked against the dish when I touched it. I didn't hear it.

A hand clamped around my right arm.

Horace probably spoke. I don't know. All I know is that I had scooped the ring into my left palm just before I woke him, not even knowing if it was the right ring. Then he groped for it, found nothing, and dug his fingers into my forearm.

I didn't think. If I had, I wouldn't have wanted to touch the vile instrument of my mother's murder, let alone wield it. But Horace jerked my arm. He was going to hit me.

I worked the tip of my left index finger just barely through the band of the ring and said, with no idea how loud my voice was, "Let go of me."

And his grip loosened.

I rubbed my left hand against my thigh in order to push the ring further onto my finger. Once it was seated, I said again, "Let go of me."

He did.

"Forget this. You didn't find me here. You didn't find anyone. You're not awake. Go back to sleep. Don't remember this when you wake up."

I reached for the beeswax in my ears, pinched it to remove it, and stayed just long enough to hear the sound of Horace settling into the sheets and breathing deeply. Then I slipped the ring into my pocket and ran out of the house.

I've been back at the Maison Laval long enough to write this entry. The ring has been sitting on my desk the whole time. I can hardly look at it. I would almost rather have been caught than to have used it.

It would be comforting if there had been some effect—if it really had drained my life, as I lied in my letter to Horace, or if it had made me sick or in some small way uncomfortable. But it didn't. I put on the ring that my father used to kill my mother, that my brother used to kill my father, that I stole from my brother, and it felt good. Powerful. Right.

I wish I'd thrown it into the river.

V BEAUCHÊNE TO J MORÈRE, FEBRUARY 23, 1824
SLIPPED UNDER THE DOOR

J—

This is a strange question, and I know it's late, but do you think you could draw a picture of a weasel for me? It came up in conversation while I was out tonight. I've never seen one in person and I'm seized with curiosity. I assume you, a child of nature, have some expertise in this matter.

—V

J MORÈRE TO V BEAUCHÊNE, FEBRUARY 23, 1824
SLIPPED UNDER THE DOOR

[*This letter includes an illustration of a weasel.*]
You need to go outside more, V. I worry about you.

PRIVATE DIARY OF V BEAUCHÊNE, FEBRUARY 23, 1824

J's weasel illustration is lovely and I want to stare at it and then collapse into bed, but I have to write this down before I forget all the details.

I ran into Savigny at the Comte de Davrance's ball this evening. He was alone. (I would have liked to see his handsome companion Quang again.) It surprised me when Savigny indicated with a nod that he wanted to speak to me, and it surprised me further when he wove through the crowd and slipped into one of the alcoves lining the ballroom.

Long mauve velvet drapes hid the two of us from the dazzling, stifling light and heat. A chill penetrated the panes of glass behind us. The cramped space provided plenty of privacy, but Savigny rested a hand on the door latch as though he meant for us to stand on the balcony in the wet, cold night. His expression was severe. That, too, was chilling.

So I said, "If you wanted me, Savigny, all you had to do was ask. No need to make such a spectacle by hauling me in here—unless that's what you like, of course."

"Is your crudeness a defense or does it bring you pleasure?" he asked.

"Oh, both, I think."

Crisply, he said, "I apologize for bringing you here, though there was no spectacle, as you called it. Our departure wasn't observed, and if you're careful, our return will also go unnoticed. I only wanted privacy. I'll be brief. You have to stop what you're doing."

"And what is it that I'm doing? Being charming? Did I flirt with someone you like?"

"I see patterns," Savigny said.

Even at the time, I recognized that with this non sequitur, he was offering me a secret, but all I said was, "And?"

Savigny's composure slid off his face like the rain down the window. He kept his voice low, but it was obvious he wanted to shout. "And the pattern I'm sensing right now is that you have the intelligence of a shit-splattered cobblestone. Your thefts leave a paper trail, you thick-headed child."

"Everything I've acquired was freely given to me. There's a written record that proves it."

Well. Horace's ring was a theft. But Horace doesn't remember that and Savigny couldn't possibly know about it.

Savigny's face was white against the black of his clothes and his eyepatch. "You tricked Taillefer into giving you that Nicolas Tilleul painting. How many times do you think you can do that before someone notices?"

"None, I suppose, since you already noticed," I said. "Is Taillefer a great friend of yours?"

Savigny is too dignified to roll his eye at me, but not so dignified that his lips didn't twist in disgust when I mentioned friendship with Taillefer. "No. You shouldn't associate with him. He's not a good person."

"But <u>you</u> associate with him," I said. "How else would you know about the painting?"

Savigny said, "Unlike you, I'm good at what I do—and <u>discreet</u>. As a favor to your aunt Sophie, I am telling you to stop this foolishness before it gets you killed."

"Fine. Your warning is delivered. Are we finished?"

"Christ," Savigny said. He pinched the bridge of his nose. "Look. Imagine a forest. There are wolves and bears and other things that kill. But those big, dangerous predators, they each have a territory. They hunt, but they mostly leave each other alone."

"They do?" I have lived in the city my whole pampered life. J's farm was the wilderness to me, and I mostly saw the inside of J's studio. We didn't have time for the forest.

Savigny let a controlled exhale pass through his nostrils. "In this analogy, you are an oblivious little weasel, sticking its nose where it doesn't belong. You don't know who else lives in this forest yet, and I advise you not to find out."

Our language gives weasels and their ilk a bad reputation, but J's illustration shows a sleek little animal with sharp teeth. Belated credit to Savigny for this comparison, which I don't mind at all.

(It's late and granted I am no expert, but I had the impression weasels were reddish brown animals. I notice now that J used a wash of color over their usual black ink, and the particular weasel they've drawn is rather blond. I can't tell if this is an insult or a compliment, or if I'm imagining a portrait where none exists, so I will blame the hour for the ache in my chest.)

"Are you also a weasel?" I asked. "Or are you one of the

bigger, more frightening animals? Do you think we could say what we mean now instead of telling a children's story about forest animals?"

"I am treating you like a child because you are one."

"I think you're upset because I'm very good at taking things from people," I said. "Perhaps I've taken something you wanted, and now we're in competition. We don't have to be. I can't give you the painting because it no longer exists, but we could work together."

"We—what? The painting no longer exists?"

"Yes, that's what I said. I'm not such a useless child after all." I don't know if J's method works on anything other than J's own paintings, but obviously I didn't say that to Savigny. I won't expose J. "You should agree to work with me."

"You're serious."

"Why wouldn't I be serious? I know you used to work with people," I said. "Sophie told me that's how she met Madame de Tourzin. You and your network of spies or whatever you were."

"You've misunderstood my role," Savigny said, ignoring my mention of the past. "I don't collect objects. I make it my business to know where they are. Who's buying and selling. I deal in information."

"You see patterns, right," I said. "Even better. That will help me so much, knowing who owns what and where this stuff comes from. I want to start by cataloguing it all, and then dig into why and how it works—"

"I only ever talked to you to keep you <u>out</u> of this," he said, aggrieved. "For Sophie's sake."

"I love Sophie, but she doesn't tell me what to do. You and Béatrix made your case for ignoring the world around me, and I declined. You cannot change my decision, nor are you responsible for it. Now let's return to our real conversation. Let's work together."

"This is a very dangerous world you're entering, Victor."

"I'm already here. And I'm not going anywhere except back to the ballroom. Think about my offer."

I turned on my heel and left. Now I will wait for Savigny to write to me.

PRIVATE DIARY OF V BEAUCHÊNE, FEBRUARY 24, 1824

[*This page is warped from a spill.*]

I've spilled Aunt S's favorite brandy, but if she asks me why I stole the bottle from her room, I'll have a damn good excuse: Isabelle de Tourzin was sitting on my bed when I returned home this evening.

The door was locked. I'm not convinced she didn't climb in the window.

Dressed in all black, with soot smeared on her face and her hair stuffed under a cap, I might not have recognized her as the elegant woman who hosted me at 9 Rue Branoux. Especially since she'd only lit one candle. White wax crawled down the column of it, and a drop splattered into the candleholder. She'd made herself at home, setting the light on my desk to illuminate Julie's portrait of Alphonse.

She'd removed the sackcloth and propped the painting up, using the wall and the desk as supports. I would have thought her entranced—though the effect of that particular painting is unpleasant—except that she turned toward me as I opened the door and said, "You look like Anaïs."

An opening line calculated to discomfit me. I <u>was</u> uncomfortable, but it was her sudden appearance and her disregard for the power of the painting that unsettled me. Regardless, I didn't want her to know. "Yes, Sophie told me that you'd spent some time with my mother."

"She was a good woman, your mother. I'm sorry you and Sophie lost her. I saw you a few times during my visits, but you never saw me." She turned back toward the portrait, toward the halo of light cast by the candle and the handsome face that seemed to watch us both. "Where did you find this?"

"A shop on the Quai de Voltaire."

"Aveux," she said.

Since she knew the shopkeeper, I suppose there was no harm in telling her where I found the painting, though I regretted giving up the information so easily. I should have made her bargain for it. My only excuse is my nerves.

"Some paintings have the power to lull their viewers into a state of contentment," she said. "Not this one."

Just like Savigny, Isabelle de Tourzin knows about the Tilleul paintings—or at least, paintings like them. I think J would hate knowing that. I said, "It's a warning. Do you know that man?"

"Do you?" she asked.

"Only by reputation." I eyed the portrait. Alphonse's painted face was making me almost as nervous as Isabelle de Tourzin's presence.

"He's not a friend, then," she said.

"No. Is he a friend of yours?" I asked.

"No. I'm looking for him. He stole something from me," she said. "Savigny told me you want to work together."

She knows about Alphonse. She <u>knows</u> Alphonse. "You and Savigny do keep in touch."

"Savigny won't help you unless I tell him it doesn't bother me. He's careful." Her dark eyes cut toward me. "You could use a little of that."

"What are you going to tell him?" I asked. "Does it bother you?"

"Everything bothers me," she said. "But if you're determined to participate—Savigny says you are—then we might as well be useful to each other."

"To lessen my chances of getting myself killed?"

"It is not possible for me to make that promise," she said. "As I said, I'm looking for that man. He's dangerous. I intend to stop him. I believe your brother, or someone in your brother's circle—Taillefer or Bertin, perhaps—may be one of his connections in Paris. I need someone who can join their little collectors' club."

"Did Sophie not explain to you that I've been disinherited? My brother hates me," I said. "But I'll help. However I can, I'll help."

"You haven't even heard what's in it for you."

"Yes, I have," I said. I didn't think Mme de T would appreciate hearing how much I love J and would do anything to keep them safe and make them happy, including murdering the man who abused them with my bare hands. So I didn't say that. "But please keep going."

"If you want to write a catalogue of objects, I can provide you with a starting point."

"Are you offering me access to your collection?"

"I am," she said. "If you use any of it to cause harm, I'll kill you. I have no desire to, but I will. Don't make me."

"You're very direct," I said, thinking of Savigny's forest animals. I decided to be direct, too. "Why do you own a collection of dangerous objects if you don't use them to cause harm?"

She showed me her teeth. "I never said that."

Mme de Tourzin left through the window. It was the least shocking part of our exchange.

V BEAUCHÊNE TO J MORÈRE, FEBRUARY 24, 1824
SLIPPED UNDER THE DOOR

J—

If you're awake and you see this note and you wouldn't mind letting me in, I'd like to see you.

—V

FEBRUARY 24, 1824

Victor stood in the hallway in their dressing gown, even paler than usual but with two bright spots of color in their cheeks. Scarlet red, maybe just a dab of gamboge yellow. They entered as soon as Julie stepped aside. She caught the faint scent of brandy as they passed.

"I had a little sip and I spilled some," Victor said. "I'm not drunk."

"Is something wrong?" Julie asked.

"I can't sleep. Can I tell you another story?" Victor sat on her bed and their dressing gown revealed the nearly transparent white linen of their nightshirt. It was far finer than Julie's.

She took their hand and drew it into her lap. "Only if you tell me what's keeping you from sleeping."

"Nothing's wrong. I'm in an excitable condition, that's all. Someone made me an offer of employment, I think."

"You think?"

"We didn't discuss the details," Victor said.

"Is this legitimate employment?"

"I don't want to distress you."

"So no, then," Julie said. "Relax, I'm not going to start a fight in the middle of the night. Given my choices, I'd rather that you tell me the truth, even about things you think I won't like. If you came for a distraction, let's do that. Is this story about the convent school?"

"No," they said. "But you can rest assured that Victorine and Julie escaped from the school and went to live in a little house in the countryside. They support themselves by writing and illustrating obscene books together and are living happily ever after."

"I never doubted it," Julie said. "So who are you in this one? Innocent school girl again?"

"Oh, I'm myself, more or less. More of a man than a woman, but beyond either category. And I'm a bit more repressed, I suppose. Innocent's not a bad word for it."

"It's hard to imagine you *less* repressed," Julie said. "But you're not really yourself in these stories. You arranged the last one so I had all the power, even when it meant imagining yourself far more naive and less clever than you are in real life. Less of a shameless flirt, too."

"When you are telling the story, you can write yourself the cleverest, most brazen, most wanton version of me you like," Victor said archly. They drew their dressing gown closed. "But I am telling this one, and our poor, inexperienced protagonist is full of pent-up longing. Also, they have a cock."

"I can't wait to hear about it."

"Good. This one happens at a party. Elegance. Opulence. All that. I meet a handsome stranger there."

"Is it me?" Julie teased.

"As it so happens, the stranger's name is... Julien."

"And what do they look like, this Julien?"

"It varies from one telling to another. Do you want them to look a particular way?

"No, you choose."

"Julien is taller than me, and has long, dark hair in a braid that hangs over their shoulder. There's something about that kind of eccentricity of style that I find very attractive." Victor tugged a lock of Julie's hair, which wasn't long enough to be braided or to hang over her shoulder, but which certainly qualified as an eccentricity. Too short to be feminine, too long to be masculine. "It's bold. Like their gaze. And they have very powerful eyebrows, of course."

Julie laughed. "Of course."

"It was rude of me to sneak a glance at their legs, but they're long and shapely. Their thighs are muscular. It's a wonder their trousers haven't split at the seams. I meet plenty of beautiful people at these parties, but none of them have ever been so alluring—"

"Do you go to lots of parties, you poor, shy, repressed thing?"

"The success of my bank depends on rich people knowing and trusting me enough to invest their fortunes, so I'm always attending their events, which are so proper it's stifling. I'm not happy, but I'm good at what I do, and I've learned to suppress my yearning for something else. That's why it's so troublesome that I feel a spark of attraction when Julien shakes my hand. I can't ignore it."

"They have a firm grip, this Julien." Victor's hand was still in her lap, so she pressed it between both of hers.

"You're joking, but it's a startlingly erotic handshake. They don't grab me or drag me or crush my hand in theirs, but I can tell their hand is warm even through our gloves, and they look right into my eyes like they know all my secrets. A shiver runs through me. I feel like I should be bowing or down on my knees instead of shaking hands.

"Julien doesn't say anything, but there's an offer in the way their hand holds mine. I could resist that gentle pull. They exert just enough strength to let me know what they want, but not enough to force me. It might seem like an accident to anyone watching, the fact that we end up closer together than we should be. But I go willingly. My eyes are level with the clean line of their jaw, where there's just a sliver of bare skin before their cravat covers the rest of their neck. The thick length of their braid is fragrant with some kind of perfume, and I can smell the scent of their soap and underneath that, their body. My cock fattens in my trousers. I'm sure Julien knows. I have to step away quickly."

"You're easily discomposed," Julie said.

"When it comes to you, yes, I am." Victor paused, distracted by the interruption. "Sorry, I suppose these stories spend a lot of time on why some version of me is so attracted to some version of you, and not very much on why you might be interested in me."

"I don't need help imagining that," Julie said, taking Victor's chin in her hand so they couldn't avoid her gaze. Her fictional counterpart always did a lot of staring in the stories. The real Victor probably didn't find it as unbearably arousing, but it couldn't hurt to try.

She pushed Victor's shoulders, guiding them gently down to the mattress, then lay on top of them. Both dressing gowns had fallen open in the shuffle, so there were only two thin layers of fabric separating them. "Let's get back to Julien's remarkable handshake prowess and how horny it makes you. Tell me what happens next."

"I'm trying not to think about what passed between us, telling myself it won't happen again. Julien is the host of this party, so they'll likely be at the head of the table, nowhere near me. And there's no way they could say anything suggestive without calling attention to themself. I'll be able to control myself and dinner will continue as usual and then perhaps when the party ends and I'm alone at home, I'll allow myself to think about them. A poor consolation, but much safer than indulging myself at this public event. The things I want... well, my desires quickly get out of hand. I can't think about that. A scandal could ruin my career."

"Your career that you hate," Julie said. She'd enjoyed participating in the last story, and she trusted Victor to make it clear if her additions were unwanted. "And this party isn't like those parties. So Julien gestures for you to sit right next to them."

"They do. It would be rude to say no. And I don't want to, even though a thrill of fear runs through me at the thought of what I've agreed to by sitting here. No one seems to notice when they put their chair far too close to mine. No one except me. Julien doesn't touch me, but I can feel the heat of their body. My pulse races like they can see every filthy thought in my head. The conversation goes on around us, with everyone else unaware. Julien maintains their composure and even contributes a remark every now and then. I, on the contrary, am struggling. Every time I stammer something halfway coherent—not insightful and nowhere near witty, you understand, just a remark that proves I am paying attention—Julien's arm brushes mine, or their leg presses against mine, or their ankle hooks over mine. They slide their fingers idly up and down the stem of their wineglass, and it drives me to madness. But every time I think I simply can't take any more of this, Julien stops. I catch my breath, and the moment of peace stretches into dullness and then absence and agony, and I feel completely unhinged because all I want is more. The only thing worse than Julien touching me is Julien not touching me."

"How am I so good at this? Am I omniscient or are you giving everything away by blushing and fidgeting?"

"Yes," Victor said instantly. "Both."

Julie reached between their bodies and shoved the hem of Victor's nightshirt up their thighs, making sure to drag her fingertips along their hot, bare skin. She stopped when she felt the first brush of wiry curls. "So even though the table is covering your lap and I've barely touched you, I can tell you're hard in those fashionably tight trousers you prefer."

"It's damned uncomfortable," Victor agreed. "I'm cursing you and my tailor. I'm mortified—or I should be—and I don't want to make a mess of myself in public, but I'm also so desperately aroused that I can't care. I love it. When you put your hand under the table in an act of brazen rudeness, no one glares or goes wide-eyed. This is your home, and people seem to expect you to act like some sort of debauched king. The rules don't apply to you. They still apply to me, though, and I know that if I gasp at the warmth of your broad hand on my thigh, everyone will turn toward us."

"You'd better keep quiet, then. And you'd better stay quiet while I make a slow, leisurely exploration of your balls and the shaft and head of your cock, which is drooling and has soaked right through your trousers. You've never been this hard. It's huge and heavy and aching. It strains at the fabric and there's no way to hide it. If you stood up right now, everyone would see."

Julie stroked her fingers along the swollen flesh between Victor's thighs. They closed their eyes and shivered.

Voice unsteady, Victor said, "I want you to keep touching me, even though I know I might come. I think I would do anything you asked as long as you keep stroking me through the fabric with one hand and gesturing through your dinner conversation with the other."

"Oh, are we still having dinner?"

"It's the dessert course by now, I think."

"A shame to waste that. You have two hands free. I think you should eat your dessert. It's one of those oblong choux pastries filled with cream."

"Julie," Victor groaned.

"Julien," she corrected. "Pick up your cutlery in your trembling hands and try not to squirt cream everywhere while you eat it, and I will keep touching you."

"I regret allowing you to tell this story with me, you wicked creature."

"No, you don't," she said. "And just think, I could have asked you to drop to your knees, crawl under the table, and get me off with your mouth. Would you have said yes to that?"

"Yes, if you asked." Victor shuddered.

Julie rewarded them with a few slow strokes of her fingers. "What a marvelous little slut you are. I love that you said yes. But that would be unkind of me—these other guests at this party, you don't want them to watch, do you?"

"No."

"If you did, I would already have stripped you naked

and fucked you in front of them," Julie said. "But it's the thrill of *almost*, isn't it? You want a near miss. You want me to wind you up in public and wreck you in private, and I am going to give you what you want. Be good and eat your pastry."

"I eat the pastry slowly and carefully, licking my fork clean after each bite. I know you'll kiss the sweetness out of my mouth later, if I do this right. It's torture, feeling the friction of your hand, trying not to come and trying not to send cream spurting across my plate. I don't quite manage the latter, and you swipe your finger through the smear and hold it up to my lips. My whole body is flushed with heat. You want me to lean forward and suck your finger clean in front of all these people. I want it and don't want it. It doesn't make sense, the way I feel, but I don't have to understand it, because you're giving me what I need. I'll feel the lovely shiver of humiliation no matter what I do, whether I rise to your challenge or not. When I wrap my lips around your finger, I don't do it because you'll be proud of me or because you'll reward me—though I hope you will—but just because it's my mouth and your finger, and I want you inside me, and that's the most powerful feeling I know."

"God, you're perfect," Julie said. "I dismiss everyone from the room with a wave of my hand, and you think for a split second that I'm dismissing you, too, that I might be so cruel as to make you walk out of here with your cock as stiff as a tree trunk and no relief. When I feel you twitch, my grip on your thigh tightens, and you stay where you are. With only a look, I make it clear that we're not leaving this room until you get what you need. It takes a long time for everyone to file out of the room, and you have to bite back whimpers while I fondle you, but when we're alone at last, I stand up from my chair, clear a space on the table by sweeping the plates aside, and tell you to bend over."

There was no massive oak table in Julie's room, so she lifted herself and pulled at Victor's hips until they rolled onto their stomach. She stripped Victor of their dressing gown and pushed the hem of their nightshirt to their waist, exposing them.

Victor said, "My first glimpse of the bulge in your trousers makes me blush like a virgin, which I am, more or less. No one has ever made me feel like this. I put my palms flat on the table and lean forward, and then you make a small, amused sound and push me onto my forearms. The new, lower position makes me more vulnerable, but the thunder of my pulse doesn't have much to do with fear. If it did, you leaning forward and dropping a kiss my cheek would calm it. The tail of your braid swings in my peripheral vision as you stand.

"You run a hand possessively down my back, and then you unbutton my trousers and shove them down my thighs. The air chills my skin, but then your hand curves around my backside, kneading one cheek and then the other. You reach around and skim your fingers through the wetness that coats my cock. There's so much. The person I was a few hours ago, they might have been embarrassed by how much—how needy I am, how badly I want this—but I don't have room in my head for that. Your hands are on me. That's all I care about."

It was almost like being instructed, except Julie didn't feel as though she'd given up any control. She had an inkling of where the story was going. Pleased and relieved that she'd begun to keep a bottle of oil next to her bed, she retrieved it along with another implement. She poured some oil into her hands.

"Then you run one slick finger down the cleft of my ass and circle the rim of my hole. It feels so good. I gasp. You slide your finger in, and it's smooth and wet just from how wet I am, and I shudder and press back into your touch. I think you could fuck me right now, and I want you to, but nobody rushes you, least of all me. You've been taking your time all night and you intend to continue. You finger me open slowly. You don't care that my cock is dripping on your fine table linens, or that I'm almost sobbing with how much I need to come."

"Oh, I do care," Julie said. "Not about the table linens, but about you. You're so beautiful. You've been waiting a long time, and you did everything I asked of you, and I'm so pleased. I bend down and kiss you deeply, tasting traces of sugar and cream on your tongue, and you lean into it, but we both know it's not tender kisses you're begging for. I like to see you desperate. I'd like to see you squirm on my cock even more. I spread you open, line myself up, and press the head against your hole."

"It's... wood," Victor said.

Julie worried she'd ruined the moment, that they wouldn't like this, that it didn't suit the story they were telling.

And then Victor said, "This was the bulge in your pocket. My God, you'll never get tired. You could pin me down and fuck me for hours."

"I could," Julie agreed. "I push inside you in one long thrust."

"Oh, God, that feels—" Victor didn't have the breath to finish.

She kissed them for it. "Good, yes, that's exactly what you say. And I stroke your back while you adjust to the feel of me inside you, stretching you open, and then I grip your hips to hold you still while I fuck you."

Julie didn't have trouble composing that part of the story, since it was just a slight variation on what she was doing with her hands. It would be nice to have a harness for the toy, to use her body to thrust, but there was an intimacy to using her hands, too. Victor was tight around the dildo, gorgeous, and didn't fill the silence with anything but wordless moans.

"If I were truly cruel, I'd make you finish the story," Julie said. Slowing her pace, she asked, "Do you want me to be cruel, Victor?"

"Julie—sorry, Julien fucks me so hard I can't see straight, and it's—uh—perfect, and I love it, but I, I mean, they, oh fuck *please* touch me, I need it."

"Good," Julie said, and reached around to cup them between their legs. Victor rubbed their cock against her fingers, grinding hard. She could feel their pulse throbbing in her hand. Julie leaned down, bit them on the earlobe, and said, "You come so hard you scream. It's loud and messy. You soak my hand and splatter the table and I've never seen anything more beautiful in my life."

She thrust once more and Victor cried out and did exactly as told.

When their breath evened out, she withdrew the toy and set it aside. Victor rolled to their knees and crawled between her legs, covering her thighs with sloppy, grateful kisses and then sliding their tongue along her sensitized flesh. It took nothing—a few quick circles of the tip of their tongue—to bring her to the edge.

Her own orgasm was quieter, but no less spectacular than Victor's. It was shattering, a burst so intense she saw white, and it subsided slowly and pleasurably in waves.

She and Victor lay next to each other, sticky and sated, and smiled.

Whatever had made Victor come in search of a distraction, she couldn't be upset about it. They'd been honest with her about the path they were pursuing. It wouldn't be free of risks, but nothing was.

She could accept it, she thought. Victor was worth it.

V BEAUCHÊNE TO J MORÈRE, FEBRUARY 25, 1824
SLIPPED UNDER THE DOOR

J—

You missed dinner and were gone all day and are, I assume, channeling your genius onto a canvas. I miss you, as you can tell from this pathetic little note. For so many reasons, I have not been able to stop thinking about the implement you used yesterday, but I am on fire with curiosity about one reason in particular: did you make it?

—V

J MORÈRE TO V BEAUCHÊNE, FEBRUARY 25, 1824
SLIPPED UNDER THE DOOR

V—

I bought it from a shop—you can buy anything in Paris—and then adjusted it to suit myself. Why? Do you want one?

—J

V BEAUCHÊNE TO J MORÈRE, FEBRUARY 25, 1824
SLIPPED UNDER THE DOOR

J—

Are you telling me it's one of your self-portraits? I didn't know you were a sculptor as well as a painter. You have so many talents.

How will I ever be satisfied with one from a shop now?

—V

J MORÈRE TO V BEAUCHÊNE, FEBRUARY 26, 1824

LEFT ON THE DESK UNDER A PARTICULAR PAPERWEIGHT

V—

Yes, it's a self-portrait. I didn't carve the wood, but I suppose I did sculpt it, much the same way I sculpt myself. I'm Pygmalion and the statue. I can always make another —in any medium—so this one can be yours.

Sorry for using your room key while you were out, but this gift doesn't fit under the door and it seemed indiscreet to leave it in the hall.

—J

PRIVATE DIARY OF V BEAUCHÊNE, FEBRUARY 26, 1824

J's absence doesn't make me happy, but I'm relieved they weren't in my room when I found their gift. Even in solitude, it is embarrassing to melt with tenderness when a person leaves a wooden dildo on your desk. Nothing could make me blush except the ridiculous—adorable—floppy velvet bow tied around the base of the wood. I held that wooden cock and gazed at it like it was a posy of flowers. (I would much rather have a dildo—this one in particular.) I only started laughing after it was cradled in my hands. An absurd moment. J gives the best presents. Filthy, but personal. I'm still giddy.

How would I know if I was in love with J?

I cannot imagine that it would feel any different from this.

PRIVATE DIARY OF V BEAUCHÊNE, FEBRUARY 26, 1824

I must be in love because it's the only explanation for not seeing this earlier:

1. J can transform material objects with magic. Proof: the dildo.
2. J can nullify cursed artifacts. Proof: <u>Landscape with Ruins</u>.
3. Therefore <u>J CAN NULLIFY THE RING.</u>

This is far preferable to throwing it into the river where anyone might fish it out and use it.

V BEAUCHÊNE TO J MORÈRE, FEBRUARY 26, 1824
SLIPPED UNDER THE DOOR

J—

Anything I write here will seem silly or insincere, and that is not the tone I wish to adopt in speaking of your gift. For now I will merely say thank you. I'll treasure it.

I know you have been very busy lately, and I know you don't want to be involved in the sorts of affairs I'm involved in, and I do respect that, but I also have a project I'd like to discuss with you when you have time. Your involvement would be limited. It's presumptuous to say this, but I think you'd enjoy it.

But even if you don't want any part of that, I want to see you. I miss you. These notes are good, but they're not enough.

—V

J MORÈRE TO V BEAUCHÊNE, FEBRUARY 27, 1824
SLIPPED UNDER THE DOOR

V—

I've never written this to anybody before, but I mean it with love: go fuck yourself. Frequently and enthusiastically.

I will think about whether I want to hear this proposal of yours.

As for missing me, you remember we're having dinner with Camille this evening, right?

—J

CAMILLE DUPIN TO JULIEN MORÈRE, FEBRUARY 27, 1824
NOT POSTMARKED

Dear Julien (Julie?),

I'm leaving one copy of this letter with you and keeping one copy for myself. This written account is as much to convince myself that what I saw really happened as it is to provide you with reliable testimony. You were, of course, present this evening, and it is my hope that you will not need my version of events because you will remember your own. As you are unconscious and I still fear for your life, I am exercising caution.

Tonight I wouldn't be able to sleep even in the softest of featherbeds, so this uncomfortable chair in this cramped little room at the Maison Laval will certainly not permit it. I may as well calm myself by writing. (Don't read this and mutter to yourself that I should have lain down in bed. You are badly wounded, or you were, and I fear to disturb you. I wanted to take you to my townhouse, but it is too dangerous to move you at the moment. Honestly, Julien, if I'd known the conditions of the Maison Laval, I would have invited you to share my home long ago. As friends, of course—I know you're in love with Victor, though you've never said it. My point is that there's no need for this meager living; comfort will not prevent you from making good art.)

Look at me, avoiding the task at hand. I intend to write down what happened this evening, but I can hardly bear to think of it. Yet it's also true that I can think of nothing else. The mind is a contradictory thing.

Here it is in its barest form:

We were returning from dinner just after ten o'clock. As it was raining, I offered to return you and Victor to the Maison Laval in my coach, and you accepted. We were having such a lively conversation that when the coach stopped in the street, I exited with the two of you, intending to walk you to your door and perhaps conclude our debate about the lost work of Master Frenhofer in the next few steps. Naturally, we didn't finish, and both you and Victor invited me for one last drink. All three of us had drunk some wine, but at least in my case, not enough to impair my comprehension. I won't speak for you and Victor. The two of you agreed that Victor's room was a better place to congregate. I assume this is because you live in artistic chaos.

The main door to the Maison Laval was shut but unlocked. Both of you remarked on this, as Madame Laval usually locks it at ten o'clock and you were expecting to enter by subterfuge. I had already been warned to be quiet, as guests are not allowed at night. Victor lives on the ground floor, so it wouldn't require too much stealth to get from the dark, silent foyer to his room.

The door to Victor's room was also shut but unlocked. A gold line of candlelight lit the gap beneath it.

"Shit," Victor whispered. He addressed the two of us. "Get out of here. Right now."

I said I was only recounting the barest facts of this evening, but I can't stop myself from speculating about this moment. I couldn't see Victor's face, but I would swear from the tone of his voice that he <u>expected</u> a visitor.

"Absolutely not," you said.

I could have run then, out the door and back to the safety of my waiting coach. But I didn't believe myself in any danger.

Victor pushed the door and stepped over the threshold. Inside the room was a man in a black greatcoat with a hat shadowing his features. He was taller than Victor and perhaps a little taller than me, but not your height. Broad through the shoulders. Blond sideburns. Anger reddened his pale face. Between his hands, he'd wrenched open a book. There were more books on the floor, spines cracked and pages wrinkled. Every drawer in the desk was open. The ripped mattress sat askew on the bedframe, straw spilling through the gash.

"Horace?" Victor said. If Victor had expected a visitor, it was not this one.

"You son of a bitch," said Horace. He hurled the book to the floor and rounded on Victor. "Where is it?"

"Where is what?"

"The ring," Horace roared.

"What ring?"

"Father's ring. I know you stole it. I don't know how, but I know it was you. I know about the money, too, you conniving piece of shit. Father told me."

"I haven't spoken to Father in months. You'll recall that he disowned me. I didn't even learn of his death until three days after it happened," Victor said. I remember thinking how remarkably calm he was, faced with the wreckage of his belongings and his large, angry brother.

"This is my room and you are here uninvited. Leave. Now."

"Or you'll hex me again? Is that your threat, you cursed lying piece of shit?" Horace reached into the folds of his greatcoat and retrieved a long, thin knife with a white handle. I have combed through my memory for further details, but there are none. He brandished the blade. "Give it to me."

"I can't very well give you something I don't have," Victor said. "I don't know what you're talking about."

"Liar," Horace shouted. "I'll kill you."

He charged at Victor. I recall the blade gleaming white even in the yellow candlelight. As in a dream, I saw only one thing. I didn't see you step in front of Victor. I can't say if Victor dodged or if you shoved him out of the way. All I know is that when the knife completed its journey, its hilt protruded from your belly.

Horace yanked it out.

You screamed. Blood spattered the floor. You swayed on your feet and Victor caught you as best he could. Horace attacked Victor next. I don't know if he wounded Victor. Certainly it sounded that way from the long, low moan Victor let out. I was grabbing him from behind, trying in vain to pull him away from his brother without hurting you.

You and Victor dropped to the floor with a thud. Horace rounded on me and I jumped away.

Knife in hand—this detail seems impossible but I swear the blade was clean—Horace charged the door. I chased after him. Possessed with fury, I hurled myself at his back and knocked him down. He bucked me off and I hit my head on the floorboards. I tackled him again.

On the floor with Horace, my mind at last arrived in

the moment. I am not small or weak, but neither am I trained in fighting. I couldn't incapacitate him. What I hoped to accomplish by tackling a large, armed man, I can't say, and it doesn't matter because I couldn't maintain the upper hand for long. He threw me off and loped toward the door, his footsteps rattling the house. A resident of the boarding house darted out of the shadows in the foyer to accost him, but Horace brandished the knife and ran. He left the door hanging open to the rainy night.

I was still on the floor to catch my breath, though I was leaning against the wall rather than prostrate. The resident came to stand over me. Wearing a long white nightshirt and, incongruously, the blue jacket with brass buttons that is the uniform of the police, the resident offered me a hand.

"Forestier, police officer."

"Camille Dupin, novelist."

His eyes widened, but he didn't stare at my long hair, now in disarray, or my trousers. He also didn't stop me from pushing myself up and forcing myself to Victor's room to see if you and Victor were alive. "Are you all right?"

Victor's coat was torn in slashes, but there was no blood. He was white with shock and covered in a sheen of sweat, but he appeared unhurt. He said, "Camille, will you please stay with Julien while I fetch the doctor I know? May I take your coach?"

"Are you sure you don't want to stay? I could go," I said.

"No, it has to be me," Victor said. "Help me move Julien to the bed."

"Excuse me," said Forestier. "Can you tell me what

happened here, Madem—Monsieur Dupin? Or you, Monsieur Beauchêne?"

I didn't correct his form of address for me. It didn't seem the time. I shifted Victor's mattress, patting its straw back inside as best I could and rearranging the sheets to cover the rips, and said, "I was accompanying my friends Victor and Julien home this evening when we came upon that man. He had entered this room and destroyed it. Victor attempted to speak with him. He was armed with a knife and he attacked Victor, but Julien stepped in and took the blow."

Forestier helped Victor and I lift your body to the bed. You were not entirely unconscious, I think, because you were still blinking, but you were pale and silent. There was less blood on your clothing than I expected.

"Did you know that man?" Forestier asked.

"He was my brother Horace," Victor said. A tight smile. "A family disagreement. I'm sure you've heard about our troubles. I'm sorry it disturbed you."

"A stabbing is a matter for the law," Forestier said.

"No," Victor said. "My friend Camille made an error in the account. There was no stabbing. You see?"

Your waistcoat was unbuttoned and your shirt was untucked—both were shredded—so Victor had already examined your belly. He lifted your clothes to reveal your skin, which was indeed whole and unblemished. There was no evidence that the knife had entered your body. What little blood marred your clothes and the floor might have come from something incidental and trivial like a nosebleed.

Your face, however, was grey and taut with pain.

"But how can that be?" I said. I began to doubt myself.

But you were clearly unwell. <u>Something</u> had happened to you. And there had been a knife.

I didn't know what to make of Victor's lie. I still don't. Perhaps it will mean something to you.

And I know I saw the point of that blade pierce your body. I'll never forget the sight as long as I live. But I can't explain by what method the skin on your belly appeared not merely healed, but untouched.

"That man brandished a blade at me," Forestier said. "You're sure he didn't attack your friend?"

"Julien has had a shock," Victor said. "As an artist, he has a delicate constitution. Camille will stay with him while he rests and I fetch the doctor."

"I suppose if there's no attacker and no wound, there isn't a need for me," Forestier said, but his tone had become cold. I can't blame him for suspecting something amiss.

"You may retire. As I said, I'm sorry to have disturbed you, but there was no crime here. As my brother, Horace has a key to my rooms. We did have an argument, and Julien was caught in the middle, and we certainly disrespected Madame Laval's rules. As your neighbor, I apologize. But no one broke the law."

"I'm still going to make a note of this," Forestier said. "I don't like any of it."

"Nor do I. If you'll excuse me, I'm going to fetch the doctor," Victor said and left.

A moment later, Madame Laval came to the door in her white cap and her dressing gown. She was displeased by my presence, but I suppose sitting by your bedside holding your hand to comfort you through your obvious suffering was the least offensive thing I could have been doing. She didn't ask me to leave and seemed appeased by Forestier's presence and brief explanation.

Forestier departed after she did, and then I was alone with you for almost an hour. The lone candle began to gutter and I had to light a second one. I apologize for this, my friend, but I lifted your clothes again to look at your belly once more. Our friendship has never involved this kind of liberty before, and I would not have done it except that I was trembling in confusion and fear. I wanted reassurance. Continuously, I imagined some sort of gash revealing itself, as though Victor and Forestier and I had simply missed it the first time. But there was no cut. Your skin was clean. It seemed to me that a dark bruise was forming under the skin of your abdomen, but I could hardly trust myself on that point.

Victor returned then. He was accompanied by a person in a voluminous dark cloak whose whole visage was obscured by the hood. "The doctor needs the room."

With great reluctance, I let go of your hand and went into the hall. Victor exited the room a moment later with a full satchel.

He was moving stiffly, which I noticed because I wondered again if it was really possible that he hadn't been wounded. His coat hung in tatters. There were a few slashes that had cut all the way through his frock coat, his waistcoat, and his shirt, so I could see the skin beneath. It wasn't bloody.

Victor sagged against the wall and pushed a hand through his damp hair. "Thanks for taking care of Julie, Camille. I'm sorry about all this. What happened to my brother?"

I described how we'd struggled, but he'd fled with the knife.

Victor said, "Thank you. I hate to impose further, but do you think you could watch Julie for a few more days? The doctor says it'll probably be safe to move her in the morning, so she could go to your townhouse. I'll write to her sister Adrienne to come to town, so you won't have to do it alone."

My friend, I have always found a certain joy in our shared rejection of categories, but I never knew you were called Julie. I don't think Victor would have revealed this about you if he had not been in such distress, and if you did not want me to know it, then I am sorry for having acquired the knowledge. I can't promise to forget it, but if it would please you, I will behave as if I knew nothing. When you wake, you can tell me what you prefer.

"Victor, please tell me what is happening," I said. "Why are you speaking as if you won't be here?"

"I can't," Victor said. "The less you know, the better. I'm sorry to have involved you, but I'm grateful for your help. Please trust me that this is not a matter for the police. I'll handle it."

"Who did you bring in my coach? Is that person really a doctor? What are they doing?"

"That person is saving Julie's life," Victor said.

"Was that man really your brother?"

A nearly soundless laugh. "He's denied it before, but yes, he's my brother."

"Are we still in danger?"

"You won't be if I leave. Take Julie to your house in the morning."

"And if she asks about you? When will we see you again?"

"I don't know," Victor said. He hunched with unhappiness.

THE SCANDALOUS LETTERS OF V AND J

I had so many more questions, undoubtedly destined for unsatisfactory answers, but the doctor came out of your room then and strode down the hall without a word to either of us. Victor said goodbye to me and followed.

I came to your side again. There was a bandage over your stomach as if you had a real wound there. I wasn't bold enough to remove it or even to peek under an edge, but from what I could see, the spreading bruise under your skin was gone. Your face looked a bit less pale and you gave the impression of being peaceful in your rest, whereas earlier your face had been drawn with pain. I don't know what the doctor did to you, or what happened in the attack, but it was a relief to see such marked improvement.

Since then, I have been writing this letter at your side, using supplies borrowed from Victor's room. I notice he cleared up a few of the books that had been strewn around the floor before he left. It was easy to find paper and ink, but there were no pens in the room. Luckily, I always carry my own.

It is deepest night now. It is my hope that you will wake with dawn, but if not, my coachman and I will carry you to the coach. I don't want to remain here a minute longer than necessary. This affair has disquieted me. I feel fear and fury for you in equal measure.

Please wake up, Julie(n).

Your friend,

Camille

PRIVATE DIARY OF V BEAUCHÊNE, FEBRUARY 28, 1824

[*This entry has so many ink blots that it is almost illegible.*]

I don't know where to start. It's almost dawn and I'm so tired and nothing is right. But it's urgent that I record tonight's events before I forget their details.

I vomited twice tonight on the gravel path leading to Mme de Tourzin's house in Rue Branoux. She witnessed the second time and merely lifted her skirts and her cloak to step over the puddle, which will be humiliating when I revisit the memory, but for now all I can think of is J, who saved my life tonight and who will be repaid with cruelty.

God, I could be sick again. This is all my fault.

Once we were outside her coach and she'd calmly ignored my distress, instead of going into her house, she said, "You didn't stay with your injured friend. You came all the way across the river with me because you intend to pursue your brother."

I was rather slow to understand. "You know where my brother lives because you cared for my mother."

"I treated her illness for a time," Mme de T corrected. "What will you do when you find your brother?"

"Make sure he doesn't come after me—or Julien—ever again."

"You can't even say the word 'kill.' I'm coming with you. You're not going to do it right."

I wondered if she meant that I was unarmed—I had the ring, but she didn't know—but she didn't elaborate. Her terse and practical companionship might have unnerved me, had she not recently saved J's life. We walked side by side for a quarter of an hour. How strange that in all the vastness of Paris, I had grown up mere minutes from Mme de T and yet I had known nothing of her or her mysterious world of magic.

Both had been in my father's house without my knowledge.

We reached the Rue d'Artois, which used to be the Rue Cerutti and might well be called something else under the next king or emperor or republic. No matter how many times the street name changes, I will always be able to find it in the dark.

My childhood home loomed over us, that grand townhouse where my father had murdered my mother, my brother had murdered my father, and I intended to complete the set.

Despite Mme de T's unfazed presence and offer of help, I trembled.

Practiced now at slipping in the back, I entered through the kitchen in silence. I thought I was guiding Mme de T, but she never hesitated. She'd come through the back entrance before. The hallway floorboards didn't betray us. We were so quiet that it was easy to overhear a conversation in the parlor.

I froze. Beside me, Mme de T melded herself against the wall and then tugged me closer. The weak light of a single lamp illuminated the slit between the parlor door and the threshold. We crept as close as possible and strained to hear.

"I have asked you for two simple things and you have failed me *twice*," said a clipped, low voice I didn't recognize. They were not shouting, but neither were they making any effort to conceal the conversation.

"If that idiot slut hadn't stolen the ring, I'd have the necklace for you by now," Horace protested. One assumes I am the idiot slut in question. "I'll get it. And I'm looking for your girl, but nobody knows her."

"Woman," the other person said. "She has the appearance of a woman of about forty. If you're looking for a girl, you've already done it wrong."

"Woman, woman," Horace said, hurried and placating. "I know, I know, she's got black hair and a stern and unforgiving face that is captivating but not beautiful and she's called Madame de Tourzin or Isabelle, I've memorized everything you said, it's just that <u>nobody has ever heard of her</u> and I'm beginning to think she doesn't exist."

Her fingers certainly existed when they clamped around my wrist.

"There isn't even a Monsieur de Tourzin," Horace continued. "Her name, it's a fabrication."

"She's real," the other voice insisted. "She's alive. I won't give you what you want unless you bring her to me. Only I know the secret of immortality, Faucheux. All the other wonders I've shown you are trinkets in comparison, and without this one, you're likely to die of the same wasting disease that killed your parents."

"I'll find her, Malbosc, I swear it," Horace said. "And I'll get you the necklace. It's only that damned shopkeeper Aveux won't tell me what he knows—"

Malbosc. The name echoed in my mind for a moment before I connected it to the author of the first book I'd read about magic. That two-hundred-year-old catalogue of cursed objects had been composed by an author named J. L. A. Malbosc.

It did not escape me that on the other side of the door, someone calling themselves Malbosc had just claimed to know the secret of immortality.

Mme de T's grip on my wrist constricted until I couldn't feel my hand.

Malbosc said, "If the shopkeeper is a problem, then torture him until he tells you what you need. Kill him afterward, don't be fool enough to leave him alive."

"Well, I, uh—what would I do with the body?"

"What concern of that is mine?" Malbosc demanded.

The carpet muffled footsteps, the light under the door receded, and then there was the distant sigh of hinges and the click of the front door. Malbosc had left and my brother had followed.

My head was spinning. I had come to kill my brother. I couldn't seem to move my feet.

Untroubled by any such perplexity, Mme de T opened the door to the parlor. Without my brother's lamp, it was impossible to see the two gilded, stuffed sofas and the matching armchairs, the glossy inlaid wood tables, the marble mantels, the sumptuous drapes. I knew where they were, but Mme de T didn't wait for guidance. She disappeared into the darkness.

I drifted after her. The door from the parlor to the foyer was outlined in light. Horace must be there, standing in front of the door or perhaps mounting the stairs with his lamp in hand.

Mme de T threw open the door, strode into the light

with her cloak billowing behind her, and caught my brother by the back of the neck. To call it a fight would be a gross exaggeration. He had the lamp in one hand and that phantom knife in the other, but his weapon made no difference. She pulled his cravat garrote-tight and yanked the knife by the blade.

I winced and clenched my own hand, imagining the cut to her palm. Two drops of blood splashed the white marble threshold, but no more.

She flipped the knife with practiced ease, then kicked my brother in the back of the knee. He fell by halting movements, one leg and then the other, and when he was kneeling before Mme de T, she pulled aside frock coat, waistcoat, shirt with one hand. The other was around his throat, and to judge from his white face and bulging eyes, it was painful.

When his chest was exposed, she stabbed the knife into his heart. I can still hear the sickening sound of it puncturing his body.

My brother gurgled and died.

She pulled the knife out. There was a squelching, sucking sound and for an instant, the scent of blood. It dissipated as quickly as the noise. As with all the other wounds, there was no mark on his pale skin.

The realization that she had pushed aside Horace's clothing to disguise the manner of his killing, so that anyone who knew nothing of that knife and its nature might mistake his death for some sudden accident of ill health; the skill and speed with which she had executed her plan and my brother; the implications of Horace and Malbosc's conversation about her; the knowledge that I was the sole witness to her undetectable murder and she was still holding the knife—well, I fainted.

Perhaps I ought to be ashamed that it was all those things, and not the stabbing itself or the death of my one and only brother, that caused me to faint. But there was hardly any blood during the stabbing—oh, but that sound —and my brother had not only tried to kill me mere hours ago, but also delighted in my misery for the entirety of my life, so I can't feel too ashamed.

Fainting is embarrassing, though.

"You didn't piss yourself, at least," Mme de T said when I woke up.

"Let's be thankful for that," I said, thinking that if she'd intended to kill me, she would have done it already.

She'd sat on the floor next to my head. Her wrists hung over her knees. I hadn't realized she'd been wearing trousers under her cloak, or boots, but these details seem trivial now. The knife lay by her boot. Horace's corpse was still crumpled on the floorboards.

"I didn't let you crack your skull on the floor," she said. From our brief acquaintance, I understand this to be a remarkable demonstration of warmth on her part. "You were injured badly, you know. Just because the knife wounds close on the outside doesn't mean they stop bleeding on the inside."

"I—"

"I shouldn't have let you come here. I should have taken care of it myself. But here we are. I healed you and your friend in one night, I killed your brother, I found Malbosc, and you're in the middle of this unfortunate affair. You were only unconscious for about fifteen minutes, by the way, but don't count yourself healed yet."

"Horace was looking for you," I said. I had to start somewhere. I felt in good health considering the circumstances, but the inside of my mouth tasted strange and I had hardly any idea what was happening. Cautiously, I pushed myself into a seated position. "That other person —Malbosc—was looking for you."

"I don't wish to be found," she said. "Are there servants in the house?"

"There are, but they sleep on the top floor and I assume Horace instructed them not to interfere with his middle-of-the-night conversations," I said. "Still, we should probably... do something about the corpse."

The corpse was the least of my concerns.

She had grabbed Horace's knife by the blade. A clever and unexpected move, one that I had assumed played on her knowledge of the knife's nature. I could have taken hold of that knife by the blade and had no scar to show for it, but there would still have been harm below the surface. My body would have been slow to heal that damage.

Isabelle de Tourzin showed no sign of any pain.

She had healed J, healed me, kept my mother alive for years. She didn't age. Aunt S had stopped just short of saying she couldn't die.

I said, "Malbosc said he knew the secret to immortality. You know it, too. Is it an object? A magical artifact?"

"I don't know it, I am it," she said. "There is no secret but me. This is just something my body does, the way yours grows blond hair from your head or Béatrix's makes magic with her voice."

"But how do you heal other—" I began and then stopped myself. She didn't let anyone see her healing not because she was using an object, but because she was using her body. Those two drops of blood on the white marble threshold lay like scattered rubies. I swallowed. "Are you... are you a vampire?"

"A vampire?"

"A creature of the living dead that drinks the blood of innocents," I said, embarrassment rising through my fear and confusion to lay like water over oil. "They can make other vampires by biting them and feeding them their own blood. They have fangs."

"Then no, I am not a vampire. Just a very, very tired old woman." She laughed, low and rich, bared her ordinary teeth at me, and stuck an arm out. "Would you like to feel my pulse?"

"No," I said to my toes.

"I am without fangs, and alive in more or less the usual way, and I don't drink anyone's blood," she continued. "It's strange and terrible how these stories circulate, you know, vicious notions of human sacrifice and rituals where someone drinks the blood of innocents. Your people use those falsehoods as an excuse to kill mine."

"My people?" I asked blankly.

"Christians and Jews, Beauchêne," she said. "My mother didn't name me Isabelle de Tourzin, but that hardly matters now. And perhaps they're no longer my people—everyone who knew me then is dead."

This was so much. Too much. I tried to find something to comprehend in it. She was Jewish, like J. That she and J could have anything in common seemed impossible.

I couldn't think of J.

She continued, "I've sometimes wondered if I'm to blame for the stories of blood-drinking and all the slaughter they've caused, but they're older than me. I'm just one woman, and as far as I know, the only one of my kind. I have sometimes offered my blood to others, as I did to you, but I always intended to heal them, not cause harm. Besides, as usual, the worst violence is perpetrated by the powerful. If you're looking for a blood-drinker, it's Malbosc you want."

"I... what?" I gathered my thoughts with desperate haste, and though they were as sharp as burrs, they slipped from my hands even as they pricked me. "You're saying that your blood heals people."

"I am," she said, resigned. "Revealing that truth has proven catastrophic for me once before, Beauchêne. I hope not to regret telling you."

"Why <u>are</u> you telling me?"

"We'll arrive there in time."

Sitting on the floor with my brother's cooling corpse, my own clothing ragged from where he'd stabbed me, I was chatting with a casually murderous, seemingly ageless woman who'd entrusted me with her secret. The thought <u>she fed me her blood while I was unconscious</u> was writing itself over and over in my mind's ledger like the world's most ghoulish childhood penmanship exercise. I had so many questions that I momentarily forgot how to form a sentence. "Malbosc? Him too? Immortal, that is."

"I don't care for that word. I prefer to think I haven't yet encountered the person or thing that will kill me. I await their arrival impatiently. Alphonse, on the other hand, might have lived a long time, but he has met his end."

It was the name, rather than her serenely vicious smile, that gave me pause. "Alphonse?"

"You own his portrait and don't know his name?"

Shocked by the revelation that this man was J's tormentor, I couldn't remember what Mme de T had said of the portrait. Just now I checked my diary for her description of their relationship: "I'm looking for him. He stole something from me." She'd said nothing more at the time. Paired with her assertion tonight that Malbosc drinks blood, those sentences paint a grim picture.

"I don't know him, but he hurt a friend of mine," I said. "Tonight is the closest I've come to meeting him."

"I'm sorry." Distress creased her expression.

"So am I. The fault isn't ours."

"It's his, of course, but it's mine, too. I should have killed him a long time ago." She inhaled and drew her spine straighter. "His full name is Jean-Louis-Alphonse Malbosc. There might be a few other family names I'm forgetting, but that doesn't matter. I won't be carving a headstone."

"You intend to kill him. With the knife?"

"I wish it were so easy," she said. "Alphonse has—or had—a great deal of my blood. Until I find his cellar and separate him from it, he is as impervious to harm as I am. But his presence in Paris, and his relationship with your late brother, suggest that he's near the end of his supply. He wouldn't look for me otherwise. I'm the only person alive who knows how to kill him."

"I'll likely regret asking, but how did he acquire a wine cellar full of your blood?"

She picked up the knife that lay next to her boot, ran one finger along the top of the blade, and rested the pad of her fingertip against the point. Not hard enough or long enough for a drop of blood to well, but her bare hand looked obscenely vulnerable. It made me shiver.

Once I'd started shaking, it was impossible to stop. The night caught up with me: Horace ransacking my room and attacking J, my flight across town to save J's life, my own injury, my wild desperation to avenge J, Horace's murder, learning the truth about Mme de T and Malbosc. Yesterday felt like another lifetime. The foyer floor was cold and hard and I pressed my hands against the planks.

"Alphonse had his own hoard of artifacts," she said distantly. "There was a necklace. Emerald, not that it matters. Once he'd put it on me, my will was his."

Alphonse must have lost the necklace before meeting J —thank God. Still, he was in Paris, and the necklace might well be, too, and J was hurt and unaware and in further danger.

I left J in the Maison Laval tonight to draw danger away from them. I thought if I ensured that Horace couldn't attack them ever again, it would be one small way of making things right.

And here was Alphonse, ruining everything.

"He asked Horace about a necklace," I said.

"Of course. He can't bleed me without that kind of iron control," she said. "He always had a particular interest in artifacts that granted him control of other people. He's covetous."

I thought of the ring in my pocket and how my father had slowly killed my mother. I thought of J falling into Alphonse's clutches in their youth. A chill glazed my skin and soaked into my bones. "My brother made it sound like Aveux knew where the necklace was."

"Aveux only cares about money, so your brother must not have offered him enough. But if even one person knows where the necklace is, it won't be long until Malbosc has it. I've told you all this because you're uniquely positioned to help me."

She'd crawled into my room at the Maison Laval a few nights ago and said something similar—that she wanted someone who could join my brother's circle of artifact collectors.

Or rather, the circle of artifact collectors that, as of tonight, no longer included my brother.

My voice emerged from my body as a slight and shaky rasp. "I gather you're not asking me to organize your archive."

"No," she said, and laid out a plan that I find equal parts sickening and exhilarating—or perhaps that's the sleeplessness. I don't know what is right anymore, but ignoring the problem of my family ended in disaster. I can't ignore the problem of Malbosc.

There is light creeping through the curtains now, and I have more correspondence to write before I can rest.

VICTOR BEAUCHÊNE TO ADRIENNE MORÈRE, FEBRUARY 28, 1824

POSTMARKED PARIS

Dear Adrienne,

I'm writing in a rush so please excuse the state of this letter. Julie was severely injured yesterday and I've been called away on other urgent business. The wound has been treated. The doctor assures me she will recover, but I don't know how much time will be required. I'm leaving her to convalesce in the care of her good friend Camille Dupin, whose address is below, but please get to Paris as soon as you can. She needs you.

I have written Julie her own letter, addressed to her at Camille's. I would be grateful if you would encourage her to read it when she wakes.

Your friend,
Victor

V BEAUCHÊNE TO J MORÈRE, FEBRUARY 28, 1824
NOT POSTMARKED

J—

I'm so sorry. For everything, but especially (1) for not listening to your warnings in the first place, (2) for causing you harm, and (3) for leaving your side. I asked Camille and Adrienne to take care of you because I know they will, but I also know you're justifiably angry with me. I have no excuse, so I will not waste the ink. Leaving while you were bleeding was a bastard thing to do. I am a bastard. You are right to be furious.

I wish I could console you, or grovel, or lavish you with gifts and kindnesses until you forgive me, but the truth is that you shouldn't forgive me. I see now what you have always known: we can't be together while I follow this path. My involvement endangers us both. That's unacceptable. What happened to you was unconscionable, and I will regret it for the rest of my life. I can't allow it to happen again.

Unfortunately, extricating myself will be difficult. As much as I would love to run away with you—if you'd have me—to a little house in the countryside where we could make a life writing and illustrating obscene books, we don't live in that story. Right now, wherever I go, danger will follow. So I can't be with you. There are some things I need to see through to the end.

I am arrogant and selfish, but not enough to ask you to wait for me. Don't do that. You are alive, J, and you should live. Be vibrantly, ferociously angry with me. Throw this letter into the fire. Smash something. Find solace with Camille, who is splendid and has more patience for aesthetic philosophy than I do. And is a rich, famous literary genius, besides. Or if Camille doesn't want to—an absurd notion—then you should have anyone you like. Two people at once. More, even. There's all of Paris to choose from, and most of them won't put your life in peril. It will be easy for you to forget me if you set your mind to it, and I know you can. Paint a lot of brilliant works. Overwhelm the Salon jury. Make the critics spill all their ink.

No one will ever forget you, J, least of all me. It's cruel to both of us to mention it, and I ought to keep it to myself, but as you are going to shred this letter into a hundred pieces and hurl them all into the fire, and have perhaps already stopped reading, I will permit myself the truth. I have encountered people who defy the limits of human ability and I have handled objects that break the laws of the universe. The only thing I can identify for certain as impossible is ever meeting another person who completes my understanding of the world the way that you do. Never have I felt so freely and fully myself. It is a joy to be alive near you. Even the bad things—fevers, nightmares, grief, Mme Laval trying to serve yesterday's stale bread at dinner, the grey days and their filthy puddles—are better for it.

I love you. I always will.

I will remain grateful to you for this glimpse of what life could be—if I were a better person living in a better world. I am not, I do not, and I think that will always hurt, knowing how close I came and how I ruined it by nearly getting you killed. Now the world resembles that painting we transformed and destroyed—faded, withered, drained of promise. I did this. It is my fault.

It soothes my broken heart to know that, at the very least, I am not condemning you to the same mean, hopeless future. You're alive. You're brave and righteous and dazzling. You'll find someone else better suited to accompany you, someone who will not put you in danger, or force you to overlook their crimes, or write you the kind of letter you have to throw into a fire.

—V

J MORÈRE TO V BEAUCHÊNE, MARCH 1, 1824

UNSENT

[*This note is scrawled in the margin of the previous letter.*]
FUCK YOU AND FUCK THIS

III
YOUNG MAN WRITING A LETTER

1824

PRIVATE DIARY OF J MORÈRE, MARCH 5, 1824

They're saying V is dead.

I just got back from Camille's house and sent Adrienne on her way. I haven't seen Sophie since before the incident, so I can't ask her. Her affairs are no longer here, so the rooms she and V used to occupy stand empty now. I assume she's gone to live with her opera singer, whose name V mentioned, but I can't recall it because I'm too angry.

Everyone was so solemn around the dinner table this evening. Even Forestier took my hand and said, "My condolences. I know you two were close." Mme Laval never liked V, but she acted all weepy like it was so sad. She got mad at me when I snatched the letter out of her hand.

It was signed Horace Faucheux and it said <u>Victorine Faucheux</u> was dead. No explanation given. I guess we're supposed to assume the cause was something unspeakable. Nobody in the house remarked on the different name or pronoun. I would say that means it was written with V's persuasive pen, but then why didn't it work on me?

I don't know what is going on. I don't even know why I survived the night I was stabbed. That knife went <u>through</u> me. I should be dead from blood loss or infection, yet here I am, with V nowhere in sight.

I've never met anybody named Victorine Faucheux. If Victor Beauchêne is dead, then who slid this obscene drawing I made back in January under my door last night? It's the one where I wrote "I don't think you have to worry too much about the fates that await respectable virgins, V."

Not funny.

And you'd better <u>start</u> worrying because I <u>will</u> find you.

HORACE FAUCHEUX TO JEAN-LOUIS-ALPHONSE MALBOSC, MARCH 5, 1824

POSTMARKED PARIS

Alphonse,

Excuse the note. Writing is so dull. Waste of time I could spend drinking brandy in the parlor or whoring at Florine's. Instead some dusty old spinster great-aunt died and now I've got to spend a week in the countryside sorting her affairs. I wanted to send a servant but they tell me it's got to be my signature.

Just wanted to assure you there's no need to worry about our projects. I'm working on it. You'll get exactly what you need. We both will.

Horace

JEAN-LOUIS-ALPHONSE MALBOSC TO HORACE FAUCHEUX, MARCH 6, 1824

SENT BY PRIVATE COURIER

Faucheux,

I certainly agree with you that your writing is dull. Do not presume to know my mind. These matters, if they must be discussed rather than resolved, are best treated in speech.

Any further letter from you will terminate our arrangement.

J. L. A. Malbosc

JULIEN MORÈRE TO SOPHIE BEAUCHÊNE, MARCH 6, 1824
POSTMARKED PARIS

Mademoiselle Beauchêne,

I hope this isn't too bold, but I asked Madame Laval for your new address and she provided me with this one. I heard the terrible news and wanted to say how sorry I am for your loss. Perhaps we could correspond on occasion?

Please accept my most respectful sentiments,

Julien Morère

SOPHIE BEAUCHÊNE TO JULIEN MORÈRE, MARCH 7, 1824

POSTMARKED PARIS

Julien, my dear, you can call me Sophie.

Your note moves me. I'm equally sorry for your loss—and I'm sorry for the attack you suffered from my brute of a nephew. Appalling.

I don't know that I've ever had the chance to express to you in what high regard I hold your person and your talents. You have a good heart, Julien. Guard it well.

If you ever do portraits, or would consider doing portraits, Béatrix Chevreuil would make a lovely subject. I have included her address. Please come see us tomorrow.

With love,

Sophie

PRIVATE DIARY OF J MORÈRE, MARCH 8, 1824

I went to see Sophie and she told me to stop looking for V. Not in those words, but I could see what she meant. She was kind about it, and clearly unhappy, but very firm. Apparently it's not safe for me or for V if I go digging into <u>where the fuck they went</u>.

I asked if there was any way to write to V, since they're definitely not dead and <u>I have some things to say</u>, but Sophie said it's not good to leave any kind of evidence that other people could find. I suppose she wouldn't like me writing this diary, but I can't speak to anyone else about this matter, so in V's absence, I'm forced to adopt their solution of keeping a diary.

I hate this.

I should teach myself one of V's ciphers, but I know I'll never be any good at that.

Béatrix was lovely. I did a quick little sketch and gifted it to her. I said I would think about a portrait in oils. They seem happy together—insofar as Sophie can be happy when V fucking disappeared, obviously with the intention of doing something boneheaded and dangerous.

And Sophie indicated to me that the two of them have a friend who has some kind of ability to heal people—V's mysterious "doctor," no doubt—and that's why I'm not dead. She apologized and said she couldn't say more than that because she was protecting her friend, but nothing bad is going to happen to me. I should be fine now. That's something, at least.

ADRIENNE MORÈRE TO JULIE MORÈRE, MARCH 8, 1824
POSTMARKED VÉZY-SUR-OISE

My dear sister,

I know I said this too many times while we were together, but I'm so sorry for everything that happened. I explained what I could to Camille—I like her very much—and was just wondering what you would like me to tell the rest of our family.

And I know you don't like me to worry about you, but I do.

Love,
Adrienne

JULIE MORÈRE TO ADRIENNE MORÈRE, MARCH 10, 1824

POSTMARKED PARIS

My dear, worried sister,

Thank you for keeping a certain name out of your letter. I would like you to continue that. I would also like the rest of our family to continue that, if you could do me the kindness of mentioning it.

Please tell them as little as possible. An accident from which I am now recovered, or some such. I know how guilt-stricken they were the first time. I came to Paris to prove I could make my own way in the world, so let me do that.

I am glad you and Camille became friends. She is exactly the sort of person I was hoping to meet when I came to Paris. Despite recent events, I don't regret my choice to come here.

I wish you and Léon all the best in your engagement and am sorry to have drawn you away from him.

Love,
Julie

J MORÈRE TO V BEAUCHÊNE, MARCH 11, 1824
UNSENT

V—

I can't even express how furious I am.

I SAVED YOUR LIFE.

THAT WAS <u>MY</u> CHOICE. MINE.

I stepped in front of a knife for you and almost died and you think you need to disappear to <u>protect</u> me? How does that make sense? What the hell is rattling around in your thick, empty skull, V? I made my choice and I chose <u>you and all your risks</u> and you <u>left me</u> and you can't do this to me, you can't

[*A rip in the page.*]

J MORÈRE TO V BEAUCHÊNE, MARCH 12, 1824

UNSENT

V—

You'll probably never see this letter, but I need to say some things.

First, even if you had to go through with your nonsense plan of disappearing, you should have told me what happened. Why I didn't die, I mean. You owed me that much.

Second, I know your life is dangerous because <u>your brother stabbed me in the gut</u> and I knew your life was dangerous when I stepped in front of his knife.

I chose you. Fuck if I can say why. Everything in the universe is composed of atoms except for you—you're made of bad decisions. And so am I. Here I am after everything, twitching at every creak in the floorboards, hoping the footsteps belong to you.

But you didn't respect my choice. You should have stayed that night and explained when I woke up and given me the chance to say what I wanted, which was <u>you</u>, you dolt. You and all your bad decisions and the risks that come with them. (Though, again, I don't know why I would need to say anything when I STEPPED IN FRONT OF THE KNIFE. I thought my feelings were evident, myself.)

Instead you left. You ignored me and made a choice for both of us. Fuck you. I don't want to be in love with anyone who would do that.

—J

NOTES FOR AN INDEX OF MME DE T'S COLLECTION, EXCERPTED, ENTRIES DATED MARCH 12, 1824

A knife. The handle is white bone. Effect: Any wound made with this weapon seals itself so there is no external evidence of its existence. Provenance: Unknown.

A ceramic pot of white face powder, sable brush included. The pot is light blue and fits into the palm of a hand. Effect: The wearer's face disguises itself, becoming indistinct and unworthy of notice in use by a novice, or, with practice, becoming the appearance of another person entirely. The change is only visual; touch disturbs it. It endures until the powder is washed off. Provenance: Unknown. Note: One might expect that such an artifact would make the wearer's face more noticeable and more appealing, cf. the two face powders described in the entries of March 10, 1824. Enhancement of beauty seems to be a common effect for artifacts of this type and disguise a comparatively rare one. Was the creator shy? Desperate to carry out some secret deed? We will never know.

An oval hand mirror in a hinged silver case. Effect: The person regarding their reflection can imagine a new face for themself. The change is only visual. While the new appearance endures for a few hours after the mirror is closed and put away, it requires continual concentration. Provenance: Paris, 1790s.

A pair of garters. Two white ribbons embroidered with red flowers and green vines, each with a brass buckle. Effect: They prevent unwanted touch for the wearer. Provenance: Paris, 1790s. Note: The original wearer was strongly averse to touch; reportedly all their clothes acquired this effect, but we only have these garters.

[*The following note is squeezed into the right margin in tiny print.*] From Mme de T's manner when she recounted this, I strongly suspect she knows who created them. She refuses to confirm.

A pen. A trimmed white goose feather. Effect: Words written with this pen are powerfully persuasive, provided the writer possesses sufficient conviction. The duration of the persuasion is variable. Success is most reliable if the reader expects to receive something written, though possible under other circumstances. Further experiments are warranted. Provenance: Paris, 1823. Note: Created in a moment of fury and desire to be understood, or at least listened to.

CAMILLE DUPIN TO JULIE MORÈRE, APRIL 20, 1824
POSTMARKED VERNEUIL

My dear Julie,

The long gaps between your letters concern me, and the contents of the rare letters you do send concern me even more. It's clear I was wrong to think you recovered, though you did your best to persuade myself and your sweet sister that we ought to leave you alone. I should have insisted that you go home with Adrienne or come to the countryside with me. I don't like to imagine you moping alone in Paris.

Get yourself to Verneuil immediately. The company and the air will be good for you. You can restore yourself by doing something virtuous like painting landscapes. Or you can brood on top of a hill. At the very least, it provides a change of scenery for your suffering.

This is not meant to make light. I am entirely serious. I'm also serious when I say I'd fuck you if I thought it would help. In our bedroom tastes we might be a bit like two magnets with the same polarity, but you are my friend and I would adapt. This is an offer of my body and not of my heart. I have no plans to give up my roguish bachelor's life for anyone, even as dear a friend as you. It doesn't have to be love, Julie. Sometimes it's just a pleasant distraction.

Anyway, you don't have to come to my bed but you do have to come to my house. That is an order. If you don't get yourself here, I will hire someone to kidnap you.

Your friend,
Camille

PRIVATE DIARY OF J MORÈRE, APRIL 30, 1824

I don't know why I'm bothering to write. This diary just makes me think of V; everything makes me think of V. Writing those letters was supposed to help me stop thinking of V. Instead I stopped doing everything.

I'm at Camille's house at Verneuil now. That's new.

She hasn't asked me for answers. I don't know what I would tell her if she did.

I declined Camille's offer of sex. We're better as friends—not that friends can't sleep together, just that I decided my friendship with Camille isn't that sort of friendship. Not right now. Sex sounds exhausting. Everything sounds exhausting. I was angry and sad for so long and now I'm just tired. I do nothing all day and I'm tired. I haven't drawn in weeks.

I suppose it's not true that I do entirely nothing. Camille makes me go on long walks with her. She also watches me at dinner like I'm a child sneaking food to the dog, even though there is no dog.

In the evenings, we sit on the sofa together and

Camille reads to me. Sometimes I put my head on her shoulder, sometimes in her lap. Sometimes she touches my hair. It's the only time I feel at rest.

PRIVATE DIARY OF J MORÈRE, MAY 2, 1824

Adrienne is getting married to Léon. Camille is going to come to the farm with me. I know I should be happy.

Camille says she's accompanying me because she wants to see Adrienne again and steal her from Léon, but the truth is that Camille knows I will lie in bed and not go to my own sister's wedding unless I have a chaperone, and the whole thing makes me feel awful. I don't want to be this person anymore. I want to be myself again.

PRIVATE DIARY OF J MORÈRE, JUNE 1, 1824

Lots of progress at the session with Béatrix today. Camille and I came back to Paris for this week and I've been sketching Béatrix daily in preparation for a portrait. She is as skilled at conversation as she is at singing. (Sophie took me to the opera to see her perform last week. I feel as though I never understood music until I heard Béatrix.)

At first I was worried that without Sophie to connect us, we might sit in silence. No matter how good my portraits are, I will never earn commissions unless I put my subjects at ease with chatter. Sometimes it seems to me that my jaw is locked. The words that do pass my lips tend to be the wrong ones. I always bring up serious matters—they're the ones that interest me instead of lighter topics.

Béatrix is perhaps even more fluent in social graces than Sophie. I don't need to worry about initiating conversations, and she's never boring. To hear her tell it, her five decades of life consist entirely of amusing anecdotes, but when I write about it like that, it sounds frivolous and self-centered, like she never asks me anything or talks of more abstract matters. She does—she excels at all of that. We have in common that she's the youngest of three siblings, preceded by a sister and a brother, and as my whole family practices the fine arts, hers practices music. She wasted no time discovering those things, eliciting childhood stories from me in exchange for her own.

I have not put it into words until this moment, but I feel content in her company. As content as I am with Camille, and perhaps happier than I am with Sophie, who, as lovely as she is, can't help but make me think of V, something I try not to do.

(I don't succeed, but I try.)

My drawings of Béatrix are good, too. My drawings are always good, but with her, it is a pleasure to make them. I think the portrait will be good. Béatrix tells me she has every confidence it will be. That is why we are sharing so much in conversation, according to her, so that I will know her and the painting will make other people want to know her.

"Not that I have any trouble with that," she said, which I'm sure is true. Her admirers are legion. She has many stories of men who lavished her with expensive gifts in exchange for a moment in her presence.

I don't even know if she likes men. She's wonderful company, but she isn't a flirt, at least not with me. Not that I'm a man, but I haven't come right out and told her that. Who knows what Sophie said about me before she introduced us. "I know a young artist by the name of Julien Morère. He's tall and quiet and rather hilariously intimidated by me. He also has unwise, overpowering feelings—love, anger, all of them—for dear, absent V. You should let him paint your portrait, he's not bad."

In truth, it's a relief that Béatrix never flirts with me. I wouldn't know what to do. She's a very beautiful woman, as all of Paris has noticed. Her dark brown skin is without flaw. Usually she wears a scarf over the tight curls of her hair, but she wanted it loose in the portrait, so I've been lucky enough to see the way it floats around the lovely oval of her face.

Today I found the courage to ask her how she met Sophie, and from the chaise longue where she was posed, she laughed her unfettered, room-filling laugh.

"When they dedicate an opera house to me, I'll hire you to paint a grand ceiling, and then I'll have time to tell you how I met Sophie Beauchêne, and all the years we waited for each other."

"You waited for her? But what about all your admirers?"

"They didn't love me. They loved the idea of Béatrix Chevreuil, star of the opera, gifted Black soprano, legendary beauty. And I needed them to love the idea—for my career, for the cause I serve. I couldn't trust them to love me as Béatrix the woman, and besides, that would have interfered with what I was doing."

"Singing?" I asked, puzzled.

"Singing, of course, even in a perfect world, I would be singing. But in this world, with all of its ugliness, I needed those rich men to give me diamonds so that I could send their money to abolitionists, Julien. I use my voice to make the world a little less ugly."

"Oh," I said. And then, because I'd never forgotten what V had written about Béatrix's voice being persuasive, I ventured, "When you say you use your voice..."

She made a dismissive noise. "I don't need magic to make men give me diamonds. They do that on their own. I need magic to protect myself from those who misunderstand the nature of gifts and demand something from me in return."

"I'm sorry they treat you that way. It's not right," I said, reeling from how casually she'd revealed her power.

"It's not right, but they pay for it," she said shortly. "What about you?"

"What about me?"

"How are you making the world less ugly, Julien Morère?"

"I'm painting a portrait of legendary beauty Béatrix Chevreuil," I told her, proud of myself for the compliment.

She laughed again, then said, "You're getting better at flattery, but don't think you can escape my question so easily. You know about my voice. I'd wager you know about more than just my voice."

"Yes," I said hesitantly. I didn't think I could explain what I can do—what I've done—as easily as she had. But I like Béatrix, and I wanted to be as truthful with her as she'd been with me, so I tried. "If I draw or paint in a certain way, I can... change the forms of things. Myself, mostly, but it also works on objects. And I used to make paintings that people couldn't look away from, but I don't do that anymore. Those were making the world uglier, I think."

Her eyes met mine. She regarded me with interest, but no judgment. "That's a lot of power, Julien," she said. "Fortunately for you, the world needs a lot of work."

LIST OF PAINTINGS, SCULPTURES, ETCHINGS, LITHOGRAPHS, AND WORKS OF ARCHITECTURE BY LIVING ARTISTS, EXHIBITED AT THE ROYAL MUSEUM OF THE ARTS, AUGUST 25, 1824. PRICE: 1 FRANC 25 CENTIMES. PARIS, C. BALLARD, KING'S PRINTER, RUE JEAN-JACQUES ROUSSEAU, NUMBER 8

Works owned by the artist are marked with a *.
MORÈRE, J.

- *Portrait of Mlle Béatrix Chevreuil*, painting
- *Béatrix Chevreuil at home with her friend Sophie Beauchêne*, painting
- *Portrait of Camille Dupin*, painting
- *Portrait of Adrienne Morère (sister of the artist)*, painting
- *Young man writing a letter*, painting*

PRIVATE DIARY OF J MORÈRE, AUGUST 26, 1824

The Salon was so crowded and overwhelming and so many people wanted to tell me they liked my work or that they didn't and all of them had to shout over the noise and now I can't sleep, but it's not because of any of that.

It's because someone walked by me and I smelled orange blossom soap.

How did I smell anything in that sweaty mass of bodies? Why have I latched onto this detail as if it means something? It's been six months. V can't be thinking of me as often as I think of them.

PRIVATE DIARY OF J MORÈRE, SEPTEMBER 2, 1824

Someone slid an envelope under my door in the night. Inside were several printed reviews of the exhibition, clipped to show only the paragraphs describing my work, with anything negative thoroughly blocked out. The result is an extraordinarily flattering collection of excerpts, like a bouquet of compliments.

I would consider it a lovely and thoughtful gift if I weren't obsessed by who sent it. There's no handwriting. Almost as if the sender knew I would recognize theirs.

If it's V—because of course that's the question—then how did they discover that I moved into my studio? I spent most of the spring and summer with Camille. I've only been living here for a couple of weeks. Did they return to the Maison Laval to seek me out? If they intend to remain hidden, that seems a foolish risk. To confirm my absence, they would have had to study the comings and goings of all the boarders. Or perhaps they remembered our afternoon of destroying <u>Landscape with Ruins</u> and came here first.

I remember that afternoon more often than I should.

The sex, but also what we accomplished together. Doing the right thing. Making the world a little less ugly, as Béatrix put it.

If V had written me a letter full of excuses or apologies, or even if they'd written these compliments themself, I think I would have been angry. There's so much I want to say to them, and to receive a letter without a return address (because I don't think there would be one) would only twist the knife.

But this... it's not about them, or us, just me. It's sweet.

Bittersweet, too.

J. L. A. MALBOSC TO CAMILLE DUPIN, SEPTEMBER 3, 1824
SENT BY PRIVATE COURIER

Mlle Dupin,

Forgive me the impertinence of this letter. Given your renown, strangers must write to you frequently in adoration of your superb novels. I do like your work, but I am writing to you about the work of another. I am told that you are a friend of the artist J. Morère, whose magnificent work I have just admired in the Salon. The work moved me tremendously. I long to meet the artist so that I might possess these beautiful paintings for myself, but it is difficult to find an address. I have taken the liberty of writing to you. Might you deliver the enclosed letter to J. Morère?

Please accept, Mlle Dupin, my highest esteem,

J. L. A. Malbosc, called Alphonse

CAMILLE DUPIN TO JULIE MORÈRE, SEPTEMBER 4, 1824
POSTMARKED PARIS

My dear Julie,

Now that your work in the Salon is dazzling the world and your fame outstrips mine, I have become your secretary. As your humble and devoted servant, I am enclosing a piece of correspondence intended for you.

Your dearest and best friend,

Camille

[*The enclosed letter mentioned above could not be included in this collection.*]

JULIE MORÈRE TO CAMILLE DUPIN, SEPTEMBER 5, 1824
POSTMARKED PARIS

[*This line is appended to Camille's letter of September 4.*]

If you receive any more correspondence from this man, burn it.

NOTES FOR AN INDEX OF MME DE T'S COLLECTION, EXCERPTED, ENTRIES DATED SEPTEMBER 5, 1824

An emerald necklace. Not in the collection, but described in J. L. A. Malbosc's book <u>A Catalogue of Artifacts</u> and spoken of by both Mme de T and Malbosc on February 28, 1824. Faceted oval emeralds, set in silver. The gems are arrayed by size with the largest oval in the center of the chain. Effect: The wearer's will belongs to the one who fastened the necklace around their neck. The necklace cannot be removed except by the person in command. Malbosc does not mention any limitations; Mme de T suspects killing the person in control would break its hold. Her abrupt departure from the room precluded further questions about her own imprisonment. Provenance: Songecreux, which may be the name of a house and not a town, thus useless information to anyone but Mme de T. Last known location: Songecreux, 1794.

A pair of linked journals. Bound in black leather. Effect: Text written on the pages of one appears on the pages of the other. They provide a method for nearly instant correspondence across space. The maximum distance is not yet known. Further experiments are warranted. Provenance: Paris, 1824. Note: Created in a moment of overwhelming loneliness and desire for someone living, but absent and unreachable by letter. (Said letter would be a dangerous proposition for both of us, and would most likely be deposited into the hearth unread anyway, which is what I deserve.) But at least this artifact seems useful.

PRIVATE DIARY OF J MORÈRE, SEPTEMBER 9, 1824

Tonight while I was at Camille's townhouse, after dinner when the candles had melted and the other guests had left, she wanted to talk about Alphonse. Even touching his letter made me sick. I burned it unopened. Still, he's alive and in Paris and looking for me. I want to die or kill something. Him, I suppose.

No, that thought sickens me as well. I don't have the constitution for killing, clearly.

I would have said that out loud to V, but I wasn't quite ready to explain the whole thing to Camille yet. Perhaps because she knows how to contact him, and that makes everything too real.

I want all of this to vanish as if none of it had ever happened. So I told Camille that I didn't want to discuss Alphonse or hear from him ever again, and then, to distract her and to satisfy my own curiosity, I asked her if she ever sees Horace Faucheux socially.

We were sitting on the sofa together. Camille rearranged her voluminous skirts, rustling them unnecessarily, trying to disguise her interest in this question. I've told her a lot of things and I'm sure she's guessed more, but we usually avoid this topic.

"The man who tried to kill you and never suffered any consequences? That Horace Faucheux?" she asked.

"I don't know if that's true about the consequences."

"What sort of punishments do you think he suffered?" she asked. "As far as I know, he's still out and about with his insufferable friends, generally being a nuisance to society, spending profligate amounts of money drinking and gambling and hunting and whoring, all the things that ruin women's reputations and make men's. Perhaps buying more mysterious knives."

"You hear about him, then," I said.

"Our paths don't cross," she said firmly. "I hope you're not trying to get into another fight, Julie. The last one didn't go well."

"It didn't," I agreed. "And then Horace's younger sibling mysteriously died."

"Julie. Do not tell me you're imagining some sort of play where the brothers switched places."

I shrugged and said nothing. I've told Camille about my suspicions before, but she thinks it's unhealthy of me to believe that V's still alive. She has no answer for who might have returned my private drawing.

With an air of great patience, though less actual patience than I would have liked, Camille said, "Fine. Explain it to me. So if Victor is posing as Horace—to what end, I won't ask—then what happened to the real Horace?"

"Well, there was a funeral. They buried someone."

"You think Horace is dead. And you began by talking about consequences, so I suppose you think someone murdered him?"

405

I'm still embarrassed about that part, so I didn't look at her.

"Julie, my dear, are you suggesting that your lover disappeared in order to murder the man who attacked you?" Camille probably had too much wine at dinner. Her voice swooped from high to low, sort of like the sound of a laugh, but she didn't laugh. "Well, that's quite a story, but if the job is finished, why hasn't Victor come back for you? Why is he still pretending to be Horace?"

I don't think Camille believed any of this, but she was humoring me.

"I think it has something to do with the mysterious knife," I said. "Or rather, the trade in other mysterious objects. I think Horace's social circle must be buying them, and Victor is... well, I hope he's trying to stop them. I don't know. But he probably feels that he can't come back because I was so adamant about him not getting involved in any of this, and now he's killed someone, and he thinks I won't forgive him."

"And would you?"

"For the murder? I don't care about that," I said. Camille didn't tell me that I should, or that I was being foolish, so I continued, "From everything Victor ever said about Horace, he was a terrible person, and as far as Horace knew, he killed me when he stabbed me. I should have died. It's only because Victor had a particular connection that I survived. So I don't care if Victor did kill him. That's easy to forgive. What's hard to forgive is Victor disappearing and not giving me a choice. Not trusting me to be part of whatever he's doing. I don't want to be protected. I could be useful."

"Ah," Camille said softly. She glanced around, looking for her wine glass, but it was empty. Her gaze settled on my face. "I don't suppose you'd care to tell me how, exactly, a person such as yourself could be useful in this dangerous deception you think Victor is perpetrating."

"Do you remember earlier this spring at Verneuil when I grew a beard?" I asked. "And then later in the summer when we, um..."

"Unwisely mixed our friendship with fucking, yes, my dear, I do remember that," she said and patted my knee. "And we had a very mature conversation about how you're lovely in all ways, including in bed, and that I am an excellent kisser—an excellent everything, in fact, except I am a failure in one domain, which is that I am not Victor, and that is why I caught you clutching a pillow and bravely repressing your sniffles afterward. I prefer my lovers to cry because they are in awe of my sublime sexual generosity. So no, I haven't forgotten the grievous blow you dealt my self-esteem, Julie."

"It doesn't seem to have suffered all that much," I said.

"I also remember," Camille went on loudly, "that we concluded that we would both prefer to remain friends and fuck other people, though I haven't noticed you doing any of that. You said 'other people' but you meant 'the scoundrel who abandoned me,' you ridiculous creature."

"This is not why I mentioned the subject," I said stiffly. "You've seen me naked. You know that I change."

"I'm not sure that I did. I knew you were unusual, but so are plenty of other people." She smiled mischievously. "I've slept with quite a lot of them. I knew you sometimes went by Julien and sometimes by Julie. You're telling me something different."

"It's all connected. I've always been this way, long before I could change my body. It's my nature that motivated me to use magic, not the other way around."

"Magic," Camille said. "Adrienne said the word to me when we were taking care of you, but this is the first time I've heard you use it. It's marvelous that you can change your body with magic, Julie, but I don't see why it qualifies you to run headlong into danger over a person neither of us has seen in six months. A person who <u>left</u> you, I must point out again, though I know it's tiresome."

"A person who saved my life. And changing myself isn't the only thing I can do," I said, and finally told Camille the whole truth: Alphonse, the Tilleul paintings, nullifying and destroying one with V. "It was exhilarating, working with Victor. It made me wonder what else I could do. I wanted to do more. And then—well. You know what happened."

"I do know what happened," she said. "And it is my opinion that you should not do anything about this wild theory of yours, and you should instead come to more parties with me and we'll find you somebody who hasn't faked their death or committed even a single hypothetical murder. But I've seen the look on your face and I know you're not going to listen."

I thought about telling her about the gift, the neat cut edges of every paragraph, the care they showed, the generosity, but despite having written a famous novel about lovers separated for years, Camille is impatient with my yearning. I think she is trying to protect me—she once loved someone who didn't love her back, and she is trying to save me from that suffering. She doesn't understand why I can't let go of V when I could just find myself another equally attractive but far less dangerous person to befriend and fool around with.

I suppose that's fair. I could do that. We go to a lot of salons and parties and I have all of Camille's connections available. There is surely someone adequate. Or if there isn't, I have friends and a loving family and a fulfilling career and that could be a life. A very good life.

Maybe it's foolish to want more.

Maybe it's foolish to want V, specifically. As much tenderness as I feel over their gift, I know we would fight if we saw each other again. But it would be a fight worth having.

PRIVATE DIARY OF J MORÈRE, SEPTEMBER 16, 1824

This morning there was a conch shell outside my door, gleaming and flawless. It is a little bigger than my hand, snow white on the outside shading into aurora red on the inside.

I don't know what it means, but it's beautiful.

[*This entry includes a sketch of the conch.*]

PRIVATE DIARY OF J MORÈRE, SEPTEMBER 23, 1824

A bird's nest today, wrapped in paper. It's of such an intricate construction and hardly damaged at all.

[*This entry includes a sketch of the bird's nest.*]

PRIVATE DIARY OF J MORÈRE, SEPTEMBER 30, 1824

My search for V—"Horace"—has been fruitless. We don't travel in the same circles, and it's not easy for a person like me to enter the private spaces a Horace Faucheux type might frequent. I suppose that's why V is committed to the ruse.

But I know two things. First, V is alive and in Paris at least some of the time. Second, my will to find them is stronger than their will to hide. The trinkets are proof of that.

I stayed up all night for the last three nights, lying in wait. A tread creaked on the stairs in the darkness this morning, and I threw open my door hoping to catch V. Instead I terrified the grimy urchin who was delivering a basket of peaches.

He told me, for an exorbitant price, that "a man" whose face he didn't see had paid him to put this basket at my door. I questioned the child about how he'd entered the building, which should be locked at night, but there wasn't enough money in the world for that answer. Suspect V paid him in money and a set of lockpicks.

So it's not possible to catch V in the act. I will continue to step outside every morning with hope quickening my pulse.

The peaches are ripe to bursting. I can't even smell my turpentine anymore, that's how fragrant they are. It's like a sun-warmed orchard forested my studio overnight. Maybe it's the lack of sleep, but they're so sweet I feel a little drunk.

[*This entry contains a watercolor sketch of two peaches, one whole and one cut to expose its center.*]

JULIE MORÈRE TO ADRIENNE MORÈRE, OCTOBER 10, 1824
POSTMARKED PARIS

My dear Adrienne,

I hope you and Léon are still in wedded bliss.

You don't have to worry about me so much. I know I've had a difficult time this year, but things are better now, and I will prove it with a funny story.

Camille and I have met lots of wonderful people recently. We attended a new salon and I witnessed Camille develop a tendre for a young woman within an instant of seeing her. In Camille's defense, the woman—Delphine—is stunning. Like one of Rubens's Graces walked out of the painting and slid her bare arms into those short, puffed sleeves that all evening gowns seem to have these days. (I know you wish for a better description of Delphine's dress, Adrienne, and I have done my best to capture its wide neckline and various ruffles in the enclosed sketch. It was bluish purple. If I were painting Delphine's complexion, I would use cream yellow and reddish white. Her hair is a lovely shade, predominantly brownish orange, like a dark topaz or a piece of amber.)

You probably know this from having spent a few days

in Camille's company, but among our set, Camille is accustomed to success. She is gracious and careful about her fame, but it can't be ignored that when she wants someone, all she has to do is say hello in a particular tone of voice and they will blush.

So I was delighted that after Camille introduced herself with her usual confidence, Delphine said, "And what do you do?" with such sweetness that it came back around to being wicked. It was clear to me that Delphine recognized Camille—in trousers and long hair, Camille cannot be missed—and simply wanted to tease her, but it was not clear to Camille. I've never seen anyone wrongfoot her like that. She's usually on top of things. It only took Delphine a few syllables to dismantle one of France's greatest living writers.

"I'm... a novelist?" Camille said.

"Oh?"

"I wrote, um, Virginie, that's what it's called."

A tilt of Delphine's head and the slightest of smiles.

"It's, uh, about a girl. But also how the institution of marriage crushes women. She falls in love anyway, though. There's a dog in it."

Delphine only stopped this unceasing embarrassment by laying a hand on Camille's arm, grinning in a wild, conspiratorial way that didn't fit with her coiffure or her dress or her general veneer of civilization, and whispering, "I know. I wept all through the ending. It was brilliant."

Camille shut her mouth like a door slamming.

"I'm delighted to meet you," Delphine said, as well as a number of other things intended to salve Camille's pride that I doubt Camille registered, since Delphine's hand was still touching her.

Camille was not restored to herself until long after

Delphine had wandered away to chat with the other guests. Her trills of laughter glittered in the air, and I caught Camille watching her several times. I hope we become friends. Sometimes the people we meet at salons are grasping, only wanting to be near Camille because they think to raise their own status, but Delphine didn't give me that impression. It was also very entertaining to watch the two of them together, and that alone is reason to hope for more. Even if it makes me ache—well, no, this letter isn't about that. It's wonderful to watch people flirt, that's my point.

So you see that life is perfectly fine here, and you can lay your concerns to rest. Tell me more about what you're painting.

With love,
Julie

CAMILLE DUPIN TO JULIE MORÈRE, OCTOBER 27, 1824
POSTMARKED VERNEUIL

My dearest Julie,

I wish you had come with me to the countryside. Then I wouldn't have to write this most pathetic of letters. Alas, you remain dedicated to your art and have forced me to put my thoughts to paper.

You saw what passed between Delphine and me at our first encounter. It was a flirtation, was it not? No matter how unbearably I performed, it <u>was</u> a flirtation.

I know she is married, but it is a loveless arrangement and would have posed no obstacle. We could have dodged her worthless husband. Here is what plagues me: why should she have flirted like that only to spend all her time in my company talking about some fool named Ali?

Her monstrous husband does not like to let her out of the house, but she's clever and we have contrived to see each other almost every day since the night we met. Strolls. Drives. Calls at home. Dressmakers. Milliners. No matter the setting, the incomparably lovely and intelligent Delphine captures my attention with her affectionate conversation and her chaste yet suggestive touches—and then she overflows with stories about Ari.

I've never met the man, but even his name is odious to me. I want to push him off a cliff, Julie, but I can't because then Delphine will be unhappy, and Delphine's happiness is of paramount importance to me.

Do I have a rival? What an unbearable cliché.

I don't know why I came here. My novel is unsalvageable and I hate all these trees.

Yours,
Camille

JULIE MORÈRE TO CAMILLE DUPIN, NOVEMBER 1, 1824
POSTMARKED PARIS

Camille, my dear friend,

The good news is that you don't have a rival. The bad news is that Ari has won. You have to give up on Delphine. Her heart belongs to someone else.

I could be mean about all the times you told me you'd never be so foolish as to fall in love again and gently (or forcefully) tried to dissuade me from my own sentiments, but I won't rub salt in your wound. Come back to the city and we'll get drunk about it.

Yours,

Julie

JULIE MORÈRE TO ADRIENNE MORÈRE, NOVEMBER 7, 1824

POSTMARKED PARIS

My dear Adrienne,

I'm glad you agree with me that Delphine sounds delightful. She is—though she's also something of a tragic figure. I saw her again tonight and thought I would share the story with you, since you claim to be leading such a dull country life. (I know the truth is that you are rapturously in love with your husband and trying not to make me feel sad and alone by writing about it all the time. I forgive you your happiness, Adrienne. Nobody deserves it more.)

I recently finished a portrait of these rich industrialists, the Taillefers. I don't like them and I wouldn't have done it, but they paid me a great deal of money and it seemed like a good way to cement my reputation as a portraitist. I know I once said I never wanted to be one, but I'm enjoying myself and it does pay well.

Anyway, the Taillefers unveiled the portrait at this absurd party and they invited me. You know how I feel about parties, but you also know how I feel about people praising my work. So I went.

The portrait, with Taillefer standing behind his seated

wife, was displayed in an enormous gilt frame in the glow of hundreds of lamps and candles in the ballroom. I'm proud of making both of them look pleasant and enamored of each other, which they aren't.

The ballroom and every other room of the Taillefers' townhouse were stuffed with people, all of us sweating into our finery. What a shame to spend a crisp November evening sweltering in a crowd of people I don't care for. Sometimes I regret my dedication to wearing suits in public—at least evening gowns allow for bare arms and necks. All those layers of skirts look hellish, though.

Speaking of skirts, Delphine was there in an absolute rustling cloud of them, looking radiant despite everyone around her wilting.

[*A small portrait of Delphine in ink.*]

I'm trying to be sensitive to Camille's pining and not make things difficult by spending time with Delphine, but tonight it was hard because everyone at the Taillefers' party was awful <u>except</u> for Delphine, who is wonderful, and who I wish returned Camille's feelings because they'd be perfect together. But it's not her fault if she's in love with someone else. All I know about him is that his name is Ari and Camille hates him without having met him. Knowing Delphine's taste in people, I imagine Ari is probably decent and not deserving of being pushed off a cliff, which Camille once despairingly suggested.

The same cannot be said of Delphine's husband.

I didn't spend much time with him at the party. She clearly doesn't care to. He's a sneering little man, obsessed with the power granted by the "de" in his family name (he's Henri de Tousserat, Marquis de Quennetière, if you're curious) and deeply insecure about Delphine's wit and charisma. For the brief moment that the three of us were together, he complained bitterly about the crowd and the heat and everything his wife did and did not do.

"You shouldn't have worn that dress. It's not flattering." (This is an infuriating falsehood. I shudder to record it.) "Then again, it's also unbecoming when a married woman of your age tries to pretend she's still beautiful, so it's good to acknowledge that you're not what you used to be."

Delphine is one of the most beautiful women I have ever laid eyes on. She is your equal, Adrienne, and you know I don't say that lightly. I also suspect she's not more than twenty-five years old. And her husband looks as pinched and shriveled as his soul.

He continued in this manner for some time, until Delphine said, sweetly enough that her words could not be counted an insult, "You seem distressed, husband. Are you feeling well? As you said, it's stifling in here. Perhaps you'd like to retire to the drawing room for a moment? You could lie down."

He sputtered with rage and left.

"When we first met, you told me that your name was Delphine Lazare," I said after a moment.

"I don't much care for being Delphine de Tousserat, Marquise de Quennetière," she replied.

"I can see why."

"It's not always so bad. He has his mistresses and his hunting and his hobbies. If I'm not right in front of him, he doesn't interfere in my life. I'm lucky, really. I can coax him into letting me out on occasion, so I still go to salons where I meet people like you and Camille. The false name I gave you wasn't a lie. It was a wish."

They live in the same house most of the time, so escaping his attention must be laborious, which doesn't seem lucky to me.

"Before I got married, I used to wind men up at these parties."

"Like what you did your husband? The drawing room, lying down, all that?"

"Exactly like that. There'd be two or three of them drooling down the front of my dress and I'd say the most insulting things in a sweet voice. Some didn't even notice. Some did, but couldn't do anything about it. It was great fun. Or what passes for fun in a place like this."

"Men don't ever leave you alone, then."

She laughed. "I like you, Julien. I hope this isn't an inappropriate thing to say, but you talk about men as if you aren't one."

I decided to trust her. "I'm not."

"Oh," she said. "Please excuse me. I didn't realize. You're... a little like Camille, then? Should I call you something else?"

I said I was, more or less, not wanting to discuss it at length in the Taillefers' ballroom, and that she could keep calling me Julien. But I am glad to have my good opinion of Delphine confirmed by her reaction. Perhaps some day you'll visit me in Paris in good circumstances and I can introduce you.

Give my love to everyone.

Love,

Julie

PRIVATE DIARY OF J MORÈRE, NOVEMBER 7, 1824

I've distressed Adrienne enough for a lifetime, so I didn't tell her who else I saw at the Taillefers' party. I wish Camille were here so I'd have someone to talk to, though Camille has a low opinion of V and wouldn't be happy that I saw them.

Horace, that is. But I'm convinced it was V.

I went to the awful Taillefers' awful party of awful people because they seem like the sort of unsavory rich people that Horace—the real one—might have socialized with. It's why I accepted their commission in the first place. I thought it might be an opportunity to make more connections among that circle.

I wasn't expecting a sighting. My name is on that portrait, after all, so if Horace/V was trying to avoid me, attendance would be a risk. I made the rounds, met some of the Taillefers' friends, performed politeness in the hopes that they might some day hire me, and then whiled away the hours with Delphine, watching her bat away would-be adulterers. I scanned the crowd again and again, more foolish and more disappointed every time.

And then I locked eyes with Horace Faucheux.

It's a chill, seeing someone you last encountered with a knife in their hand. The sight snuffed out everything else in the room for me. No roar, no press, no heat. All the way across the room, just one glance, and I knew. Objectively, Horace is good-looking: tall, muscular, symmetrical, unmarked. He has the same golden coloring as V, but no one could ever mistake them for each other, and it has nothing to do with size. There's a lightness, a quickness to everything V does. Horace doesn't have it. He's stony.

Tonight, the person who looked like Horace—they flinched.

They flinched exactly like I've spent months imagining V would flinch, if I ever saw them again.

And then they melted into the crowd.

It's not much to go on. But between that letter announcing the death of Victorine Faucheux and the series of little offerings at my door, I know what I saw.

I gave chase into the smoke-filled billiard room and the empty study and the cold, dark garden, far from the anguished ballroom violins. A flash of blond, an apology, an understated hello—I would have accepted anything as a victory. What I wanted was to slam them into a wall and kiss them furiously. But there was never anyone there.

PRIVATE DIARY OF J MORÈRE, NOVEMBER 8, 1824

If I had any question about the source of these gifts—I didn't, not really, though I've been reluctant to write anything down—today's delivery clears me of all hesitations. It's an obscene novel, but tucked into the pages was a small flat object made of two copper disks, each one with an alphabet printed around the edge. I know from a long-ago conversation with V that this thing is a cipher disk. I have a vague notion of how to use the disk to match up one alphabet to the other and decode a text.

The illustrations in the novel aren't any good. The text isn't much better, but I fiddled around with the cipher disk and I don't think I'm meant to decode anything here. The book was a wrapping for the disk—a signature of sorts, making sure I knew who sent it. As if I could ever have harbored a doubt.

I await a letter.

PRIVATE DIARY OF J MORÈRE, NOVEMBER 10, 1824

I can't believe V writes their whole diary in code. What a colossal effort. It took me hours to unravel this letter and it was agonizing.

I didn't understand how to use the cipher disk until I realized that the letter—of course—starts with "J."

V BEAUCHÊNE TO J MORÈRE, NOVEMBER 7, 1824
SLIPPED UNDER THE DOOR

J—

Your work on the portrait is magnificent as always, by the way. I can't believe you made the Taillefers look like people I'd want to spend time with.

I apologize for last night. I didn't want you to see me like this, and I won't pretend it was all selfless desire to spare you the sight of the man who attacked you. (Though it was that, a little bit.) I'm ashamed, not merely because I'm hideous in this disguise, as I think we can agree, but also because I've behaved abominably toward you, as we can probably also agree. So I didn't imagine you'd want to see me or Horace, and then I fucked up and showed you both. I imagine the overlap is even more unsettling for you than it is for me, and I have been sick over this fraud for months.

Here is a short but incomplete list of things for which I am sorry:

- leaving you
- not explaining anything

- seeing you unexpectedly last night
- leaving you (again)
- not explaining anything (again, but please don't stop decoding this letter yet)

God. Why are you letting me write to you? <u>Are</u> you letting me write to you? Maybe you've tossed this letter out the window along with everything else I've given you. (You haven't, at least not yet. I've been checking the alley.)

I want to tell you everything, at least everything that is within my rights to share, but you should know that (1) the truth will put you in danger (2) it will not make you any less unhappy with me (3) everything is shit. If you still want to know, leave a note outside your door.

I don't wish you had caught me, but I do wish you had caught me. I wish I had been myself, or not myself, but some other me. You'll have to be some other you in this wish, because I am not at all sure what the real you would have done.

I wish, after we locked eyes across the ballroom, that I had been just a touch too obvious in my escape. Afterward, you wonder if I did it on purpose. I could have slipped away, you think. With all those mirrors in the hall, doubling the crowd and the chandeliers, it would have been easy. My clothes are fashionable, a suit of deep blue heavy with gold embroidery, and they might have stood out on any other evening at any other party, but here color and glitter are camouflage. There are so many wide skirts and long wigs to hide behind.

When I threaded my way through the crowd, you lost me. Your long-awaited opportunity for justice, or vengeance, or reunion, or all three, gone as soon at it appeared. You stare at the throng, bereft. Whatever it was you wanted me for, you did want me.

You refuse to lose me a second time. You vow to ask every guest, to check every room.

But you don't have to. Because I make a mistake—if it is a mistake.

I exit the glow of the ballroom. I push through one of the glass doors into the garden. A few guests are gathered on the stone patio, close to the light spilling through the windows, but not enough to hide me. I stride across the patio, heading for the sloped lawn down into the garden, with its fountains, its hedges, and its high stone walls.

You cut through the crowd and follow me into the night, one hand on the smallsword sheathed at your side. An accessory to your finery, more decoration than weapon, but the tip is still lethally sharp. Sometimes people assume that because you don't fight a lot of duels, you don't know how to use it. You've never bothered to correct them.

But I know your skill. It's one reason I'm running.

I'm also a coward and a scoundrel besides. I shouldn't have come here, but I can never resist an opportunity to see you—even from a distance. Even when I know you might see me.

You follow the sound of my shoe soles scraping the packed earth. You can't see me, or even my shadow, but the hum of the night doesn't hide my footsteps. Left down the path, then right, then left again, zigzagging deeper into the hedges. Each turn feels like the one I would take, and a spark of rage lights in your heart as you wonder if I am making this too easy, if I want to be tracked—or worst of all, if you know me so well that tracking me isn't a matter of listening for my footfalls and the occasional exhale, but the two of us being drawn to each other despite everything. I broke your heart. My behavior was shameful; your anger is righteous. You tighten your grip on the hilt of your sword.

At the next turn, a shoe lies stranded in the path. You kick aside the heeled slipper, a delicate thing meant for floating through stately dances in ballrooms, not fleet-footed nighttime hunts. A few paces onward, its twin suffers the same fate. You wonder why I am wandering this maze in my stocking feet, and then come across my abandoned frock coat, moonlight picking out the embroidery rippling over its folds. I couldn't have taken it off while running, so I must have slowed down.

You're not surprised to see me around the next corner, but you are surprised that I'm halfway up the stone wall that borders the garden, my silk-clad toes shoved into the mortared ridges and my arms straining for the top. My shoes and tight coat wouldn't have allowed me to make this escape attempt.

It's undignified, a little bit ridiculous, and it saps your will to charge forward. It's not that you expected me to have the courage to stand and fight. My naked cowardice is honest; I've acknowledged your superior skill before the duel has even begun. If you weren't furious, you might find it funny or even flattering. But how should you treat an opponent who is willing to discard dignity, propriety, honor? A more ruthless person would have grabbed my ankle and yanked. You could have me in a heap on the ground. This could end now. You hesitate just long enough that I scramble to the top.

While I am still crouched and panting, you launch into motion. The wall is easier for you, with your long limbs and your strength, but you still have to leave your coat and shoes on the ground and you resent me for it.

The stone chills the bottoms of your feet through your stockings.

You rise to your full height, balanced like you were born for this. It steals my breath. I should toss my sword aside and jump down into the forest outside the garden wall. I might cut my feet and sprain my ankles, but the thicket could hide me. The trees would protect me from your sword. It would give me a chance to evade you.

Instead I glide along the top of the wall, thinking of how smooth and sturdy it is, and not of the precipitous drop on either side. I put distance between us, but it won't take you long to close it, especially not after you unsheathe your sword. You level it at me, its long thin blade tipped with moonlight.

I'm a fool, but not so much of one that I'll let you point a sword at my defenseless back. I turn toward you, drawing my own sword. I don't want to hurt you, not again. I don't want to run, either.

I want this. You. If the only way I can have you is in a fight, then we'll fight.

You lunge. Always surefooted, the narrow width of the wall doesn't trouble you. Metal slides against metal as my blade blocks yours. A second thrust. You advance, I retreat. I've never been the duelist you are, but I'm slippery. I twist and swoop and duck out of the way. We go on like that until we can hear each other breathing. The lengths of our swords separate us, but this is closer than we've been in a long time. I imagine the line of your neck gleaming with sweat. A few strands of your dark hair have worked free from the clubbed queue you wear and they're plastered to the skin above your collar.

The distraction costs me. I wobble and nearly fall off

the wall as I dodge your next attack. When I find my footing again, I focus only on the fight.

New constellations appear between us, your sword piercing the darkness. You hit me with a shower of attacks like meteors, streaks of light that I catch from the corner of my eye, and I lose ground. We're nearly at a corner of the garden wall now. I don't trust myself to step over the column that marks it.

Inside the garden, the hedged paths have given way to an open space filled with a circular fountain. A statue of a naked nymph pouring water stands at the center, but the basin in her arms is as empty as the garden. The wide pool of water at her feet lies undisturbed.

Outside the garden, the forest goes on for miles, thinning into rivers and pastures and little villages on occasion, but mostly thick, shadowed, impenetrable. It's my only real exit from this duel. I can't win, but I can run.

I hop backward to avoid your latest strike, landing on the balls of my feet, the backs of my heels just scraping the column capital that marks the corner of the wall. Balanced there for an instant, I pivot and plunge down into the garden. Landing sends a shock through every bone, but I don't break anything. I get up, dust my breeches off, and back away from the wall. You loom over me, poised on top of the wall, sword held loosely at your side. We are both panting.

I honestly don't know if you'll jump down here and run me through. It's not only the darkness that renders you inscrutable to me. You're angry. You're right to be angry. But are you angry enough to stab that sword right through my heart? In this moment, which might be one of a dwindling few, shivering with exhaustion and exhilaration, I think I wouldn't blame you if you did. I think maybe I would stand still and let you, if only you'd let me look at you one last time.

You land so much more gracefully than I did. You unsheathe your sword and renew your attacks. Metal whispers and shrieks against metal. I dodge. I parry. You return relentlessly. We circle the fountain, once and then again, and I would go around a third time, a fourth, all night, if a stumble didn't send me one step out of line. I find my footing again, but now my back faces the wall and you're advancing, shrinking the distance between us even as I retreat until my shoulders hit the stone.

The cold tip of your sword traces under my jaw, lingering over the hot, frantic pulse in my throat.

I don't move except to open my hand. My sword lands in the dirt beside us.

Slowly, you withdraw the sharp point from my skin. You don't sheathe your weapon. I lift my trembling hands in surrender and drop to my knees. Your sword hovers, ready to pierce my heart or slice through my clothes. The night hums around us, our breath mingling in the cool air. My body shudders with the force of my heartbeat, and I will it to be quiet. I am at your mercy.

What are you going to do next?

—V

J MORÈRE TO V BEAUCHÊNE, NOVEMBER 11, 1824
LEFT OUTSIDE THE DOOR

[*This letter contains an illustration of two figures, one kneeling and one standing. The standing figure points a sword at the other's throat. There is one line of text written as a caption to the image.*]

I don't want to kill you, little weasel. I just want you to tell me the truth.

V BEAUCHÊNE TO J MORÈRE, NOVEMBER 13, 1824
SLIPPED UNDER THE DOOR

J—

Here's an account of what's happened since we last saw each other as ourselves. I've tried to be truthful even when the truth is unflattering to me. It's ciphered, but I'd prefer that you destroy it after you've read it—unless you were lying about not wanting to kill me, in which case I suppose you can put these pages in the post and have done with it.

It was strange to attend my own funeral.

Stranger still to stand by the grave, dressed as my brother, knowing it was him in the ground. If it had been Horace's funeral, I wouldn't have been allowed to go to the cemetery as Victorine Faucheux, since the graveside overwhelms delicate female constitutions. I wouldn't have been allowed there as Victor Beauchêne, either. Horace made sure that no version of me could ever watch the first shovel full of dirt tumble down onto his casket.

So I watched it as him, instead.

A magnanimous gesture, Horace Faucheux making sure his father's second child was buried in the family plot even after being disinherited. Nobody expected such grace from

Horace, but perhaps this series of tragedies—his mother's death several years ago, his father's recent passing, and now the youngest family member as well—has changed him. That's what they said around town.

What really changed my brother was bleeding to death from an internal wound made with the phantom knife.

I owe you an explanation for why Horace came to the Maison Laval that night. He was angry because he believed I'd stolen a ring from him, and he was correct. But I didn't steal the ring to further my own ambitions. I didn't want to wield it at all. My father had visited me at the Maison Laval and revealed that he'd worn this ring for years, using it to influence everyone around him, but my mother especially. It was her resistance to his commands that caused her to fall ill and eventually die. Horace stole the ring from my father, and my father had come to demand that I steal it back. He was dying of the same thing that killed my mother—resisting the ring's influence. I had no desire to help him, but I knew it would be wrong to let Horace keep such an artifact. Because I hesitated to act, my father had time to tell Horace that I was a threat, that I'd stolen from the family fortune. So despite my precautions, when the ring disappeared, Horace suspected me.

That was why he came to the Maison Laval on the night he attacked you. It was my fault. I had taken the ring. The only reason he didn't find it in the wreckage of my room was because I'd hidden it among Aunt S's things, and Horace didn't think to search her room. He always discounted her.

You know the rest of the story of that night, or as much of it as I can tell you: I saw you'd been wounded with a cursed artifact and went to find someone with the ability to heal you. After that, I left to kill Horace, that he might never harm you or anyone else again.

I was wounded in the fight and needed help from the same person who helped you. That person also accompanied me to my family's house. Their part of the story is not mine to tell, and I want to protect them.

It's foolish to write any of this down, of course, but it feels even more extravagantly foolish to name anyone else. It's not that I don't trust you, J. I trust you more than anyone and that's the only reason I'm taking the risk of writing this letter—though God knows <u>you</u> shouldn't trust <u>me</u>.

What matters here is that Horace wasn't alone when we found him.

He was being threatened by a man with whom he had an illicit business arrangement, Jean-Louis-Alphonse Malbosc. They were looking for my colleague as well as for magical artifacts that grant control over other people. I mention this because Malbosc is the same man who abused your talents when you were younger. He is also the author of the first book I read about magic.

It was published in 1620.

His crimes against you are not his only crimes, so it will not surprise you to learn he has kept himself alive so long through wicked means. My colleagues believe Malbosc cannot be killed—not while he still possesses that which keeps him alive. They wanted me to discover where he keeps it so we could retrieve it. (I have acquired some new skills over the course of our separation, though mine don't equal my colleagues'.)

I couldn't return to the past and erase the decisions I'd made that put you in danger, but I could keep you out of future danger by stopping Malbosc. To do that, I had to get close enough to discover his secret. He is, of course, guarded and distrustful, even with people in his circle.

So I had to become one of them.

Horace's death was the perfect opportunity. As siblings, we already looked a little alike, and since I lack your transformative talents, I needed that advantage. (If we ever meet in person again, I would love to talk to you more about your work. Among so many other things.) At first, I sewed persuasive letters into the linings of all Horace's clothes—I'm so good with the pen now that if I channel enough of my will while writing, people don't even need to read the words—and then later, I did it with stitching instead. Simpler to use the materials at hand. There's face powder involved in the deception as well, and a few other items, but dress and attitude go a long way. One drawback of constructing my illusion with clothing is that it doesn't quite hold if anyone touches me. I am not as tall as I appear. So I try not to be touched. But the relief of using the clothes is that I can take them off and <u>not</u> be Horace. I have to breathe sometimes.

I don't enjoy looking like Horace, but I won't lie: inventing the techniques that allowed me to steal his life was exhilarating. Tricking his horrible friends was satisfying, too, at least for the first few times. There's a fine edge between terror and excitement. I stumbled back to the townhouse in the middle of the night after those first few outings—I always pretend to drink more than I actually did—and then lay in bed with my heart racing. It was working. It was going to work.

I thought, back then, that it would be over in a matter of weeks. Infiltrating Horace's life was easy; I was good at it. His friends ascribed any small difference in behavior to distraction or fatigue. No one thought Horace was grieving me. They knew I'd caused him trouble and assumed he'd taken care of the problem, but they were all impressed by how cleanly he'd done it. Burying me in the family plot was a nice touch, they agreed. His friend the Marquis de Quennetière—a monster I now address as Henri—slapped my back over that like I'd told a good joke. That's the kind of contact I have to avoid, but luckily he was drunk at the time. They're all drunk a lot.

Horace's friends are brutes and louts, interested only in their own pleasure, and for most of them, pleasure includes crushing other people under their heels. They do this with money, political power, physical strength, and where those things fail, they do it with magical artifacts. Malbosc is similar, and he cultivated their loyalty and siphoned their money, a sort of Tartuffe. His rare appearances at their club or occasionally their homes were met with reverence. (They didn't have much reverence for anything or anyone else.) He was the source of all their knowledge and a good many of the objects they coveted. He'd brought them into this new world, made them feel powerful.

I can only speak to Horace's—my—relationship with him, but perhaps he drew all the others aside to make secret bargains and I simply don't know it yet. Malbosc's arrangement with Horace was tailored to Horace's particular fears and desires. Horace watched our mother waste away while she tried to resist my father's poisonously magical suggestions, and then he inflicted the same fate on our father. He lived in horror of a similar end for himself. Malbosc promised him the secret of immortality in exchange for Horace's help finding one of my colleagues, whose name I have kept out of this letter, and an artifact

THE SCANDALOUS LETTERS OF V AND J

that grants total control of another person's will. (An emerald necklace. I hope you never see it.)

Needless to say, Malbosc did not deliver immortality to my brother. My life depends on his ignorance. I have spent more time than I wish in his company. I know him well now—not well enough that I can end this charade, but well. You do, too, of course. He wants money and power, but he's drawn to a particular kind of power that operates in secret and that controls, diminishes, suffocates anyone he pulls into his orbit.

Before I embarked on my deception, I had a memorable conversation with my colleague. I said, "So Malbosc doesn't want to insinuate himself into the king's circle?"

"If the whim took him, he might, I suppose. But that sort of thing was never his goal—ruling a nation, moving armies around, appearing in ceremonial processions. Not that he wouldn't enjoy adoration from the people, but it's too much work and it doesn't provide what he craves. What he likes best is to control a devoted few. The world at large bores him. His world is his own enjoyment and whoever he can lure near him to suck out their life like a leech."

Malbosc is a private sort of monster, not a public one. I was struck by the metaphor. "Is that how he's lived so long?"

"Yes," my colleague said and closed our conversation.

Malbosc is a parasite. Unfortunately, even after months, I still haven't discovered his secret. He is not susceptible to my persuasive pen, and even if he were, he forbade me to write to him. My wretched family heirloom, a ring that allows me influence over people, occasionally dissuades him from threatening me, but it cannot contravene his will, so it's useless for ferreting out the answers I need.

Fortunately, he doesn't have what he wants, either. I have lied and lied to keep my colleague hidden from him. There has been no sign of the necklace. Perhaps I no longer have the right, but I shudder to think what might have happened if he'd had such an artifact when he'd known you. I remain grateful for Adrienne's intervention. I wish I could say that I've prevented any such harm in the future.

While perpetrating my deception among Horace's friends, I passed a lot of information to my colleagues. They retrieved a number of dangerous artifacts, but our real goal remained out of reach. This hardly consoles me when I think of the wasted months, every hour I spent feeling further and further degraded by their company. I am sparing you the details, which are both dull and appalling, of things they—<u>we</u> said and did. Sometimes I worry that I am permanently contaminated by the way these men think and speak and act. After a certain time, getting away with the charade no longer excited me and the goal felt so far away. I missed you. I missed myself.

Is it any wonder that I broke? I came as close as I could to visiting you: I went to the Salon. Not as Horace, because it would have been unbearable, and not as myself, because it would have been dangerous, but as someone else. I'd perfected the trick with the clothes by then, and with access to my late family's fortune, ordering a new suit is no trouble. I can change my face, too, with the aid of the face powder and this little hand mirror a colleague gave me. It's all illusory, a change for the eyes and not the hands, and I maintain my false face with force of will alone. I couldn't manage it in front of <u>Young Man writing</u>

a letter. It was too hard to look at your portrait of me and be someone else. The illusion slipped from my grasp. I had to dab at my eyes with a handkerchief to cover my face and then push my way out of the crowd.

The loss of the illusion was, perhaps, not my only reason for dabbing at my eyes. I know I don't deserve your sympathy for how often I have cried over you. I don't have any right to be proud of you, to delight in the success of your work, but I can't help that, either. I shouldn't have been relieved when gossip turned away from your alleged liaison with Camille toward Camille's new flirtations. I shouldn't be giving you gifts, no matter how discreetly. I shouldn't have been thrilled when you wrote back to my first letter; I certainly shouldn't be writing this one. My self-control suffices to spend months pretending to be someone I am not, except when it comes to you, J. Thinking of you—even when it hurts—is the one happiness I can never deny myself. You asked for the truth and I'm telling it.

It has not all been despair. Sometimes I slip away from this life to meet with my colleagues, who I suppose are my friends now, though I'm no expert in that matter. Horace had more friends than I ever did, and now I've stolen his and I wish I hadn't. But my colleagues do care for me in their way.

One of them has a companion who keeps himself apart from our affairs, but still spends time with us. I like him best of all. He's cheerful and kind. It soothes me to have even the briefest encounters with someone outside this world. Though he isn't really outside it—he knows what his beloved does. I do occasionally wonder if, in another life, you might have accepted such a compromise. It's too late for that now that I've ruined everything, of course. I don't expect you to forgive me for leaving or lying. As I said, I would let you run me through with a sword if that was what you wanted. This written list of my failures falls far short of that.

This friend I was discussing, the one whose lover is one of my colleagues—the pair of them encouraged me, not so long ago, to abandon this project, since it hadn't borne fruit and was making me miserable.

But I worry too much about what Malbosc will do if he gets what he wants.

He's in Paris again. Sometimes he retreats to a distant country estate to which I have not yet received an invitation. My courage might fail me if I did. But the Faubourg Saint-Germain and its surrounding neighborhoods are familiar enough territory, and I am to see him tomorrow.

I don't know if I'll be able to write to you again, J. There will be no more gifts for some time. It would be dangerous for me to further entangle myself in your life as I spend time with the man who used you and made you afraid. He can't know you're here. Over the course of my deception, I've learned that your skills are extraordinarily rare even among people familiar with magic. Malbosc undoubtedly still wants you for your power, and I've encountered far too many cursed artifacts that would grant him control over you. Be careful, J. Stop doing things like painting portraits of the Taillefers. Find some <u>nice</u> people to paint.

I will be careful, too. I must take my leave. Even if I can't see you or write to you, at least I can know you're alive, making beautiful paintings. That will have to be enough.

—V

IV
THE EMERALD NECKLACE
1824-1825

CAMILLE DUPIN TO JULIE MORÈRE, DECEMBER 15, 1824
POSTMARKED PARIS

My dear Julie,

I know you're brooding furiously over some painting or another, so this note is to remind you that Delphine is hosting another one of her my-awful-husband-is-out-of-town salons this evening and I am giving a reading. My plan is to do such a good job that she falls in love with me immediately. Your presence is required for moral support. Wear something that doesn't have any paint on it—but don't look better than me.

Don't make me drag you from your studio.

Your dearest and best friend whose force of will is stronger than yours, don't test it,

Camille

CAMILLE DUPIN TO JULIE MORÈRE, JANUARY 15, 1825
POSTMARKED PARIS

My dear Julie,

I know I failed to make Delphine fall in love with me at last month's reading, but she did flirt with me, so I have decided to believe in incremental progress. She is hosting another salon—mercifully, the Marquis leaves town frequently—and that Haitian poet Marie Lapointe is reading, so we simply can't miss her. I will drag you, etc., etc.

Your dearest and best friend whose optimism in regard to Delphine's affections is not at all pathetic,

Camille

CAMILLE DUPIN TO JULIE MORÈRE, JANUARY 16, 1825
POSTMARKED PARIS

My dear Julie,

Did you, right before my eyes, finagle a portrait commission from the object of my affection so that you will be spending hours alone with her <u>without me</u>? Do <u>not</u> be handsome or charming in her presence, Julie, I implore you.

If I put aside my own <u>profound</u> feelings of betrayal, I can see that it would be good for you to spend time outside of your studio with someone who is not me.

Your dearest and best friend, or so I thought,
Camille

JULIE MORÈRE TO CAMILLE DUPIN, JANUARY 17, 1825
POSTMARKED PARIS

Dear Camille,

There was no finagling. She asked and I said yes. I hope you know I would never betray you in the manner that you're suggesting. I have no intention of seducing Delphine and wouldn't accept if she tried to seduce me. While I will allow that I am handsome (one must be proud of one's own work), I am not in possession of much charm, and regardless, you don't need to worry. I just want to paint her and earn my commission.

You don't need to worry about my social life, either. I have several other portrait clients and I've been to see all of them, and just two days ago, I had coffee with Laurent and Auguste. So you see I do leave my studio without your urging. Besides, it is not melancholy that keeps me here. It's passion.

Your friend,
Julie

CAMILLE DUPIN TO JULIE MORÈRE, JANUARY 19, 1825
POSTMARKED PARIS

My dear Julie,

You'll think me paranoid for this, but please tell me that Delphine was in good health at your most recent portrait session. She has stopped answering my correspondence, which is out of character. Before you ask: no, I did not suggest anything untoward that might have prompted her silence. I am the soul of propriety. Delphine is the one who writes outrageous things—when she writes, that is.

I can't stop thinking about her odious husband. I am distressed.

Your friend,
Camille

JULIE MORÈRE TO CAMILLE DUPIN, JANUARY 20, 1825
POSTMARKED PARIS

Dear Camille,

You are not paranoid. I was going to write to you, in fact. She was not herself at this morning's session. As far as I can tell, she is in good health, but her spirit is gone. She hardly speaks except when I ask her a direct question, and doesn't move unless specifically instructed. Normally I have to ask my portrait subjects to stop moving, or to adjust them so they're in the original pose, but today she sat so still that I had to ask her to move. It was like working with a living statue.

I have a terrible suspicion of what caused this, but I fear to write it down. I will watch over her as best I can.

Your friend,
Julie

PRIVATE DIARY OF J MORÈRE, JANUARY 20, 1825

I went to the Marquis de Quennetière's townhouse today to draw Delphine. She was in the same condition as yesterday, eerily still and not speaking, and in all the same finery, so it was as if I was working with a doll. I'm sure she's been cursed—I know from V's letter that her husband is part of the same circle as Horace and Taillefer, and I strongly suspect the emerald necklace around her neck is the same one V mentioned—but I don't know how to fix it.

Despair and frustration don't help me draw, so there was almost nothing on my page when I heard the front door open and two loud, deep voices laughing and chatting in the foyer next to the parlor where I was drawing. The Marquis de Quennetière's arrival is always an unpleasant surprise, and on a day where I had nothing to show for my time spent with Delphine, I dreaded him even more. He clearly suspects me of trying to seduce his wife, or perhaps the other way around, even though he also sneers at me for being unmanly. (If he only knew how right he was.)

The second voice I did not recognize, but I heard the Marquis invite his friend to come into the parlor.

In a panic, I dashed out an outline of Delphine's head and shoulders in three-quarters view, including the long ringlets framing her face and the enormous strand of emeralds she's wearing for the portrait. My outline wasn't good, but the Marquis is not a connoisseur. He's only discerning enough to tell the difference between a blank page and one that has lines on it.

"Horace Faucheux," the Marquis said behind me, "I present to you my wife, Madame la Marquise de Quennetière—say hello, Delphine—and Julien Morère, the hack my wife has hired to preserve what's left of her fading beauty."

I stiffened. Delphine, of course, did not react to the insult. She did dip her chin and say, "A pleasure to meet you, Monsieur Faucheux."

I didn't miss that her husband had explicitly instructed her to do that. We'd done three sessions together and I'd learned that a direct instruction—I hated to think of it as a command—would stir her to respond. If her husband hadn't told her to say hello, would she have stayed silent?

The Marquis de Quennetière's introduction, abrupt as it was, had given me the time to pause my work and face them, as I should have. I couldn't move. V might be practiced at deceiving people, but I'm not.

I lowered my hand to drop my charcoal into the tray of my easel, and in somebody else's voice, V said, "No, no, please don't stop on my account. I'd like to watch you draw."

I felt V move close enough to touch me, but no touch came. The air between us was charged, magnetic. Still, V's instruction reassured me. My hand didn't shake as I picked up the vine charcoal again and put it to the page. The scratch resounded in the silence.

"You're a shrewd man, Henri, always trying to trick the rest of us into thinking your wife isn't beautiful. Now that I've seen her, I know she's stunning. You just want to keep her for yourself."

The Marquis de Quennetière, who I suppose is called Henri by his friends—ugh—laughed loudly. "I've seen what you like, Horace. Your taste can't be trusted. And it doesn't do to tell women they're beautiful. They get a high opinion of themselves and start to want things."

"Unbearable," V said, and since the Marquis didn't punch V, I suppose he interpreted the statement as "women wanting things is unbearable."

This was not my interpretation.

I wonder if it gave V a secret thrill, performing for me? They don't like posing as Horace, but until today, they'd never been in the room with anybody who understood the truth. As petrified as I was of turning around and seeing their face—<u>not</u> their face—being so near to them and cradling their secret excited me.

"I've solved that problem for myself," the Marquis said. "She's no trouble anymore. Isn't that right, Delphine?"

"Yes, you're right," she said in a voice with all its edges dulled. Her mouth moved, but the rest of her face remained inert.

I could only think of Delphine in the ballroom, slyly asking her irate husband if he needed a nap. It's a horror, what he's done to her.

"Ah," V said. "You've given her a gift, then?"

"Exactly. You don't think she bought those emeralds herself, do you?" he chortled.

So it was the necklace, then. It didn't look evil, just

obscenely expensive, each oval emerald ringed with silver and a few tiny diamonds. The large gems caught the light in a whole range of greens: verdigris, apple, grass, sap, siskin. Once I knew the necklace was cursed, the fact that it rested so close to the base of Delphine's neck, nearly choking her, took on a sinister aspect.

Next time I was alone with Delphine, I'd remove it.

Loudly, V said, "I should take my leave. I've taken enough of your time."

"Well then, I'll let you go," the Marquis said, and they both walked out the door they'd come in, which kept them mercifully out of my sight.

I heard them in the foyer making their goodbyes. The door swung open and shut. The Marquis trod heavily on the stairs up to the second floor. A moment later, much more quietly, the door opened again.

"Excuse me," V said to the footman, their new voice carrying purposefully. "I just realized I dropped a hairpin while I was in the parlor. I think it felt out of my pocket. I don't want to trouble you with finding it—it's quite small and will be very hard to see—and it's not valuable, except to me, since it belongs to a particular friend of mine. Could you allow me a moment to look for it?"

The footman could, apparently, because a moment later V was in the parlor with me. They entered quietly, but they were standing in front of the windows, casting a long shadow across the room. To my surprise, the shadow bent down to search the floor. There was some truth to the hairpin story, or at least, V intended to act like it.

"Julien," they said softly, crouching on the ground near my feet, dragging their fingers through the pile of the floral carpet. "This cannot happen again."

"Then you'll need to stay away until I've finished Delphine's portrait. You are the one with a choice."

"You're in danger. He comes here sometimes."

My heart stopped. They meant Alphonse. Malbosc. Whatever name he goes by now, I still fear him.

"It's been years. He may not recognize me," I said. It was weak and I knew it.

"He will know your talent."

V's trick with Horace's clothes was good, and it made them seem much larger, but sometimes I'd blink and the illusion would vanish. I know too well what it looks like when V is kneeling at my feet. The golden curls at the back of their head looked the same as always, but the rest of the wavering illusion disconcerted me.

I wanted and did not want to see their face.

I kept my eyes on Delphine, seated on the sofa in perfect stillness. "I won't leave her like this."

It didn't matter if V saw me remove the necklace, so I decided to try it right then. I crossed from my easel to the sofa and said to Delphine, "I need to adjust your necklace, if you'll allow me?"

"I do not permit it," she said in an icy tone I had never heard her use.

I hesitated, even though I knew she wouldn't have said that if she hadn't been affected by the artifact. In my place, V would have said, brisk and cheerful, "Nothing to worry about, I just need to slide the clasp behind your neck. It slipped to the front and now it's in the picture." So that's what I said.

I reached for the necklace and Delphine grabbed my wrist in a bone-grinding grip. "I do not permit it," she repeated.

"Could you do it for me, then? I think if you unclasped it, we could reposition it nicely."

"I cannot."

"You can't unclasp it?"

"I cannot," she repeated.

"Likely only the person who clasped it can unclasp it," V said.

I made the mistake of looking. It was Horace's face I expected, handsome in a hewn-from-granite way, framed with thick sideburns. A blink dispersed that image. Then I could see V's face, clever and quick, observing Delphine with sharp curiosity. No matter that I had memorized that face well enough to paint a portrait in V's absence, the sight of the real thing made me ache.

"Stop," V said. "I can't be him with you gazing at me like that. Can't you look like you hate me?"

"No," I said. "I can't."

They'd given up their search for the hairpin and were kneeling on the rug. They rose to their feet and came to stand next to me. A double awareness came over me: V as I knew them, shorter than me, and Horace, a little taller. It made me dizzy.

"Don't think about it," V said. "Sav—a colleague said that if he stopped thinking about my real appearance, the illusion didn't bother him. Expect Horace, see Horace. It works if you let it work."

"I don't want it to work."

"This is why we can't be in a room together," V said harshly. And then, almost inaudibly, "I don't want it to work, either."

"How do we help Delphine?" I asked.

There was a long, uncomfortable pause. "You know my project."

"So you're just going to let this happen? Vict—"

V's hand sliced the air and I caught myself.

"She's my friend," I said. Lowering my voice back to a whisper took great effort. "And you said you were sometimes able to—"

V's hand cut me off again. They said, "We can't discuss this here."

Instead of taking their hands in mine, I stepped closer. "Don't walk away from me again. I won't forgive that. I won't forgive you if you abandon Delphine, either."

V took a step back and said, either as a warning or an appeasement, "Julien."

"I won't let you do it," I said, advancing on them. Their back met the flax-flower blue brocade wallpaper beside the door. I closed in. The wall was smooth and cool under my palms. "Tell me how to find you. It's not fair that you can contact me, but not the other way around."

"It's not meant to be fair, it's meant to be safe."

"You need my help," I said. "You've been working on the same goal for almost a year and haven't achieved it. You need me."

V reacted like I had slapped them. Eyes wide, cheeks glazed scarlet.

"Commission me," I said suddenly. "Horace Faucheux met Julien Morère today. There's a good reason for me to come see you at your townhouse. I'll paint your portrait."

"No," they said. "I couldn't—I don't want—"

"I see you," I said. I cupped their face in my hand and closed my eyes. "It doesn't matter what you look like, I see you."

The first time I'd touched their skin in months and it was like striking a fuse. Their face was soft, certainly, and warm, but skin is skin—there are different colors and textures, but one ordinary young person feels much like the next. I could have touched a hundred beautiful people in V's absence if I'd wanted to, run my hands over the velvet warmth of their bodies, and it might have been a pleasant way to pass the time. But it wouldn't have quenched my longing. I can't explain why touching V's skin lights me up in a way that no one else's does, except for the knowledge that it's V.

A patter of footsteps in the hall outside the door. Creaks in the wooden floor. Voices.

Some instinct made me shield V with my body, pressing us both into the wall as the door next to us swung open. We held our breath.

In retrospect, this was foolish—I should have gone back to my easel, where I was supposed to be. V could have explained their own presence in the parlor. They'd made up that hairpin story with ease. But if I hadn't hidden us behind the door, I wouldn't have such a fresh memory of our chests and stomachs and hips meeting, and that was worth all the risk.

On the other side of the open door, a small child cried "Maman!" in delight.

"Stop right there," a woman's voice scolded. "Your mother is busy. She'll see you later. My apologies, Madame la Marquise, he's very spirited today."

I couldn't see Delphine, but she made no sound. I've never seen Delphine with her son, but from what I know of her, I simply can't imagine her ignoring him in silence. It was so wrong.

Some rustling and some protests from the child. The door swung shut. The governess must have scooped him up. She murmured to him, but it wasn't loud enough to overcome my heartbeat. Or perhaps V's heartbeat. I could hardly tell ours apart.

V exhaled against my neck. "You can't come to the townhouse. It's too public."

"Pick somewhere private, then. In person. No more decoding."

"Fine," they said softly. "I'll come to you."

PRIVATE DIARY OF J MORÈRE, JANUARY 21, 1825

V came to my room last night. I don't know how I knew it was them and not an unknown intruder. I woke at the whine of the door hinge, lifted my head from my pillow, and said, "I didn't give you a key."

"You need to put oil on this hinge," they said. "I don't want your neighbors noticing my entrance."

V didn't sound like Horace. I wanted to see their face. I sat up. My hand knocked against the lamp I'd left next to my sleeping pallet.

V said, "I'd prefer you didn't light that. I'll be gone soon anyway."

"Ah," I said. "So you've come here to tell me you're sacrificing Delphine in this quest of yours. You don't intend to help."

"Julie," they said, their voice much closer to me. They'd learned to walk silently—and, I suppose, to pick locks. All the time we'd spent apart, V had learned and grown and changed without me. It hurt to think about that. We should have been together.

They didn't sit on my pallet. I wanted them to even though I knew it was a bad idea.

"Tell me what you came to say," I said.

"I'm so close, Julie. All I need is a little more time, a little more knowledge, and we'll have Alphonse. I am sorry about Delphine, but if we free her and the Marquis de Quennetière connects it to me, all my work will be lost. Months and months of work wasted. You know Alphonse will hurt more people if we don't catch him."

"The Marquis de Quennetière is hurting Delphine now."

"I know. It's terrible. But I can't get involved." They paused and I almost snapped at them, but just as I was opening my mouth, they said, "You could, though. If that's something you're willing to do now."

Not being able to see V sharpened my listening, and I heard bitterness in their tone. I countered it with salt. "I thought stepping in front of your brother's knife demonstrated my willingness to be involved."

"Christ."

Having this conversation in the dark frustrated me. If V didn't want me to see them, I would have settled for sitting close enough that I could feel their weight on the pallet. I could have comforted myself, imagining that I heard small movements and intakes of breath. Instead I had the agony of waiting for V to speak.

"I will always regret that night, Julie—both the harm you suffered and the way I abandoned you. I thought I was protecting you."

"I know all that," I said, irritated. They're clearly sorry. It's not that I don't forgive them for keeping things from me and making decisions for me in the past. It's that I don't trust them not to do it again in the future.

463

I want them to let me in.

I also really really want to go to bed with them, even though I know it's a bad idea.

I didn't say any of that last night. What I said was, "I'm involved now. Let's talk about how to get that necklace off Delphine's neck."

"I, ah, looked into how it was removed from the previous wearer."

"And?"

"It wasn't the necklace they removed," V said with a bitter note of apology.

It took me so long to understand that I might as well have been going through that remark letter by letter with V's cipher disk. When I decoded it at last, I matched the bitterness in their tone and said, "The object is to save Delphine, not cut her head off."

"The simplest way to break her husband's hold over her is almost certainly to kill him. It will significantly complicate my plans if you do, but I won't stop you."

"As much as I hate him and think his death would improve the world, I'm not sure I want to be the one to cause it, not if there are other options," I said. I don't know why I felt the need to pretend that I wasn't shocked and horrified by the suggestion. I don't care if the Marquis de Quennetière lives or dies, but that's a different feeling from holding the knife that slits his throat.

"I'm guessing he has to be the one to unclasp the necklace, so either persuade him or force him," V said. "Or you can attempt to nullify it while she's still wearing it."

"By... painting it into something else, you mean?"

"Unless you've developed some other skill in my absence, yes, that is what I mean."

"I'm not the one who disappeared to learn new things,"

I said mildly. "Will it hurt Delphine if I try to change the necklace while she's wearing it?"

"I don't know," V said. "The real question is whether it will hurt more than what she's already enduring."

"When you put it that way, it's worth a try," I said. "I haven't practiced that skill. Not since that gift I gave you."

"The dildo," V said, and even without a lamp, I knew the delighted little smile they were wearing.

I shouldn't have brought it up, but it was unfortunately relevant. I once transformed an object into something else merely by painting it repeatedly—drawing it, in fact. That's good because it's too messy to take paint into Delphine's parlor. I don't know how many drawings will be necessary to change the necklace, if it's even possible.

"I don't know if I can do it," I said.

"I'm not worried about that. I'm worried about Malbosc. And what you're going to do when you succeed."

"What do you mean?"

"You can't leave Delphine in that house after you remove the necklace. Her husband will be enraged that his hold over her is broken. But if Alphonse sees you, none of that will matter."

"Camille would offer her coach to help Delphine and her child, I'm sure, and they could go to the estate at Verneuil. But that's only a temporary solution." Killing Delphine's husband began to sound simpler.

V asked, "And Malbosc?"

"I don't expect to encounter him. There hasn't been much company in the townhouse during my visits. I was surprised to see you this morning."

"That is not a plan, Julie." A rustle. V's shoes scraped the wooden floor. They shifted their weight and there was more rustling. "Don't take this the wrong way."

"Are you undressing?"

Cloth whispered against skin. "Here. This will keep anyone from touching you. It's not enough, but it's something."

I held out my hand and V let an embroidered ribbon of fabric pool in my palm, carefully not touching me. They must have bent over or crouched in front of me, since my pallet was so low that I was practically seated on the floor, but their shape was invisible in the darkness. How they'd found my hand without fumbling mystified me.

At the end of the embroidered ribbon in my palm was a buckle, its metal still warm from their body. Almost a touch. A twin item landed atop the first. I closed my fingers over them and said, "Why are you giving me your garters?"

"I forget that not everyone can feel it," they said, putting their clothes to rights. "These are... they came into my friend's collection from someone who hated being touched—hated it so powerfully that all their clothes absorbed the sentiment. These garters were the only thing I could wear discreetly, but they deflect people well."

"They didn't deflect me."

V dropped abruptly onto the sleeping pallet, the straw crackling under their weight. No part of our bodies came into contact, but I was close enough to hear V swallow before they said, low and reluctant, "They prevent unwanted touch."

That made my heart swell, but I tried to stay on topic. "You were wearing these. You need them."

"I've also become very good at dodging. Don't worry about me," V said. "When I was wearing the garters, people would reach for me and then just... think better of it. As if they'd suddenly realized I was covered in spines, their hands would find somewhere else to land. I noticed, but they never did."

"And if I want someone to touch me?" I asked.

"Take them off."

"What about if I touch someone while I'm wearing them? Will they find it unpleasant?"

"No."

"You tested that, did you?"

"They prevent unwanted touch for the wearer, nothing else," V repeated, staunchly refusing my real question.

"Your letter was very factual," I said. I set the garters aside. "It made me miss when you used to tell me stories."

"Like the story about the convent school?"

"Well. Not only that. You used to tell me stories about the people you met when you were out with your aunt. Like the night you met Béatrix for the first time."

"Ah," V said. In a brisk tone, refusing my obvious attempt to elicit something further about their life, they continued, "You should still run if you encounter Malbosc, you know. He's too clever to be deterred from you for long, and I know him well enough now to know that if you're within his reach, he'll seize you."

"I know," I said. "He wrote to Camille in September, asking for my address."

"What?"

"Obviously she didn't give it to him. I've ignored it and he seems to be ignoring me."

"September—he saw your work in the Salon, then. He doesn't have to look for you, Julie. He knows you'll exhibit more work in the future. He's not ignoring you, he's waiting."

"Meanwhile, you've spent almost a year in his company, perpetrating a deception that he would undoubtedly kill you for if he knew," I said. "We're both in danger. I meant what I said earlier about helping you, Victor."

A tiny inhalation softened their rigid posture. "I don't get called that very often anymore. It's... good to hear it. It's good to hear it from you."

"I would say it more often if you'd give me a chance."

"Julie, we can't—I shouldn't be here."

I moved then, groping through the darkness until my hand landed on their arm. Even through all the layers of their clothes, touching them satisfied some hunger I'd harbored so long it was almost forgotten. "But you are here."

V didn't recoil from my hand. I stroked from their shoulder to their elbow and they leaned toward me even as they said, "I should get out of your bed. I have things to do in the morning and besides, I was with <u>them</u> before this; I reek of brandy and tobacco."

"It's only your clothes. You already took them off once."

"I—"

V's reticence was a reversal of our usual positions, and it distressed me. They had never been anything but eager. I like directing things in bed, but not like that. "I'll stop if you want me to stop."

Their arm shifted under my hand as they dropped their head into their hands. "You make me feel too much myself. I want it too much. It makes it harder to be him."

"You said yourself that you have to breathe sometimes. It could be here. With me."

"You surprise me. I didn't think you'd want anything like this. Didn't think you'd trust me."

"I missed you, Victor. No matter how obstinate you're being, that outweighs all my other feelings." I found their hand and squeezed it. "All I've wanted since the day you left was for you to come back."

"God, Julie, I missed you, too."

They sniffled. My resolve to constrain myself to small touches broke. I dragged them into an embrace. It was awkward with both of us seated in bed, and their hair did smell like the smoke-filled club. I pressed my nose into it anyway. They clutched at me like I was the last plank of a sinking ship, then let go, still insistent on returning to the townhouse.

It was cold after they left. I closed my eyes, but didn't sleep.

J MORÈRE TO CAMILLE
DUPIN, JANUARY 22, 1825
POSTMARKED PARIS

Camille,

I have a plan to help our friend. I need a few days to work. After that, I might require your help—and your coach.

—J

CAMILLE DUPIN TO JULIE MORÈRE, JANUARY 23, 1825
POSTMARKED PARIS

My dear Julie,
    Anything you need, just say the word. I'm ready.
    Your friend,
    Camille

PRIVATE DIARY OF J MORÈRE, JANUARY 24, 1825

I wore V's garters. I can't tell if it worked; people don't touch me much in the course of a normal day, especially not with Delphine so absent from her own presence. Perhaps some people gave me a wider berth on my walk through the Faubourg Saint-Germain? The only people I saw in the townhouse were Delphine and a couple of servants.

Frustrating, repetitive work today. It's the only way to change a physical object, drawing it over and over and making tiny little changes in each one. I can't just look at an apple, draw an orange, and be done. I wish. Delphine would already be out of that house and on her way to Verneuil if I could.

I'm making the smallest possible change to the necklace—adding a tiny flaw to one of the silver links between the emeralds. With each successive drawing, the flaw grows, and soon the link will crack. My final few sketches will show the necklace draped loosely around her neck, unclasped. It's my hope that when she stands up, it will slide to the floor and she'll be restored. Unfortunately, even this very small adjustment is laborious, and I've begun a second work that will take more time. The changes are slow to take effect, so I'll know more when I see Delphine again tomorrow.

Every day I spend in that townhouse is a day I risk being discovered by the Marquis de Quennetière or Malbosc.

Luckily, the Marquis has shown no interest in my work, and he doesn't often have visitors. Still, I won't breathe easy until it's finished.

I hope V comes to see me tonight.

PRIVATE DIARY OF J MORÈRE, JANUARY 25, 1825

V took so long to arrive last night that I almost thought they'd decided not to come. But then they slipped through my door and sat next to my feet on the pallet where I sleep.

I am sure V, posing as Horace, sleeps in a grand wooden bedframe on a mattress stuffed with feathers. My pallet on the floor must appall them. It's not even as nice as the bed I had at the Maison Laval. But a real bed would take up too much space, and it's a silly expense since I can sleep anywhere—except when I am lying awake waiting for V.

Respecting their wishes, I didn't reach for a lamp after I woke. But the night wasn't as cloudy as their last visit. There was a little moonlight from the windows. It reflected in the freestanding psyché mirror I keep in the corner, and I could see the outline of their hunched shoulders. They didn't look like Horace to me. That glimpse soothed the hunger that was gnawing at me, even though it wasn't enough to satisfy.

V asked a lot of questions about my progress and my

safety, which I answered, and then I thought they were going to leave, which made me desperate to continue our conversation.

"You were out carousing with Horace's friends again?" I asked. They'd carried the scents of smoke and liquor into the studio with them. "Do they do that every night?"

V nodded and yawned. "Most nights. They all sleep late."

"But not you."

"Not most of the time. I'm at Isabelle's every morning, cataloguing her collection, looking for something that might help us."

The name Isabelle sounded familiar, like one of the stories V used to tell me about meeting the elite of Paris, but I couldn't place it until I went through my saved letters. Isabelle de Tourzin, a knowledgeable but mysterious old friend of Sophie's. V must have forgotten that they'd written to me of her. At the time, that letter and their pursuit of magic made me angry. Now, what little information V is willing to let slip, I cherish. I want to know their life. But I was afraid if I asked about Isabelle, they'd realize they'd inadvertently revealed a name. So I said, "You must be tired."

"God, yes."

The urge to tell them to lie down in my bed almost overpowered me, but I didn't want to be told no. "It sounds miserable, spending every night with people you hate."

"It hasn't all been bad. Cataloguing the collection is a genuine pleasure. My whole life, I've had too much curiosity and it's finally useful to someone. And I've met a few people whose company I enjoy. Not Horace's friends, obviously, but my colleagues. And one of the women at Florine's."

"Is that a brothel?"

"Sorry. I shouldn't have mentioned it." There was a crackle of straw as V shifted. "It's a bad idea for us to—"

"I know," I said, although I didn't and still don't understand why V will come to my studio in the middle of the night and sit close to me, but not fuck me or even touch me. They won't even let me light a candle. Shouldn't I be the one who's not ready to fall back into bed? "I'm not asking for that. I just want to know what you've been doing."

"And if you don't like what you hear?"

"What I don't like is not hearing anything," I said. "You can't do worse."

V huffed. "Well."

"Tell me about this work you love so much."

"I'm compiling an encyclopedia of sorts. Every known item, what it does, its origin, its location, everything about it. I put your paintings in it—even the one we nullified."

"You do love a list," I said, thinking of the first page I'd ever seen covered in their handwriting, the index of sex acts in The Education of Young Denise. I read the book. It wasn't nearly as thrilling as V's meticulously organized and annotated list.

There'd been lists in their letters, too. And after the Salon, they'd sent me those clippings of reviews, which was surely the result of exhaustive research. They'd always liked to curate things, to record them, to encode and decode the world.

V continued, "The goal isn't just the accumulation of knowledge, although it is that, but also learning how things are made and unmade. Some magical objects are good and useful, but some need to be contained or, if possible, destroyed. You were right about that."

I couldn't ignore how happy V sounded, talking about their work. They'd always been passionate about learning, and now they'd found an application for their talents—if they could survive their entanglement with Malbosc. If we could survive it. I asked, "And have you found ways to destroy the cursed artifacts?"

"Not really, no," they said. "None more reliable than you."

If I could have grabbed hold of that praise and clutched it to my chest, I would have, but luckily the words passed into the darkness and I didn't embarrass myself. "And how many objects are in your book so far?"

"One thousand two hundred and seven, but most of the entries are incomplete," they said. "I think it might take me the rest of my life."

"You sound like you could use some help."

Once we were on the subject, V dropped their guard and spoke freely. "I have some—the entries are mostly from Isabelle's collection, and I've been interviewing her about each item. She has an astounding memory. She doesn't always know the origins, but it's been fascinating to learn what these items do. Some of them are old, very old, and they're still carrying traces of some long-dead person's most forceful feelings. Their needs. Their will. To think of all the hands these artifacts have passed through, all the generations, to hold a little remnant of someone else's life... it gives me chills." V paused. "Sometimes in a bad, shuddering way, because a lot of the objects are products of violence and hatred. But it's not always like that. Sometimes it's pure awe. A person made this. A person who was just like me—and yet completely different from me."

"I understand that, I think," I said. "I feel that kind of awe when I see a masterpiece."

"Most of the artifacts are mundane. The kind of thing you might touch every day."

"Unknown masterpieces," I said.

"Maybe," V said. "In some cases, their magical nature might be the result of the kind of deliberate skill that goes into a masterpiece. For you and many other people, magic and art overlap. I don't think it's because magic is art, though. I think it's because magic and art are both made by people. Plenty of magic is unintentional. That's how I stumbled upon it, and I'd wager that it's more common by accident than on purpose. Regardless, when I first discover something new in Isabelle's collection, whether it's the purposeful labor of a lifetime or the crystallized expression of some overpowering instant, it's a marvel to me. I learn something so intimate about a stranger. And they're so varied—so individual. There are so many ways to be human."

"It sounds like worthy work," I said, my voice half-caught in my throat. I'd nearly kept them from this pursuit of knowledge, this thing that made them happy and made the world a little less ugly. Then again, their life in disguise had kept them from me. Living apart made both of us deeply unhappy. We had to find a better way. "Is it only Isabelle who helps you?"

"Not only her, no. Savigny's been invaluable for telling me about all the things Isabelle doesn't own. He knew about your paintings and he's been able to warn me about some of the things Horace's friends own. I've discovered a few of those myself. On a couple of occasions, we've been able to remove things discreetly."

"Steal them, you mean."

"Yes," V said without remorse. "I'd rather see dangerous things go into Isabelle's dusty storage room than into the hands of Maximilien Taillefer or the Marquis de Quennetière. I'm sorry we weren't able to get the necklace before it ended up around Delphine's neck."

"What else do you know about the necklace?"

"Malbosc used it on Isabelle."

"That's terrible," I said. I didn't know Isabelle, but no one deserved to have their will crushed like that. "I wonder how Isabelle freed herself? Getting Delphine out of that house safely is taking a long time."

"If it's any consolation, the incremental changes you're making are probably saving Delphine's life. All the other ways I've found to destroy magical objects are volatile. I singed off my eyebrows twice. Took me ages to restore the illusion afterward."

I laughed softly. "And yet you love your work."

"I do. That part, anyway. I don't like pretending to be Horace. If it had only been a few days, I wouldn't have minded so much, but it's been a long year."

"It has," I said, and then before either of us could think too hard about that, I said, "I like knowing about your life and the people in it. When I said you could use some help, I meant from me."

"You keep saying that."

"I wanted to suggest it a year ago, before Horace. When we worked together on that painting, it felt like the right thing to do."

We could have lived such a different year if I'd said so sooner. Or if V hadn't left. Neither of us mentioned that.

"Julie," they said, touched. "I would love that. And you could meet Isabelle. She's very grouchy, always acts like she doesn't want to meet people, but I think she would like you, even if she'd never say so out loud. And Savigny has a stick up his ass, but he'd be impressed by you despite all that. And his companion Quang is so beautiful and warm-hearted. He's not involved in our affairs, he's just—he lives with Savigny. I thought he was involved, at first, and I wrote him this note asking if he could teach me to throw a punch—Quang has the most incredible arm muscles—and he wrote back and told me that his arms were like that because of all the heavy cargo he lifted at his shipping company, and that as a rule he didn't punch people, but that he would like to be my friend, and Savigny would be happy to teach me any kind of violence I wished to learn."

"And did you learn to fight?"

"Ugh. Savigny was so disdainful—at our first training session, he said, 'You wrote to Quang because you think I'm too effeminate to be good at this.' I had the sense not to correct him that, in fact, I thought he was too old. And he walks with a cane and has one eye!"

"He trounced you."

"He annihilated me. I'm sore and embarrassed just thinking about it."

"Did you improve?"

"Not much."

"And your other colleague—Isabelle—couldn't teach you to fight?"

"Her style is... not suited to anyone else," V said. "Besides, I may not be good at fighting, but I excel at running away. No compunctions at all about that."

"I would've preferred to hear that you know a dozen ways to kill a man."

"Oh, well, that's easy," V said. "There are at least five hundred items in my catalogue that can cause death. I suspect Malbosc can recover from all of them."

"A worthy experiment," I said.

"A risky experiment," V replied. "Even for my taste."

"I have an idea. But you have to trust me, or it won't work."

"I trust you, of course I trust you."

"Enough to tell me everything and let me risk my life like you? Or do you intend to keep me in the dark for the rest of our lives?"

"Julie, I—" V stuttered, marshaled their forces, and said, "I want to see you again."

"And stop Malbosc."

The slightest release of air, not a sigh and not a laugh, and then V said, "That too."

I laid the foundations of a plan, telling them of the preparations I'd already begun, and they listened attentively. Afterward, they crept out of my studio with reluctance, going back to their townhouse to sleep.

PRIVATE DIARY OF J MORÈRE, JANUARY 26, 1825

Maybe I should stop pretending I'm using this diary to record my progress in freeing Delphine (slow, frustrating) and be honest that I'm just recording everything I remember of V's visits so I can relive those moments in V's absence.

I've stopped pretending to be asleep when V arrives. I still undressed and got into bed this evening, but I spent a few hours trying to read a book of aesthetic philosophy that Camille gave me. I didn't comprehend a word of it, so all I did was waste lamp oil. Had to extinguish it in a hurry when V arrived. They didn't make a sound even though I would have sworn the door had a creaky hinge. I just heard their voice say, "Extinguish the light, please."

"Sorry."

"No, I'm sorry. I know it's a strange thing to insist on. It's just—hard, being two people at once."

"Of course," I said, and then ventured, "What do you do when you're with your colleagues? Surely you and Isabelle can't be compiling a catalogue in darkness, and

Savigny would have needed to be able to see to teach you to fight—"

"It's you, Julie," they interrupted. "If we lit a lamp—and you looked at me, the real me—I'd—"

"You'd what?"

A shaky little laugh. "Fall apart, probably."

"And why can't you?"

"Because I'm spending tomorrow evening at Malbosc's townhouse in the Faubourg Saint-Germain. Ugh, I'm nervous. I haven't been nervous in months."

"Even though you spend most of your time with people who would try to kill you if they found out you weren't who you said you were?"

"I hardly notice that anymore. This is new. This is different."

"Victor," I said. "Why did you come here tonight?"

"I wanted to see you. And I suppose I was afraid," they said haltingly. "If things don't go according to plan, this might be the last time."

"If this is our last time, I have a few ideas—"

"Julie," they said. "We can't."

"You're trusting me with everything else. Trust me with this, too. You've continued this deception of yours for months without getting caught, which means you're excellent at it, and one night of rest won't ruin you. It'll do you good."

"I don't deserve this. You."

"You making decisions for both of us is what got us into this mess," I said. "I choose who receives my affection, and I want to give it to you. Do you want it or not?"

"Yes," they said. "But can we—maybe if you didn't touch me. If we just talked. In the dark. I'm sorry. I know it's not what you want."

"Don't apologize," I said. "I love it when you talk to me. What do you want to talk about? Your friend at Florine's, maybe?"

"Ha. That's not what you think."

"So what is it?"

"I was scared shitless the first time Horace's friends dragged me there," V said. "I can't undress when I'm Horace. Even in my disguise, I didn't think I could fool anybody who'd been with him, so I insisted that I only wanted new women. I found one, made her my favorite, and now I pay her double to keep up the pretense that we're fucking."

That sparked so much curiosity, it was like gulping down too much coffee. I buzzed with questions, but I didn't need to say anything. V had been so long without talking to anyone that it poured right out.

"Her name is Louise, but everybody calls her Butterball. You'd like her, I think. We've spent a lot of time together, and I've been awake for some of it. She has this voice like what I imagine a princess would sound like, so high and light and delicate, but she shouts with laughter at filthy jokes—even if she's the one telling them. If you think I'm good at telling stories, you should hear hers. I told her she could write a great obscene novel, but she hates writing. She's not very good at reading, though I keep trying to teach her."

"Wait, how can you sleep in front of her? Wouldn't the illusion fall apart?" I asked. "And doesn't her repertoire of stories make you worry that she talks about you?"

"I keep my clothes on while I sleep and ask her to extinguish all the lamps. It's not a perfect defense, but I'm paying her enough not to ask questions. As for telling stories about me, we're something like friends now—and I don't think I've done anything comical enough to merit it."

"I'm sure the handsome rich stranger who pays her double to pretend is of no interest," I said. I'm partial, but if V were repeatedly visiting me in the night to chat and teach me to read and catch a little sleep, I would be in love with them.

Of course, I already know how to read.

"She did say once, after a few months of acquaintance, that my lack of desire for her shook her confidence," V said. "I thought she was joking—I've never met a more confident woman, which I suppose is natural when most nights, she sees people who are absolutely dying to touch her. Paying prodigiously for the privilege, too. But she was sincere, or as sincere as Louise ever gets, since she's always playful. She liked me; I was hurting her feelings."

"Oh?"

"I explained, as delicately as I could, that it wasn't a lack of desire on my part. I found her sublime. I said—because I'm accustomed to lying now—that I simply did not care to be touched or looked at, and didn't wish to impose my strange requirements on her. You can imagine what she said to that."

The tone of V's voice made it clear where the story was going, but all I said was, "Tell me."

The moonlight showed that they'd relaxed, their legs stretched in front of them and their shoulders supported by the wall. I risked sitting up to match them, my shoulder next to theirs, not quite touching. It was almost like old times, except V was fully dressed.

"She laughed and said I was already imposing my strange requirements on her, she just wasn't getting any orgasms out of it. And besides, strange requirements were her work, and did I really have the arrogance to believe I was the first man who'd wanted to tie her up and blindfold her, that was nothing special, just a usual night for her, and if that was all I needed, I should have fucked her already. I had the impression she was put out at having to ask."

I smiled. "And did you give her what she wanted?"

"Not as quickly as she wished. I asked her a lot of questions about what she liked in a lover, which she found amusing. She knew I was stalling and said what she liked most in a lover was a swift decision. She was teasing me, but there was some truth to that, I think—she enjoyed it when someone else made the choices. Particular choices, naturally, ones that would please her. She didn't care for pain, which was a relief to me, and she didn't want to do any work, which was even more of one. She wanted to lie back and be adored. I thought I could do that.

"So I promised that next time, we could. I was nervous, but exhilarated. It had been a long time since I had done anything for my own pleasure."

"Since me?" I asked.

"Ah," V said. "Not quite."

"Oh, there was someone else, was there? Someone other than Louise?"

"Well, Savigny and Quang have this arrangement—they're in love, but Savigny doesn't want sex, and Quang does. So there was one night—"

"Only one?"

"Only one," V said. "And in truth, while it was good, it was... too close to what I wanted, while not being exactly what I wanted. Anyway, that's not the story I'm telling, and I don't suppose you've been celibate, though I hope you haven't been bringing your lovers here. I know Camille wouldn't stand for that. The gossip makes it sound as though you two are... intimate. Though it also sounds as if Camille has a long list of intimates."

Perhaps it was wicked of me to find amusement in their forlorn tone. "You've paid attention. Did you make an index of people I might have fucked?"

V hardly noticed my teasing. "I never stopped thinking about you, Julie. Even when I was with someone else."

"I know how that feels," I said softly, and then, bringing us back to what was important, "But you really never stopped thinking about me, not even when you were with the sublime Louise?"

V laughed. I hadn't heard the sound in almost a year, and even as soft as it was, it rolled through me like I was standing next to a church bell that had just been struck.

"Especially not with Louise. I wish I could draw it for you, the way her chestnut curls brushed her nipples but couldn't cover her breasts, the way the sweet, sulky pout of her lips was the same pink at the tips of her breasts and between her thighs, the way her arms trembled from being extended for so long. I didn't expect to like that, you know. I thought I'd spend the whole time wishing I was tied up in her place—and I did, but sometimes it feels good to want something, even something you can't have. I'd never seen her unclothed before, but she'd slipped out of her silk peignoir before getting on the bed. She looked luscious, naked and waiting for me, and I wanted to press my whole body up against the softness of hers, but that was one of the things I couldn't risk. I'd stripped my coat off, which was already bold, and rolled up my sleeves, but I couldn't do more."

"Fuck," I said. The story had turned from teasing to torture. I curled my hands around two fistfuls of scratchy sheets and tried not to think about the heat gathering between my thighs. About how easy it would be to twist and kiss V.

V said, "I consoled myself by thinking about you."

My throat had gone so dry that my voice rasped when I said, "I don't have the impression that Mademoiselle Louise reminded you of me."

"No, I didn't think about you tied up and blindfolded. I thought about <u>being</u> you. What you would <u>do</u>. Your certainty."

The unexpected compliment rendered me speechless, but the small adjustment I made when I shifted my weight sent a crackle of pallet straw into the silence. Heat licked a slow path down my skin. I wasn't allowed to touch V, but I wasn't forbidden from touching myself. The wrinkled wool blanket lay across my lap, and underneath there was only the thin fabric of my nightshirt. It would be easy to slip my hand between my legs, but I waited.

V continued, "My voice failed me—I was too afraid it wouldn't sound right—but my hands were steady. I caressed the outside of her thigh, her hip, her belly, both glorious breasts, the soft, quivering flesh of her upper arms, the line of her neck and the curve of her face, and then I pressed the pads of two fingers into her plush bottom lip until she opened her mouth and let me slide inside. She obliged me by sucking my fingers deep into her mouth, and when they were wet, I withdrew and turned my attention to her sex. I parted the wiry, dark curls and slipped my fingers inside. She was so hot and slick, I groaned.

"She hummed a little laugh and said, 'So you do like me, Monsieur Faucheux,' which made me snap, 'Don't call me that.' Then I had to apologize, and we settled on just 'monsieur,' since I couldn't explain to her why I reacted so strongly to what she thought was my name. We recovered, though. I took my time until she became impatient, and then I took a little more time just because I could, and—"

V paused for effect. I was so coiled with tension I thought I might be stuck that way forever, and I could feel hot, sticky liquid dripping down my thighs. "And?"

"And when she was begging for more, I took your dick out of my pocket and slid it right in."

That startled a suffocated laugh out of me. "You fucked her with my dick?"

"I fucked her with your dick and she loved it."

I meant to offer some appreciation, but what came out was a wordless grunt. I wanted to push V flat on their back and tear their clothes off, or failing that, to thrust my hand between my thighs, but instead I gripped the sheets hard enough that I'm surprised they didn't rip.

"God, I wish you'd been there—I suppose you were there in a way. It was so gorgeous, the way she shoved her hips down and writhed. I felt powerful, but also... humble, or in awe. And envious and desperately aroused, of course. I shoved one hand into my trousers and came in two strokes. But most of all, I missed you, Julie. I missed you so much." V let their head drop back against the wall. "Fuck."

"I missed you, too," I said. "You only slept with two people, but you must have touched yourself."

"Sometimes. In the dark."

"It's dark now."

A long exhale. I imagined hearing, in that sound, the decision to trust me. "Tell me what to do."

"Unbutton your trousers. Drag them down your hips. No need to worry about the rest of your clothes. We'll be quick about this, because I can tell you need it." I could tell I needed it, too. I inched the hem of my nightshirt up my thighs. "Can you put your hand between your legs?"

"Yes. It's tight with my clothes still on, but—yes."

"Good. And what do you feel?"

"It's hot. Like all the heat of my body collected right here."

"Yes. Dip your finger inside."

"Oh, it's wet, it's so wet."

I had to touch myself so I didn't die of envy. V was right: sometimes it feels good to want something, even if it's something you can't have. I shuddered at my own touch and said, "Take two fingers and fuck yourself the way I'd fuck you."

"God, Julie." The end of that sentence was wordless, a high, falling sound.

"Slower," I said, willing myself to take my own advice. If it had been V's hand instead of my own, they'd have been quicker, but I was too close to the edge for that. "Deeper."

It was nearly fatal to sit there in the dark, not quite touching, with only the faint sounds of V's hand and their breath as proof that my words were having any effect. The warm, earthy scent of sex dispersed into the still air of my studio, barely there. I licked my lips as if it would give me a taste.

"Since you've taken up pretending to be me," I said. "What would I be doing to you right now?"

"Asking me questions." They huffed. "Tracing a little circle around my clit, pressing hard. Maybe pushing against the rim of my hole or sliding a finger in."

"Do that, and we'll find out if you like it." At the wild sound they made, I said, "It seems you do. Did you know you weren't the only one pretending?"

Their breath was coming too fast and shallow for conversation. "I—you?"

"Mm," I said. "I had to be subtle. I couldn't get shorter or blonder, but if you could see me naked, you'd know. I missed touching your smooth chest and the slight curve of your belly. Your soft thighs and hips. The beautiful wet cunt between them."

"Julie," they said, urgent.

"I never sounded like you," I said. "So you'll have to remind me. Come, Victor."

My name again, a strangled cry, and then a string of obscenities and groans that I don't have the list-making skill to reproduce. I couldn't feel Victor clenching around my fingers, but I could feel myself tightening and releasing in rhythm as pleasure shattered over me. I didn't care, in that moment, that it was my hand and not theirs, or that we weren't touching. We were together. Nothing about it felt solitary. It was the closest I've been to anyone in months.

Still, I would have licked their fingers if they'd let me.

They didn't. They emptied their lungs in a sigh and slumped against the wall. "Fuck, that was good. It'll be a long walk to the townhouse. I don't think my bones are quite solid anymore."

"Why would you leave?" I asked. "I said one night of rest won't ruin you. Surely it's in character for Horace to go out all night. Stay here."

"And sleep on this pallet?"

"And sleep in my arms," I said.

Their bones hadn't melted, but their resistance had. "Well, in that case," they said, and began to strip.

It was cold to sleep naked, but I wanted to be skin to skin, so I found us a second blanket and pulled off my nightshirt. In bed, V curled toward me and ran their hands over my torso, belly, and hips, exploring. My nipples were stiff from the cold and then, as they traced the shallow arc under one breast, from the heat.

"Is it vain if I like this?" V asked.

"I don't know," I said, laughing softly. I laid my hands on them, too. "Not to undermine my efforts, but touching you still feels entirely different from touching me. And if I'm allowed to touch the genuine article, there's no reason to settle for an imitation."

Their fingers brushed my cheek, which was still stubbled, and then my upper arm, which was still thick with muscle. "Not an imitation, an homage."

"I only do exact counterfeit when I have no other choice."

"I know. I did listen to your plan," they said. "And I love you in any shape. Will you kiss me?"

I did that and more. We were quieter the second time, but it was no less intense. V let me hold them afterward and we fell asleep together. I haven't slept so deeply in a long time.

I wanted to wake up next to them, to watch the light of dawn paint them gold, but they were gone by morning.

JANUARY 27, 1825

The following day, with flawlessly clear winter light raking through the windows of Delphine's parlor, Julie finished her work on the necklace. The flaw in the link of the emerald necklace fissured. The weight of the gems pulled the broken chain to the carpet, where it landed with a muted sound.

Julie seized it, the metal still warm from Delphine's neck, and executed the most important step of her plan. Her heart pounded, alternating triumph and relief, as Delphine awoke.

"Julien," she said, touching her own face and neck tentatively, assuring herself. Life and feeling rushed back into her face. With horror, she regarded the necklace Julie had planted at her feet. "How did you—"

"There's no time," Julie whispered. "Your husband is in his study in a meeting. A coach is waiting. Walk south to the corner and Camille will find you. You need to go right now."

"Not without Octave," Delphine said.

As Delphine discreetly sent a servant to fetch her son,

493

Julie's sense of triumph collapsed. She'd planned so carefully, and yet hadn't realized how much time it would take to bundle Delphine's independent, curious child into his coat and coax him into the coach. It took mere minutes, but any minute could ruin everything. Shaken, Julie wondered what else she'd forgotten.

Octave, thankfully, was quietly happy in Delphine's arms and watched her with big dark eyes as she spoke to him. "We're going to see Mademoiselle Dupin, Octave, you remember her."

Julie walked them to the door, trying not to cringe at every sound they made. Delphine crossed the threshold into the sunlight and the brisk cold air, then turned and said, "Aren't you coming?"

From the shadowed shelter of the foyer, Julie shook her head. "I have more work to do. Get yourself and Octave to safety."

Delphine frowned, but she didn't miss her chance. She hurried Octave down the steps. There wasn't time to watch them walk to the corner, but Julie trusted that they would find Camille.

Victor had done their part, arranging for Delphine's husband to be occupied in his study. No sound made its way from that room, sequestered at the back of the house, all the way to the foyer. Julie had imagined the meeting as a low murmur of voices behind the heavy, closed door, but perhaps it was over.

When she went back into Delphine's parlor, she was no longer alone.

The dark silhouette of Alphonse's frock coat as he studied her drawing interrupted the serene blue tones of the room. He rendered the long, high expanse chilly and menacing. It was silent except for a small clink every few seconds. Alphonse was idly dropping a strand of emeralds from one hand to the other. Julie had left it on the floor. He let the gems pool in one palm, caged them in his fingers, and then flipped his full hand and started again. The faceted gems flashed green through his fingers.

He didn't turn from her easel. "Morère. You figured it out at last. I always thought you would."

Her chest constricted. She forced breath into her lungs and movement into her feet, little though she wanted to go closer. The parlor was too civilized for this confrontation; her feelings were more suited to cutting through a tangle of wilderness and jumping back from the gleaming slither of a snake. At the end of her cautious approach, she said, "That necklace doesn't belong to you."

"On the contrary, I am its original owner."

"It's your design, then?" she asked. Victor had suspected as much. They'd enjoy the confirmation. The thought brought her a measure of peace. So did her height. In memories, Alphonse always towered over her. Now she could level her gaze with his.

"I suppose you know its secrets, since you just helped the Marquis de Quennetière's wife flee," Alphonse said. "What I can't figure out is why you'd leave it on the floor —or why you'd come back."

"I intend to destroy it," Julie said.

"More fully than you already have?" he asked, pinching the broken link between his fingers to close it. The connection came together, but not enough to withstand the weight of the gems. "It's of no use to me like this. I wonder if I might undo the damage?"

He cast a speculative, raised brow glance at her and then swiped his index finger through the charcoal drawing of Delphine on the easel, slitting her neck with a horizontal smear. The drawn necklace disappeared in the blur. The one in his hand remained broken.

"Interesting," he murmured. "Would a simple physical repair suffice, do you think? Or will you have to draw it whole?"

"I won't," she said. Miraculously, her hand didn't tremble as she reached for the necklace.

His grasp tightened as she tugged. The gems and metal hadn't been in his hand long enough to warm. They felt lighter than the burning weight in her pocket.

"Ah, Morère," he said. He held the necklace taut. "Unfathomable power and you only want to use it to break beautiful things."

"We disagree about what is beautiful." She'd once mistaken him for handsome, after all. Now she knew what his smooth, youthful face masked. Uncanny and untouched by time, he repulsed her.

"That we do," he said. "But you broke something of mine, so now you must fix it. I think we can come to an agreement. We have a friend in common who can arrange it."

"What friend?"

"I know your friend as Horace Faucheux, but I suspect that's not his name. He awaits us at my townhouse. If you don't come with me, I'll kill him. Crude, I know, but you've destroyed my more elegant method."

He tugged on his end of the necklace. In shock, Julie let go of hers.

"Take it," she said. "What have you done?"

"You cannot give me permission to take what is rightfully mine. As for the rest, we'll see what you have to offer me in exchange."

JANUARY 27, 1825

Alphonse lived in a stately townhouse from a hundred years ago or more, ensconced behind high stone walls in a narrow street of the Left Bank, close enough to the river that the winter air was wet with its scent. The house was only twenty minutes on foot from the similarly grand residence that Delphine had just escaped. With other company, less rigid with terror, Julie might have found the walk pleasant. She straightened her spine as she passed through the wrought-iron gate and across the courtyard.

Alphonse led her to a parlor, bade her sit in a plush chair upholstered in red, promised to return momentarily, and disappeared into the depths of the house. At the the Marquis de Quennetière's townhouse, servants quietly going about their business were never far away, but this place was a tomb. Julie was alone.

She'd wanted this. She'd planned it. Victor had tried for months and months to delay and dissemble, to prevent Alphonse from getting what he wanted, and it hadn't worked.

Julie's plan hadn't worked yet, either, but Alphonse had returned with Victor, so there was no more time to think.

Victor was still disguised as Horace, wearing last night's evening dress, black and white and as rumpled as she'd ever seen them. Their face wavered in her vision, Victor one instant and Horace the next. It was dizzying, but she wanted Victor too much to abandon herself to the illusion.

They weren't bruised or bleeding, at least. Alphonse wasn't dragging them, but they were in chains: a strand of emeralds was clasped around their neck, sitting unevenly atop their cravat, one silver link smashed together in haste. The jewels brought a greenish cast to their face, equally pale and tired in both disguise and reality.

Julie stood to greet them—or to rush forward and yank it off their neck. Alphonse brandished a knife. She halted. It was the same long, wicked blade that Horace had used to stab her, the one that had sealed the wound it made.

"I took this from him. Sit," Alphonse said to Julie, waving a hand, but it was Victor who sat right down on the Persian carpet. The disguise vanished. Only Victor was there, gazing at the air an arm's length from their face, as dull-eyed as Delphine had been when she'd been under her husband's control.

It was not how Julie wanted to see them.

Cruel enjoyment curled across Alphonse's face as Julie meekly returned to her own seat. He kept the knife visible, aimed in her direction, sunlight collecting along its sharp edges. "Yes, I've caught this little liar now. Tell the truth. Did you kill Horace Faucheux?"

"Isabelle de Tourzin killed him," Victor answered.

"And you took his place. Where is Isabelle de Tourzin?"

"She lives in the Rue Branoux."

"Under my nose all this time," Alphonse said, shaking

his head with sad amusement. "I suppose you didn't arrange for the Marquis de Quennetière to find the emerald necklace before me."

"No," Victor said. "He found it himself. I didn't want that to happen."

"Incompetent in addition to dishonest," Alphonse said. "But you saw it around Delphine's neck and didn't inform me."

"I was giving Julien time to work," Victor said.

Alphonse eyed her with that same hard stare she'd once captured in his portrait. "Julien," he said, tasting her name in a way that made her shudder. "Not that I'm not impressed with your painstaking efforts to retrieve the necklace, but you do realize you could have just killed the Marquis and saved yourself some time? Not that it matters, since I've done it for you—though you were the last known visitor to his home, which I imagine could cause you some trouble."

"You killed him," she said. Damn. She should have predicted that. She'd told Victor to arrange an encounter between Malbosc and the Marquis de Quennetière. He'd accomplished that perfectly. The failure lay with Julie, who'd envisioned the two men negotiating over the necklace. Her imagination wasn't violent enough. Of course Alphonse wouldn't bother negotiating. He probably hadn't even listened to the Marquis de Quennetière's last words.

"The world is going to assume *you* killed him," Alphonse said. "I was a dear friend of his, a fellow wealthy man, and you're a degenerate artist who wanted to fuck his wife."

"If you want me dead, the knife would be quicker," Julie said.

"You know neither of us wants that," he said. "I'll take

care of everything if you'll lend me your talents. I'll even set your little liar friend free. Though you shouldn't care so much for him, you know. He's the one who told me where to find you and what you could do. He has a treacherous nature. Fortunately for you, I know how precious your talent is and would never harm you."

"Then put away the knife."

"I can't. I have no such certainty that you won't harm me, Julien. What do you say to my offer?"

"No."

Like a doomed saint, Alphonse cast a glance heavenward, though Julie knew he believed in nothing beyond himself. "Do you care for your friend here? I offered to free him. Perhaps we should ask him what he thinks. Tell us your feelings for young Morère, you, whatever your name is."

"My name is Victor," they said, and Julie's breath caught; Victor was limited in affect by the necklace, but whatever followed would be the truth. "I love Julien Morère with all my heart. I would die for him."

"Good," Alphonse said, handing Victor the knife. "Stab yourself in the stomach."

"No!" Julie jumped to her feet. "Stop, don't, I'll do whatever you want."

"Ah," Alphonse said, his features serene and smug. "As I thought."

Behind him, Victor crouched and swung the knife in a deep, slicing arc across Alphonse's abdomen. He yelped and gagged, eyes bulging, as a thin splatter of blood hit the carpet. Then he sank to his knees. He splayed a hand over his bloodied clothes as if to hold in his entrails. Julie knew from experience that the lack of exterior wound did not mean the injury was painless.

Alphonse spat red-tinged spit on the beautiful, undeserving Persian rug and glared up at Victor. "Idiot. You know this won't kill me. I can't say the same for what I'll do to you."

"You don't want to ask how I escaped your control?" Victor asked, pulling at the necklace. It snapped where Alphonse had tried to repair it. Victor dangled it in front of him. "It's very clever, I'd love to tell you about it."

"Morère," Alphonse rasped. "Morère painted a fake."

"Indeed," Victor said. "And brilliantly. But that's not the cleverest part."

Julie stepped forward, drew the real necklace out of her pocket, and pinched the soft metal of the broken link together. The fragile connection barely held against the weight of the emeralds. She didn't know if it would work.

As she clasped it around Alphonse's neck, he struggled ineffectually. He pulled at her wrist with one hand. "Let go," she said, and he did. Relief flooded her. With the power of a full, easy breath, her voice didn't shake. "You will tell us, clearly and truthfully, every location in which you are storing Isabelle de Tourzin's blood or any other magical objects. Include instructions for how to find these places as well as what traps you might have laid in them. Omit nothing."

From their pockets, Victor produced a tiny notebook and a stub of vine charcoal that looked suspiciously like the kind Julie bought for herself. Then they began to make a list.

Alphonse was compelled to answer, but his injury left him short of breath. His labored speaking and the scratch of Victor's writing were the only sounds in the room for a long time.

"That's all," Alphonse said at last.

"I'd find this impressive if I didn't hate you so much." Victor tapped the list, and then demanded a second, thankfully shorter list of servants in the house and whether their presence was coerced. To Julie's surprise, Alphonse had few servants, and all of them worked for him of their own volition in exchange for high wages.

Victor scribbled a long note and then said, "Well, Julie, you know he's going to kill me and torture you, Isabelle, and many others if we leave him alive."

"I know."

"Do you want to kill him? Or would you prefer that I do it?"

Alphonse curled over his knees, trapped and wounded. He'd hurt her once. He'd hurt a lot of people. He'd lived a long, long time and it had only made him worse. Julie would be relieved to know he was gone. Just like when Victor had proposed killing Delphine's husband, she balked at wielding the knife herself.

"It's not cowardice if you don't want to," Victor said. "I didn't want to take it from you if you wanted it."

"I don't."

"Then allow me."

Julie turned away, but the sound of the butchery was impossible to miss. When at last it was quiet, there was less blood than expected, but Victor had managed to separate Alphonse's head from his neck. The head was so far from the body that Julie could study the carpet's pattern of twining vines in the gap. Victor plucked the emerald necklace, only slightly blood-spattered, from where it lay.

"You won't mind destroying this?"

"It would be my pleasure," Julie said. "Didn't you tell me that Isabelle was freed from the necklace by beheading? She must have survived."

"Yes, but *she's* the source of the magic. Malbosc doesn't have that advantage. I suspect her head was close to her body, and her magic healed the damage. I've taken a step to prevent that, as you can see. And now that I've told Isabelle where he was keeping everything, she can reclaim it. Perhaps we should adjourn to another room for a moment while I sort things out with her."

"You've told her? How?" Julie followed them into another lavish parlor, unsettled by how well they knew the house.

Victor sat at a round table and laid the tiny notebook on its mahogany surface with an uncharacteristically shy smile. "Do you like it?"

Julie opened the book, flipped through the pages of locations and the list of servants, and then arrived at a note that said *Malbosc killed the Marquis and plans to frame J. We are still at house.*

Below that, while she watched, letters in another hand appeared, spelling out *I'll take care of it. Leave DISCREETLY.*

"Is this... Isabelle wrote this last bit?"

"Yes. She has an identical notebook."

"Something from her collection, no doubt."

"Actually, I made them."

"You can make magical objects deliberately now?"

"Ah," Victor said. They swiped a finger through the message about the Marquis de Quennetière's murder, smearing it into oblivion. "It was more a consequence of yearning to write to one particular person and being unable to do so. But after the initial accident, I was able to refine the usage."

"So for months you've had a magical object that would have allowed us to communicate—which you created specifically for that purpose—and yet you didn't use it?"

"For most of those months, I wasn't sure you'd write back."

Julie thought back to the earliest of Victor's gifts—the newspaper clippings, the shell, the nest, all given with no expectation of a response. "I suppose I understand that. You should have risked it, though."

"I know," they said. "I should have given you the chance to express yourself. I promise to consult you about everything from this moment forward. You were right about everything in there and your plan was the only reason we succeeded. Speaking of, Julie, I said something in the other room that was true, but I don't want you to think I only said it because I was playacting in front of Alphonse."

"I don't think that," she said. "Still, I'd like to hear you say it again. Perhaps somewhere other than here."

Victor offered her a genuine smile then, as bright and visible as dawn.

V BEAUCHÊNE TO J MORÈRE, JANUARY 27, 1825
NOT POSTMARKED

J—

You've asked me what I'm doing, and I know it's absurd to write you a note when you're standing so near, but you deserve to see this in writing. Really you deserve to see it carved in stone and ten meters high, but I only have this pen and I've already made you wait too long.

I love you. I am continually amazed by you, principled and brilliant and courageous, not to mention splendid in appearance(s) and in possession of a very nice pair of thighs, and it is the great joy of my life that you share any part of yourself with me. Every moment I am permitted in your presence is a gift. I will work to stay in your good graces, not only so I might gather as many of these moments as you will allow me and hoard them until I die, but also that I might try to make you as happy as you make me.

I hope to fill many more diaries and spill a great deal more ink writing to you and about you, J.

—V

PRIVATE DIARY OF V BEAUCHÊNE, JANUARY 28, 1825

My pen wobbled as Julie ran a warm hand down my inner thigh. Only a few minutes to write something that deserved hours of contemplation and already she'd become impatient. I tsked.

She said, "I haven't had the chance to look at you in the daylight in almost a year and you're bending over the desk very provocatively. I don't know what you expected."

"I didn't sit down because I wanted to demonstrate how very quickly I was going to compose this precious document that contains all my hopes and fears. Would you read it, at least?"

"I did," she said and leaned forward to kiss my temple, enclosing me between the desk and her body. "Your backside is distracting, but I do know how to read."

"And?"

Her hand traveled up the inseam of my trousers. She began a slow, maddening stroke between my thighs. "And I wouldn't be trying to seduce you if I didn't like what you'd written. We have unfinished business."

"We do?"

"You wrote me a very exciting story about a swordfight," she said. "And we never arrived at the end."

"You illustrated a scene as I recall," I said. "Just a moment."

I hadn't wanted to return to the mausoleum of this townhouse, but J had convinced me. The bed here was softer than the tragic ascetic pallet on her studio floor. The house was also usefully stocked. I left the room and returned a moment later.

"This is a sword," J said, holding the blade flat across her spread hands.

"Yes." I knelt before her. "It's ordinary, but sharp."

"Why did you give me a sword? I don't want to hurt you," she said, panicked.

"You won't. No one has steadier hands. Now think about it: I kneel before you. I am at your mercy. What are you going to do next?"

She set the point under my chin and lifted. The metal was cool and hard, but didn't dig into my skin. Still, there was tension. I had to strain to look up at her face, but I would have stayed in that pose as long as she wanted.

"You really do trust me," she said.

"I do. The sword is the least of it." At her instruction, I'd told Malbosc where to find her and what she could do—undoing all the work I'd done to keep his attention away from her. That had been the worst of it, the part that made me sick with fear. It was gutting to feel like I'd betrayed J. I hadn't, but I had to remind myself constantly. Anyone who could have heard my thoughts would have been subjected to a recitation of "I trust her, she chose this, I am doing as she asked" over and over. In comparison, allowing myself to be taken captive hardly registered, except for the fear that I might be powerless to stop

Malbosc from hurting her. The necklace had been false, but the danger had been real. During those long hours alone in his house, at any point he might simply have decided to kill me.

I met her eyes. She knew.

"I will always want to know your mind," I said. "Even if we don't agree. I won't hide anything from you."

"Good," she said and dragged the tip of the sword through my cravat. For the sake of fantasy, let us pretend the fabric parted effortlessly and slid to the floor, and that the clothes I had worn to disguise myself as Horace met a similar fate. In reality, not trusting her sword nearly as much as I trusted her, J insisted on a safer and more ordinary method of removal. It pleases me to imagine those clothes in shreds.

Kneeling naked, the pile of the carpet and the uneven planks it covered ground into my knees. My bare toes were cold. I was happy.

J made a long, leisurely study of my body, holding the sword to my throat until the metal was warm from my skin. Nothing else touched me. Everything in me grew hot and tight and aching.

"It's good to look at you," she said. "I missed you so much."

She tossed the sword aside and knelt in front of me, her clothes rustling. The dark waves of her hair swung loose, brushing the tops of her shoulders and curtaining her face until she swept them aside. She caressed my cheek and gripped my chin to force me to look at her.

"I'm sorry I made you feel like you couldn't tell me what was happening with your family—or anything after that," she said.

"I know," I said. "You had your reasons."

THE SCANDALOUS LETTERS OF V AND J

She kissed me hard, setting my heart pounding, and then said, "Lie on your back in the bed. I want to ride you."

I retrieved the toy from the table beside my bed, slicked it with oil, and lay down. She was half-stripped by then, as if it wasn't a display to be savored, as if I wouldn't have watched her slip every button from its hole. She dropped her clothes with careless grace. When she crawled across the bed to straddle me, I made a crude, small noise of helpless awe.

"Is it my imagination, or do you look a little different already?"

"Always," she said. She tapped the dildo. "Hold this still while I fuck it."

There was a narrow trail of dark hair leading from her navel to the thicket between her legs. I caught the barest glimpse of pink as she lifted her spread thighs to settle herself over the wooden cock. She slid down until the length disappeared. Her body pressed against the tight circle of my hands. She raised her hips and slammed back down, and then again, moving with magnificent force. Under her, I was breathless, trying not to squirm, desperate to touch myself or thrust my fingers into the dripping slick of her cunt.

Her thighs rippled with muscle and her small breasts bounced. It was hypnotic. I imagined how tight she was squeezing and moaned. She closed her eyes and rode until she came, softly and and quietly but in wave after neverending wave.

She lost no time after that, plucking the toy from my trembling hands and tossing it aside so she could dive between my legs. Wild with lust, I could have come from the tiniest touch. Instead, she took her time, dipping her fingers into the sweet wetness of her cunt and then circling one around the rim of my hole until I let her slide it in. Slow and careful, she added a second finger. The fullness made me groan with pleasure.

Then she put her mouth on me and licked and sucked until I screamed.

I came down gradually, my breath ragged, and she crawled next to me and kissed me. We washed and slept and fucked again, and then slept until morning. The room smelled of us, as though we'd cleansed the house and claimed it for ourselves. I stroked J's hair from her face and smiled.

ISABELLE DE TOURZIN AND VICTOR BEAUCHÊNE, JANUARY 28, 1825

WRITTEN IN A PAIR OF LINKED NOTEBOOKS

I resolved the matter of the Marquis.

You did?

Malbosc made it easy for me—he used the phantom knife, so there were no exterior wounds. It appeared that the Marquis had simply collapsed.

So Malbosc was making an empty threat against J.

Yes. Unfortunately, by the time I arrived at the house, a servant had notified the police. I had to hide, but I overheard the officer when he recognized Julien's name.

What? How?

The easel was still in the parlor, and he asked about it. The servant explained that Julien Morère had been working on a portrait of the Marquise. The officer said, "Julien Morère who used to live at the Maison Laval?" and the servant said "I don't know, sir."

> Forestier.

Yes. That was his name.

> He's a snoop. I don't think he knows enough to do anything. Still, let's keep an eye out.

He determined that no crime had been committed, so it may come to nothing. When he asked where the Marquise was, one of the maids answered that the Marquise's visit to her friend's country estate was planned long in advance.

> She must like the Marquise. Did he believe it?

He conspicuously chose not to ask why the easel was set up in the parlor if the Marquise had planned a journey out of town.

> That's surprising. But good for us.

One last note—Savigny and I emptied Malbosc's house and dismissed all his servants. We burned the body.

> And the head?

We did not find a head.

> Fuck.

He can't have traveled far. I'll find him.

VICTOR BEAUCHÊNE TO SOPHIE BEAUCHÊNE, JANUARY 29, 1825
POSTMARKED PARIS

My dearest Aunt S,

I am so very sorry to have vanished from your life for so many months. It pained me to do it, but I was trying to keep you safe. I cannot say that there will ever be a time without danger, but I judge the risk greatly reduced. Could you find it in your heart to allow me in your life once more?

With love,
Victor

SOPHIE BEAUCHÊNE TO VICTOR BEAUCHÊNE, JANUARY 30, 1825
POSTMARKED PARIS

Victor, darling—

Who hasn't faked their death and disappeared for a time? You young people think you invented everything. Just come home.

With love,
Sophie

DELPHINE DE TOUSSERAT, MARQUISE DE QUENNETIÈRE TO JULIEN MORÈRE, JANUARY 31, 1825
POSTMARKED VERNEUIL

Dear Julien,

Please accept, once again, my profound gratitude for everything you did to save me. My son and I are quite happy here in the countryside. It is generous of Camille to host us, though she's been locked in her study writing most of the days we've been here. I do hope she's well.

My late husband's sudden and unspeakably tragic collapse has given me quite a shock. Never did I dream of such an event. I am corresponding with the family lawyer; he assures me I will find a way to continue. I think he may be right.

Your friend,
Delphine

CAMILLE DUPIN TO JULIE MORÈRE, FEBRUARY 1, 1825
POSTMARKED VERNEUIL

My dear Julie,

Have you ever seen a dog chase after something much larger, like a carriage or a horse? Pure joy of the chase drives the dog forward and it spends not one instant contemplating what might happen if it catches its quarry.

Delphine is not a quarry, but I feel a bit like a dog. For months I have wanted nothing but time alone with her, and now I have it, but she's trapped here with me and her life is in turmoil. I can't possibly pursue her. What kind of reprehensible rake takes in a stranded, wounded woman and then seduces her? She deserves better than that.

I know you can't write about what you've been doing, but I hope you are safe and that you found what you've been seeking.

Your friend who's mired in self-doubt,
Camille

JULIE MORÈRE TO CAMILLE DUPIN, FEBRUARY 3, 1825
POSTMARKED PARIS

Dear Camille,
    I am safe and I did find Victor.
    Talk to Delphine.
    Your friend,
    Julie

V MORÈRE TO J BEAUCHÊNE, FEBRUARY 3, 1825
CIPHERED AND SENT BY PRIVATE COURIER

J—

I have moved my affairs from the townhouse to Sophie and Béatrix's apartment, so that is where you will find me tonight. If you can join us for dinner, they will be delighted to see you, and have made several unsubtle promises to go to bed early, sleep soundly, and so on.

I thought it would please your Jacobin heart to know that I plan to sell the townhouse and will disburse the remainder of my family fortune. I will keep a reasonable amount of money—our definitions of reasonable likely differ—and earn a salary from Isabelle for continuing to archive her collection.

Speaking of Isabelle, she wishes to invite you to visit. I explained your ability to her and she is fascinated. Needless to say, there are many items other than the emerald necklace that could be rendered less dangerous, some of which are in her possession already. If this work interests you, she could pay. But I understand if you prefer to focus on your portraiture.

I await our next session with impatience.
—V

J MORÈRE TO V BEAUCHÊNE, FEBRUARY 3, 1825

WRITTEN IN PLAIN TEXT AND SENT BY PRIVATE COURIER

V—

We have to spend more time together because it takes me too damn long to read your codes.

I'd love to dine with your aunts tonight, no matter how unsubtle they are. And please tell Isabelle I'd love to see her too. It would be my pleasure to work with you in this and any future endeavor.

To ease your impatience, I am enclosing a sketch.

—J

[*A small watercolor sketch of a blond weasel reclining on its back with one tiny paw thrown over its face in a pose reminiscent of a human. The setting is a loosely painted cave, all shadow except for a narrow ray of bluish white light piercing an opening in the rock. The moonlight caresses the weasel.*]

V BEAUCHÊNE TO J MORÈRE, FEBRUARY 3, 1825

WRITTEN IN PLAIN TEXT AND SENT BY PRIVATE COURIER

J—

Is this a sketch of Endymion as a weasel? How is it that you send me the most foolish, bizarre things and yet I clutch my heart in a fit of emotion? I must be in love with you.

I have saved all your letters and all your drawings, you know. It is my nature to keep records. Some day I'll gift you something of equal worth—you deserve a whole book —but until I write it and for the rest of my life after that, I offer you myself.

—V

THANK YOU FOR READING

I hope you enjoyed V and J's story. If you did, please consider posting a review or recommending it to friends who might like it. Word of mouth makes a huge difference for indie books like this one.

Turn the page for a sneak peek of the next book, which is the story of Delphine, Camille, and the mysterious Ari.

For more of my writing, you can find me online at FeliciaDavin.com.

SNEAK PEEK

ARI LAZARE TO DELPHINE DE MONTFLEURY, AUGUST 9, 1822, UNSIGNED, LEFT BEHIND A LOOSE STONE IN A CHURCHYARD WALL

My darling,

I need to get lost, but I want you to find me. I have left you the means to do so, hidden under the floorboards of a top-story room in the Maison Laval, the one where the garret window faces the Rue de la Montagne-Sainte-Geneviève. The current resident is called Forestier. He's unaware of what I have put in his room, and has a generally unpleasant air, but I'm reasonably certain he won't stop you from retrieving the package. I trust your skills; you've charmed sterner men.

When you do, you will find my compass—your compass, really, as you were the one who divined its unusual function—and a linen kerchief shoved into one of my old stockings. Don't touch the kerchief with your bare hands. I've used it to forget something I can't know right now. Keep it hidden for me. I'll remember some day when it's safe.

I don't know where my journey will take me, but the compass will tell you.

Avoid Maximilien Taillefer at all costs.

DELPHINE DE MONTFLEURY TO ARI LAZARE, AUGUST 12, 1822, UNSIGNED, WRITTEN IN DUPLICATE, ONE COPY LEFT IN THE CHURCHYARD AND THE OTHER HIDDEN

My darling,

What do you mean by this alarming letter? You make me fear you will never read this, but I write in hope. I know I once complimented your alluring air of mystery, but I meant your serious, dark eyes and tendency to gaze into the distance while lost in thought. Leaving me bizarre instructions and then disappearing is not at all the sort of mystery I enjoy.

I wish I thought you were joking, but I'm the funny one. To be clear, since I know you are not well-versed in humor, in case you <u>were</u> attempting a joke: this is not funny, and I would never do it to you, and I would like you to come back now.

I did do as you asked. It took me two days to plan my attack, hence the delay in my response. You know it's not easy for a girl of my status to stroll into a shabby boarding house on a whim. (To think that you lived in such a place and refused all my offers to pay for somewhere better! You do know that the purpose of a roof is to keep water outside? A man with your scientific education ought to know that.) My parents have become fanatical about

SNEAK PEEK

marrying me to that ogre and won't let me out of their sight, so I had to make use of all my cunning wiles and enlist a lot of help. Fortunately for me, I am rich in wiles and friends.

It's also not easy for a girl of my status to get her hands on a crowbar to pry up floorboards—I did not even know the word "crowbar" before I embarked on your quest—but I did that, too. F*** was as gruff as you said. I regret that your trust in me was misplaced, but he was unmoved by my pretty face, my ample bosom, my social graces, my fluttering lashes, and my many other wonderful qualities, except he did smile a little when I slid the world's shortest, daintiest crowbar out of my skirt pocket. I interrogated him about your comings and goings prior to your disappearance, but he knew nothing useful. Thankfully, he asked no questions about why you'd buried something for me under the floorboards of his room. He doesn't know what it is, as he pointedly averted his gaze. He must think all this was something disreputable related to our love affair, which is, I suppose, not false. I made him promise to contact me if he learns anything. He was surprisingly amenable to that, offering me one full, silent nod of his head.

I have your compass in hand, and whenever I think of you, the needle points south and slightly east. Every so often it wobbles, but it always aims south and east again in the end. What am I meant to do with this information, you handsome riddle? Where are you? You know I cannot wander Paris until this device leads me to you, as it once led you to me. I remind you: girl, status, parents, marriage, ogre.

Regarding that impending marriage, there is something

SNEAK PEEK

I need to tell you, but I think it best not to record it in writing. The spot where we exchange letters remains undiscovered, and my name isn't attached to this paper, so it isn't entirely secrecy that stops me. There are some things that ought to be shared face to face and hand in hand.

As for M*** T*** and your warning, the idea that <u>you</u> would need to tell <u>me</u> which men are vile and untrustworthy lechers is laughable, though I wouldn't characterize it as funny. I will continue to avoid him as I always have. Why do you think I've spent so many years honing my wiles? It isn't to ensnare men—until you vanished, I had the only man I wanted—but to repel them.

Ah, but you, you I would track down and ensnare and keep forever if only I knew how.

DELPHINE DE MONTFLEURY TO ARI LAZARE, SEPTEMBER 7, 1822, UNSIGNED, WRITTEN IN DUPLICATE, ONE COPY LEFT IN THE CHURCHYARD AND THE OTHER HIDDEN

My darling,

I have sent A*** to check for a response every day since my last letter. Sometimes twice a day. She humors me because she's very kind and she can see how your absence haunts me.

I have also sent L***—he works in the stables and always smiles at me, and I gave him a silver bracelet for his troubles—to search for you on several occasions. Teaching L*** to use the compass required telling him who you were, not merely in name but in character. It took quite a few stories before he could reliably make the compass needle point toward you as I can. He knows now how much I love you, but I deemed the search worth that risk.

Every time L*** has followed the compass, he's gone southeast until he's surrounded by pastures, and still the needle urges him on. You are not in the city. I don't have enough silver bracelets to send him on an unknown journey outside Paris.

No letters and no movement. Your compass needle has not so much as quivered in seven full days. I sleep with it under my pillow. Every morning and every evening I hold its brass case until the metal is hot and clammy from my desperate grip. South-southeast. South-southeast. South-southeast.

Either you're dead or you abandoned me in my condition—in which case you're not my darling. I know you didn't know because I never had a chance to tell you, so it's not your fault, but still there is a little ember of anger lodged in the ache of missing you. From a great distance—a cosmically great distance—our collision of catastrophes is almost funny. How dare you get in trouble when I was already in trouble. One of us ought to have waited their turn.

In either case, dead or gone, I shouldn't be writing to you, but this letter is the least of my futile grasping. I am so very alone.

I know, I know, I've just mentioned A*** and L***, so I do have people who can help, but there isn't any help for these circumstances. A*** is in my confidence and she offered to find someone who could "solve the problem," but even if it wouldn't kill me, which it might, I don't want that. I might possess the last trace of your life. It's not you, but what if it's the closest I can ever come? I have failed you in everything else. I would do anything to preserve this remnant of us. Sometimes envisioning our child is the only thing that gives me hope.

In a matter of days I will marry.

I dream of you climbing through my window in the darkness to whisk me away from my dire fate, but if you're going to do that, you need to do it now. Admittedly my novelesque imagination fails me after the scene where you slip in and lift me from my bed—in addition to scaling the walls of my parents' townhouse in the dead of night, you can also carry me effortlessly in this fantasy, your soft, intellectual physique and my rather more generous one notwithstanding—and I am not sure where we would go, or how we would find shelter or food for ourselves, let alone keep alive (nurture? educate?) the other consequence of our actions, but I know in my heart that if you were here, we could find a way.

I'm the one who needs to climb in through your window to rescue you. But I don't know how. Too much of the world is south and east, and in any case, I am not free to explore.

Please don't be dead.

DELPHINE DE TOUSSERAT, MARQUISE DE QUENNETIÈRE TO ARI LAZARE, FEBRUARY 15, 1823, UNSIGNED, WRITTEN IN DUPLICATE, ONE COPY LEFT IN THE CHURCHYARD AND THE OTHER HIDDEN

My darling,

It's been months since I've written, but I suppose in the absence of any response, it doesn't matter. I'm a mother now. He's named after a Roman emperor, and I had no more choice in that than I did in his family name.

But I love him. I wanted to tell you that.

DELPHINE TO ARI, OCTOBER 2, 1823, UNSENT, HIDDEN

My darling,

You know I've never overflowed with spiritual feeling, but the scent of fresh bread is heavenly. I missed you so much that I sent Amélie to a bakery in the Marais to bring me some of the challah you once described. It was delicious. A little less so after being splashed with tears, but it didn't go to waste.

I wish you to think of me beautifully overcome with sadness like a woman in a painting, draped over a bed with tears shining in my lashes, perhaps robed in folds of cloth that artfully cover my nudity, rather than splotch-cheeked and sniffling into a loaf of bread. But I suppose you don't think of me at all, or read these letters, so it doesn't matter.

In February, I asked Amélie to put a letter in the churchyard wall, and when she did, she found the previous one I'd asked her to deposit. The paper was spotted with mold and the words were illegible. She brought them both home. I will not bother to leave a copy of this letter.

Thinking of you is the sweetest of bittersweet things. I would have gone back to that bakery myself every week if only my husband didn't forbid me to leave the house. (That isn't the bitterest of all bitter things, but it's tongue-shriveling enough.)

You and I used to talk so endlessly about what an unacceptable match we made—myself wealthy and Christian, beautiful and uneducated except in manners, and you, poor and Jewish and educated in all things except manners, and beautiful, Ari, <u>beautiful</u>. I must write it twice. Since you never write back, I can at last say that to you without argument. I miss your rough dark stubble and soft lips. I miss the way your formidable brows used to draw together when you were giving solemn consideration to whatever idly curious question I posed about how to make Thénard's cobalt or how steam locomotion works. No one else ever takes me seriously, you know. The frills and the giggles put them off, but not you. It is my favorite of your many wonderful qualities, though I also love your less wonderful qualities—an excess of spleen, for instance, and a strong inclination toward distraction and forgetfulness, and a sort of simmering anger about the world that never causes you to raise your voice, but manifests instead as fatigue and disgust. I miss all these things. I even miss how you stoop your shoulders out of habit because the ceiling in your room slopes so low. I know I'd be happier shivering in your leaky garret than I am being titled marquise and married to a villain.

I didn't do it for the money, Ari. I'd wither if you thought so. You're the one who made me think about where all this money comes from, and how wrong it is for a few to have so much while most have so little.

I did it for Octave. We'd have starved otherwise. Yes, I know that's a question of money; what I meant is that I didn't do it for the riches. I do need food and shelter, and more importantly, so does Octave. My own happiness is a trifle, but I would carve out my own heart before I would see him suffer. So I married the villain and did my best to scramble my tracks on the question of when Octave was conceived. No need for jealousy. Drowning that particular fish was ghastly work, but necessary.

Fortunately, my husband is a dullard, lacking both

curiosity and perception. It is his best quality. Well, that, and the fact that he ignores our child. He probably thinks he'll have ten, but I use a sponge and drink an eye-watering brew that Amélie makes every month. I gag every time and I would drink it morning, noon, and night. This secret refusal is the only power I have.

You see how unsuitable I am for my well-matched marriage? Duplicitous and adulterous. I'll have to burn this letter, but it feels good to write freely.

Amélie, by the way, has no need of her own brew at this time. She is solely devoted to Marthe, Octave's nursemaid. I discovered their love by accident. Marthe had taken Octave into the garden to give me a rest—I spend more hours a day with my child than is proper, according to my husband—but I was taken by a sudden whim to hold him again. When I entered the garden, Marthe and Amélie were kissing. It was quick and discreet and seemed to me the greeting kiss of long-time lovers. They broke apart when they noticed me.

I could think of no way to make Marthe trust that I wouldn't tell except to give her a secret of my own—Amélie, of course, already possesses my most valuable secret—so I said I wanted sponges and anything else they knew of that could prevent children. They proved enormously resourceful. Marthe even knew of a shop that sold unusual artifacts and found two different wedding rings there with contraceptive properties, but if I wore a new ring to bed, it would raise suspicion. A sponge, at least, can be inserted unseen.

We have also had several illuminating conversations on the appeal of women kissing other women. Marthe and Amélie have been in love for some time, though Marthe is married to a man named Eugène who works in the stables.

She reports that he is decent, both a good friend to her and a good father to their daughter Caroline, a sweet girl of the same age as Octave. Imagine that! To be friends with one's husband! He is not troubled by Marthe's liaison with Amélie because he has a male lover of his own. It is a situation of some complexity, but everyone involved seems happy.

These conversations with Marthe and Amélie have made me reconsider some moments of my youth—I know, I know, I'm only twenty-three, but marriage has aged me. Anyway, reflecting on all that made me think of you, because everything does. (I still check your compass every day.) Do you remember how flustered you were when Hassan flirted with you, and then again when I asked if you'd tell me what you liked about men? You did it, though. You always did what I asked.

Since I will throw these pages on the hearth, or lock them away and bury them, or devise one of your strange magical objects that will make these words illegible to anyone but us, I can first tell you about Octave, who makes life in this wretched house almost bearable. He can crawl on his belly now. Five hundred times a day, he grabs my skirts in his little fists and pulls himself to standing. Every time he sees me anew, he smiles with his whole face and flaps his arms. He makes the sweetest cooing sounds when he's fascinated, which is most of the time since he's so avidly curious. He has your big brown eyes and your unfairly lush fringe of lashes. His face is mostly cheeks and he doesn't have much hair yet, but something in the brows and the shape of the lips reminds me of you.

Oh, damn it. These pages won't burn if I soak them with tears. I wanted to tell you something happy. Every happiness in my life is like watered wine now. The flavor is familiar, but it used to taste better.

If you come back, I'll be drunk so fast that my face will redden and I'll trip into your arms. Entirely unsuitable, but I never wanted to be suitable for anyone but you.

DELPHINE TO ARI, OCTOBER 10, 1824, UNSENT, HIDDEN

My darling,

Even though I will not send this letter, the urge to beg your forgiveness for not writing is almost overpowering. It's been a year. I suppose I've resigned myself to your absence—except that I'm writing.

My husband is as hateful as ever, but I've become adept at wheedling my way out of the house, or sneaking if he forbids it, and going to a few parties and salons has made me feel almost myself again. That's not why I'm writing, though.

I'm writing because <u>I met Camille Dupin</u>.

I had to buy myself a new copy of her novel <u>Virginie</u> to replace the one we read together, you know. After I carried that poor, beloved book in my skirt pockets for all those months, it was quite worn. You must remember the thrill of reading it. There was always the slimmest chance we'd encounter each other at some gathering and be able to hide ourselves away in a corner and read a few pages together—among other things. I've never read such a good novel so slowly, but I couldn't stand the thought of turning the page without you. We sustained the pleasure of reading far beyond the end of the book, too, discussing it constantly and then cataloguing every bit of gossip we could find about its mysterious, androgynous author.

SNEAK PEEK

She—Camille is a she, though she wears trousers (seeing a woman in trousers is a revelation, in case you haven't been so lucky, and it made me question what kind of world we live in that would frown on such a wonderful thing, though in a strange way it was the forbidden nature of the sight that thrilled me—well, that, and her bottom, to be perfectly frank, though I tried my best to exercise subtlety in looking)—oh I've tangled my sentence and will have to start over. This is how it goes with my embroidery, too. I should spend less time thinking about Camille's bottom, but I won't. I don't want to.

In her suit, Camille was very handsome. She's only a bit taller than me, but managed to appear far more imposing through means unknown to me, and I think her handsomeness is the same way. It has little to do with her features—brown hair, brown eyes, an unremarkable mouth, a long, narrow nose in a long, narrow face—and everything to do with her presence. You know how dearly I appreciate a well-dressed person, so it's her clothes, certainly, but also her postures and expressions. She has an air of such strength and confidence that it almost crosses the line into haughtiness and disdain, but I overheard her speaking voice before we were introduced and it was low and warm like a banked fire.

Can you blame me for wanting to stoke it?

Camille was preceded by her reputation of having many lovers, and on seeing her, I understood it immediately and wished to add my name to the list. I will, but the game itself is a joy. To give up before we'd even played would be such a disappointment. From the way she smiled at me and said her name, she was clearly accustomed to an easy victory.

It pleased me to refrain from falling at her feet. "And what do you do?"

"I'm... a novelist?" Camille said.

"Oh?"

"I wrote, um, <u>Virginie</u>, that's what it's called."

Ari, the thrill of flustering my favorite novelist nearly sent me floating to heaven. I could have beamed, I could have giggled, I could have grabbed her by the shoulders and hauled her into an embrace. Instead I tilted my head and offered a sliver of a smile to encourage her to continue.

"It's, uh, about a girl. But also how the institution of marriage crushes women. She falls in love anyway, though. There's a dog in it."

She blinked and drew her brows together, adorably stunned and mortified. I swear I am recording exactly what she said, Ari. You know I love to dismantle men, but until then I'd never had the pleasure of discomposing anyone else. The only thought in my head was <u>Camille Dupin finds me attractive</u>. I was soaring so high I think I heard angels.

I laid a hand and my most wicked grin on her, closing my fingers around her arm as I leaned in to whisper, "I know. I wept all through the ending. It was brilliant."

The realization that I'd been teasing her caused Camille's jaw to snap shut. I don't usually bother to soothe anyone else afterward, but I wanted her to like me, so I did more or less fall at her feet then. She was still too frazzled to do anything about it, but I am determined to see her again. It will be a bit like after you met me and followed me all over the city for days, except I won't use your compass for anyone but you, so I'll have to devise some other means of finding her.

SNEAK PEEK

I wish you'd been there. Your presence wouldn't have prevented any coquetry on my part—indeed, the opposite—but you would have found it amusing, having such common ground with Camille Dupin, and you do love her novel so very much.

∽

The Mischievous Letters of the Marquise de Q is available November 14, 2023.

FELICIA DAVIN TO READERS WHO MADE IT THIS FAR, JANUARY 9, 2023

Dear Readers Who Made It This Far,

I am so grateful to you for reading *The Scandalous Letters of V and J*, or even just for skipping right to the acknowledgments, if that's what you did. I have been working on this series in one form or another since late 2018. It's been scrapped and rewritten and scrapped and rewritten more times than I care to think about, and every time it came back, it got more niche (now it's in letters!) and horny (with funky storytelling sex scenes) and queer and trans (this time *both* protagonists are nonbinary). The small part of my brain that plans how to market books was trembling with fear, but the rest of me was having a great time. Every book I write is the book of my heart, but this one especially.

This book is, years after the fact, the only real use I have made of my doctorate in French literature, other than occasionally making Delta Airlines call me "doctor" just because I can. Itemizing all my influences is beyond me, but in case you wanted more detail, here's a little.

To Honoré de Balzac, I owe some story premises (your rich cruel dad kicks you out to give your inheritance to your brother, so you end up in a boarding house full of sad outcasts; a youth comes to Paris from the provinces to follow their ambitions), some notions of magic (a weird antique shop on the Quai de Voltaire where you might buy, say, a cursed, wish-granting donkey skin), and many, many character and place names in shuffled variations. (This includes my pen name, which is a variation on a pen name Balzac once used himself, borrowed from his friend journalist Félix Davin.) Probably more than that, really, this whole project started as something I was calling "Balzac, but horny and queer and magic," which I had to amend to "Balzac, but with explicit sex and a happy ending," because original-flavor Balzac is, in fact, already horny and queer and magic. You can hardly turn a page in Balzac's sprawling, interconnected world of novels and short stories, *La Comédie humaine* (The Human Comedy), without coming across a young man who is beautiful because of his feminine hips or his smooth young girl's face, or a woman with masculine strength and dark hair on her upper lip. I love *La Comédie humaine*, but it's steeped in nineteenth-century prejudice and doesn't always treat my favorite characters right, so I took a few elements and did whatever I wanted. My result bears little resemblance to Balzac's work, but he still belongs first in my ingredients list.

To George Sand, I owe both gratitude and an apology. In my defense, Balzac wrote real-person fiction about George Sand while she was alive and they were friends—she inspired his character Camille Maupin. So mine is the copy of the copy, a shadow on the cave wall, and not meant to resemble the historical George Sand. She *was* a cool, suit-wearing nineteenth-century literary superstar, though.

V's namesake is, of course, *that* Victor (Hugo), not for any resemblance, but because *Les Mis* is a goldmine of information about life in early nineteenth-century Paris and I'm thankful. And because "Victor" is similar to "Victorine" (Taillefer), the unfortunate Balzac character who gets disowned by her heartless family of rich bankers and has to move into a boarding house with her aunt. Also, less excitingly, "Victor" is both a common nineteenth-century French name and easy for anglophones.

J's namesake is both the most famous French epistolary heroine of the eighteenth century, *Julie, ou la nouvelle Héloïse*, by Jean-Jacques Rousseau, a novel I did not care for, but could not pass up as a reference, and also the real 17th-century queer opera star and duelist Julie d'Aubigny. (Also, I wanted a name where the "masculine" and "feminine" forms were only one letter different, so Julie/n worked out neatly for my purposes.) An epistolary novel I do care for, and to which I owe this project and my entire life, is *Les Liaisons dangereuses* by Pierre Choderlos de Laclos. The GOAT. It has a monstrous woman for a villain/main character. She's horrible and I love her.

Thérèse philosophe is a real work, an anonymous eighteenth-century philosophical and pornographic novel. *The Education of Young Denise* is a fake work, a sort of parody synthesis of a lot of the philosophical porn that I read years ago in grad school.

I made a couple of visits to the Musée des arts décoratifs in Paris (MADParis) while working on this book. MAD is part of the Louvre and thus well-funded and not in need of my recommendation. Nevertheless it's a great museum full of beautiful objects, and you can pretty much have the whole place to yourself. If you're in Paris, you should go.

I also made extensive use of Gallica, the French National Library's online catalog, while writing. How cool is it that a few clicks can get me multiple different 1820s maps of Paris? That said, in tribute to Balzac, who wrote a story set in Egypt without, say, checking whether panthers live in the Egyptian desert (they don't), or doing any research at all ever, I too have often ignored reality in favor of storytelling. Historical accuracy? I don't know her.

That said, if you want history, there is some wonderful academic work being done by actual historians. Anne E. Linton's *Unmaking Sex: The Gender Outlaws of Nineteenth-Century France* studies intersex people in memoirs, novels, and medical literature, and there is much overlap with transness and queerness. If you don't have academic library access, I recommend episode 2.11 of Jessica Cale's podcast Dirty Sexy History, where Cale interviews Linton. Less relevant to this novel, but also good reading is Jen Manion's work on "female husbands" in the United States; one of their essays is freely available online.

As I mentioned in the content guidance, and will repeat here, I am indebted to Xan West/Corey Alexander, may their memory be a blessing, for their writing about trans and nonbinary erotica.

Thank you to K. R. Collins, Valentine Wheeler, A. J. Cousins, and Skye Kilaen, all of whom read early drafts and offered comments and support. Thank you to Chace Verity, who provided a valuable tutorial on designing a print cover.

Thank you to my mom, image librarian and art historian, who helped me figure out how to license a high-resolution digital image of Adélaïde Labille-Guiard's *Portrait de femme* (1787) for the cover, and who provided me with a lovely print copy of *Werner's Nomenclature of Colors* (1821), the source of all the wonderfully specific color names in J's point of view. Thank you to my dad, painter and art professor, for answering a *lot* of questions about painting, art supplies, and where to find out more about the lives of nineteenth-century French artists and students at the

École des Beaux-Arts, including John Shirley Fox's memoirs, source of the naked paintbrush duel anecdote.

Thank you to my beloved, physical chemist and all-purpose speculator about how things work, for answering questions about paint pigments (even more on this topic in book two!), cryptography, and whether particular writing choices were "too much" ("babe, everything about this book is too much"), for cooking a lot of delicious meals, for keeping our ceaselessly active and curious baby from bonking his head on *every* surface, and for unwavering support and belief in me. I love you.

And I love you, too, Readers Who Made It This Far. A novel is always a cooperative experience. These words don't do anything if you don't apply your brain to them. For this book to exist, I need you as much as you need me. Only you know how your reading went, but I hope we made something remarkable together.

Please accept, dear Readers, my most respectful sentiments,

Felicia Davin

ABOUT THE AUTHOR

Felicia Davin (she/they) is the author of the queer fantasy trilogy *The Gardener's Hand* and the sci-fi romance *Nowhere* series. Her novel *The Scandalous Letters of V and J* was described as "a string of natural pearls, each a luminous gem on its own but even more exquisite in sequence" by *The New York Times*.

She lives in Massachusetts with her partner and their cat. When not writing and reading fiction, she teaches and translates French. She loves linguistics, singing, and baking. She is bisexual, but not ambidextrous.

She writes a biweekly email newsletter about words and books called *Word Suitcase*, which is available at feliciadavin.com.

ALSO BY FELICIA DAVIN

THE GARDENER'S HAND

Thornfruit
Nightvine
Shadebloom

THE NOWHERE

Edge of Nowhere
Out of Nowhere
Nowhere Else

CO-AUTHORED AS L.K. FLEET

Errant, Volume One
Errant, Volume Two
Errant, Volume Three
Errant: The Compendium

Made in the USA
Monee, IL
13 December 2024